# *Lucky Like Us*

## BOOK TWO: THE HUNTED SERIES

**AVON**IMPULSE
*An Imprint of HarperCollinsPublishers*

Excerpt from *The Right Bride* copyright © 2013 by Jennifer Ryan.

Excerpt from *All or Nothing* copyright © 2013 by Dixie Brown.

EPub Edition APRIL 2013 ISBN: 9780062271327

Print Edition ISBN: 9780062271334

10 9 8

*For my best friend and husband, Steve.*
*I'm lucky to have you.*

## Chapter One

A WISP OF smoke rose from the barrel of his gun. The smell of gunpowder filled the air. Face raised to the night sky, eyes closed, he sucked in a deep breath and let it out slow, enjoying the moment. Adrenaline coursed through his veins with a thrill that left a tingle in his skin. His heart pounded and he felt more alive than he ever remembered feeling in his normal life.

Slowly, he lowered his head to the bloody body lying sprawled on the dirty pavement at his feet. The Silver Fox strikes again. The smile spread across his face. He loved the nickname the press had dubbed him after the police spoke of the elusive killer who had staged eight deaths. Who knew how many more? He did. He remembered every one of them in minute detail.

He kicked the dead guy in the ribs. Son of a bitch almost ruined everything, but you didn't get to be in his position by leaving the details of a partnership to chance.

They had a deal, but the idiot had gotten greedy, making him sloppy. He'd set up a meeting for tonight for a new hit, but hadn't done the proper background investigation. His death was a direct result of his stupidity.

"You set me up with a cop!" he yelled at the corpse.

He dragged the body by the foot into the steel container, heedless of the man's face scraping across the rough road. He dropped the guy's leg. The loud thud echoed through the cavernous interior. He locked the door and walked through the deserted shipyard, indifferent.

Maybe he'd let his fury get the best of him, but anything, or anyone, who threatened to expose him or end his most enjoyable hobby needed to be eliminated. He had too much to lose, and he never lost.

Only one more loose end to tie up.

## *Chapter Two*

San Francisco
Thursday, 9:11 P.M.

LITTLE DEVILS STOMPED up Sam's spine, telling him trouble was on the way. He rolled his shoulders to erase the eerie feeling, but it didn't work—never did. Something was wrong and he'd learned to trust his instincts. They'd saved his hide more than once.

Sam and his fellow FBI partner, Special Agent Tyler Reed, sat in their dark car watching the entrance to Ray's Rock House. Every time someone opened the front door, the blare of music poured out into the otherwise quiet street. Sam's contact hadn't arrived yet, but that's what happened when you relied on the less reputable people of society.

"I've got a weird vibe about this," Sam said, breaking the silence. "Watch the front and alley entrance after I go in."

Tyler never took his eyes off the door and the people coming and going. "I've got your back, but I still think we need more agents on this. What's with you lately? Ever since your brother got married and had a family, you've been on edge, taking one dangerous case after another."

Sam remembered the way his brother looked at his wife and the jealousy that had bubbled up in his gut, taking him by surprise. Jenna was everything to Jack, and being identical twins, it was easy for Sam to put himself in Jack's shoes. All he had to do was look at Jack, Jenna, and their twin boys to see what it would be like if he found someone to share his life.

Sam had helped Jenna get rid of her abusive ex-husband, who kidnapped her a couple years ago. Before Jack had come into her life, she'd been alone, hiding from her ex, simply existing, she'd said. Very much like him.

At thirty-six, he had no kids, no wife, no home of his own, and a job where burnout could get him killed. The last woman he'd dated—a copy of all the rest—couldn't stand the hours he worked, the way he sometimes had to dress to go undercover, the fact he disappeared at the drop of a hat for days on end. His job consumed his life, leaving nothing left for him to give to a woman daring enough to catch his attention for more than a few days.

"Sam. I'm talking to you, man." Tyler's voice intruded on his wandering thoughts.

Preoccupied, dangerous in his line of work, Sam focused on the here and now. "What? Sorry, I was thinking about that visit with my family. My sister-in-law gave me some advice."

"Did she tell you to get laid and keep your mind on the job?"

Sam sent a dangerous glare Tyler's way that intimidated most people. Tyler, however, ignored the look, completely unfazed. It would take a hell of a lot more to rile an ex-Special Ops guy like his partner.

"She told me to get a life before I didn't have one left."

"Take that advice. Stop working like a maniac. You need a break. Something is off with you, and I can't say I'm happy about it. My ass is on the line here too."

Sam glanced at his watch. "I have a bad feeling about this setup. Scott should be here by now and the bar is crowded. It'll be difficult to keep an eye on everyone."

They'd agreed to meet at eight when the bar would be less crowded. Just after nine, the bar was rowdy with bikers, hookers, and others looking for a good time. The clientele was a rough crowd, and they would keep their mouths shut when it came to people conducting unlawful business. The kind of dark, seedy place you'd meet a guy to set up a hit.

Sam's contact, Scott, was an insurance salesman. Sometimes, when the situation and the money were right, he played middleman, setting up "accidents", ensuring the insurance paid out. Scott hadn't wanted to meet anywhere they might be recognized, so he'd chosen this bar on the outskirts of the city.

Scott made contact with him after Sam went undercover, posing as a customer at the insurance agency, looking for a lucrative life insurance policy for his "wife". He'd subtly hinted about hiring someone to kill his "wife", so he'd get paid for all the grief she put him through. A plausible cover to get to the hit man himself, known to the FBI as the Silver Fox. Tonight they'd settle the details, payment, and provide how and when the "wife" would be killed. After the meeting, Sam and Tyler would follow Scott and hope he would lead them straight to the Fox.

"I'll go in and find a corner at the back and watch for him. That way I can get a feel for the crowd, see if there's any threat. If something is off, I'll come out the front with my sleeves pushed up. You can ride in for the rescue, and we'll get the hell out of Dodge. Otherwise, I'll meet with Scott and try to set up a meeting with the Fox. Then we'll go from there."

"Your bad feelings usually pay off. Are you sure you don't want to rethink this?" Tyler glanced at him before scanning the area around the bar again. "I can only see so much from here. You'll be completely on your own. If something goes wrong, I won't know."

Tyler might be right. Maybe Sam was losing his edge. After solving this case, he'd hand over his other cases to Tyler and take a long vacation. He needed one. Some time to regroup, refocus, get his priorities in order. Hell, decide what his priorities are, and find that elusive life he should be living.

"Let's get this done and get out of here."

Sam slid out of the car before Tyler made any more protests. He headed across the street and down to the bar. Once inside, he'd have to rely on his training and instincts to keep himself alive and protect innocent by-standers if things went sour.

ELIZABETH WAS IN her kitchen mixing up another batch of sweet treats for the local children's hospital. She delivered them every Friday, and the kids expected her, rain or shine. She'd filled a dozen racks with cookies and needed to pack them up. Her mother used to iron; she baked to relieve stress. The smell of chocolate chip cookies filled the room and had a way of smoothing out the rough edges better than any pill.

Vigorously stirring a bowl of cookie dough, she stared out across the Great Room, hoping to release her anger before her arm gave out.

Elizabeth had converted a two-story building into a home, complete with her dream kitchen when she bought the building a few years back. From the outside, you'd think it was simply a warehouse, but the inside resembled any other living space. Hardwood floors the color of melted caramel spread out to whitewashed brick walls. Like an old weathered farmhouse that hadn't had a new coat of paint in a hundred years, the bricks were fading back to red in many places. She'd kept the old-world feel of the large space but added the modern conveniences, including the restaurant-size refrigerators and ovens.

Some of the other buildings on her street had already been converted into chic lofts and apartments. Several warehouses nearest her still stood empty, so the area was usually quiet. She loved sitting up on the roof in her

Adirondack chair, drinking tea and looking up at the stars, or out across the great city of San Francisco. A quiet life was all she wanted, especially coming from a family like hers.

The phone rang. Elizabeth wasn't in the mood to talk to anyone, but she couldn't let it go unanswered. It might be a family member calling to check on her. It better not be Jarred, or she'd be pissed.

Checking the caller ID, a wave of relief swept over her. Kay. Best friend extraordinaire. Calling to the rescue. They loved and teased each other, fought, laughed together, and generally shared their lives like siblings. Even Elizabeth's brothers thought of Kay as a sister.

She picked it up on the third ring, and while she licked cookie dough off her finger said, "Hi, Kay."

"Spill it. What happened today?"

"Jarred waltzed into the shop and told Amy we'd gotten back together and had a lunch date. He said we were moving in together."

"He didn't," Kay gasped.

"Oh yes he did. Can you believe his audacity? When I came back into the shop, Amy was so excited and happy for us. She looked downright crushed when I told her the restraining order was still in place and under no circumstances would I get back together with him."

"That's just creepy."

"It's beyond creepy. He's moved past nuisance and straight to stalker. Amy told him I was out shopping, so he covered by saying he must have gotten the time for lunch wrong." Elizabeth jabbed the spoon into the cookie dough in frustration. "He got what he wanted. Amy gave him a bunch of information about me, least of which is that I've been invited to the Governor's Ball next month."

Amy, nineteen, a nursing student at UC San Francisco, still believed handsome men were all knights in shining armor coming to kiss the damsel and sweep her off her feet. Amy hadn't learned that some men, even handsome ones, were dragons in disguise, waiting to breathe their fire and scorch you on the ass.

Elizabeth sighed and wiped her cheek, inadvertently spreading flour across her face. "She didn't realize he was baiting her and fishing for information. I had a long talk with her about giving out my personal business to anyone. Why can't he take no for an answer? Of course, no one ever says no to him, so I shouldn't be surprised. Look at Amy. She took one look at his handsome face, ate up his charm, and spilled her guts."

"What do you think he really wants?"

Elizabeth took a finger full of dough from the bowl and licked it clean. "The same thing he's wanted for over three months, us back together, living his version of happy. Dad annoyed me when he insisted on the restraining order, but now I'm thinking it was a good idea. Jarred's really starting to creep me out.

"I still can't believe he told her we were moving in together. How demented is that? First it was showing up places unannounced, which got out of hand when he followed me without so much as trying to hide it. I received those creepy letters and the messages sent with the flowers. Then I don't hear anything from him in almost two weeks, and now this. Remember the time he showed up at my uncle's party, telling Uncle Charles I'd invited him? He cut in on Pat and me while we danced. Pat almost decked him right in front of all the guests before I stopped him."

"Patrick and Daniel had to escort Jarred out," Kay remembered. "That was pretty ballsy, but this is even worse. He's talking about you guys moving in together and ignoring the restraining order. A lot of good that thing is doing you, by the way. I hope you're still documenting everything."

"I am. He's too obsessed with who he thinks I am."

"You know, you're right," Kay agreed.

"He only sees me as the daughter of the extraordinary Judge John Hamilton. I don't care about all the parties and the people in the same way Jarred cares about them. He's using me to see what he can get from me and the people I know."

Elizabeth wished she'd meet someone who saw her as a singular person and not a piece of the Hamilton family and fortune. Her brothers had the same problem with women chasing after them for their money and social standing, but it never seemed to get them down like it did her.

"I always wondered if you realized those men were using you. You seemed so detached and hardly ever dated them for more than a month or so. It must be difficult. I'm sure you'd like to have someone in your life who really loves you for you."

Elizabeth let out a heavy sigh. "Now that would be a

truly remarkable man to take me on and not notice my family."

"Maybe you should stay with your parents for a while. Put some distance between you and Jarred. All that security at the Hamilton Mansion will keep him away. He obviously can't take a hint—or a restraining order," Kay added, as exasperated as Elizabeth.

"I'm not involving my parents. It makes me so angry. He thinks he can walk into the shop and bother my employees. He knew I wasn't there because my car wasn't out back. He's nothing but trouble."

"Let's go out this weekend and have some fun. Maybe you'll meet a really great guy who can kick his ass the next time he tries to bother you. I know, we'll go to some cop bar and find you a hot cop to date. That would be the perfect solution."

Elizabeth laughed at her friend's enthusiasm. "I don't need another guy. I need Jarred to stop dogging me. His behavior is so weird lately. I'm starting to wonder if he'll try to harm me. I keep getting crank calls with UNKNOWN CALLER on the ID. The other day I could have sworn someone had been in my house, even though nothing was out of place or missing. I'm afraid of my own shadow when I'm alone."

"You better be careful. We've all seen news reports about some jilted boyfriend or husband who goes after the woman and ends up killing her. I don't want to see that happen to you." Deep concern laced Kay's voice, sending a chill down Elizabeth's spine.

"I don't know what to think anymore. He better not

show up on my doorstep with his bags packed," Elizabeth said, jabbing the spoon into the dough bowl again.

"You need a big, mean-looking dog. A Rottweiler would do the trick."

"I don't think the Muffin Man would like a dog. He's very happy being the only man in my life."

"There's something wrong with that cat. He hates everybody and either runs and hides, or hisses at you the whole time."

"He doesn't like people invading his space. Siamese are temperamental."

"I'll give you the mental part," Kay said with a laugh. "What are you doing tonight?"

"Baking cookies for the children's hospital."

"Right. What else have you made?"

Baking as an emotional escape sometimes had a downside. Half the time, Elizabeth lost herself in the process. Hours later, she'd find herself buried under mounds of cakes, pies, and cookies.

"Peach pie, some berry tarts," she confessed. "Come over. We'll have a sleepover and eat ourselves into a sugar coma."

"How many pies and tarts did you make?"

Elizabeth smiled and mentally tallied the confections around her. She'd gone seriously overboard, but the food would never go to waste. She'd take them to the local homeless shelter tomorrow. People from all over the city lined up at her shop to sample her fare. They'd be jealous if they found out she gave her goods away for free.

"I baked six pies and three dozen tarts," Elizabeth

said, thinking a piece of pie and some vanilla bean ice cream was just what the doctor ordered.

"Good God. Are the extras for the shop tomorrow?"

"No, the crew is taking care of the orders and stock for the store. I needed the distraction." No sense lying about her quirky behavior.

*Pop!!!*

Elizabeth jumped and turned to look out the bank of windows. "I heard something outside. Hold on while I check it out."

"It's probably just a car. You really should get a guard dog, until people fill the empty buildings around you. There's no telling the kind of people who hang out at night down there."

"Hey, I like it here," she scoffed into the phone and made her way to the front windows. "It's normally quiet, and I have all the space I need. It's close to the shop."

*Pop!!!*

Elizabeth jumped. "There it is again. Sounds like firecrackers."

"It's not even close to the Fourth of July or Chinese New Year," Kay said, concerned. "Maybe it's some kids fooling around. It better not be Jarred hoping to wine and dine you, especially at this hour. It's almost ten."

Elizabeth peered out the wide bank of windows overlooking the street. The lights in this part of her home were off, so she could see outside with ease.

"Kay, hold on. I see someone outside, lying in the road. He might be hurt. I'll bring the phone out, but it might drop the call if it's too far from the base."

"Don't you dare. What if it's Jarred? Or worse, some criminal. Or some ax murderer who wants to hurt you."

Elizabeth rolled her eyes at Kay's overactive imagination and remembered how much fun they'd had as kids watching horror movies and trying to scare each other.

"He's lying in the street, no ax in sight. Hold on."

Elizabeth stepped out onto the sidewalk in front of her place. Her Suburban was parked at the curb and she walked past it toward the man. She approached cautiously and stood over him. Lying on his back, his arms flung out to his sides, she could only see one side of his face. A cut above one eye bled into his long blonde hair, a black and blue bruise bloomed on his scruffy cheek, and several bleeding scrapes ran along his jaw. As far as she could see, no major injuries. He'd probably been in a fight and passed out in front of her place.

"Hey, are you okay?" She gave him a nudge in the shoulder with her foot. He didn't make a sound or move. Kay was probably right: he was drunk and lost his way after leaving some local bar several blocks away.

Tires squealed, an SUV came out of nowhere and sped toward them, revving up to top speed. Elizabeth's heart pounded, adrenaline kicked in, and her mind screamed for her to run. Caught in the headlights, the car bore down on her and the man at her feet. Without thinking, she screamed into the phone for Kay to call the police and tossed the phone aside. She made an attempt to drag him by the shoulders, but only managed a foot before giving up. He mumbled incoherently so she threw herself on top of him. Grabbing hold of his shoulders, focused on her

Suburban parked a few feet away, she thought, "This is going to hurt."

"Roll," she ordered.

She used all her strength and pulled the man over. With minimal help from him and a grunt and massive effort on her part, they rolled once, twice. Her back grazed the underside of her car, tearing her blouse and cutting her back, but adrenaline masked the pain. They'd made it under the Suburban not a second before the SUV rammed into her car, nearly running over them.

The noise from the crash made her ears ring. She shook her head to stop the annoying sound. The car pulled away, only to rev up and ram her car again. She scrambled to move further back toward the curb, dragging the man by his black sweater. Tall and heavy, she couldn't gain any leverage with so little room to maneuver him.

*Oh God, buddy. I hope you're okay.*

The other car sat idling. Metal crunched and squeaked and the driver pushed against the door to get out.

For a split second, she thought to turn her back, slide out the other side of the car, and run for her life. The man let out a moan so filled with pain, she couldn't possibly leave him. Her protective instinct flared to life and fed her determination to get them both out of this unbelievable mess alive.

She moved down along the man's side, so she could get between him and whoever was trying to kill them. At his feet, something hard under his pant leg pressed against her ribs as she moved over him. Pulling up his jeans, she found a gun and a knife strapped to his ankle.

Grabbing both, she slid up to the man's side. She'd never used a gun.

*Point and shoot. How hard can that be? Someone is trying to kill you.*

*I watch far too much TV.*

The unconscious man stirred again. He spotted the gun in her hand and grabbed it, trying to take if from her. Weak, but unwilling to give up the gun, he fought for it. She feared she'd accidentally shoot him, or herself.

"Please. I'm trying to help you. He's getting out of the car. Let go."

The driver's shoes scraped the pavement, moving toward them. She didn't have time to wrestle over the gun. Reluctantly letting it go, she held on to the knife and rolled to confront their attacker and protect the man behind her. A loud pop echoed and a fiery sting shot across her arm as she stabbed the knife through the driver's foot. Her hearing went hollow. She tried to pull the knife out to keep a weapon, but the driver bent, grabbed her wrist and held tight, crushing the bones together painfully. She lost her grip. The man used his other hand to pull the knife free of his foot. Blood dripped from the blade on to the asphalt near her head, making her stomach pitch and roll. She swallowed the bile rising in her throat.

*What have I done?*

"You little bitch!"

He grabbed her other wrist and dragged her out from under the car, scraping her arms and side on the pavement. Kicking and screaming, she pulled and fought to free her arm and tried to scoot away, anything to get free.

"Let me go," she begged, using her fingers to try to pry his gloved hand off her arm.

"You'll regret stabbing me, bitch." He dragged her up by her hair and threw her up against the smashed Suburban. Reaching up to rub her stinging scalp, her hand never made it to her head. He backhanded her across the face and punched her in the ribs, pitching her forward at the waist. With his hand around her throat, he pulled her back up, shoving her against the car, choking her until she gagged.

"You're a hellcat." A touch of humor laced his deep voice. He lifted her off the ground by her throat. Pressing his body to hers, every point of contact meant to show her he had her right where he wanted her, could do whatever he wanted to her. Fear left a sour taste in her mouth.

A euphoric look came into his dark eyes and his body shuddered against hers. "You're a determined little thing." His body pressed hers into her car's wrecked metal, shooting pain up her back. His cruel voice whispered close to her ear, "I like it when you fight."

With her feet dangling off the ground, her toes scraping the pavement but never gaining purchase, she fought with every ounce of energy she had left. She scratched at his wrist where he held her throat, but he wouldn't let her go. Desperately trying to take a breath, she couldn't fill her lungs. Her ears echoed her heartbeat like a chugging train slowing into a station and her vision tunneled. She kicked her feet, hitting both the car and the guy's shins in a futile attempt to escape. He was too strong.

His cold dark eyes stared at her through the ski cap.

She made a grab for it and tore it off his head, scratching his cheek in the process. Right in her face, his nose brushed against hers. Eyes locked an inch apart, he spat out, "Now you've done it. You sealed your fate."

He threw her to the pavement and kicked her in the ribs, making her fall flat on the ground. Her diaphragm convulsed from the blow, she tried in vain to gulp in the much-needed air she'd been denied moments ago.

Sirens sounded in the distance, but too far away to help her. Palms planted on the road, she dragged her legs under her. The man's ominous presence behind her sent a chill up her spine. Two terrible explosions echoed over her attempts to gulp in oxygen. Fire and pain erupted in her back. Then a bolt of lightning struck her leg.

The man's shoes scraped across the pavement, moving away from her. Metal crunched as he got into his SUV and slammed the damaged door. Tires squealed. All that was left was the whining drone of sirens and the numbness engulfing her.

Her eyes focused on the dark outline of the man lying motionless under her car. Her vision closed in and spotlighted him. *Please be okay. Help is coming.*

Before everything went black, she feared they were too late to help her.

# Chapter Three

LOCAL LAW ENFORCEMENT investigated alongside the FBI, but nothing had been determined as of yet. Even Tyler was in the dark about what happened tonight, and he'd been with Sam.

The FBI had been investigating this criminal for quite some time. The only problem: no one had ever gotten an accurate description of the hired gun, known as the "Silver Fox". Wanted for more than eight known hits involving insurance fraud, the deaths had all convincingly appeared natural, or staged to look accidental to collect the life insurance money. And now he'd gone after an FBI agent.

Deputy Director Davies cornered Tyler. "What happened? Why weren't you with Agent Turner? You were supposed to back him up. How did he end up over here?"

Tyler had recently joined the San Francisco office after leaving Texas and knew Davies by reputation only.

Extremely good at his job, he'd earned his subordinates' utmost respect because he gave respect to everyone.

Davies liked things orderly and done by the book, so Tyler began his overview. "We don't know, sir. I was holding my position outside the bar. I expected Agent Turner to come out through the front door, but he never showed. Several cars and motorcycles entered and left the alley to the back parking lot. Nothing appeared out of the ordinary.

"Agent Turner was scheduled to meet our contact from the insurance agency. I believe the Fox may have shown up for the meeting and made him for a cop. After thirty minutes, I went into the bar to check things out and discovered Agent Turner missing. The waitress remembered him, but didn't see him with anyone else. I questioned the bartender, but he didn't see anything."

"Nothing new there. Too frightened to rat out their worst customer," the Deputy Director said, frowning.

"Exactly. Agent Turner had a bad feeling about tonight, but he still wanted to go forward." Tyler glanced at the ambulance holding his partner. "It was supposed to be a simple in and out. Follow our contact and see if he led us to the Silver Fox."

Tyler ran a hand over his head and watched the controlled chaos of the scene. "Anyway, a woman named Kay called 911 stating her friend was in trouble and needed police assistance. When they arrived they found a woman severely injured in the middle of the street and Agent Turner passed out under the smashed Suburban. After I'd put out the call about our missing agent, the local PD put it together and notified the local office they'd found him.

"Skid marks down the street indicate another vehicle accelerated at high speed and rammed the Suburban. Probably more than once, considering the damage. My guess, the driver tried to kill Agent Turner.

"We believe the woman lives here, in this converted warehouse. We found the door open, cookies burning in the oven. The noise must have startled her and brought her outside. She was shot twice and stabbed in the thigh. We did find blood by the Suburban and splattered underneath. At this time, we can't ascertain if it's hers. It doesn't appear to be Agent Turner's."

"Where's Agent Turner now?" The Deputy Director took in the scene with a sweep of his eyes.

"In the ambulance, two gunshots to the back. He wore his vest. We haven't spoken to him yet. Unconscious when we arrived, probably drugged, he hasn't woken up. We found his gun by his side, one round missing from the clip. His knife is in the woman's thigh. The paramedics are working on her, but they don't think she'll make it."

"You better hope she makes it. Do you know who that is? That's Elizabeth Hamilton."

A woman approached, makeup-stained tears streaming black down her face, lips trembling. Disheveled blonde hair fell to her chin. Several strands stuck to her skin, turned dark by the wet tears. She practically mowed down three cops to make her way toward them. Shifting her focus back and forth between them and the woman lying in the middle of the street while paramedics worked on her, she seemed to have a hard time deciding which direction to go.

Deputy Director Davies took the lead. "You're telling me that's Judge John Hamilton's daughter? Good God. What the hell is she doing here?"

"She lives here. I'm Kay, her best friend," she said around a sob. "We were on the phone and the line went dead. I don't even know what happened." Crying uncontrollably now, apparently overwhelmed by all the police and seeing her best friend bleeding in the street. A female officer came over and put an arm around Kay and led her into the victim's house. Distraught, all she could do was follow.

"I didn't think this case could get any worse." Davies surveyed the scene again. "Judge Hamilton's about to come down on us like softball-size hail."

Davies stared at Ms. Hamilton intensely. Tyler wondered if he tried to will her to get up and announce she was fine. It would certainly make things a lot less complicated.

"Tell the paramedics to do everything possible for Ms. Hamilton, keep her alive, and get her to the hospital ASAP. Whatever it takes. Contact the hospital and let them know who's coming. I'll contact Judge Hamilton and let him know his daughter's been injured and to meet us at the hospital."

Tyler winced. The situation was dire. "She's critical. You may want to prepare him to see her."

"Do you want to be the one to tell Judge Hamilton his daughter got in the way of an FBI investigation and will probably die because she tried to help one of our agents?"

"No thank you. His temper is legendary."

Tyler hated to admit it, but Judge Hamilton was on his short list of people you didn't mess with—ever.

"Christ. Heads will roll if anything happens to his only daughter. I don't even know if she helped or harmed Agent Turner. Is it clear who shot her?" Davies asked, letting his frustration show.

"I can't say. We're still collecting evidence. We need to speak to Sam. I'll light a fire under the paramedics and get them moving to the hospital. Looks like the ambulance carrying Sam is leaving now."

The police measured skid marks, marked possible evidence, and took photographs of the entire scene. Officers interviewed people who had come to gawk, and several officers and firefighters stood near the paramedics working on Ms. Hamilton. Tyler took it all in and hoped they'd sort everything out soon.

The paramedics loaded Ms. Hamilton into the back of the ambulance. Tyler caught them before they left. "How's she doing? Will she make it to the hospital?"

"If we can get her there, she might have a chance. She's lost a lot of blood. Looks like she might have scratched someone. Several nails are broken, and we bagged her hands for evidence. She's not conscious, but mumbles like she's trying to get something important across to us."

"This is Judge Hamilton's daughter, Elizabeth." Recognition dawned on the paramedic's face. "Make sure she makes it to the hospital alive. Tell the attending doctor who she is and Judge Hamilton and his wife are on the way. Hospital administration will want to put measures in place for dealing with reporters."

"No problem. We've got to go. Time is critical. She's holding her own right now, but that could change in a second."

Once the doors were closed, Tyler slapped the back of the ambulance, indicating they could go. He walked into Ms. Hamilton's house and found Kay sitting with a cup of coffee in her hands, answering questions for an officer. As soon as he approached, she jumped up to confront him, spilling soiled tissues from her lap and coffee down her hand, the burn unnoticed.

"How is she? Is she okay? What happened? They keep telling me Liz is in good hands." A new flood of tears cascaded down her cheeks. "If anything happens to Liz, I don't know what I'll do. We've been best friends since we were kids."

"She's on her way to the hospital," Tyler said softly in hopes of soothing the poor woman. "She'll need emergency surgery. She's lost a lot of blood. They said she's holding her own right now."

"Surgery? Why does she need surgery?"

"She's been shot and stabbed." Tyler hated to be the bearer of such news.

"Oh, God. Oh my God. No. I have to call her parents and her brothers. I have to tell them what's happened. Where are they taking her?"

"St. Mary's, along with our man."

"Was he shot too? Is that why he was in the street?"

"We aren't sure of the extent of his injuries."

Kay's hands trembled. Hell, her whole body shook. She probably couldn't put together two coherent thoughts to save her life.

"Can I get a ride to the hospital? I don't think I can manage on my own and call Liz's parents and brothers at the same time."

"An officer will take you," Tyler assured her.

"What about Liz's home? I should lock up." The place was crawling with police and smelled like a cookie factory. "If Liz were here, she'd serve everyone coffee and pie. She'd want you all to make yourself at home. You're cops. It isn't like you'll steal anything," Kay rambled.

Tyler put his hand on Kay's shoulder to reassure her. "We'll take care of everything and lock the place up tight when we're ready to go. Don't worry."

Tyler had seen a lot of victims like this. He was used to them going from hysterics to wondering if they'd dropped off the dry cleaning. Kay needed to think of ordinary things. Her mind didn't want to think about her friend, bloody and lying in the street, and how she'd ended up that way. It was too much to process.

He wished his own mind could switch to ordinary things. Instead, he worked over everything that had happened and wondered what they could have, should have, done differently.

Tyler shouldn't have let Sam go in alone. Unless Sam provided a clear description, they might never find the man who did this. Attempted murder of an FBI agent and a federal judge's daughter would send anyone into hiding for the rest of their lives. He didn't even want to think about the danger Sam or Ms. Hamilton could be in if either of them could ID the Silver Fox.

## Chapter Four

"YOU NEED A hospital," the doctor admonished for the third time.

"Do the job I'm paying you more than your net worth to do and keep your mouth shut."

Settled into the deep leather chair, his foot propped on a matching ottoman, he leaned his head back and exhaled his frustration. The doctor pushed the needle through his numb skin and tied off another stitch.

How did everything go so wrong? With his partner and the cop out of the way, he'd almost gotten away clean. Then the woman showed up and threatened everything he'd worked so hard to conceal. Elizabeth Hamilton. Damnit, did she recognize him? What difference did it make? Still, killing a beautiful, spirited woman like her left him unfulfilled. He'd have liked to keep and enjoy her for a while. Ever since he'd allowed himself to explore the undiscovered depths of his darker side, the more alive and the less dissatisfied he felt in his everyday world.

The sting of the antiseptic against the scratches on his cheek brought him back to reality. The doctor had finished stitching and wrapping his foot. He wiggled his numb toes, thankful the short blade hadn't done any major damage.

"Get out," he ordered once the doctor finished applying ointment to his face. Without a word, the doctor dropped a bottle of antibiotics and pain meds on the side table and left.

Alone, he stared out the bank of windows of his highrise condo. The city view usually calmed him, but tonight nothing soothed his frustration or disappointment. With Elizabeth and the potential to experience another new dark fantasy gone, he'd have to learn to live with it.

## Chapter Five

Friday, 6:27 A.M.
St. Mary's Hospital

JUDGE HAMILTON AND his wife waited for the doctor to update them on their daughter's condition. They hadn't slept and were on pins and needles hoping for any word. Not known for his patience, waiting had completely zapped him of his limited stores. He'd already raised the roof with the doctors and administrators upon arriving last night, demanding to see his daughter and that she receive the best possible care. No expense would be spared to save her.

His name and occupation opened all sorts of doors, but it didn't mean anything when his daughter was in someone else's hands. He was still left waiting for word on her condition, drinking burnt coffee, sitting in hard, vinyl-covered chairs, his shoes squeaking on the lino-leum floor while he paced.

His wife, Rachel, sat with Kay by the windows, holding hands, praying and hoping Elizabeth would be okay. Deputy Director Davies hadn't been forthcoming about the extent of Elizabeth's injuries, but stated it was imperative they get to the hospital immediately; Elizabeth's life was in jeopardy.

The dreaded phone call every parent feared and hoped would never come. These kinds of things happened to other people, right? Not to his family. Not to his baby girl. He wished he could wake up from this nightmare.

The doctor came out the double doors leading to the surgical rooms. John hurried to meet him at the entrance of the waiting room. "How's my daughter? What's going on?"

"Judge Hamilton. Mrs. Hamilton. I'm Doctor Watts. We're still working on your daughter. Things have been touch and go, but she's holding on. We've taken out both bullets and repaired her liver and removed her spleen. We've cleaned and stitched the gunshot wound to her arm. It wasn't severe, and actually just left a long furrow in her skin and muscle. We're about to fix her thigh where she was stabbed. We've stopped the bleeding temporarily so we could take care of the bullet wounds, but we still have to repair the muscle and tissue damage."

"Will she make it, Doctor?"

"It's too soon to tell. She's been through a lot. She lost a lot of blood. It will be a couple more hours before she makes it to the recovery room. I'll come back out as soon as we've finished with her leg."

"Doctor, tell us. What are her chances?" He worked

with the law, encountered the many shades of gray in his line of work. This was black and white. He needed to know, absolutely, if his daughter would make it.

"I don't want to give you false hope. Life is fragile, and sometimes even when people have a great chance things turn out in the worst possible way. Elizabeth's condition is extremely critical." Doctor Watts put his hand on John's shoulder. "If I had to guess, I'd say she's a fighter. That can make all the difference in a case like this one. We're doing everything we can for her. Let's get her out of surgery and into the ICU. I'll let you see her for a few minutes once she's settled."

"Thank you. I'll be waiting."

The doctor hurried back to the operating room where John's Ellie Girl lay waiting for him to save her. John held his wife while she held hands with Kay. Both women cried softly.

"Oh, John. She has to make it. She has to. What was she doing out in the street? How did this happen?" Rachel asked while she held him tight, her face buried in his chest.

They'd all asked that question more than a few times over the past eight hours. He didn't have an answer, except for what little information Kay had provided. He shuddered thinking about it.

John knew his daughter. She was the type of person who would climb the tallest tree to save a cat. She fed the homeless, was a friend to everyone, and her trust was given without strings attached. He loved her ability to see the good in everyone. He had no doubt she'd gone out to help the agent, and when danger presented itself she'd done everything possible to help save him at her own risk.

Deputy Director Davies returned to speak with them again, another reminder of how Elizabeth had gotten here. "Judge Hamilton. Any word on your daughter?"

"She's still in surgery. They took out both bullets and repaired her liver, took out her spleen, fixed the gunshot wound to her arm. They're repairing the stab wound to her thigh."

John took a menacing step toward the agent. "Let's see if that list covers the damage done to my daughter when she tried to save your agent's life."

Losing his temper and shouting at the agent didn't help, but the FBI had a lot of explaining to do. His daughter shouldn't have had to provide backup for a federal agent. The fact that only one agent was found at the scene weighed on his mind. He was clearheaded enough to realize whatever case the agent was working had gone terribly wrong. If there had been more agents, maybe his daughter wouldn't have been hurt.

"What the hell happened, and how the hell did my daughter get involved?" he bellowed.

"Nothing I say will make you or your wife feel better. Unfortunately, I haven't put all the pieces together."

Before John could go off again, he continued, "Our agent suffered a beating, was drugged, and shot twice in the back. His bulletproof vest saved his life. The doctors gave him something to counteract the drug he was given, but he hasn't regained consciousness." Deputy Director Davies sighed and put his hands on his hips. "I don't know what happened. The assignment was a simple meeting with a contact. Something went wrong, and he was taken out of the rendezvous place, past the agent watching outside. We don't know how he ended up six blocks away at your daughter's home."

"My daughter saved his life. She told Kay there was a man—alone—in the street. Not under her car. Elizabeth must have somehow gotten him to safety. What happened to her after is another matter entirely. Obviously, had Agent Turner been doing his job, he wouldn't have endangered innocent civilians," John shouted.

Kay stepped up to them. "Wait, I just remembered. She said she heard a sound like fireworks. That must have been the shots fired at your agent. I didn't remember until now, but everything happened so fast. One minute we were talking about Jarred, and the next she's telling me to call the police."

Deputy Director Davies nodded his agreement. "How Agent Turner got under her car, who rammed the car, and how she got hurt are still questions I want answers to as much as you do."

"When Agent Turner wakes up, I want to hear his explanation about how Elizabeth ended up almost . . ." John couldn't finish the sentence. He couldn't say *almost dead*. It was unthinkable.

"I'll let you talk to him, but you have to understand, Judge Hamilton, he was drugged and may not remember. Also, you know he can't comment on the case. Agent Turner won't be able to tell you who hurt Elizabeth, especially if it was our suspect in the case."

"I want to know what happened to our daughter." He gave his wife's shoulder a squeeze. She'd been holding on to him and listening to the whole exchange, though he figured her mind was in the operating room with his Ellie Girl.

"I want to know that too," Patrick added, walking into the waiting room to join his parents. He had no idea what happened to his sister. When he'd checked his voicemail and heard the message, he'd gone directly to the airport, catching the first flight home. He'd tried his father's cell a number of times with no luck and decided better to get there and find out what happened to his little sister than waste time.

"Patrick. I'm so glad you're here. She's still in surgery." His mother transferred her grip from his dad to him and held tight, probably thanking God he was safe and sound.

"You said in the message she'd been hurt and to get here. I'm here. Now somebody tell me what's happened to my sister."

Patrick, their younger brother, Daniel, and Elizabeth had their family squabbles and petty rivalries, but they were friends. They talked often and looked after each other. He'd had several girlfriends who wished he'd talk to them as much as he talked to his sister.

Patrick listened intently as Kay and Deputy Director Davies filled him in on what happened. The looks on his parents' faces said it all. Elizabeth was barely hanging on.

"My God. Will she be okay?" Patrick ran a hand

through his hair and gave his mother a squeeze. The feel of her, real and warm at his side, was a comfort.

"The doctor said he'd be back out in another hour or two." Deep lines etched his father's face with concern. He didn't want to see any of his children hurting. The fact that Elizabeth lie helpless in the operating room, and his father was unable to help her, had to be sobering for the man.

"Another hour or two? How long has she been in there?" It had taken him a while to get a flight out of Los Angeles and make it to the hospital. He'd received the call hours ago. Had she been in surgery all this time?

"Over eight hours," his dad confirmed, eyes filled with worry.

The FBI agent took his leave from the family.

"Has anyone talked to Daniel?" Patrick wanted to see his brother. If he couldn't get to his sister, at least he and Daniel could keep vigil together.

As if Daniel had been summoned from thin air, he appeared behind their father looking solemn and disheveled. Patrick took in his brother's bent six-foot frame, shoulders slumped. His dark eyes were grave. Daniel's hair, thicker and straighter than Patrick's, was a mess. Elizabeth shared the same brown hair, but Elizabeth had their mother's sky blue eyes. Patrick hoped he'd get to see them full of mischief and love again.

"Am I too late? Is she . . .?" Daniel swallowed hard and stared down at the floor. The thought of life without his sister was too much to bear for either of them.

Patrick embraced his younger brother and gave him

the news that Elizabeth was still in surgery. He walked Daniel over to a small couch by a window and explained what they knew so far. Their mother joined them and they all sat looking out the window at the dawn of a new day, a day they all hoped Elizabeth would live to see.

Their dad paced the room and watched over the family. They sat waiting for the doctor to bring news of their beloved Elizabeth. Kay came back with coffee for everyone. Two hours of waiting turned into more than three before the doctor finally arrived.

Deputy Director Davies joined the family to hear the doctor's report.

"She's out of surgery and in recovery. We're sending her up to ICU. We repaired the damage to her thigh, though it was touch and go for a while. We lost her once on the table, but we got her back. I want you to understand the severity of her injuries. They are life threatening. We'll take her recovery one hour at a time. To say she's lucky, well, I'm sure you can all imagine how lucky she is. We'll keep her heavily sedated, and she probably won't wake for several days. I'll let you see her for a few minutes once she's moved into the ICU. Two at a time would be best. I suggest after that you all go home and get some sleep. Do you have any questions?"

"Her mother and I want to stay with her. We don't want her to be alone."

"You can see her for a few minutes, but after, I really insist you go home. There's nothing you can do for her. The best thing for her right now is rest.

"Give us time to get her settled. I'll send the nurse out when you can go back and see her. She isn't out of the woods. We'll see how things progress."

The doctor walked away, and Patrick hoped he'd never see the terrified looks on his parents' faces ever again.

## Chapter Six

*Friday, 11:13 A.M.*

PEOPLE WHISPERED IN the room, saying something about a woman. Sam tried to fight the black ooze that crept in and stole his every thought and sent him back into the darkness. Someone touched his arm, probably to check the IV line he felt taped to his skin. At least now he knew he was in a hospital, though he couldn't figure out for how long, or even how he got there.

"She doesn't look good."

"Looks like someone used her as a punching bag before they shot her. Her lip needs to be cleaned, and we should wash her face and hands before her family comes in to see her."

"Set up the monitors."

"Her fluids and meds are all in good shape. I've calibrated her doses,"

Who were they talking about? A flash of memory came of a woman lying on top of him, before they tumbled over each other. He was under something, and she tried to get away. The harder he tried to concentrate, the foggier his brain, and the images dissipated into nothing. Too weak to hold on, he let the blackness close in again.

He came back to himself some time later. Someone held his hand. They whispered close to his ear. Their warm breath brushed his cheek. He tried to concentrate on the familiar voice, someone he loved. He fought to hear them clearly.

"Please, Sam. Wake up. Come back to us."

He recognized Jenna's voice, soft, warm, loving. She clutched his hand. No matter how hard he tried to open his eyes, he couldn't quite make it happen.

"Sam. Please. Wake up. Can you hear me? Jack is on his way. He's terrified. Please, Sam. Wake up."

Unable to open his eyes, he used what little strength he had to squeeze the hand holding his. He hoped she'd know he heard her. Her voice whispered with sadness and a trace of fear. His beautiful sister-in-law, he wanted to see her. What was she doing here? Wasn't she in Colorado with Jack?

"I felt you, Sam." She returned his squeeze. "You can hear me. You're going to be fine. They gave you some medicine to counteract the drug you were given. Your bulletproof vest saved you. Your back is severely bruised, so don't try to move around. It will hurt. Your face is beat up, but you're still the second most handsome man I've ever seen. I love you, Sam," she said and kissed his hand. "Open your eyes for me."

Sam was relieved to know they knew he'd been drugged. He remembered feeling like he was floating, and he couldn't think or reason anything out after his mind went fuzzy. He tried to answer Jenna's plea. He couldn't manage to open his heavy eyelids. The black ooze came in and closed over him like a wave. He let it take him.

Over the next few hours, he went in and out of consciousness. Jenna's voice coaxed him to wake up, and he heard other voices he didn't recognize, but he listened to them and tried not to slip away. They spoke about someone named Elizabeth. Somewhere inside him, he knew she was important. He wished he understood why.

Sam slept restlessly. Never sure when he was aware of her, Jenna talked to him, hoping he heard her and knew he wasn't alone. "You heard me, that's all that matters. I need to leave for a few minutes and call Jack on the jet. He should arrive in San Francisco soon with the boys and Summer and her family. Everyone is coming. Jack is beyond frantic about you.

"The whole family's been worried about you for months. You've withdrawn from us and no one can figure out why. Your job's stressful and takes up every bit of your time and energy. You've been riding the very edge of burnout for months, but something more is affecting you, Sam.

"Jack and I wish we could convince you to take some time off to reevaluate your job and life and come back to us. You've been so distant lately. We miss you.

With all you endure being undercover, you need your family to ground you. We're here for you whenever you need us."

Jenna stepped toward the door. Judge Hamilton and his wife, Rachel, walked in. She'd met them on several occasions when she attended social functions representing Merrick International. She wondered why the Judge and his wife were here.

"Judge Hamilton. Mrs. Hamilton. I'd say it's nice to see you, but this doesn't seem the place."

"Call me Rachel, dear. We're here to see our daughter." Rachel indicated the woman in the bed next to Sam's and the light dawned.

"Oh, I'm so sorry. Deputy Director Davies told me she was involved in what happened with Sam. I had no idea she was your daughter, only that they were put in the same room with the guard outside for security. He didn't tell me her name."

"Elizabeth. She's our Elizabeth." Rachel looked over Sam before her gaze rested on Elizabeth, a frown marring her beautiful face. "Turner? Sam is your husband? I thought his name was Jack."

"Sam is my husband's twin brother. Jack is flying in now. I sent the jet to pick him and the kids up, along with my sister-in-law and her family. I was in town on business. When I got the call about Sam, I came right away. I must have missed you earlier when they settled Elizabeth. How is she?"

Jenna turned toward the woman in the bed. The Judge sat next to her, holding her hand, rubbing his thumb in circles on the back. He didn't look like the energetic, sometimes cantankerous man she'd met many times.

"Did Deputy Director Davies tell you what happened?" Rachel asked.

"Only that she must have found Sam in the street and tried to help him. I know how worried and upset you must be, but I have to say, I'm so grateful to your daughter for what she did. From what Deputy Director Davies told me, I think whoever did this intended to kill Sam."

"Elizabeth was shot three times and stabbed in the thigh. You can see from her face, he also hit her and the bruises on her neck tell us he choked her. She suffered so much. She's a kind and gentle person with the strength and will of both her brothers. She's everything to the family and me, but especially to her father. They're so much alike, she's his little girl. Always has been. Men stand before him in his courtroom and shake when he thunders. Not Elizabeth. She gave as good as she ever got from him. Whenever they'd argue they'd stand toe-to-toe. He admired her for her strength of conviction. I'm hoping that strength will pull her through this.

"How is Sam? They said he was poisoned, shot too, but one of those vests protected him."

"The doctors think he'll make a full recovery. It'll be slow and painful, but thanks to your daughter, he's alive. Because he got medical attention so quickly, they were able to give him an antidote to whatever poison he was given.

"I was talking to him. He heard me. He squeezed my hand." Tears filled Jenna's eyes and clogged her throat.

That small recognition had meant so much to her. She loved Jack, but she also had a special bond with Sam. Maybe because they were twins she figured she understood Sam as well as she understood Jack.

"I hope he'll wake up soon and tell us what really happened. I want to know who did this to my daughter."

Jenna understood. "I don't blame you, Rachel. I won't rest until I know the whole story, that your daughter and Sam are safe from whoever attacked them. I hope he'll be able to tell us."

"Excuse me, please. I have to call Jack and tell him Sam heard me when I spoke to him."

"Of course, dear. I'll watch over him while you're gone. Not to worry."

Jenna held Rachel's hand to let her know she appreciated it and offer comfort during this distressing time. "Thank you."

Jenna left the room and headed for the pay phones in the waiting area. She couldn't use her cell in the hospital and knew Jack was desperate for any word on Sam.

RACHEL SAT IN the chair next to Sam's bed and put her hand over his. She stared at the man for a long time. She'd seen Jack several times. Sam had longer hair and a rough growth of beard. Must be part of his cover for working for the FBI. The cuts and bruises on his face added to his rough-and-tumble look. His appearance was that of a common street thug, not an FBI agent. When she thought of FBI agents, she pictured men in navy blue suits with black shiny shoes. She studied his face and decided he was a good man. His strong square jaw showed strength and confidence, even in sleep. A line creased his brow indicating he was too serious and often lowered his eyebrows when he was angry or intent. No laugh lines around his mouth. She thought it a shame he might not laugh often enough.

"What are you doing, Rachel? That man is responsible for what happened to Elizabeth."

"Now, John. This man didn't hurt Elizabeth. If he was in trouble, you can't blame him for Elizabeth's actions. She's a strong woman, and you know as well as I do she'd have helped anyone who needed it. Remember the time she made her brothers take the grate off the sewer drain by the house, so they could lower her down to rescue the mother duck and her babies."

Smiling slightly, remembering it fondly, he said, "She was six. When she came in smelling, well, like a sewer, I was furious. She could have been hurt. She was so proud of herself, insisted I drive her and all those ducks down to Stow Lake in Golden Gate Park. She wanted the ducks to have a good home. She had cuts on her knees and palms from crawling after the ducklings down the sewage tube. I must have put half a tube of antibacterial ointment on her cuts. She never complained, because I promised to take her to the lake if she'd let me clean her up before we left."

"That's right. Now look at your daughter and tell me if she's the kind of woman who would leave a man lying in the street, no matter the danger to herself."

"No. She wouldn't." He pressed her palm to his cheek. "We can't lose her, sweetheart." He glanced up, tears glistened in his worried eyes, and he whispered, "She's my heart, as much as you and the boys are."

"We won't lose her. This young man is going to wake up and tell us the most amazing story about how our daughter saved his life. I'm proud of her. She'll make it through this. You watch and see." Rachel brushed the hair away from Sam's forehead and kissed him lightly where she'd removed his hair and just above the cut over his eye. Sound asleep, she didn't think he knew she was there.

Rachel went to her daughter and did the same thing, careful where she touched Elizabeth. Everywhere her eyes fell, Elizabeth was injured. Her left leg hung from a sling suspended above the bed, her thigh completely bandaged. A sheet covered the other leg and up to just under her breasts. She was dressed in a hospital gown that opened in the front with string ties. Rachel made sure her daughter was covered properly, though it didn't really matter as her midsection was also bandaged. They had her propped on her side, so the pressure was taken off the gunshot wounds to her back. A tube stuck out of her ribs for drainage. Elizabeth had an IV stand on both sides of the bed with lines going into each arm. A couple of the bags were medication for pain and to keep her asleep. The constant whirl of the respirator and the beep of the heart monitor filled the room. The steady beat comforted Rachel. She touched her precious Elizabeth's hand and closed her eyes, praying her daughter would be okay and wasn't in any pain.

"He better wake up soon," John grumbled crossly. "I don't have the patience to wait and see. What if the guy who did this to her comes back to finish the job? Look at our girl, so small and still. She's just so still."

"Relax, dear. The hospital posted a guard at the door just in case. Elizabeth will be fine," she assured him, needing the reminder herself.

They stayed by Elizabeth's side, keeping watch every minute the nurses allowed. They tried to give her their strength and willed her to get better and come back to them.

PEOPLE WERE TALKING again. Sam didn't recognize the voices, but tried to figure out who and what they were talking about. Nothing made sense. He tried to fight the darkness and break through the fog clouding his thoughts. Who was *"just so still"*?

Another flash of memory came to him. A woman trying to take his gun and knife. She was going to hurt him. He grabbed the gun and fired. He hit her in the arm before he'd collapsed back to the hard ground and hit his head. Oh, God. Is that the woman in the other bed? Why was she still? He'd only shot her in the arm. Hadn't he? Who was she? He let out a frustrated mumble, the only sound he could manage, and a soft hand brushed his forehead and another hand rested on his shoulder.

"Shh. You're all right, Agent Turner. You're in the hospital." The woman's voice. Not Jenna's. The other one, talking to . . . Elizabeth?

"Rest."

Rest. Yes, he'd rest, and then he'd figure out what the hell happened. The black swallowed him again.

## *Chapter Seven*

---

*Saturday, 9:36 A.M.*

THE ALARM WENT off, but he didn't want to get up yet. He should roll over and toss the damn thing against the wall. Anything to get it to shut the hell up. His head pounded, his mouth tasted like shit. Still groggy and out of it, he wanted to fall back into sleep, but the insistent alarm blared.

Opening his eyes, everything came back to him. Not home, the hospital. Nurses and a doctor crashed through the door, heading across the room. Barely able to keep his eyes open, he managed to turn his head and see the woman in the bed next to him. One of the machines hooked up to her sounded the alarm. Not a good sign.

A nurse stepped to the side and he got a good look at the woman's face. In addition to the split lip, a bruise bloomed in vivid color on her cheek and jaw with some scratches that reminded him of road rash. Her leg was bandaged and held up in a sling. A flash of memory came to him again and the other night crashed down on him. He closed his eyes, trying to remember.

He was in the bar looking for his contact, Scott. He wasn't one of the faces in the crowd. Before Sam made his way to the back corner and set himself up in a position to watch the door and his back, someone jabbed a needle in his arm, wrenched it behind his back and led him through the side door. Thrown on to the floor of a car, someone punched him again and again, trying to subdue his lame attempts to escape. They didn't drive far, and Sam remembered his head swimming. Everything was fuzzy and seemed unreal and hazy. When the car came to a stop, he jumped out and tried to get away, but his legs were like rubber. The earlier beating made his ribs, side, and back ache. Someone chased after him. The sound of shots rang out. Two shots.

He turned and hit the ground hard on his back. And then what? Someone landed on top of him. Her. She rolled him under a car. How the hell did she manage that? A loud crash echoed as a car rammed into them. She'd tried to take his gun. Oh, God. She'd saved him, and he'd shot her. Someone dragged her from under the car. Her frightened scream echoed in his head. The overwhelming feeling of helplessness washed over him even now. He'd wanted to get up and save her, but his body refused to cooperate. He'd gotten lost in the haze, unable to help her or himself.

Opening his eyes, he stared at the woman in the bed beside him. The nurse mercifully turned off the alarm. The pounding in his head had been keeping rhythm with the incessant beep, and now it pounded out the thrashing beat of his heart.

*Please let her be okay.*

The nurse gazed over and saw him staring at them. "Doctor, Agent Turner is awake."

The doctor turned to him, but never left the woman's side. "Agent Turner, how are you feeling?"

"I feel like the fogs rolled in and it weighs a ton. There's an elephant stomping on my brain and banging a drum in my ears," he said irritably.

"Give it time and you'll become more and more alert. We've counteracted the drug you were given. How does your back feel this morning? Are you in a lot of pain?"

"I don't really know yet." His voice came out thick and slurred. His tongue stuck to the roof of his dry mouth and his eyes began to droop when another alarm went off. "What's the matter?"

"Elizabeth, if you can hear me, you're in the hospital. You're safe." The doctor laid a hand to her forehead and applied pressure, probably to reassure her someone was with her. Her heart rate steadied and dropped.

"What's wrong with her?" Sam couldn't take it anymore. He had to know if she was going to be all right. She had to be. It was his fault she was here, and the guilt ate him up inside.

"I think she was either dreaming or in a panic. She's been through a lot in the last day. We lost her once in surgery, and although we're pumping her full of meds, I don't know if it's enough."

"I shot her. I don't know what happened, but I know I shot her." He closed his eyes, tried to cut himself off from the pain and despair. She'd tried to save his life, and he'd tried to kill her.

"You grazed her arm. We stitched up the wound. It wasn't serious. We'll have a plastic surgeon fix it up in a few days, so she'll barely see the scar."

"If the wound wasn't serious, why is she here? And what happened to her face and leg?" Upset and agitated, the possibilities of what happened to her after he'd blacked out stirred his emotions into a roil of fear and fury that someone hurt her and he didn't protect her.

"Sam, calm down. You don't want to get agitated. It will only hurt your back and head more. Your back will spasm."

The pain finally became part of Sam's conscious thinking.

"It's really something to see you go pale, considering you're already gray from the drugs. Relax. Stop moving around before you hurt yourself more.

"Deputy Director Davies wants to talk to you about what happened. You remember shooting her in the arm, but after that, my guess is the man who was after you punched her a few times in the face, kicked her in the ribs, and then . . ."

"What? And then what?" He tried to sit up, tried to see her better, but his back protested painfully, sending him flat against the pillows again.

"He shot her twice in the back and stabbed her in the leg."

The doctor whispered to one of the nurses before going on, Sam reeling as he stared at Elizabeth. The doctor had called her Elizabeth. Such a pretty, old-fashioned name.

"Elizabeth and your bulletproof vest saved your life. You were shot at very close range. It's a miracle you don't have any broken ribs, though four are cracked. Elizabeth's actions saved you and got you here so we could give you the antidote in time. Another half hour and you'd be dead."

"Is she okay?"

"I don't know. We're taking things one hour at a time. She made it through the night with minimal problems. We're keeping her heavily sedated. She's breathing on her own and that's a good sign. Although she's had several of these anxiety episodes where her heart rate skyrockets, I believe it's the trauma, or she's in pain."

"Can't you give her something? Don't leave her in pain. You can't do that. Help her, damnit."

The nurse inserted a syringe into his IV line.

"We're doing everything we can for her. Rest, Sam. You need to regain your strength."

Sam's eyes rolled back and he gave in to the medication, numbing his body and mind, but he tried to hold on to hope for Elizabeth.

## Chapter Eight

*Sunday, 12:00 P.M.*

"COME ON, BUSY BEE. Open your eyes for me," Patrick pleaded. "Mom and Dad are so worried about you. They went home to get some rest. They'll be back soon. You should see Dad, he's in rare form. I've never seen him so subdued. Mom says he's moping around the house when he isn't here.

"I've been staying at your place. Everyone we know has sent flowers to your house. They can't send them here to the hospital, because you're in ICU, so your place looks like a garden exploded. You'd love it, Bee."

He stroked his sister's hair and spoke to her with a tenderness born of years of sharing a close relationship. "What's with all the chick food in the fridge? I swear there wasn't a steak or hamburger to be found. I ate that huge piece of salmon you had in the freezer. I had to throw out some of the vegetables in the bin, but you still have half a vegetable and fruit stand in there. It was kind of nice making an omelet this morning. You've got twelve dozen eggs. Maybe I'll buy you some chickens and your own chicken coop for the roof. You can collect them each morning. I bet you'd love that.

"The Muffin Man is acting up more than usual. I think he misses you. I gave him some of the salmon I made last night, and he actually meowed at me without hissing.

"Daniel went to the shop today to check on things. I'm sure everything is running smoothly, but he needed something to do. He'll check the books and make sure the staff is keeping to your standards. I'm sure he'll have a full, *detailed* report when he gets here. I have to say I was disappointed to find the cops had eaten all the treats you'd made. Kay asked Amy to come to the house on Friday morning to pack the cookies. A few of the officers took them to the children's hospital. I bet the kids got a kick out of having the police visit.

"Speaking of cops. Sam, you can stop pretending to sleep. I know you're awake. How'd Bee do last night? Any trouble?"

Sam wanted to ignore Patrick, but his sister was in the hospital because of him and he couldn't lie there and ignore the worry in Patrick's voice. Turning his head, he glanced at Patrick, the stress and worry written in the lines on his face. Dark circles marred his eyes, his hair was in disarray from running his hands through it in frustration.

"She set the bells and whistles off twice. Once around midnight and another time around five this morning."

"Was she in pain?" Patrick stroked his sister's arm, brushed his fingers over her pale cheek.

"God, I hope not." Sam rubbed the heels of his hands over his eyes, the muscles in his back protesting the movement in his arms and shoulders.

"You're worried about her." Patrick didn't sound surprised.

Sam was grateful Patrick understood he wasn't callous about Elizabeth's condition. "When you guys aren't here, I watch her. She doesn't move, she doesn't make a sound, and the longer she doesn't, the shittier I feel."

"Well, I guess that's something. I know you didn't mean for this to happen, but you do understand as soon as you're well, I will deck you for getting my sister hurt."

"Understood. If it was my sister, I'd do the same."

Sam welcomed it. He should be punished for what he'd done. He spent hours watching Elizabeth and playing the "what if" game in his head. What if he'd listened to his instincts? What if he hadn't gone into that bar? What if he'd called in more backup? On and on, his mind tortured him, and she was still lying there fighting for her life.

"Are you feeling better today?"

"You just can't wait to beat the hell out of me. Sorry to disappoint, but I feel like someone stomped on my head and is sticking red-hot pokers in my back. Actually, I'm sure that doesn't disappoint you at all. I feel like shit. Happy?"

Patrick smiled sheepishly. "A little. But Elizabeth would want to know you're okay. She's one of those people who always thinks about everyone else. She calls me several times a week to see how I am and what I'm doing. She's got a great sense of humor. She makes up names for the women I date. So far she hasn't liked a single one, and I can't blame her for that. None of them has seen past the name and the money. The last woman I dated she called Oleander." At Sam's raised eyebrow, Patrick explained, "Beautiful to look at, but poisonous, just like the flower."

"I imagine the Hamilton name can be a blessing and a curse."

The Hamiltons came from old money. One of the original Hamilton's had been in the shipping industry and made a fortune that had probably expanded exponentially over the years. The family still held interests in shipping, but the present Hamiltons were rooted in the law. Patrick was a successful defense attorney and Daniel was in corporate law. They took after their father, the Judge.

"Why isn't Elizabeth married? She's beautiful and seems to have a good heart."

"The best. She suffers the Hamilton curse more than Daniel and I do. Men look at her and try to figure out how to use her to get to us and the people we know. She hardly dates. When she does, it only lasts a couple of weeks. I think the last serious relationship she had was in college. She was nuts over this guy, and they dated for several months. Right before graduation, he asked her if Dad or I would help him with some contacts to start a business. She refused to ask us, and he dumped her the next day. Since then, whenever a guy even hints at wanting to get close to us, she shuts them down and never dates them again. Most of the time they're after some invitation to a party, or an introduction with someone she knows. She has so much to offer on her own. They don't see her."

"That's rough. She must be lonely." Sam knew the feeling well. A lot of women liked the idea of dating an FBI agent. It always started off with them romanticizing what he did for a living. The danger seems exciting and could be a great aphrodisiac, but then reality showed its ugly head. He worked long hours, days turning into weeks when they didn't see him, and they hated worrying during those long silences. So far he hadn't found a woman willing to put up with his job and its demands. Or maybe they couldn't put up with him.

"I think she is lonely. She loves kids. I think she'd like to have a family of her own. She'll be a great mother someday." He stroked his sister's arm. "She has that natural way of taking care of people. She can't help herself. She's got a great business sense, she's funny, beautiful, I wish someone would see all of that and everything else about her without wondering what she can do for them."

Patrick wished he could find someone like his sister, Sam thought. There was a lot of love there.

"What shop does she work for? What does she do for a living?" Patrick had told his sister Daniel was checking on her shop.

"She owns it. She has an MBA and opened her store a few years ago. Ever heard of Decadence?"

"The bakery and café?" Sam asked impressed.

"Yeah. Ever been there?"

"Hasn't everyone who comes to the city? There's usually a line out the door and around the block. Jenna, my sister-in-law, stops by and picks up something whenever she's in town. I don't think there's been a time she's come to the city without there being a white box with the Decadence logo left on the kitchen counter. By the time I get to it, the box is empty, and it pisses me off every time. I bet the officers on the scene the other night were happy to eat up whatever she'd baked."

"Apparently the racks were filled with several pies and a bunch of tarts. Kay said they cleaned every pie plate and tart tin. Elizabeth will be pissed when she wakes up and discovers she can't use her arm to stir up a batch of cookie dough. You'll have hell to pay for that one."

Sam already felt bad about shooting her, now he felt worse. He'd shot her in the right arm, and he'd bet she was right-handed. "If she'd wake up, I'll spend a year mixing up bowls of dough for her."

He didn't know what to say to Patrick about having shot his sister. I'm sorry didn't seem to encompass his feelings. He needed to get up and stretch. The doctor had told him to take it easy, but lying on his back hurt, and he figured if he wanted to get out of this place he'd better be able to stand.

He used the bed control to lift him into a higher sitting position. Throwing off the blankets, he swung his legs over the side of the bed slowly. Facing Elizabeth and Patrick, he sat holding on to the side of his mattress. He hissed out a breath between his clenched teeth and waited for the pain in his back to subside. His cracked ribs ached from the punches he'd taken, but his back was worse. The muscles protested and went into spasm with every movement, large or small. He broke out in a sweat just sitting there. His head pounded with the beat of his heart. He wasn't wearing a shirt. Thanks to Summer and Jenna bringing him some pajama bottoms, he didn't have to wear a hospital gown with his ass hanging out. He stared down at his feet. Someone had put a pair of socks on him while he was passed out. He had to smile at their thoughtfulness.

He pulled the monitors off his chest, ready to try to get up on his own. Might as well use the restroom while he got some exercise. He was supposed to ask the nurse to help him up, but he figured he could make it ten feet.

"Man, I had no idea your ribs and stomach were so bruised and beat up. That must really hurt. I mean your face looks bad, but that looks livid."

"Yeah, thanks. If I hit the floor, will you pick me up?"

"Sure, right after I stop laughing."

Sam would have laughed himself if it wouldn't hurt like hell. Unable to get to his feet quite yet, he decided to wait another minute to get the pain under control.

"I don't know how she does it." Exasperated, Daniel stormed into the room. "I spent an hour with an angry bride trying to convince her that Lizzy was not able to do her cake next week, no matter how much she pleaded. She's convinced the staff at the bakery can't do the job. The woman has no compassion. She's only obsessed about having the perfect wedding cake. It's a cake, for God's sake."

He softened his voice and held his sister's hand. "Come on, Lizzy. Wake up for me. I don't want to deal with any more Bridezillas." Daniel put his hand on top of her head, brushing her hair down. He leaned over and kissed her cheek softly. Looking at Patrick, he asked, "How is she?"

"The same. Sam said she had two attacks last night."

Sam had just gotten to his feet when his gaze collided with Daniel's furious eyes.

"I want her to wake up. I want to hear her laugh and see her smile again." Daniel's anger simmered in the way he stood, fists clenched at his sides. He took two menacing steps toward Sam and made him stumble back. "This is your fault, asshole."

Sam fell back on his ass on the bed. Every muscle in his back protested the sudden move. His cracked ribs throbbed so he tried to sit up straight, only to send a fresh wave of pain down his spine.

Daniel stood over him. "You hurt my sister. Now I'm going to hurt you."

"Jesus, Daniel. The guy just stood up. Wait until he's out of the hospital to punch him." Patrick chuckled, but Sam caught a glimpse of regret as his vision cleared then doubled again.

Elizabeth's heart monitor sped up, the beginning stages of another attack.

"Now look what you did. You've upset Bee," Patrick said in a tone he probably used when they were kids and Daniel annoyed him. He bent over his sister to soothe her. "Bee, can you hear me? It's all right. Calm down."

"Lizzy, relax. He's fine. I didn't hit him."

Her heart monitor raced. Sam's stomach rolled until he had to swallow hard to keep from throwing up, thanks to the aftereffects of the drugs and the overwhelming pain. He groaned, feeling like someone had stuck him with a fork and roasted him over a fire. The searing ache in his side throbbed. He rose to his feet again—not an easy feat in his condition—and squeezed in next to Daniel near Elizabeth's head.

Leaning close to her, he cupped her face in his hand and whispered. "Sweetheart, you're okay. Calm down. Everything is fine." He turned to the monitor next to him and watched her heart rate. Steady for several beats, it finally slowed. "That's it, relax. Listen to me, you're going to be all right. Rest, Elizabeth."

Touching her face with his fingertips, he listened to the monitor slow to a steady beat. Patrick was also watching Elizabeth's face. He noted the worry and concern her brother showed for her. Patrick turned to Daniel and his expression changed. Sam caught sight of Daniel staring at him. After Daniel forced him back onto the bed, he must be even paler, but he didn't understand the look of horror on Daniel's face. Elizabeth's parents stepped into the room and gawked at him too.

Patrick came around Elizabeth's bed to stand beside Daniel, all of them continuing their intense scrutiny.

"What's the matter with all of you?" The room remained completely quiet, except for the now steady beat of Elizabeth's heart monitor. The way they stared made him uneasy.

Rachel regained her speech first. "Sam, your back. I had no idea. You must be in terrible pain."

The muscles in his back were taught and swollen. The black and blue marks spread out from two very angry-looking bruises, one on each side of his spine just under his shoulder blades. If he hadn't been wearing his vest, he'd be dead. Both shots would have gone straight through his heart. He turned back to Elizabeth, not letting them see how empty he felt. After all, she was a lot worse off.

Sam kissed her on the temple before shuffling off toward the bathroom. Each step hurt. "I'm fine." He closed the door on them and turned on the shower. He'd give them time alone with their daughter and see if the hot water could work out some of the tension in his muscles. Then he'd get some more drugs before he collapsed in a heap of pain and misery.

"I shouldn't have gotten in his face like that," Daniel addressed Patrick, his voice contrite.

"What do you mean?" John was angry too, but knew Agent Turner hadn't meant to hurt his daughter. He saw the way Sam looked at her and gently kissed her, he'd give anything to take back what happened. That said more to him than any words Sam offered. He didn't like the fact his son had lost his temper and taken it out on Sam. They were usually cool-headed, except when it came to family, and especially Elizabeth.

"I came in to check on Elizabeth and update her and Patrick on the shop," Daniel tried to explain. "He stood up from the bed, and I don't know what happened. All the anger I've been feeling about Elizabeth became too much. He was standing, and she hasn't even opened her eyes."

Patrick thought he'd help and added, "Bee heard the angry words and got upset. Maybe she knew what was going on. I think the only thing that got Sam up again was Bee. It must have taken every ounce of strength the guy had do it. As soon as he talked to her, she calmed down. I think she heard him."

They'd been talking to her for days hoping something was getting through to her, but Sam had the most impact on her. John thought that was interesting.

"You boys had better leave that poor man alone," Rachel addressed her sons like they were naughty children, taking him back to better days. "Can't you see he's hurting, and I don't mean his back and ribs? Think about what he must see in his line of work and the things he has to do. Better yet, ask your father to tell you about some of the horrific cases that come into his courtroom. Cases I'm sure Sam has had to work on. He's probably spent every second since this happened hoping and praying for her to be okay. Maybe more than we have, because he feels responsible for what happened.

"I bet if you asked him, he'd tell you he'd trade places with her in a second. This wasn't his fault. He didn't cause this. Let's not forget the man was drugged and a killer was after him.

"You guys want to start doling out blame, there's plenty to go around, but it won't do us any good, and it certainly won't help your sister. She needs us to stand together *with* Sam. She risked her life to save him. When she wakes up, she'll want to know he's okay and her brothers haven't killed him." She gave them the look she'd always used on them when they were little boys. She got the proper apologetic looks and went to Elizabeth's side.

John gave his sons a glare, letting them know they'd deserved the whip of their mother's tongue.

"There you go, baby girl. I put your brothers in their place. You rest. Sam is fine." Rachel kissed Elizabeth and held tight to him while he frowned at his sons. He had to admit, his wife could be formidable when it came to her kids. And people thought his temper was fierce.

## Chapter Nine

*Monday, 10:30 A.M.*

TYLER ENTERED DEPUTY Director Davies's office ready with his update on the Silver Fox case. Tyler received the forensic analysis this morning, along with the ballistics report on the bullets recovered from Elizabeth's body. The attempt on an agent's life left Sam injured and made the case a top priority. Every available resource was being used to find out what happened and identify the man behind the Silver Fox name. Tyler wanted to solve this case more than anything, because he'd been partly responsible for Sam's abduction and near death. He couldn't even think about what Elizabeth Hamilton had been through with the Silver Fox.

"What have you got?" Davies motioned for Tyler to take the seat in front of his desk.

"Quite a lot, actually. The blood recovered near the

vehicle was type A negative. Elizabeth Hamilton's blood type is B positive. I should have the DNA analysis this afternoon, along with the analysis on the scrapings we took from under Elizabeth's nails."

"Good thing the paramedics thought to bag her hands."

Tyler nodded his agreement and went on. "In addition to Elizabeth's blood on the knife, we also found the suspect's blood type. I think she stabbed or cut him, which I'll verify with Elizabeth when she's able to speak to us.

"We've got an analysis of the skid marks, confirming the vehicle was a Toyota 4Runner. The police found an abandoned burned out one several blocks from the crime scene with a smashed front end. The vehicle is being processed for evidence, but due to the fire the likelihood there's anything worthwhile is next to nil. The most helpful evidence came from Elizabeth herself. Once we have the DNA profile, we can check the databases for a match and the Silver Fox's true identity. I have a feeling we won't be that lucky, however."

Davies frowned. "What about the bullets recovered from Elizabeth and Sam's vest?"

"Ballistics came back this morning. All of the bullets recovered came from the same Ruger 9mm. We found it in the suspect's vehicle. The fire destroyed any prints we might have gotten, and of course the serial number was filed off. The lab guys are trying to recover the serial number and any other evidence."

"So pretty much we have evidence, but none of it points to any one particular person. The DNA profile probably won't amount to anything. Our guy isn't stupid. He's not in the system anywhere. That would be too easy. Basically, we need to know if Ms. Hamilton can identify this guy. Sam's a dead end. He's not cooperating. What do you make of that?"

"Sam is on the fast track to burnout. This may have been the last straw for him. Shooting Ms. Hamilton messed with his head. Not to mention the fact he feels responsible for what happened to her because we screwed up."

"We? You take responsibility for this mess too?"

"I shouldn't have let him go in alone. Both of us felt something was wrong. We should have called in backup. Of course, knowing what we know now, it's easy to say that. If we'd called in a bunch of agents and the meeting went down without a hitch, it would have been a huge waste of time and resources."

"Exactly. Based on the information you had at the time, you both did the right thing. It didn't turn out well, but you followed protocol. So far, Judge Hamilton is taking this well. He hasn't threatened a lawsuit, and he's wound down to threatening to kill Sam every few hours instead of every five minutes.

"On the other hand, I'm concerned about Sam. He's working himself to death, and his cases have taken an emotional toll. Because of the shooting, he'll be on paid administrative leave until the investigation is over and he completes his routine visits with the mind benders."

Tyler cocked the corner of his mouth. "Mind benders, sir?"

"I hate those guys. I know they're necessary, but do you really think they'll get a man like Sam to open up and dump out his feelings? He'll give them the answers they want to hear, so he can get back to his job."

"Sam will jump through their hoops and get himself cleared to work again, but I don't think that's a good idea at this point. He needs a break. He's been hip deep in the shit for too long. He needs a beach and a babe."

Davies smiled. "Doesn't every man need a beach and a babe?"

The pause in conversation worried Tyler. Deputy Director Davies contemplated some unknown topic, then spoke deliberately. "If you don't think Sam is ready to come back on the job, he isn't."

Tyler wasn't often stunned. Deputy Director Davies's show of confidence was unexpected, but uplifting. Relatively new to the San Francisco office, he still had a lot to prove.

"I'll suggest Sam take his vacation and go to Colorado with his family."

"I don't know if Sam will heed that suggestion."

"If he won't, I'll make it an order. Time away will help him gain some perspective. I want to know the results of the DNA profile and if you miraculously get a hit."

Deputy Director Davies sat stone-faced for another moment. Something in his bearing concerned Tyler again. Weighing his words carefully, he began with, "I don't think you're leaking privileged information."

That ominous statement hung between them. Tyler

didn't move or say anything. What could he say? He had no idea where this conversation was headed.

"I got a call earlier from someone looking for you. They left a message."

"Who was it?"

"Morgan."

Tyler masked any outward spark of eagerness, but inside he came to full alert. So Morgan was the turn in conversation.

"What's the message?" Tyler's heart raced. He'd been trying to find Morgan on and off for the past three years. She'd disappeared as quickly as she appeared. One moment she was there, dropped a bombshell on him, and then she was gone. He never had the chance to thank her. He'd even considered over the years she wasn't real at all, but a figment of his imagination. She sporadically left him cryptic messages with a clue to one of his cases, but never spoke to him directly. She kept him guessing, and it pissed him off.

Deputy Director Davies read the note on his desk. "She said not to blame yourself for what happened at the bar. The blonde agent couldn't prevent what happened and neither could you. She said to tell you the Fox is hiding in plain sight, the woman has a double threat, and the blonde needs to mind his back. On your other case, you'll find the Rose Princess under the grand oak, and when you find the King of Hearts you'll solve the case."

Tyler had listened carefully, weighing and remembering every word. "Was there anything else?"

"No. She made sure I got the wording right and hung up."

Tyler thought hard, looking into nothing, trying to link the last part of the message to one of his cases. "Did you happen to get the number she was calling from, or anything that would tell me where she is?"

There wouldn't be, never was.

"No."

See. Figures.

"She stayed on the line less than three minutes, and I didn't think it necessary to try to find out where the call originated. What I want to know is who this woman is, and how she knows so much about your cases? Are you giving her information, or using her to help you with the cases? Is she an informant?"

"I don't know who she is, except her name is Morgan." Deputy Director Davies wouldn't let him off the hook with a short answer. He hated having to explain himself, but Davies was his superior and a damn good agent.

"A few years ago, I lived in Texas. She sat down at a table next to me while I was having dinner at a restaurant one night. She ordered her food and sat quietly eating. She was a young kid, maybe eighteen or nineteen, probably a college student. She carried a beat-up backpack with her. She never looked at me, or said a word. I finished my meal and left the money for the bill and tip on the table. Before I passed her table, she grabbed my wrist, looked me in the eye, and told me to go to the yellow house and find my sister. If I didn't go and get her that night, I would never see her again."

"She knew your sister?"

"No."

Davies's eyes grew more intense.

"Morgan was so intent and serious, she really made me believe something could be wrong. I hadn't seen my sister in several weeks. She and I had communication problems. I played the protective brother all the time, and she wanted to be left to live her life, despite the consequences of some of her poor choices.

"Anyway, I believed Morgan's warning, despite the fact I had nothing to support her claim. I went to my sister's boyfriend's house, the yellow house, and found her. Stoned out of her mind, the boyfriend was nowhere to be found. I took my sister to the hospital. Beyond thankful I'd come to get her, she was afraid to call and ask for my help when she'd screwed up so badly. She stayed overnight at the hospital while the doctors cleared her system of the drugs. Luckily, she wasn't that bad off and motivated to stay clean.

"The next day, the police and fire department were called to a house explosion. The boyfriend was cooking up a batch of meth in the kitchen and blew himself, the house, and half the house next door to hell. Had I not gone to get my sister, she would have been killed.

"I asked my sister about Morgan, but she didn't know anyone by that name, or with her description. I can't explain how Morgan knew about my sister, or how she's known about some of my other cases. She's like a ghost. Sometimes I don't even think she's real. Over the last three years, she's contacted me a handful of times with a cryptic message. I don't know how she found out I'm FBI, or how to contact me. I don't even know how she knows my name. I haven't spoken directly to her since I met her in that restaurant."

"Is she some sort of psychic or something?"

"She's something all right. If she's psychic, she's the real deal. Every tip she's given me has resulted in my solving a case."

Deputy Director Davies accepted Tyler's explanation with a nod. "Well, what does the message mean?"

"I don't know. Don't take this the wrong way, but are you sure that was the exact message?"

"Yeah, she made me repeat it back to her." He clipped out each word.

Frustration and exasperation laced the Deputy Director's voice. He didn't like to be questioned about his ability, especially in taking a simple message. Asking had been difficult for Tyler.

"I only ask because she left a message for me once on a case I worked in Kansas. The message was to find the green man hiding in the flour, f-l-o-u-r, although I didn't know that at the time. I only figured it out after we solved the case. Anyway, the person who took the message didn't understand the message and told me to find the green man hiding in the flowers. You know, like roses. I got it stuck in my head that I was looking for someone who worked with plants and flowers. Turned out a local flour mill sectioned off each work area by color. The workers wore jumpsuits specific to the section they worked. The green man turned out to be the brother-in-law of the victim."

"Are all the messages some sort of imagery or obscure

reference? The Rose Princess and the King of Hearts? What does that mean?"

"That's just it. The messages are obscure. But once I solve the case, they make perfect sense. She never says, go find Bob at the local fried chicken shack. Like the other case, the message didn't make sense until I narrowed down the suspects to the family members. When I set up the interview with the brother-in-law, and he told me to meet him after work at the flour mill, it dawned on me the message might refer to flour and not flowers. He worked in the green section and wore a green jumpsuit. After I caught him in a lie, we got a warrant and found a bloodied jumpsuit in his locker. The message made perfect sense, once I had all the information available to me. I'll have to check the evidence and case descriptions I'm working and see if the new message makes any sense. More than likely, I'm close on one of the cases and the message will help me put the final pieces together. That seems to be the pattern."

"I can't wait to see how this turns out. It's a little strange," Deputy Director Davies said intrigued.

"Try being the one she calls and having her messages come true. I don't even know how she finds me. She probably calls the Bureau and finds out which office I'm at. But still, it's weird having someone who knows what I'm doing and which cases I'm working."

"Keep me posted on the Silver Fox case and whether you figure out the message. You better tell Sam to mind his back. That's kind of strange she used the word *mind* and not *watch*."

"That's why I asked about the way she said the message. 'Watch your back' means one thing, but 'mind your back' means something else entirely. Sam said he had a bad feeling the night he went into the bar. He should have *minded* his back."

"You'd better figure out what the double threat to Elizabeth means, too."

"I'll do that." Tyler left the office with more questions than answers. He'd check over his cases for the Rose Princess and King of Hearts before going to the hospital to check on Sam and tell him about the message on the Silver Fox case.

He wondered what Sam would think of his ghost. Maybe he needed to see the mind benders.

## Chapter Ten

*Monday, 2:00 P.M.*

"I SWEAR TO God, Sam, as soon as I get you home I'm taking a pair of scissors to that hair and a razor to your face and turn you back into the gorgeous man I know is hiding under all this scruff."

Summer couldn't stand seeing him looking so bad, it went against her grain. She couldn't do anything about the cuts and bruises, or the way he felt, but she was good with a pair of scissors. Sam had no doubt the first chance she got, she'd tie him to a chair and start cutting.

"You think you can take me, little sister?"

"I most certainly do." A wicked grin added to the challenge. "You're no match for me and my scissors." She grabbed his hair and gave a tug while she leaned down and gave him a smacking kiss on the forehead.

"Is that so? And what do you mean, turn me back into

a gorgeous man? You know I'm the best-looking guy in this room." He smiled and tickled her ribs under the arm she used to hold on to his hair. When she squealed, it eased the tightness in his chest.

"You're the only man in this room." Her grin faded and she turned serious. "It's nice to hear you joking. I was afraid you'd never come out of your stupor. She'll be okay, you know. It wasn't your fault." She stood back and glanced over at Elizabeth, silent in the other bed.

"It is my fault. I shot her."

"You shot her in the arm. You never meant to hurt her. You were protecting yourself. You didn't know if she was a threat. You're a trained agent, and if you really thought she was going to hurt you, you'd have shot to kill."

"I'll second that." Tyler strode into the room and nodded a hello to Summer. He took a critical look at Sam, obviously not liking what he saw. "You look like shit, friend."

"Some friend. I blew the op and got myself shot. I shot an innocent woman and passed out while the asshole I'm supposed to arrest strangled, beat, shot, and stabbed her." Tyler knew all that, but Sam needed to say it, repeat it, so he'd never forget what his mistake had cost.

"And that's my cue to leave, so you two can talk." Summer gathered up her purse and jacket. "Sam, we'll visit you later. Tyler, it's nice to see you again."

"You too."

Sam nodded at his sister, but kept his attention on Tyler. "I think that pretty much sums up my part of the operation. I hope Davies didn't chew you up and spit you out."

"Nope. He told me we handled the situation well within protocol, and even if we had called in backup, things could have turned out the same or gone the other way. You know that as well as I do. It should have been simple. I'm as much to blame as you are for what happened. I should have covered the alley, or moved in sooner."

Sam shook his head. Tyler was right. He'd sat in that bed for the last couple days replaying the whole thing over and over. No matter what, it all came down to one fact. You could wish for things to be different, but they are what they are. He couldn't change what happened to Elizabeth. He prayed she'd wake up and forgive him for what he'd done.

"Let's not do the whole 'if only' thing. I've done nothing but run scenario after scenario in my mind of what I wished I'd done. It doesn't get me anywhere, except angrier. You did what I told you to do. Who knew the guy would stick me with a needle and toss me in a car? I should have been more careful and watched my back." He shifted on the mattress. He hated being laid out while Tyler stood over him at the end of the bed. "What are you doing here? Do you have any useful information on the Silver Fox?"

"I've actually got a lot to tell you and some questions." He cocked his head toward Elizabeth. "No change, huh? She's still out?"

"Yeah." Sam put his head back and turned to look at Elizabeth. His mind playing the same message it had for hours, "*Please, wake up.*"

"Here's what we know. Obviously, we believe the Silver Fox showed up for the meeting. I'm sure you agree." Sam nodded, so he went on, "After you got out of the car, he shot you in the back twice. The rounds were recovered and matched to a Ruger 9mm. We recovered the gun from the vehicle we found abandoned and burned several blocks away. No serial number or prints. How did you get under the car? Did she drag you?"

"No. She threw herself on top of me, held on, and rolled me under the car."

"Really. God, that girl is smart. I couldn't figure out how she got you under there. You outweigh her by fifty pounds, at least. I thought maybe you had come to and gotten under there yourself."

Sam shook his head no.

"What do you remember once you were under the car?"

"I shot her." Sam glared at Tyler. The guy, obviously, knew he didn't want to talk about what happened, but here he was poking an open wound, hoping Sam had the magic answer and they'd identify the Silver Fox.

Tyler treaded on quicksand. Sam blamed himself for what happened and no one, including Tyler, could talk him out of it. The longer he spent in that room looking at the evidence of what happened, the deeper he sank into despair.

"Tell me about her. What did she do? Do you have any memory of her fighting with the guy?"

"You know something. What is it?"

Tyler was fishing for something. Sam wished his mind wasn't such a muddy mess.

"Tell me what you know first."

"You'll show me yours, if I show you mine." Sam stared coldly. He didn't want to play games, but Tyler remained impassable. "Fine. She got me under the car and found the gun and knife at my ankle. She was beside me when I saw the gun and grabbed it. She let it go, and I shot her. She still had the knife. I must have closed my eyes to steady myself because she was there, and when I opened my eyes again, she was gone." *She screamed.* He didn't want to tell Tyler the scream blared in his ears even now.

"That's it. You didn't see if she stabbed the guy or cut him? Nothing after you shot her and she was gone?"

Sam shook his head no, and Tyler let out a sigh. "Shit. I hoped you had more information."

"Sorry to disappoint."

Tyler ran his fingers across his brow and clamped down on his jaw before going on. "We found blood by the SUV. Type A negative. We found the same blood type on the knife after it was removed from Elizabeth's thigh. Her blood type is B positive."

Sam turned back to Elizabeth and watched her.

"She scratched him. The paramedics noticed her broken nails and bagged her hands. We recovered the guy's DNA. I'm waiting for the analysis to come back, but I'll bet the blood and skin from under her nails will be a DNA match."

"She must have really fought the guy," Sam said, never taking his eyes off her.

"Sam, we think she saw him. We think she can ID him, and that's why he shot and stabbed her."

Sam ran both hands through his hair and thought about all that statement implied. "He'll try to kill her if she can ID him. She's the only one who knows who he is. Even Scott admitted they'd never met in person. They set things up by phone and used drop sights for the money exchanges."

"We won't know for sure until she wakes up, but she provided us with a lot of evidence. Even with all we have, we probably won't find him in the system."

"The guy's too smart. I have a feeling he's been playing this game a long time. He's not stupid enough to be caught and wind up in our database."

"There's something else. It's kind of strange." Tyler almost looked away, but he held Sam's gaze.

"Lay it on me, man."

Tyler hesitated, and Sam found it odd, since the guy was usually a straight shooter.

"I got a message today from someone who has helped me solve some of my cases. She left a message with Davies. It sounds strange, but the message was for you. She said that we couldn't have prevented what happened the other night, and you need to *mind* your back. She also said there is a double threat to Elizabeth, and the Fox is hiding in plain sight."

"Have you been calling 1-800-PSYCHIC again? You should really lay off the sauce late at night. Get a girl. Spend some time doing something productive between the sheets besides calling 800 numbers." Sam smiled wickedly at Tyler's indignant face.

"You realize the only thing keeping my fist out of your face is the fact you're laid up?"

"Is that so? Bring it on. I couldn't feel any worse than I do right now. Maybe you could knock me into next week and this nightmare will be over."

"Listen, I know you're feeling like shit about all of this, but the message is as real as it gets. This girl, she knows things. Because of something she told me, my sister is alive today. Every time I get some strange cryptic message from her, I remember my sister is attending nursing school and alive and well. So, what do you think about the double threat to Elizabeth?"

Tyler was serious and believed the message was genuine. Sam would assume the same and see if it gave them any help in solving the case. He'd like nothing better than to see the Silver Fox behind bars for what he did to Elizabeth. The FBI used psychics. At times, they were a good tool, and other times it was just a bunch of BS. Sam would give Tyler's message the benefit of the doubt.

"Well, if she can ID the Silver Fox, that's most likely one of the threats. Maybe her injuries are the other threat." Sam hoped that wasn't it. He wanted to believe she'd wake up any minute. "Or maybe more than one person was there the other night. I only remember one guy hitting me, but there could have been someone else. Has anyone found Scott?"

"He's gone underground. No one has seen or heard from him."

"He's a loose end, but I don't think he's a threat to Elizabeth. He's small time, and he's never been involved in a violent crime directly. He's an insurance salesman who found a way to make some extra cash. He doesn't actually get his hands dirty with any of the murders."

"Okay, what about the Silver Fox hiding in plain sight? Other than the fact we believe the suspect is someone working for the insurance industry, who knows how to get past the red tape and ensure the payoff of the life insurance policy, we really don't have any one person we're looking at."

"I agree. We don't have shit. I'm glad you came to give me all these answers." Sam rolled his eyes. "Got any more questions we don't have answers to?"

Tired and irritable, the news Tyler had brought wasn't what Sam wanted to hear. Nothing had changed and that pissed Sam off even more because he was stuck in the hospital, unable to do anything to help Elizabeth.

"All right, I'll get out of here and leave you to your wallowing. Davies told me to tell you, officially, you're on paid administrative leave until the investigation into the shooting is completed and you go to all your psych evals. Have fun with that, by the way. Oh yeah, don't forget to *mind* your back."

"Mind my back, not watch my back. Your 1-800-PSYCHIC has a sense of humor. If I'd been minding my back, I wouldn't have gotten shot in the back."

"I don't know if she has a sense of humor. I've only spoken to her once, and that was for less than a minute." He let that sink in with Sam. "Like I said, she only leaves me messages. I think it was a friendly reminder to trust your instincts from now on. It's good advice for both of us, especially with the kind of work we do."

Tyler shrugged and stood to leave. He looked back over his shoulder at Sam and then to Elizabeth. "She's something. She did everything she could to save your life and make sure we had evidence to get the guy for trying to kill you. I don't think she thought about herself for a second. It wasn't your fault, Sam. Everyone but you knows that, and I'll bet she'd say the same thing."

Tyler left the room without another word. Sam tried taking what he said to heart. The guilt and self-recriminations were too great to overcome at the moment.

*Chapter Eleven*

*Tuesday, 9:31 P.M.*

THE DOOR CLOSED. Judge Hamilton and his wife must have left for the night. Sam avoided the Hamilton family. He also avoided Deputy Director Davies and his own family, though they were more insistent he speak to them. Not that he said much. They were probably getting tired of his one-word answers and his aversion to talking about what happened. He'd told Deputy Director Davies he knew as much as he did.

Sam simply allowed them all to think his memory remained foggy, with missing pieces because of the drugs. While that had been the case for the first day or so, he now recalled almost the entire incident up until he'd blacked out under the car after hearing Elizabeth's scream. He woke up in a cold sweat more than once, her scream ringing in his ears. He didn't think he'd ever go to sleep again without waking up to the sound of her scream.

He didn't want to speak to anyone, especially after he'd talked to Tyler.

Why didn't they all leave him alone?

He needed to get out of this room. Every time the alarms went off on Elizabeth's machines, he panicked and prayed to God nothing more happened to her. He wouldn't be able to live with himself if she died because of him.

They rolled her out of the room yesterday and back into surgery for the plastic surgeon to repair the stitches on her arm and thigh. They'd discovered she had an infection deep in the muscle. Now, they pumped even more potent antibiotics into her system to help rid her body of the infection.

Waiting for them to bring her back had nearly undone him. He couldn't imagine everything she was going through with the surgeries and being in the black empty space. He knew what it was like to be in that void, feeling so alone and not knowing how to claw your way out of it.

He tried to avoid her family, but they caught him pretending to sleep every once in a while. Her brothers had calmed down, since their last encounter. He understood Daniel's anger. Dealing with his sister's condition wasn't easy. Being young, Daniel figured he was still invincible. He'd learn soon enough, if he hadn't already, life is fragile. Look at Elizabeth. She was holding on to hers with both hands.

Sam always got the feeling the only thought Daniel

had for him was, "Do you see what you've done?" He knew all right. They were all angry with him and wishing he was hooked up to all those machines, lying half dead in Elizabeth's place. He wished for that with every breath he took.

The Silver Fox had somehow known Sam was an FBI agent. If only Sam had been more careful, or minded his back before he ever went into that bar.

Oh yes, he knew Elizabeth was here because of him. He put both hands over his bearded face and scrubbed them up and down, trying to wash away the images of her holding his gun and knife and telling him she was only trying to help him. She hadn't even known he was an FBI agent. She'd just wanted to help some guy lying in the street. He rubbed his hands over his face again and turned to stare at her like he did when they were alone together. Rachel sat beside Elizabeth, staring at him.

"I was wondering how long you'd ignore us. You're quite good at pretending to sleep." She gave him a half smile. "Don't worry, the Judge went to make some calls. He won't be back for a while yet. How are you feeling, Agent Turner? Better, I hope."

Sam had almost dropped dead when he found out Elizabeth was Judge John Hamilton's daughter. Just his luck the daughter of a federal judge saved him. "I'd think you'd hope I was on my deathbed."

"Nonsense. Aside from needing a haircut and a shave, I have to say you look much better. I'm sorry about what happened on Sunday. Daniel is, well, young and impulsive. I'll bet when you're all cleaned up, it's hard to tell you and Jack apart. At first, I thought you were Jenna's husband. We've met them at several social functions, and when I saw her here a few mornings ago, well, I thought you were Jack."

Sam dismissed that. He was used to being mistaken for his twin. "You call her Elizabeth. Everyone in your family calls her something different. Lizzy, Busy Bee, Ellie, Liz. I've never heard one person with so many names. You always call her Elizabeth though. For the Judge, it's Ellie Girl."

Rachel smiled. Sam Turner was an observant man. "She's all of those names. Each of us knows her and sees her in a different way. She's Elizabeth to me because from the moment she was born, she seemed so regal. Even now, she has this air about her that makes her stand out. It's the way she carries herself. Even when she was a baby she had this way of looking at you." Rachel stared at her daughter, and like a slide show, she saw her grow up into the beautiful woman she was today. "She's Ellie Girl to John because she's daddy's girl. He loves her with everything he is. When they argue he calls her E-liz-a-beth, dragging out each syllable with his exasperation because she's usually right, or puts up a really good argument for her case. After one of their arguments, he always comes to me shaking his head and says, 'That Ellie Girl, she's really something.'"

She stroked the back of her hand down her daughter's cheek, stood, and went to the chair beside Sam. Propped up in the bed, when she sat, they were eye to eye. "Her brother, Patrick, calls her Busy Bee. When they were young, she'd trail after him everywhere he went, like a bee going from flower to flower. He made quite a fuss over her 'buzzing' around him, but he liked it. Daniel has called her Lizzy since he started talking. Like a little mother to him when he was born, she thought I'd given her a live doll to play with, and he adored her. She's so close to her brothers she has an uncanny way of knowing when they need her. They tell me all they have to do is think about her and she calls them. Have you ever had that happen?"

"Jack and I have something like that. We always seem to know when the other one needs him. When we were kids, we finished each other's sentences. We were inseparable. He told me the night this happened he felt like someone had locked him in a dark closet and he couldn't breathe. That's exactly how I felt when I was going in and out of consciousness."

"They say that about twins. There's a connection. She has that with her brothers."

"How do you think she's doing?" Sam asked in earnest.

"You've heard everything the doctors told us."

"I know what they think. She's doing well. She's holding her own. She needs time to heal. They're keeping her medicated and sedated. Yeah, yeah, yeah. You know her. What do *you* think?"

Serious, concerned, his need to know poured off him like a raging river.

"Elizabeth is one of the strongest people I know. Think of what it must have taken for her to get you under that car with another car speeding after you, trying to run you over."

Sam closed his eyes hoping to avoid the memory of what happened, but closing his eyes only made it easier to see the replay in his head. "I remember her on top of me. She grabbed my shoulders, clamped her feet to mine, and she rolled and used the momentum and my weight to propel us under the car. She must have scraped the hell out of her back, not to mention the strength it took for her to move me without any help."

"She and her brothers would do that down the grass hill at our lake house. It was a game they'd play when they were very little. 'Jack and Jill tumbled down the hill,' I think they used to call it. So much joy, she'd laugh and scream. I heard her delight all the way in the house."

She took a moment to relish that memory of her children playing when they were small, thankful they were still so close. "Her shirt was torn up pretty bad, she has some cuts on her back from under her Suburban. Lucky for you, she drives a car that has a lot of ground clearance.

"It's been hard to see all the damage to her body. She's almost completely covered by bandages. I imagine she looks worse than you do."

Sam winced at the thought. She did look worse than him, because although he was severely bruised from the gunshots, Elizabeth had holes in her back where the bullets entered. She had surgical cuts on her abdomen where they'd repaired the damage. He'd seen a lot of victims of gunshot wounds and knife attacks and knew the damage would leave a lot of scarring.

"I've been trying to piece all of the events together. It seems I was awake then asleep then awake so many times. I couldn't keep track from one moment to the next. Things were hazy and out of sorts. I think, after she got me under the car, the suspect rammed her car and she tried to get in front of me. Maybe she wanted to move me further back under the car toward the curb. She found my gun and knife in their holsters at my ankle. She had them when she was beside me and . . ." He covered his face again with his hands and ran them through his hair, and stared at Elizabeth so still in her bed.

"And you took the gun from her and shot her in the arm."

He closed his eyes as Elizabeth's mother spoke the words he didn't want to say and didn't want to be true. "I remember seeing the gun. I grabbed it, but she held on. She said something, but another crashing sound made it impossible to hear her. The other car rammed us again. Everything happened so fast, or so it seemed. I remember, now, what she said: 'Please, I'm trying to help you. He's getting out of the car. Let go.' I didn't let go though. When she held the knife in her hand, I guess I only saw her as a threat, and I fired. I shot her. She was there one minute and gone the next. She screamed. That's all I hear now."

He leaned his head back and closed his eyes. "I don't know what happened after she disappeared, but I remember her scream. I'm sorry. You probably don't want to hear this. I don't want to hear this. I don't want to see it play in my head over and over. It should be me lying in that bed unconscious with all those wounds, or dead on the street. She should be home baking cookies. Is that right? She was baking cookies?" He thought how sweet and innocent an act, a woman at home baking.

"Poor Sam, tormenting yourself with guilt over what happened. Don't. She wouldn't want you to."

Sam didn't deserve the gentle way she touched his shoulder to reassure him. It didn't. Nothing would. Except Elizabeth waking up.

"She bakes cookies every Thursday and delivers them to the children's hospital on Friday. The police took the ones she finished over to the hospital the next day. They apparently ate the pies and tarts she'd made up that night."

Sam's eyebrows drew together and he frowned deeply in outrage. Rachel laughed.

"She wouldn't have minded. She loves to bake, and when she's upset about something, she bakes a lot. Kay, her friend, who called the police that night, told me she'd been upset." Rachel shrugged like it was common knowledge everyone bakes when they're upset. "If she hadn't been incapacitated, she'd have fed all the officers there that night. It's what she does."

"Incapacitated. That's putting it lightly, don't you think? You're awfully calm about all of this. Your sons are agitated and upset each time they come in, but you and the Judge, you're always so calm when you sit with her. You talk to her and tell her she's going to be fine. The Judge told her he expects her to wake up in time for Sunday dinner, or else."

Rachel smiled. "I love John. He's demanding in the most loving ways. We have Sunday dinner once a month.

No one is allowed to miss it. It's to be this coming Sunday, and I suspect the Judge does expect Elizabeth to wake up in time to have supper with her family. I have a feeling she will too. She hates to disappoint her father."

"I hope she wakes up soon. Every time I hear those alarms go off, my chest hurts and I can't breathe for hoping she's okay."

"You're a nice man, Sam Turner."

"Nice. I shot your daughter."

"Oh, calm down. You're getting all worked up over something you wouldn't have done had you known she was trying to help you. Besides, you barely grazed her arm. You weren't the one to shoot her in the back or stab her in the leg. So stop beating yourself up over something you couldn't have prevented. Let me tell you something about my Elizabeth, she'd as soon set her hair on fire then stand by and not help when help is needed. She can't stand to see anyone or anything suffer."

Sam wasn't appeased in the least.

"We have a three-story house, here in San Francisco. When she was a little girl, eight I think, she went out onto the roof on the third floor with a hammer. She was taking up the spike strips that her father had put up to keep the pigeons from landing and making a mess up there. When her father found her out on the roof, she stood up with her hands on her hips and told her father if he wanted to have a house in a place with lots of birds and not enough trees, then he'd have to share the roof. She took every last strip off and her father hired a crew to come and clean each month. Does that sound like someone who would leave a man lying in the street, even if she might get hurt herself?"

He didn't know what to think. "Why did he leave her up on the roof? She could have killed herself if she fell off."

"She could have, if he hadn't insisted on tying a rope around her while she worked."

"He let her have her way."

"She was right. It's hard to argue with an eight-year-old's logic. What you missed about the story is that an eight-year-old girl was out on a three-story roof helping a bunch of birds. No fear for herself, just get the job done and save the birds. That's who she is, and why she went out to help you. Don't dwell on what you did. You know you wouldn't have hurt her if you'd been in your right mind. She's probably lying there wondering if you're okay rather than thinking about herself."

"That's for sure," the Judge said, walking into the room. "My Ellie Girl thinks about everyone but herself."

Sam almost flinched when the Judge approached. Unsure what to say or do, he waited for the Judge to rage at him. He deserved it and accepted the responsibility for everything. He looked into the Judge's eyes and couldn't speak. Flashes of him shooting Elizabeth went off like rockets in his mind. Rachel held his hand, and he was thankful for the support.

"Don't look so glum, boy. It's not your fault what happened to my Ellie Girl. Sounds like the guy you were after got the best of you. I'm sure you won't let it happen again. She'll be fine. Right as rain for Sunday dinner. You'll see.

I expect you'll join us. We'll have dinner here, of course. Six o'clock. Sharp. No excuse for being late."

"Sir, it's my fault she's here. I knew something was wrong before I ever went into the meeting. I went in anyway."

"Like I said, you won't make those mistakes again. If Ellie Girl doesn't see you up and walking around for herself, she won't rest. She'll want to know you're okay, and I don't mean physically. It'll hurt her if she thinks you're blaming yourself and beating yourself up over what happened. Don't make my girl upset about saving your life."

Sam couldn't believe his ears. They let him off the hook. Maybe they were right about Elizabeth thinking about him. "She had another anxiety attack last night. I went over to her bed and told her she was okay. She was safe. She spoke."

The Judge and Rachel exchanged a glance. "What did she say?" the Judge asked, his voice hoarse.

"She barely whispered, but I heard her clearly. She said, 'Save him.'" He leaned his head back and stared at the ceiling. Rachel squeezed his hand.

"She spoke. She actually spoke. See, she's getting better. The doctor said in the next day or so they'll cut back on the sedatives and see if she wakes up on her own. She's not in a coma, but a deep sleep. It's best to keep her calm, they said." Rachel smiled softly, pleased to hear her daughter had managed to speak, even if it was only a couple of words. Tears filled her eyes.

The Judge gave Sam a brisk pat on the leg. "The nurse

told me you sat with her most of the night. She said you held her hand."

"I wanted her to know someone was here with her. After she calmed down and the nurses left, it was quiet. I think she might have been aware no one was sitting with her. Her heart rate sped up, so I let her know I was still here. When I held her hand, her heart rate went down."

Rachel stood next to Sam. She leaned over him, holding his gaze. "You're a nice man, Sam. If it had been her lying in the street, I have no doubt you'd have done for her what she did for you. Get some rest. I hear you're going home tomorrow. I hope you'll come back to check on her. We'll see you on Sunday. The Judge does not accept excuses for Sunday dinner." Before Sam said anything, Rachel leaned down and kissed his forehead. She whispered, "You're a good man."

He sat in silence while they said goodnight to their daughter. He thought about his own parents. They weren't able to come to San Francisco, and he was sorry for that too. His father had a heart condition and finding out his son was injured and in the hospital had caused a mild episode. Sam had spoken to them every day on the phone, but it wasn't the same. He missed them. Elizabeth Hamilton was a lucky lady.

## *Chapter Twelve*

*Wednesday, 2:40 P.M.*

JACK AND JENNA brought him home that morning and surrounded him with family. His sister, Summer, and her husband, Caleb, along with their children were happy to see him home. His niece and all three of his nephews played in the living room while all the adults watched him. Sam knew he looked like hell, but figured his outside should reflect what he felt on the inside. He couldn't muster up enough energy to do anything about his appearance or his attitude.

He'd sat there for over an hour watching the two families interact, until he couldn't take it anymore. Not the scenes in his head, the scream echoing in his ears, the love between Jack and Jenna and Summer and Caleb, the children happily romping around the room. He couldn't take himself another minute. Rising from where he'd planted himself on the couch, no small feat since his back was killing him, he went to the bar. Everyone's eyes bored into his back, but he didn't care. Pouring a double shot of whiskey, he knocked it back in one long gulp. When the sting in his throat and gut subsided, he poured another and knocked it back just as quickly. Jack came up behind him, and just for spite, he poured himself another. Before he downed that one too, his brother clamped a hand over the glass and held it down.

Sam refused to look up. "Don't you have a ranch in Colorado to run?"

Jack leaned into his ear. "Don't you think drinking yourself into oblivion is a stupid idea considering the amount of painkillers you've already taken?"

Jack wasn't about to let Sam self-destruct. Sam was sinking into depression. The doctor had warned them before they left the hospital. They didn't need the doctor's opinion, however, because they could see for themselves Sam wasn't thinking clearly about anything.

Before walking out of the his hospital room, he'd turned back to Elizabeth. Nearly five minutes passed as Sam stood like a statue staring at her, probably trying to will her to wake up.

"I'm worried about you, Sam. This isn't like you. You've been undercover before and things haven't gone the way you expected. People have even gotten hurt. It's never affected you this deeply. What makes this case so different?"

What was different? Sam didn't know what was different.

Yeah, there'd been lots of other cases and people sometimes got hurt in the process, but they were usually other agents, or the bad guys. Rarely was a civilian involved.

What was different? He was different. He didn't listen to his instincts and allowed himself to be abducted by the Silver Fox. He hadn't been able to tell the difference between Elizabeth trying to help him or hurt him.

"Elizabeth," he whispered on a ragged exhale.

She was the difference. She'd been home baking cookies for sick children. Now she was in the hospital holding on to her life by a thread because of him. He couldn't stand it. He turned away from the bar and walked past his staring family and went to his room, slamming the door behind him. He would have thrown himself down on the bed, but his back hurt something fierce and the whiskey rolled around in his gut. Sitting on the edge of the bed, he did something he hadn't done since he was a very young boy. He cried. He let the tears slide down his cheeks. Burying his face in his hands while he rested his elbows on his thighs, he let the despair and sadness wash over him and swallow him up. He fell to his side on the pillow, put his legs up on the bed, and even though sleeping on his side hurt like a son of a bitch, he finally fell into a deep sleep. The drugs and alcohol would at least give him the blackness he had once tried so hard to escape, and now welcomed.

### Thursday, 12:35 A.M.

HE COULDN'T SLEEP. He'd spent the day avoiding his family locked in his room. Jack had come in several times to check on him, and each time Sam had either pretended to sleep, or simply yelled at him to go away.

With the house quiet and everyone asleep, he snuck out of the penthouse and went for a walk. He needed to get out, get away. Too bad he couldn't escape his own thoughts. The cool night air helped to clear his mind. He tried to concentrate on the city, the lights, the noise. Even at this late hour, people were out and about. He passed by several bars, music pouring out and people talking and playing pool. Many of the restaurants were closed, but the streets were filled with lights and people everywhere.

No direction or destination in mind, he aimlessly cruised the streets. After a half hour of wondering downtown, he hailed a cab and ended up at the hospital. He needed to see her and make sure she was okay.

He entered the ICU and the staff greeted him. They knew where he was headed, straight to Elizabeth's room. No one objected to his late-night visit.

They had removed the tubes in her chest for drainage. He figured that was a good sign. Her internal injuries were healing, leaving less of a chance of infection. The sheet was pulled up under her arms and her hands lay still by her side.

Someone had pulled her shoulder-length brown hair away from her face and used a headband to keep it in place. She looked so young with her face exposed like that. Her lip wasn't swollen any longer. The bruises on her face and neck were fading to mostly ugly yellow and green colors now. Dark circles stood out under her eyes.

For someone who'd slept for a week, she sure didn't look rested.

A bandage covered her right upper arm where he'd shot her. Her leg had been taken out of the sling and lay hidden under the sheet, probably still bandaged. They didn't have her leaning on her side any longer. He supposed the bullet holes in her back must be healed enough for her to lie flat.

He stood beside her bed looking down at her taking in every inch of her body. She was a beautiful woman. He wanted to see her smile and know the sound of her voice. He wondered if her laugh was soft or whole-hearted. He wondered what color eyes she had. Where they brown like her father's and brother's, or blue like her mother's, maybe a shade all her own? She liked to bake, but he wondered what else she liked to do. Did she prefer the city, or would she like the ranch in Colorado? She apparently liked birds, and he wondered if she liked horses, and had she ever been riding? He'd like to see her atop a horse with her hair flying in the wind. Hell, he'd like to see her do anything besides lie like a statue with her skin as pale as white marble.

"She's doing better. The doctors took out the tubes and sewed up her chest. They've decreased her sedatives and hope she might wake up in the next couple of days. She's a strong one, hasn't had an anxiety attack since before you left."

Sam hadn't heard the nurse come in; he'd been so focused on Elizabeth, taking inventory of every injury and mark on her body. "She is strong. She moved me from the middle of the street under a car. I probably outweigh her by sixty pounds, and I'm at least four inches taller than her."

"Determination can help you do just about anything, I imagine. I need to change the bandage on her thigh. You can stay if you like. I'll only be a few minutes, and then I'll leave you to your visit."

The nurse uncovered Elizabeth's leg. Very gently, she bent Elizabeth's knee and unwrapped the gauze holding the bandage in place. When she took the bandage off to reveal the long stitched cut, Sam winced. About four inches long, the wound was bad. She cleaned it, put a new bandage on, and wound gauze around her leg again. She gently put Elizabeth's leg back down on the bed and covered it with the sheet.

"It looks good. The infection is under control and probably gone by now with all the antibiotics she's had over the past week. They had to repair the muscle and ligament, that's why the cut is so long. The knife wound was only the size of the blade, I'm told. The knife was still in her leg when they brought her in. I believe the FBI took the knife and bullets as evidence."

The nurse left after that comment. She was trying to be helpful by giving him the information, but he really didn't want to hear it.

Sitting in the chair next to Elizabeth, he took her hand in his. The warmth of it always surprised him. He sat staring at her face hoping beyond hope she would wake up and tell him she was fine, that it was all a bad dream, some sick joke on him. Not going to happen, but he wished for it all the same. Softly rubbing his thumb on the back of her hand, he watched her sleep. Everything about her peaceful.

Although he'd pretended to sleep most of the day to avoid everyone at home, the late hour and fatigue weighed on him. The pain medication and muscle relaxers weren't doing him any good. If he moved too fast, his back went into spasms that shot pain up his spine and down his legs. Every breath made his cracked ribs throb.

He thought he might get a few things off his chest. They were alone. She was unconscious. It didn't really matter what he said, she wouldn't remember anyway. Right?

*Someone is holding my hand. She tried to come back to herself. Floating in the depths of a black ooze. Everything muffled around her, so empty and dark.*

"It's me, Special Agent Sam Turner. I'm the one you helped. I wanted to say thank you for what you did. I know you must be hurting. I know what it's like to be in that empty darkness I imagine you're in, like I was after I was drugged and you saved my life. I came tonight because I can't stop thinking about you."

*She heard him, but it was like listening underwater, all muffled. He was talking. Her father? Maybe one of her brothers. No, it was someone else. Who was here? The man who attacked her? Worry and fear engulfed her.*

"I hope you wake up soon. I'd really like to thank you when you're conscious and will remember that I'm truly grateful for what you did for me. If it hadn't been for you, I'd be dead."

*Thank me. Who wants to thank me? It's the man in the street.* She tried to open her eyes, but her lids felt like hundred pound weights.

The heart monitor sped up, and Sam hoped it didn't signal another anxiety attack. "You're okay. No one will hurt you. Can you hear me?" He remembered hearing Jenna that first night. "If you can hear me, try to open your eyes, or squeeze my hand."

*She tried to open her eyes, but it was no use. Her hands didn't heed the commands from her brain. All she managed was a tap of her index finger against his rough skin.*

"You can hear me. I'm Sam, Sam Turner with the FBI. I'm the guy you found in the street." She moved her finger again. He didn't think something so simple could make him feel so good. She heard him, and she tried to respond.

"Are you okay? Are you in pain?"

*Now, how am I supposed to answer that question? The darkness tried to swallow her again, but she liked his voice and fought to hear more from him. He was okay. She saved him. She hurt everywhere and wanted to tell him before the darkness took over. She wanted to sink back into the ooze and not feel.*

She moved her finger one time. He remembered seeing a movie once where the guy couldn't speak, so he blinked. One was yes and two was no, or was it the other way around?

"Okay. Let's try this, one for yes, two for no." She moved her finger once. "Yes. Okay. We're in business. Are you in pain?" One move. "Oh God, sweetheart. I'm sorry. Do you want me to get the doctor to give you more pain medication?" Two moves. "No. But you said you're in pain." Two moves. "Okay. No more meds. Probably just knock you back into the black oblivion." One move. He hadn't expected an answer, but now he knew she was probably holding on before the blackness swallowed her again. "Are you comfortable?" Two moves. "Of course not, you're in pain. Stupid question." One move. He smiled. "At least you have your sense of humor." One move.

*She liked him. He had a nice deep, rough voice, and she really wanted to open her eyes and look at him. Tired, she wasn't sure how long she'd be able to hang on. She wanted him to keep talking, so she could feel alive a little longer.*

"I don't know what to say. You're going to be okay." One move. "Good. I'm glad you agree. I've been worried, since you haven't woken up in a week." She pressed her finger down on his palm and her heart rate accelerated.

*A week! She'd been unconscious for a week. Oh, God. Her business. Her family. They must be so worried.*

"It's okay, sweetheart. You were hurt pretty bad. Do you remember what happened?"

Nothing. She didn't move. He was about to sit back and relax when her heart rate jumped. She pressed down on his palm again. One move. Yes.

"It's okay. It's over. You're safe. The nurses will come in and make me leave if you don't calm down." Two moves. "No, huh. Don't want me to go." Two moves. "I'm not going anywhere. Not as long as you're communicating. I can't sleep anyway. I keep replaying that night in my mind." One move. "You too?" One move. "I wake up in a cold sweat hearing you scream." Two moves. "Yes. All the time." He didn't want to think about it anymore. "Are you getting tired?" One move. "Okay, I'll sit here with you. You go to sleep and when you come back to the surface again, I'll be here." Two moves. "I thought you wanted me to stay?" One move. "Okay. Stay and what? Do you want something?" One move. "Well, how am I supposed to figure that out?"

*She didn't know. All she wanted was for him to keep talking. The sound of his voice was soothing and helped her keep the darkness at bay. She would probably fall asleep soon, but she wanted to hear him. She thought she'd give her voice a try. She couldn't get her eyes open, but maybe she could get out a word or two.*

"Talk," came the soft whisper.

"I heard you, sweetheart. That's good. I heard you."

He held her hand to his cheek. He felt good for the first time in a long while and all it had taken was for Elizabeth to whisper to him.

"Talk, huh. That's a lot to ask an FBI agent, and a guy for that matter. I'm trained to keep my mouth shut and let everyone else do the talking. You can learn a lot from listening to other people. Let them talk long enough, they usually reveal a lot more than they intend. I don't know you that well. I was passed out in the bed next to you for several days. I was drugged when you found me in the street. Let's stay away from that night, too many bad memories for both of us.

"I've met your family. Your brothers want to kill me. Daniel got in my face the first time I actually made it out of bed and to my feet." Two moves. "Yes, he did. He's really angry about what happened, and I don't blame him. You heard him yelling at me and set off all the bells and whistles. You've given us quite a few scares over the past week." One move. He squeezed her hand to let her know it was okay. "Your father wanted to kill me, but decided I was just stupid for making a mistake. He warned me not to do it again. Your mother is something else. She treats me like I'm one of her kids. She listened to me complain, and she kissed me on the head. I've been invited to Sunday dinner here in your room with your family." One move.

"You want me here too?" One move. "I don't know why you would. I'm the reason you're in the hospital in the first place." Two moves. "No, huh. Well, we can argue about that when you're strong enough to open your eyes and speak more than one word." One move. He smiled and squeezed her hand. "I imagine with a judge for a father and two brothers who are lawyers you're pretty good at arguing." One move.

"You're probably wondering about me." One move. "Let's see. I have a younger sister, Summer. She's married to my brother's best friend, Caleb. They have a beautiful little girl named Lily and a little boy named Jacob. My brother, Jack, is married to Jenna Caldwell Merrick, now Turner. She runs Merrick International. They have twin boys, Sam and Matt. Oh yeah, Jack is my identical twin." One move. "Yeah, we look exactly alike. Well, at least we do when I'm all cleaned up, and I haven't been undercover for months. Anyway, they live on the family ranch in Colorado. Jack and Caleb run the ranch. Summer takes care of the children when Jenna comes here for business. She and Jack have a penthouse here, and I live there. I spend a lot of time undercover and working cases all over the place, so when Jenna's in town, she's in charge of keeping track of me. I don't mind. She's really great. I helped save her from her ex-husband a couple of years ago. You may have heard the story." Two moves.

"No. I'm surprised. It was in all the papers. Well, it's a long story, but at least it'll allow me to keep talking to you." One move. "Okay, I'll tell you what happened and how Jenna became part of the family."

He talked about his family and all that had happened over the past couple of years. He told her how he was getting burned out on his job, and how he'd ended up not listening to his instincts the night she saved him. He didn't know when she'd finally fallen back into a deep sleep. He didn't care. It was cathartic to sit and talk to her, even if she couldn't talk to him. Maybe that's why he felt better for it. He emptied himself of his burdens without having to listen to someone tell him he was stupid, or what he should do. He could figure that out for himself. He didn't need someone to tell him he needed time away from the Bureau to center himself again, or he'd be no good to himself or anyone else.

## *Chapter Thirteen*

*Thursday, 2:46 A.M.*

JARRED HAD BEEN trying to get past security and the doctors and nurses. Only family was allowed into ICU and getting to Elizabeth had taken him several days. The guard outside the room had gone to the bathroom and asked a nurse to watch the door. A patient alarm drew her away.

He tried to find out what happened to Elizabeth, but the vague reports in the papers didn't appease his need for details. They called her a hero. Each morning he checked the papers for any more information, and every night he watched the news, hoping they reported on her. The Judge must have shut the press up. The hospital refused to answer any questions. No one in her family returned his phone calls, and he'd worked himself into quite a rage.

After all the months he'd dedicated to her, showing

her how much he loved her. They belonged together. He planned to tell her they were getting married. Then she'd gone and gotten herself hurt. When she became his wife, he'd make her leave that so-called house of hers. They'd buy a mansion in Marin and host lavish dinner parties, entertaining friends and rubbing shoulders with the many influential, rich, and famous people she knew and refused to discuss with him. Not anymore. They'd share everything and attend all the society parties she'd refused to take him as her date. He'd partner with her father and brothers on business deals and investments. They'd have a perfect life together.

Her father was behind the restraining order. She didn't want it. She wanted him. Her parents might not approve of him yet, but that was why she pretended to go along with them. Eventually, she'd tell them she loved him and couldn't live without him, and they'd have no choice but to accept him.

When she was out of the hospital, Jarred would make her stop playing these games.

Standing inside the door, he studied her through the dim light beside the bed. She didn't look all that bad. Her face was scratched and bruised and she had a split lip, but nothing major. The machines gave him pause, but as far as he could tell she didn't appear to be hurt too badly. Why was she in the ICU then?

He walked to her bedside, his back to the door. He doubted anyone would be in to see her until shift change at six. He had all the time in the world to look at and be with her. Her arm was bandaged. She must have cut it on some glass, or something, in the car accident. An oxygen tube ran across her face and into her nose. IVs and wires were attached to her and the equipment.

His heart beat faster just being close to her. She was so beautiful. Someone had brushed her soft hair back from her face. He remembered touching her hair when he'd put his arm behind her neck in the car as he drove her home. They'd spent only a short time together before she'd decided they should step back. She needed some space.

Yeah, right.

She wanted him. Jarred felt it in the shy way she kissed him. She may have pulled back before he'd wanted to end the kisses, but he sensed the passion under the surface. She wanted him to be the aggressor. No problem there. He enjoyed taking the lead, demanding his lovers gave everything over to him.

He grew hard thinking about kissing and touching her. She was right there in front of him. She'd never allowed him to touch her, except in the most innocent of ways, and having her in front of him now made him want to reach out and feel the softness of her skin. He ran a hand down her arm, over her hip and thigh. She didn't move or respond. He kept his hand on her leg, stroking and squeezing, imagining all the ways she'd please him. The throbbing in his groin grew more insistent as he took her all in.

Leaning close to her ear, he whispered, "Hello, baby. Did you miss me? I've missed you so much."

*Oh God. The pain. Someone was touching her leg and*

*the pain shot up her thigh and hip and into her back. Please, stop! Oh, God, stop! Who was hurting her? Sam? No, he knew her leg was hurt, he wouldn't touch her like that. Someone else, someone whispered to her.*

"Come on, baby, wake up and look at me. You've been cooped up in this hospital room over a week without me. When you get out of here, we're getting married. I'll make you my wife. We'll be so happy together."

*Jarred. How had he gotten into her room? Married. Over her dead body. Maybe his, if he didn't leave her alone and stop pressing on her thigh.*

*Where are you, Sam? He said he wouldn't leave, but she'd fallen back into the black ooze, and he must have gone home. Maybe it wasn't even the same day. How long had she been under this time? Sam had told her she'd been asleep for a week. It could be hours, or days, later. She didn't know.*

*Someone help me. Please, someone help me.*

She wouldn't open her eyes, and it pissed him off. "You better wake up, you bitch. I want to talk to you about your attitude and these stupid games you're playing."

He leaned over her, his hands planted on the bed beside her, and yelled, "Open your eyes and talk to me."

Sam had gone for a cup of coffee and spoke to Doctor Watts about Elizabeth's condition. He'd filled the doctor in on the conversation he had with her earlier. The doctor said she was doing better and would probably be more lucid over the next day or so if she continued to progress at the same steady pace she'd kept so far.

When he got back to her room, he entered quietly so

as not to wake her again, or startle her. He was surprised to find a man standing over her. Yelling at her.

*Where the hell is the guard?*

He thought about the message from Tyler. *Elizabeth has a double threat.* Maybe this guy was one of those threats. Or maybe he was the Silver Fox. Sam *minded* his back, used extreme caution and approached Elizabeth and the unknown man.

Stepping around the bed without making it obvious, he grabbed Elizabeth's hand, and casually took a sip of the coffee in his other hand. He set the cup on the table and studied the very surprised man standing on the other side of the bed with his hand on Elizabeth's thigh, resting right over where she'd been stabbed. Sam imagined she was in a lot of pain if he'd pressed on the wound, but he had to play this cool.

"Who the hell are you?" the guy asked like he owned the place. "You're not a doctor."

Sam wasn't about to give anything away, until he got some answers of his own. "Who the hell are *you*? You're not one of her brothers. I've met them. You must be a cousin."

"I'm her fiancé."

Well, that's a surprise. Certainly unexpected, but Sam hadn't heard a word about a fiancé from her parents or brothers. He'd met more than his fair share of liars over the years, and Sam knew a lie when he heard one. This guy was good though. He *sounded* convincing.

*No, Sam. He isn't. Don't believe him.*

Two moves. Not the fiancé. Jilted lover perhaps. Patrick

had told him Elizabeth didn't date anyone seriously, and usually not for more than a few weeks because they always turned out to be some bloodsucker trying to get something from her. This must be the head of all the bloodsuckers. The thought of this guy touching Elizabeth made his skin crawl.

Why the hell was he feeling so possessive? Maybe it was because she'd saved his life. He felt responsible for her. She was helpless at the moment, and the last thing she needed was some guy yelling at her and grabbing on her when she couldn't so much as tell him to stop.

Maybe he was jealous. It had been a long time since he'd had a woman in his life. Although she was barely conscious, she was the closest thing he had to a friend besides his family.

"Fiancé, huh. If that's the case, how come you haven't come to see her in the last week?"

"I've been out of town on business. I just got back."

"What exactly do you do for a living that is *so* important you can't come to see your *fiancé* when she's been critically injured and hasn't woken up in over a week?"

*Answer that asshole, because I know you aren't the fiancé, and you sure don't belong here. You better have a really good answer too.*

"I'm an investment banker. Elizabeth understands my work is important. I would have been here sooner, if not for work."

Dickweed made a good show of looking concerned and rubbed his hand over Elizabeth's thigh again. Sam read the possessive posturing. He felt he had a claim to Elizabeth and wanted Sam to back off. Not going to happen.

*Asshole! Stop touching me! Go to hell! The only thing that's important to you is getting to the people I know.*

Two moves. Sam figured she either didn't understand his need to work, or she didn't care.

"You haven't answered my question. Who are you, and why are you in Elizabeth's room at this hour?"

Sam took offense to the tone, but let it slide. For now. This guy was too cool, or at least acting like it. He certainly wanted Sam to believe he had a right to be here.

"I'm a friend." One move. Sam almost smiled, but he needed to keep his mind on the guy in front of him. "I could say the same thing to you, about the hour I mean. It's a strange time to visit. What's your name? I find it odd her family never mentioned she has a *fiancé*."

"I'm Jarred Palmer." He probably shouldn't have given his real name. The Hamiltons were bound to discover he'd been to see Elizabeth, but he didn't care. When he married her, they would have to accept him. All he had to do was ask her and they'd plan the wedding and the rest of their lives. She'd be his forever.

"You must not be close to her family if you've never heard them talk about Elizabeth's and my relationship," Jarred said defensively.

Jarred hoped this man wasn't connected to the Judge and his wife. They certainly wouldn't back up his claim to be Elizabeth's fiancé. He'd been to a few parties with Elizabeth and her family, and he'd never seen this man, so he bluffed. Besides, this man was definitely not the type to attend a charity benefit or corporate party. His hair was too long, he needed a shave, and he was wearing worn jeans, scuffed-up work boots, and a black T-shirt. A worn black leather jacket hung over the chair beside Elizabeth's bed. He looked like he belonged in a biker bar. The bruises on his face were probably from some bar fight.

Where had Elizabeth met him? Maybe he was a customer at her bakery, though Jarred doubted it. He appeared more likely to frequent some diner dive than an upscale café.

"I wonder if Elizabeth would say you two have a relationship."

"Looks like she can't say much of anything right now," Jarred said.

Who the hell was he, trying to make it seem like he and Elizabeth didn't have a relationship? It wasn't his fault she was playing hard to get. When she woke up, she'd realize how much she loved him. After all, when people went through a traumatic time, they often realized what they wanted most in life. Elizabeth would wake up wanting him.

"You'd be surprised what she can say. For instance, I'll give you two seconds to remove your hand from her thigh. You see, she's telling me by her heart rate that you're hurting her."

Dickweed finally heard the heart monitor and understood its meaning. It had been a steady slow beat when Sam had left to get his coffee, and now it raced like she'd jogged a mile in a minute flat.

"She endured over eleven hours of surgery, and her thigh is still stitched up. I imagine it hurts like a son of a bitch with you rubbing and squeezing it each time you get irritated with me." He glared at Dickweed. "I'm sure you agree, touching her thigh is a bad idea."

*She pressed down hard this time to let him know she was in a lot of pain. She hoped he would understand. Please, Sam, make him go. The dark is closing in, and I don't want to pass out knowing he's here.*

Sam gave her hand a squeeze. She was either panicked about Dickweed being there, or in a lot of pain. He'd assume it was the pain, since she must know he would protect her if Dickweed tried something.

"Since you're her *fiancé*, you've been in contact with her family and they've filled you in about her many severe injuries. Makes me wonder why you'd come in here yelling at her to wake up and grab her thigh when you know that leg's been injured. Can't you hear the heart monitor? It's about to start sounding alarms and calling every nurse and doctor into this room to see what's wrong with her."

The threat sank in and Dickweed's jaw clenched.

"Why would you do that to someone you're supposedly marrying? Do you get off on hurting the woman you supposedly love?" One move.

Well, Sam hadn't expected an answer from Elizabeth, but he'd certainly find out if the guy had hurt her in the past, or if he was just a jerk. Maybe he'd do some digging into the guy's background and find out what kind of guy Dickweed truly was.

Sam wanted to rile the guy. Hell, he wanted to severely piss him off for touching Elizabeth and hurting her. She'd been through enough without Dickweed showing up and making things worse.

"There's no supposedly about it. Elizabeth will be my wife."

Well, Dickweed certainly thought so.

Two moves. She paused and made two moves again.

*Don't believe him, Sam. You're with the FBI, check with the police. There's a restraining order. Make him go.*

"I didn't realize this was the thigh they operated on, or I certainly wouldn't have touched it."

Yeah, right. Dickweed didn't know anything about her injuries. He'd removed his hand, but uncertainty filled his eyes as they swept up from Elizabeth's legs to her battered face. He'd given himself away in too many ways for Sam to ignore.

"I wanted her to know I was here. Why are you here?"

"Like I said, I'm her friend. I think it's time you left." One move.

She wanted this to be over. Every once in a while she'd push down on his palm. She must have thought she was pushing hard, but actually it was a constant pressure, and each time she did it with less force. She was getting tired, and he needed to get Dickweed out of the room so he could talk to her alone.

"I think *you* need to leave. I'm her fiancé, and I want to spend some time alone with my future wife. I haven't seen her since she got hurt, and she'll be comforted knowing I'm here."

Overly confident and assertive, something about Dickweed set off all Sam's protective instincts and sent every nerve ending down his back into overdrive. Sam still didn't know who he was, definitely not the Silver Fox. No. The Fox was meticulous in his planning and would never allow someone to see him and live. Dickweed was definitely a threat, but not a cold-blooded killer. Sam got a completely different vibe from him. This was something personal. And personal could turn dangerous.

*I most certainly do not want to be alone with him. Sam, don't leave me alone with him. Make him go.*

Two moves. Rest. Two moves. Rest. Two moves.

The heart monitor picked up steam now. Elizabeth was about to panic. Sam needed to get rid of the guy and quick. She kept telling him no.

"Well, you see, I can't leave her. She's very important to me. I can't stop thinking about her and what she did for me." Dickweed had no idea what Sam was talking about, since the real details about what happened had been left out of the papers. "You are not her fiancé. I don't know why you're lying about that fact, but you can bet I'll find out."

Dickweed came around the bed and grabbed Sam by the front of his shirt and got right in his face. "She's mine. You got that. When she wakes up, she'll realize we belong together. We're getting married."

Sam had to give the guy credit. He had balls, but he was also about two inches shorter than Sam and not as big or strong. Dickweed wasn't a threat to him, but he could certainly hurt Elizabeth. She'd indicated he had hurt her in some way, making Sam angry. His back spasmed and exploded with pain after Dickweed grabbed him. He did his level best not to show it. He clamped his hands over Dickweed's wrists and got right in his face.

"Assaulting an FBI agent is against the law, number one. Number two, she's not marrying you, because she's marrying me." He didn't know why he said it, probably to piss the guy off, and hopefully make him understand Elizabeth certainly wasn't his. He threw the guy off with little effort when his statements stunned Dickweed momentarily. "Number three, I better not find you in here again, or hear you've been here, or you'll regret it."

Elizabeth put her finger in his jeans' back pocket and pulled. He turned and found her awake and looking right at him.

Elizabeth wanted to piss off Jarred. She managed to open her eyes and see Sam. A handsome man hiding under all that scruffy hair. His blue eyes were intense. Sam Turner, FBI agent, had a lot going for him, and all of it intrigued her. "You'll do." She gave him a warm smile before her lids fell closed again, too weak and tired to keep them open. She hoped Jarred got the picture and would finally leave her alone.

Sam's heart stopped in that moment. Did she say he'd do? God, she was great. Her brother, Patrick, was right. She had a great sense of humor. For a moment there, when his heart stopped working, the thought of her marrying him had seemed like a great idea. He'd have to think about his reaction to her statement another time. Right now, she was awake, and he wanted Dickweed gone.

"Get out. Now." His glare and tone left no room for argument. He turned back to Elizabeth and leaned close to her. "You woke up, sweetheart." He kissed her on the cheek.

Jarred knew when to retreat. He'd get to Elizabeth another time. When she was alone. If she thought she could disregard him and marry this guy, claiming to be with the FBI, she was sorely mistaken. He wouldn't be deterred so easily. He had plans for her.

"We'll talk about this later, Elizabeth." Jarred's irritation laced through his clipped tone. "I knew you were faking sleeping."

"You don't know shit," Sam snapped. "Get out before I call security and have them throw you out." He'd do it himself, but he was in too much pain at the moment. Besides, if he laid his hands on the guy, he just might kill him for upsetting Elizabeth when she'd finally managed to wake up.

Dickweed opened the door and found the security guard blocking his path. Sam called out, "Make sure he leaves and doesn't come back." The guard nodded and swept his hand out in the direction of the elevator, indicating Dickweed should precede him out.

The door swooshed closed and Sam turned back to Elizabeth overwhelmed with relief.

"Blue. Your eyes are blue. I've wondered about that, you know. Are you still awake?"

She managed to turn her head, open her eyes a slit, and look at him. Talking was too much work.

"Hi, sweetheart. Are you okay?" He sat down in the

chair and raised her hand to his cheek, holding it there, overwhelmed with happiness. Seeing her eyes open was too much for him.

"Hurrrrt."

"Do you want me to get the doctor? He can give you some more meds."

She pressed once on his cheek. She couldn't talk anymore. Her eyes drooped closed, even though she wanted to look at him. Handsome, that voice of his made her feel warm all over.

"Come on, sweetheart. Stay with me for a few minutes more. I'll get the Doc to give you some more meds in a minute."

One move. "That's it. It's probably too hard to stay awake for too long. Let's get right to it then. He's not your fiancé. Who is he?"

She couldn't open her eyes, but she wanted him to know Jarred shouldn't be there. "Restraining order," she sighed out.

"You have a restraining order against him. He's an ex-boyfriend."

Two moves. "No restraining order? But you said you had one against him."

One move. "Yes to the restraining order, no to the ex-boyfriend. He wasn't a boyfriend. Someone you dated or just knew?"

One move. *You're getting it, Sam. Hurry up. The black is coming back.*

"Yes. Okay. I'll look into the restraining order and find out what's going on. I'll ask your Dad about it."

Two moves. "Don't ask your Dad?" Two moves. "You don't want him to know about Jarred coming here." One move. "You don't want them to worry." One move. "Okay, sweetheart. I'll ask . . ."

"Kay," she cut him off.

"Okay, sweetheart. I'll talk to Kay and get the details. Are you okay?" She'd gone still again. A fine sheen of sweat broke out over her skin. Opening her eyes and talking had taken every ounce of energy she had.

Two moves. "What can I do for you? Do you want me to call your parents and have them come down to sit with you?"

Two moves. *You stay Sam. Talk to me some more.*

Elizabeth pressed her palm to his face, and he leaned into her hand. "Okay, sweetheart. You go to sleep, and I'll stay with you. I pressed the button for the nurse. She'll be here in a second, and I'll get you some more meds." He shifted in the seat and moved her hand back to the bed while he held it by linking fingers with hers. He took the painkillers out of his pocket and opened the bottle. She must have heard it because she squeezed his hand. "Just popping a couple of pain pills. My back is killing me."

*Why did his back hurt? She didn't think she'd hurt his back getting him under the car. She kept squeezing his hand trying to get him to tell her what was wrong.*

"It's okay. My back muscles are going into spasms because of the gunshots."

Her eyes flew open, and she squeezed his hand harder.

He stood and bent over her. "It's okay. I wore a bulletproof vest. It saved me, but I have a couple of cracked ribs and nasty bruises. The muscles in my back hurt like hell, especially when they tighten up on me. They'll be fine in a few days."

*She squeezed his hand once. The darkness crept in, but she was thankful it wasn't all-encompassing like it had been before. Maybe being awake for a little while had helped to keep her from sinking so deeply into the black ooze.*

He leaned over her, his face close to hers. "It's nice to know you care." He kissed her softly on the lips. She rocked him to the soles of his feet by that brief contact. He wasn't about to let her know she'd sent a bolt of lightning through his system. So beautiful, and she came from a really influential and rich family. Way out of his league.

He was well off, thanks to Jenna's generosity, more than capable of supporting a wife and family. But Elizabeth had grown up in a world he didn't understand. He'd been raised on a ranch and worked in a profession women ended up hating. He felt the loss of a relationship he'd never even had with her. He settled back into his chair and held her hand while she went back to sleep.

*Wow! She wished she could wake up enough to get him to do that again. Who knew such a simple touching of lips could send warm waves through her system and make her feel as if the sun was shining on her. She hoped Sam Turner, FBI agent, stuck around. Maybe Kay had been right. She needed a new man in her life, and a cop just might be the perfect choice. Well, an FBI agent anyway.*

## Chapter Fourteen

*Thursday, 6:30 P.M.*

SAM STAYED WITH Elizabeth until after shift change that morning. She slept, and he thought about everything that happened with Dickweed and the restraining order. He thought about how great it was she'd finally woken up. His thoughts always circled back to two things: he'd said something about marrying her and he'd kissed her. Just an innocent peck on the mouth, but it stirred something primal in him. The longer he sat watching her sleep, the more he thought about her and how she'd gotten under his skin. If he wasn't careful, she'd work her way right into his heart, and he didn't know what that would do to him when she woke up completely and remembered what happened to her, thanks to him. She'd want to get as far away from him as possible, as soon as possible.

He scared his family half to death when he walked through the front door that morning to find them all having breakfast at the dining room table. They all thought he was asleep in his room. The smile on his face when he got home startled them. He told them about his night with Elizabeth, leaving out the kiss and marriage business. They'd read too much into it, and he already knew a relationship between him and Elizabeth was a dream without a chance of ever becoming a reality.

His job was slowly turning into a burden where it had once provided him with a sense of pride and accomplishment. His personal life was suffering. If he was honest, he was suffering and needed to find some kind of balance in his life. The shooting had opened his eyes to everything lacking in his life.

*Get a life, Sam.*

Jenna's voice echoed through his memory. Getting older, the years passing by barely noticed. If he didn't watch out, he'd be too old to play ball with the kids he really wanted. Time to refocus, find a wife and have some babies, a real life. Jack made it look so easy, and Jenna was such a great mother and wife. He wanted those things for himself more than anything.

Since he hadn't slept the night before, he went to sleep after breakfast with his family. Two little giggles from beside the bed woke him. Turning to his side, he peered over the edge of the bed and into the big blue eyes of his nephews, Sam, named for him, and Matt. So cute. Their little blonde heads peaked above the mattress as both of them stared at him.

"What are you two doing in here?" He scrunched up his face in a silly way and they laughed.

"Mommy says, eat," they said in unison.

"Eat, huh. Dinner time?" Both little heads bobbed up and down. "Okay, cowboys, I'll be right there." They didn't move from the side of the bed. Both looked like they had something on their minds. "What's the matter?"

Sam looked at Matt and Matt looked at Sam. Apparently, Sam was elected speaker in their silent exchange. "You don't look like Daddy anymore."

"I don't, huh. You want me to look like Daddy again?"

Both heads bobbed up and down. "You look scary," Matt said, biting his lower lip, his eyes filled with worry.

Well, that hurt. He scared his own nephews. He needed a haircut and a shave, but he didn't think he looked that bad. Maybe the bruises and cuts on his face scared them. "Are you guys afraid of the cuts and bruises? They'll go away soon."

Both heads shook side to side. "What's the matter?"

"You look mean, like a lion," Sam said into the mattress.

"You look like a bad guy," Matt chimed in, not to be outdone by his brother.

Sam sighed. "You know Uncle Sam loves you, right?" Both heads bobbed up and down. "I don't want you guys to be afraid of me. We like to play, right?" Little heads bobbed. "Crawl up here, munchkins. Uncle Sam wants a hug." Both little boys climbed up onto the bed, and did exactly what Sam expected, but knew would hurt like hell. They jumped on top of him. His back screamed out in protest, his ribs burned and throbbed, clenching his jaw against the pain, he held his nephews tight. He gave them each a tickle and rubbed his scruffy beard against their bellies. They laughed uncontrollably and crawled all over him. They certainly weren't afraid any longer.

"Okay, you guys are killing me. Go get Aunt Summer and tell her to bring her scissors. I'll look like Daddy in a few minutes."

Both boys sent up a cheer and ran from the room. Sam rolled slowly out of bed to his feet, painfully, and headed for the bathroom rubbing at the muscles in his back, his other arm pressed against his aching ribs. He'd shave while he waited for Summer to come and do her thing with his hair. She'd threatened him at the hospital. He had no choice now. They were so cute wanting him to look like Jack again. He wondered if they understood not everyone had an identical twin. They weren't even two yet, but they were smart.

He'd just finished trimming his beard down and shaving half his face when Summer entered the bathroom. Turning from the mirror, he rubbed his hand over her rounded belly. Baby number three gave him a kick and he smiled.

"Who put the boys up to saying I was scary looking?"

Summer did her best impression of looking confused. "I don't know what you're talking about?"

"Yeah, right. I'll be done in a second, and you can chop off the hair. Apparently, I don't look like Jack and that disturbs the boys."

"It disturbs me too when you look like a member of the Hell's Angels. You seem better. Did you sleep?"

"I did. Thankfully."

"You're happy she woke up and spoke to you."

Sam rinsed off his now clean-shaven face and talked to Summer in the mirror. "I can't tell you what a relief it is she woke up. The doctors thought she should have been up two days ago. I've been holding my breath since this happened, but when she didn't wake up when they expected, I almost lost it. I don't know what I would have done had she died. She saved my life. I couldn't live with myself if she lost hers because of what she did for me."

Summer hugged him from behind and talked to him in the mirror. "I'm glad she's doing better. You know I couldn't live without you, and neither could anyone else in this family. We love you, Sam. We're happy you're feeling better."

"Thanks. Okay, make me look like Jack before the munchkin men start calling me Simba."

"What?"

"They said I look like a lion. They don't like the long hair and beard."

"I don't like it either. You're so handsome, even when you look like a criminal."

"Great. I wonder if Elizabeth believed I'm an FBI agent, or some thug hanging out in her room."

Summer didn't say anything. She cut Sam's hair to match her brother Jack's. She would have to talk to Jenna about Sam's inadvertent admission that he cared whether Elizabeth saw him as a respectable FBI agent or a thug. She didn't think Sam realized what he'd revealed with that simple statement about his appearance. Summer found it very enlightening. Sam had a crush on Elizabeth, and maybe something more. Summer hoped it turned into a lot more. Sam deserved some happiness. Now that Elizabeth had woken up, he was finally starting to get back to being the fun, loving, happy guy they all knew and loved.

# Chapter Fifteen

*Friday, 8:09 A.M.*

SAM SAT IN his cubicle reading through the Silver Fox files. He glanced up when Tyler stopped beside him.

"What are you doing here? You're supposed to be on leave. You look like a new man. Haircut, clean face, not sitting home brooding about what happened. You must be feeling better."

"My nephews thought I looked more like a bad guy than a good guy. I'm here for my meeting with Vernet about the internal investigation into the shooting."

"Doesn't that guy hate you and have it out for you? I heard he reviews all of your cases, hoping to bring you up on charges and get you fired."

"I don't know about every case, but he does watch my every move. You make a guy look like an idiot in front of his boss one time and he never lets you live it down. Can I help it if the guy can't take a joke?"

"I heard his boss didn't think it was a joke, and Vernet had to attend some class on ethics."

"Let's hope he learned something, because he's about to get his wish to have me fired granted, if he can prove I shot Elizabeth knowing she tried to help me. I don't know how she remembers the events, but I remember them quite clearly now. I might be up shit creek without a paddle if her memory and mine don't match. Vernet is looking for any excuse to go all the way and flush my career down the toilet."

"I didn't want to say anything, because the investigation is supposed to be ongoing and confidential, but I spoke with Vernet yesterday about my part of the operation. He's on a witch-hunt and you're the one he wants to tie to a stake. He's trying to make it seem like we didn't have proper backup at the bar, and perhaps you knew the Silver Fox was going to show up instead of Scott. He thinks you were hot-dogging again."

"I don't hot-dog anything. I'd be dead if I went off half-cocked all the time."

"Just be prepared when you go in and tell him what happened outside Elizabeth's place. Davies is backing us up on what happened at the bar. As for the shooting, you and I both know you were incapacitated by the drug you were given. You would have never fired your weapon unless you thought you were in mortal danger. You didn't even draw the gun yourself. She had it and appeared to be a threat. Besides, you nicked her in the arm. It's not like you killed her."

"Thanks, I feel so much better about shooting an innocent woman." Sam held up his hand to stop Tyler from protesting further. "I know what happened, and Vernet can't change the facts. Even if he wants to say I shot her on purpose, the fact I was drugged and unable to think clearly and rationally is in my favor. I'm not worried about him, it's such a pain in my ass to jump through all these hoops."

"Give him the facts. Be the man of few words you are. Make him work for it."

"That's what I intend to do. On another subject, have you looked through some of these cases? Since I'm on leave, you've been stuck with all my pending files. The most pressing one is the missing person I got the day before all this happened." He rifled through the files on the desk and came up with the one he wanted. "Here it is. Dianne Wales. She's seventeen. Went missing about two weeks ago. No one has seen or heard from her. No troubles at home, suggesting she ran away, no witness has come forward or ransom demanded to suggest an abduction. She disappeared after school one day. The police are doing a good job of putting the word out and distributing her picture." He handed the photo of Dianne over to Tyler.

Tyler scanned the high school graduation photo of a young blonde. Short hair, blue eyes, an all-American girl. The girl next door. She wore the standard black cap and gown, along with a pearl necklace with a gold charm. He looked more closely at the pendant, a rose in full bloom. The message from Morgan hit him all at once. He remembered the news reports, years ago, about the death of Princess Diana of Wales. They called her "England's Rose," or something like that. Dianne Wales was the Rose Princess from Morgan's message.

"She's the Rose Princess."

"Excuse me? The what?"

"Remember I told you about the message Morgan left for me about you and Elizabeth. She also left a message about another case. I think it's this one. She told me the Rose Princess is under the grand oak, and I need to find the King of Hearts."

Sam's eyes held a skeptical gleam.

"See here, in the picture. She's wearing a rose. Her name is Dianne Wales. Princess Diana of Wales was known as 'England's Rose.' Don't ask me how I remember that. I recall seeing all the coverage of the princess's funeral. That's a pretty good tie-in to the message and the young girl who's missing. Dianne resembles Princess Diana in some ways. It could work."

"Okay, let's say she is the Rose Princess. Who's the King of Hearts?" Sam asked, surprising Tyler with his easy acceptance of Morgan's message.

"I don't know. I'll have to go through the file. I'll head over to the police station and talk to the detective in charge. Maybe I can come up with some viable suspects for the King of Hearts from their people of interest."

"Let me know what you discover, or if you want to bounce ideas off me. I can't be an active part in the investigation until I'm cleared, but I'll go nuts sitting around doing nothing."

"Why don't you head to Colorado and hang with your family for a few weeks?"

"Not until I know for sure Elizabeth is all right, and we have some kind of closure with the Silver Fox. He's still a threat to her, until we can figure out whether or not she remembers what he looks like."

"Vernet, Davies, and I are meeting with her today to hear her official statement. It should be interesting to see Vernet try and coax her into taking you down."

"Elizabeth will surprise him. She's not one to let anyone tell her what to do or what to say. Don't forget Judge Hamilton is her father. I understand she's the only one in the family that goes toe-to-toe with him. I have to say, I'd love to see that. He's notorious for his brilliant arguments and his temper. She's probably quite something to see going up against him in an argument."

Tyler grinned, recognizing Sam's infatuation with her. Not surprising, since they'd been through a traumatic experience together, but Tyler thought it a good sign Sam wasn't as close to burnout as he'd thought.

"I'll get to see her in action later today if Vernet pisses her off."

"Don't let him upset her. She's been through enough and with that dickweed, Jarred, showing up the other night, she doesn't need any more stress during her recovery."

"I'll try to keep things calm and remind Vernet she's our only link to the Silver Fox at this point. We need her cooperation. If she can ID the Fox, I'll have a sketch artist work with her on a drawing of the guy. We can have her look at mug shots, but I don't think this guy has ever been arrested. We didn't find anything on the DNA profile in our system. As for Dickweed, the local police paid him a visit and warned him about contacting or seeing Elizabeth again. It seems the restraining order ran out. She'll have to petition the court for another if she still believes the guy is a threat."

"He is a threat. He grabbed her leg and hurt her. And then, the guy says she's marrying him. He's completely delusional. He won't stop harassing her."

"Yeah, well, I'm sure her father will make sure the restraining order is put in place again. I understand he was the one who insisted she have one in the first place."

"He did. She's very important to him. Watch out for the brothers too. If they find out you were there that night and lost track of me, you might get decked. The young one, Daniel, is a hothead when it comes to his sister."

"Sounds like there's a story there."

"He got in my face the first time I got out of bed."

Sam ignored Tyler's cocky grin. "Let me know about the missing girl. I'd love an update after you see Elizabeth. I don't want to be blindsided by Vernet if things don't go well."

"I'll be in touch. Good luck with Vernet."

"Thanks." Sam rolled his eyes and got to his feet prepared to face anything Vernet had in store for him.

## Chapter Sixteen

SAM WALKED INTO Vernet's office without so much as
knocking. Taking a seat in front of Vernet's desk, he
glared at the man staring at him. Vernet was one of those
people who thought everyone else owed him something,
but never worked to earn anything on his own. He hadn't
qualified as a field agent and decided to be part of the internal investigations of people he thought didn't deserve
to hold the spot he should have had himself. At least,
that's what he thought.

"Don't you knock?"

"You knew I was coming for our meeting, so let's get
on with it." Sam kept his voice cool.

"I'm glad to see you cleaned up your look for our
meeting and you're taking this matter seriously."

Sam didn't care what the guy thought about his appearance. Let him assume Sam gave a shit about anything the guy had to say, as long as it got him out of that

office and back to doing his job. He needed to get back to working the Silver Fox case and eliminating the threat to Elizabeth and anyone else the Silver Fox planned to kill.

Vernet expected Sam's attitude, but he'd get the answers he wanted and file his report detailing Sam's incompetence and culpability in the shooting of Elizabeth Hamilton despite it.

"I've already met with Deputy Director Davies and Agent Reed, who detailed what happened. I'd like your accounting of the Elizabeth Hamilton shooting."

Vernet put a small recorder on the desk and pushed the record button. He gave the date, time, and their names for the record. He sat poised behind his desk with pen and paper waiting for Sam to begin.

"Agent Reed and I were outside Ray's Rock House waiting for our contact to arrive. We had a meeting to discuss the final details of the contract murder for hire. Our contact was late, so Agent Reed and I decided I would go into the bar to wait.

"I entered the bar and scanned the room for my contact. He wasn't there. Before I made it to a secure position, someone stuck a needle in my arm and drugged me. They grabbed me and took me out the side door. Dazed and unsteady on my feet, I never got a look at him. I was thrown into the backseat of a vehicle and punched multiple times. I fought to get away without success. When we drove away from the bar, I was disoriented and trying to remain conscious.

"The car stopped, and I jumped out and tried to escape. Someone shot me in the back twice. I turned toward the suspect and fell to the ground, apparently, outside Elizabeth Hamilton's home. The drugs incapacitated me. I was groggy and in and out of consciousness. My sense of time was off. I can't say how long I was in the street, or how long I had been in the car.

"The next thing I remember is Miss Hamilton lying on top of me. She rolled me under a car. I heard a loud crash. When I came to again, I discovered a woman beside me with the gun and knife from my ankle holsters in her hand. I believed she was a threat, and I took the gun away from her. She still had the knife in her hand, and I shot her. After I fired, I don't remember anything until I woke up in the hospital on Saturday."

"That's it. You have nothing further to add or explain?"

"No."

"If you knew she got you under the car to protect you, why would you then shoot her?"

"I was drugged. I vaguely remember a woman landing on top of me and rolling me over and over. I didn't know why. I remember hearing a loud crash, but at the time I couldn't have told you what it was, or that it was the threat and not the woman. She had my gun and knife. She appeared to be a threat."

"Why weren't you wearing your regular weapon holstered under a jacket? I believe you prefer to wear a shoulder holster."

"I do. I didn't want to blow my cover. The meeting was with a middleman of sorts to set up the hit on my fictional wife and draw the Silver Fox into the open so we could arrest him. If my contact noticed the gun, he'd make me for a cop, so I only had my backup weapon."

"Did you suspect the Silver Fox would show up in place of your contact?"

"No."

"Did Miss Hamilton say anything to you before you shot her?"

"Not that I remember."

"Did she at any time indicate she was trying to help you?"

"Not that I remember."

"Did Miss Hamilton threaten you in any way prior to you shooting her?"

"Do you mean besides disarming me and holding my gun and knife in front of me?" Sam's anger tugged against the tightly held reins he'd put on it.

"Did she indicate she meant to harm you?"

"She had two weapons. I was drugged and incapacitated. She held the knife up in the air, and I shot her in the arm," Sam said, losing his patience.

"So you shot her because she was going to stab you."

"No."

"No, she wasn't going to stab you?"

"Exactly."

"You said she had the knife in her hand, raised in the air."

"She did."

"So you believed she was going to stab you."

"She had the knife in her hand," he said sarcastically.

"I suggest you cooperate with this investigation.

You're lucky Deputy Director Davies only put you on administrative leave. In my opinion, you should be suspended until this investigation is complete. You shot an innocent woman."

"Yes. I did." Sam kept his voice even, belying the emotions those words invoked inside of him.

"So you admit that you shot her."

"I already said I shot her."

"Are you saying you shot her knowing she tried to help you?" Vernet thought he was so close to finally getting Sam to admit he'd screwed up and shot an innocent bystander.

"No."

Vernet thought he had him on something, but the recording would show exactly what Sam wanted it to show. Vernet wasn't after the truth, but to make Sam look like he'd done something wrong.

"Give me a straight answer?"

"I did."

The muscles in Vernet's jaw twitched, his fists clenched in front of him on the desk. No wonder he hadn't made it to working in the field. He couldn't control his emotions and everything showed in his face and body language. Right now, Vernet wanted to seriously harm him, and Sam thought it was hilarious.

"You are evading and being uncooperative. I want to know what you knew about Miss Hamilton prior to shooting her."

"I didn't know anything about her, except she had my gun and knife. At the time, in my altered state, I believed she meant to harm me. I did everything possible to protect myself."

"So you shot her because you thought a woman who weighed at least sixty pounds less than you and is about six inches shorter than you posed a mortal threat."

"She's only about four inches shorter than me."

"That isn't the point."

"You brought it up. You apparently think her size and weight have bearing. She may be smaller than I am, but that doesn't make her any less dangerous when she's armed and I'm incapacitated."

"But you had taken the gun from her. Why not try to take the knife away? You're much stronger than her."

"I am stronger when I'm not drugged and going in and out of consciousness. I did what I thought necessary to eliminate what I believed was a threat. Let's cut to the chase. I didn't shoot her without reason. She had a knife. Had I known she was trying to help me, I wouldn't have shot her. It's that simple."

"I beg to differ. I believe you shot her without determining whether she was a threat or not." He watched Sam closely for a reaction, but Sam continued to sit, unreadable.

"Did you identify yourself as an FBI agent as is standard procedure?"

"No, I did not identify myself as an FBI agent," Sam admitted.

"So you didn't follow procedure and as a result shot an innocent woman."

"No."

"Excuse me, you said . . ."

Sam cut him off. This had gone on long enough, and he wouldn't let it continue. "I followed procedure. I didn't identify myself as an FBI agent because at that point I couldn't determine if Elizabeth was the Silver Fox, or working with the person who is. Identifying myself to the wrong person might have blown my cover and months of work, not to mention getting me killed.

"Now, I've answered all your questions, and you have my statement of the facts." Sam emphasized the last word. He got up and turned to leave when Vernet stood up to address him again.

"We'll see what Miss Hamilton has to say about you shooting her. I'll bet she has a lot to say. I wouldn't be surprised if she told you she was trying to help you."

She had said those very words. He didn't register what she'd said until he lay beside her in the hospital, but Vernet wouldn't take that into consideration. Let Elizabeth tell him. He'd simply state he didn't remember her saying it at the time. He'd already spoken words to that effect and it would be reflected in the recording.

"I think you'll be surprised by what she has to say, because I have no doubt she'll tell the truth about the events that happened that night. That is, if you don't distort her words like you're trying to distort mine."

Vernet puffed himself up to his full height. "I'm doing my job and investigating a shooting involving an agent who is on the verge of burnout and went into a situation he knew had the potential to be dangerous. You didn't call in backup, even though you felt something wasn't quite right about the situation at the bar. You put Agent Reed in danger and an innocent woman has paid an extremely high price for your recklessness."

"Is that so? Agent Reed was never in any danger. We work as a team. We both agreed calling in more backup would have been a waste of time and resources. We had no indication the Silver Fox would attend the meeting himself, and even if he did attend the meeting, we don't know how he found out I'm an agent. We still have to find out why, knowing I'm an agent, he would show up with the intent to kill me. He could have stayed away. We have no idea who he is. So why would he come just to kill me? These are the questions that need to be answered, not whether or not I shot Elizabeth out of malice. I've answered that question, and I'm sure Elizabeth's statement will support that fact."

"We'll see. We both know you've been skirting protocol and taking on the most dangerous cases without regard for yourself or your fellow agents. This latest incident proves you need to be pulled out of the field, and someone needs to seriously consider whether or not you're capable of continuing as an agent."

"And I'll bet you're that someone. You'd like nothing better than to see me go down, even if you have to manipulate the facts to make that happen."

"I do want to see you go down. I think you have little respect for the position you hold, and your lack of discipline and your recklessness with your life puts others in danger. Your little joke cost me a promotion. Payback's a bitch."

Sam made a show of looking at the recorder on the desk. He waited until Vernet realized what he'd done.

"Threats and accusations will get you fired. I thought you would have learned that in your ethics class. The facts of this case stand on their own. But for the official record," Sam leaned in close to the recorder, but kept his eyes on Vernet the entire time, "I shot Elizabeth because she wielded a knife and appeared to be a threat." Sam stood to his full height and continued to stare down Vernet. "I'm sure the recording will be transcribed in its entirety and provided to Deputy Director Davies for his review, as well as your superiors. I'd also like to request a copy of the transcript from your interview with Elizabeth, once it's complete. As is my right under the guidelines of the investigation, and since you seem hell-bent on proving something that is false."

Sam left Vernet's office without saying another word. If Vernet was carrying a gun, he'd have likely shot him in the back. Vernet either needed to alter the tape or let the recording stand with his threat and admission that he wanted to see Sam go down, even if it meant putting a slant on the facts. Sam left knowing Elizabeth's account of what happened would back up his recollection.

Stopping by Tyler's cubicle, he gave him an abbreviated version of what happened with Vernet and asked Tyler to call later and let him know how things went with Elizabeth. He wanted to be there with her, but couldn't because the investigation was about him. He'd go home, spend time with his family before they went back to Colorado and not think about her. Yeah, right.

## Chapter Seventeen

*Friday, 4:10 P.M.*

ELIZABETH SPENT MOST of Thursday dozing off and on. The doctors were pleased to see her stay awake for several minutes at a time and later in the evening more than a half hour. They moved her out of intensive care and into a private room. Her parents and brothers were thrilled each time she woke up and spoke to them for even a few minutes. Her father had been sweet and kind. His eyes misted over when she called to him from the bed. He told her it was the sweetest sound he'd ever heard, hearing his Ellie Girl call him Dad after so many days spent worrying about her.

Her whole body hurt. She felt as if she'd been run over by a Mack truck and all eighteen wheels had flattened her. Her back throbbed where she'd been shot, her ribs ached from being kicked, her abdomen was sore from surgery, and her arm and thigh ached constantly. The doctor upped her pain meds, but it didn't take the edge off and only made her groggier.

Sam had asked the doctors to give her a double dose the night before, after Jarred's visit. She'd fallen asleep holding Sam's hand and listening to his deep voice.

Each time she woke up, the memories flooded her mind and she couldn't shut them off. The terror and fear of what happened came back to her like crashing waves. She tried to hide her fear and the trembling in her hands when her family visited, but when she was alone it was much harder to keep the emotions at bay.

She'd only felt safe over the last couple of days when Sam was with her. Maybe because they shared the trauma of almost being killed. She liked the way he opened up and talked to her. Maybe it was that he'd talked to her about his family and his job, and she felt like she knew him better than most, because he didn't seem like the kind of man who opened up to many people. Perhaps it was the connection between them. She needed to know someone understood how she felt, how scared she had been that night, and since then, lying helpless in bed.

The FBI agents were due to show up for the interview they insisted couldn't wait any longer. She knew what they wanted to know. Could she identify the man who tried to kill her and Sam? Hell yes, she could ID him. She'd like to fillet him and feed him to the sharks in the San Francisco Bay for what he'd done to her and Sam. Her only consolation, she'd managed to fight the man and hurt him before he'd almost killed her.

She raised the bed so she wasn't lying flat on her back when the agents arrived. The minor change in position sent pain shooting throughout her body. She accidentally tightened the muscles in her thigh to adjust her position. Pain shot down her leg and up into her hip. She broke out in a fine sheen of sweat over her skin. The three men who entered stared. She hoped she wouldn't pass out before she had a chance to talk to them.

Her parents and brothers wanted to be with her for the interview, but she'd insisted they stay away. She wanted to say what happened without them asking questions, or becoming upset about what she'd been through. She wanted to spare them the strain of hearing her tell the story. It would be easier for them, and for her, if they got the details from Deputy Director Davies.

"Miss Hamilton, I'm Special Agent Tyler Reed. Are you okay?"

Was she okay? No. She hurt, and she wanted that hurt to go away so she could rest. At least when she was in the black ooze, she could block out everything. Now that she was awake, she wished to be afloat in that nothingness. The doctors told her she'd feel better in a day or so as she began to move more and heal.

She ignored the agent's concern and asked, "Where's Agent Turner? I thought he might be here for this." She reached up with her wounded arm to move the pillow and winced.

Agent Reed came forward to help her get settled. "I was Agent Turner's partner the night you were hurt. He won't be here for the interview, since he's the focus of this investigation."

"What do you mean? He's being investigated?" Elizabeth didn't like the sound of that. "Tell me you're joking."

Agent Reed moved aside and another agent stepped up to the bed to address her. "Agent Turner shot you. Any agent involved in a shooting is subject to an internal review and investigation to determine whether disciplinary action, or legal action, is required."

The man's eyes lit up at the thought of some sort of punishment being meted out to Sam. That didn't sit well with her. She'd have to watch this guy. He had some sort of vendetta to settle with Sam, and she refused to help him accomplish it. She knew a lot about people with hidden agendas.

"Then you're wasting your time with this investigation."

Agent Reed tried to hide a smile, letting her know she'd pegged things right with the other agent.

"Miss Hamilton, we'd like you to recount the events, and maybe answer some questions. Do you think you're up to telling us what happened?" Agent Reed asked, his voice coaxing.

"Hasn't Agent Turner told you what happened?"

"We've all heard Agent Turner's version of what happened. We would like to hear your version, so we can determine the truth of the matter." The agent took the chair next to her, taking out a recorder, paper, and pen to take notes.

She thought of a weasel. She pictured him as Ebenezer Scrooge, sitting at his desk counting out his money and having no thought for anyone else. This guy was exactly like that. He was only after what he wanted and not the truth, no matter who he hurt.

"The truth of the matter." She glanced at Deputy Director Davies, discreetly standing back from everyone, watching the events as they transpired. She'd already met him and found him to be a good man. He understood what was going on, and although he appeared mildly bored by the entire scene, he was taking in every detail of what the agent said and did. Agent Reed, although he hid it well, looked uncomfortable. Undercurrents radiated here, and she wouldn't let this man smear Sam's name or reputation because of what happened to her.

"What's your name?"

"I'm Agent Vernet. I'm in charge of the internal investigation into Agent Turner's actions the night of the incident. We have Agent Reed's statement about what happened at the meeting place where he and Agent Turner were prior to arriving in front of your home. I'll be recording your statement for the report."

"Well, Agent Vernet, I'm sure you'll find the *truth of the matter* is as Agent Turner told you already."

"We'll see. Ready to begin?"

Oh yeah, Tyler liked her. Very much. He discretely took out his cell phone, held it by his side, flipped it open, and hit the speed dial for Sam's cell. Tyler left the connection open and hoped Sam heard everything that came next. Elizabeth was about to put Vernet in his place and defend Sam with a vengeance. He couldn't wait to talk to Sam after this.

Elizabeth pointedly looked at the phone, and he gave her a wink. God, she was observant. He didn't doubt for a moment she didn't know exactly what every player in the room was thinking and doing.

"Yes, let's begin to uncover the *truth of the matter*," Elizabeth said and settled back against the pillows.

Home with his family, Sam pulled out his phone. Tyler's name showed on the caller ID, and he answered. He thought the line went dead, but then Elizabeth's voice came over the phone, saying something about uncovering the truth. Sam stood from the couch where he'd been talking with Jack and went into his room, so he could hear everything.

Something must be going on and Tyler wanted him to hear. Sam wondered what Vernet was up to with Elizabeth. He better treat her well, or he'd put Vernet in his place again. He didn't want anyone to hurt her anymore.

He listened intently.

"Let's begin with your account of what transpired that evening. We'll allow you to tell the entire story. If we have any questions, we'll ask them at the end."

Agent Vernet began the recording by stating the date, time, and the names of the people present.

Elizabeth began. "Fine. I was baking cookies and talking on the telephone with my friend, Kay."

"What were you talking about?" Vernet interrupted.

"None of your business," Elizabeth snapped in a tone that left no doubt of her annoyance.

Agent Vernet indicated for Elizabeth to continue. He held his lips tightly pressed together, they almost disappeared altogether. Agent Reed coughed to stop himself from busting up laughing. Elizabeth's and Kay's conversation was completely irrelevant. Agent Vernet's nosiness irritated her further.

"I heard a noise outside, the same sound twice. It sounded like a cork popping. I went to the front of my home to investigate. I checked outside through the windows and saw a man lying in the street. I stayed on the phone and I went out to see if he was hurt."

"Why didn't you call the police? The man could have harmed you," Vernet said.

"Well, let's see. A man was lying in the street, unconscious."

Sam almost burst out laughing. Not many people would leave someone lying in the street. Vernet was an idiot, and he pissed off Elizabeth. She'd handle Vernet. She was doing a great job so far.

"My first thought was to make sure he was okay. I thought you wanted me to recount the incident before you asked questions?"

Elizabeth huffed out a deep breath. Sam heard the bed sheets rustle, probably Elizabeth adjusting her position again. Her voice sounded tired but firm, and she continued her side of the story.

"As I said, I went out to see if the man was all right. He wasn't moving, so I tapped him in the shoulder and asked if he was okay. He didn't respond, and I thought perhaps he was drunk and passed out."

"Did Agent Turner smell like alcohol? Is that why you thought he was drunk?"

Sam's anger intensified. Vernet would try anything to find something Sam had done that looked even remotely inappropriate. Sam never drank on the job, unless undercover and he had to drink in order to maintain his cover. Even then, he only sipped at a beer and tried to make it last as long as possible and make it less likely the alcohol affected him.

Elizabeth sighed. This was going to take forever with Agent Vernet asking question after question and fishing for dirt on Sam. "Absolutely not. Lying flat on your back in the street is not normal behavior, and I made a rash assumption. May I go on?"

"Yes. Please continue."

"Thank you." She noted Agent Reed's smirk. "A dark colored vehicle, an SUV, accelerated suddenly, heading directly for Agent Turner and myself. I told Kay to call the police and tossed the phone."

"How could you be sure the vehicle was a threat?"

Elizabeth ignored Agent Vernet. "I lay down on top of Agent Turner, grabbed his shoulders, locked my legs around his, and rolled with him under my Suburban parked nearby at the curb. Seconds after I got him to relative safety, the other car rammed mine. I was afraid the person would try to harm Agent Turner further, so I tried to get in front of him to protect him."

"Why would you say you were protecting him and not yourself or both of you?" Agent Vernet asked, and Elizabeth thought it a very stupid question.

She looked to Deputy Director Davies and to Agent Reed to see if they understood her position and reasoning. Both stood silent, bored and exasperated. "The guy wasn't after me. He was obviously trying to kill Agent Turner. Since Agent Turner was incapacitated, I was the only person there to help and protect him. Haven't you ever been in a dangerous situation? You don't exactly think about yourself, or what could happen. You react. That's what I did. Someone tried to kill Agent Turner, and I acted to protect him."

Agent Reed smiled, Deputy Director Davies nodded his agreement, but Agent Vernet didn't look convinced. Obviously, he'd never been a field agent, and perhaps resented Sam and his position with the FBI. Sam represented everything he wanted but could never be. Elizabeth felt sorry for Agent Vernet. Then she remembered he was being vindictive toward Sam and her sympathy disappeared.

"Did Agent Turner at any time indicate he was with the FBI?"

"No."

"So you didn't know he was an FBI agent. Why would you risk your life to protect him?"

"He's a human being and someone tried to kill him. That's all the reason I need. That's all the reason anyone should need. Anyway," she said at length, "I tried to get around Agent Turner. Something hard at his leg jabbed me in the ribs. I pulled up his pants and found a gun and knife strapped to his ankle. The man in the other car backed up to ram my car again. I grabbed the gun and knife and worked my way up to block Agent Turner. The other vehicle rammed my car again. The person struggled to get the door open, the damage to the vehicle prevented it from opening easily, giving me some time. Agent Turner woke up and tried to take the gun from me. We struggled. I told Agent Turner I was trying to help him and the person was getting out of the car. He wouldn't let go of the gun, so I let go and turned with the knife in my hand toward the person coming toward us. Agent Turner fired the gun from behind me, the bullet grazed my arm at the same time I stabbed the man in the foot."

Agent Vernet wanted to interrupt her again, but she didn't give him the chance and went on with the story. "The man grabbed the knife and my wrist at the same time. He pulled the blade out of his foot before pulling me out from under the vehicle. He punched me in the face. Then he grabbed me around the throat, pushed me up against my car, choking me . . ."

Elizabeth lost herself in the images in her mind, looking into nothing, remembering the terror and the fear. She ignored the tears streaming down her cheeks, blurring her vision. She replayed the event in her mind, lost in that moment of fear. Agent Reed wiped her face with a tissue, bringing her back to herself.

Her voice trailed away, and she was having a hard time remembering what happened to her. Sam wished he was there with her. He'd hold her hand and reassure her everything was all right. She was safe. He didn't remember anything that happened after he shot her. He really wanted to hear the end. He knew the details of the injuries she'd sustained, but he didn't know the events that had led to her lying in a bed beside him in the hospital.

Elizabeth went numb, she stared straight ahead. She shook off the visions and her fear.

Agent Reed put a hand on Agent Vernet's shoulder and squeezed to keep him from asking the question on his lips. "Miss Hamilton, would you like to take a break? We'll give you a few minutes to collect yourself and your thoughts," he said gently and put his hand over hers on the bed. He kept the phone next to him in the other hand, hidden behind his leg. She wished Sam were here, not just listening, too far away.

"What? Oh, no. I'm sorry. It's a little overwhelming. I haven't actually spoken the words out loud. I've replayed it in my head so many times, but telling it out loud is completely different. I'm sorry. Where was I?"

Agent Reed squeezed her hand. "The man choked you."

She wiped her face and continued. "Um, yes. He held me off the ground against the Suburban with one hand, and I was kicking him and the car, and he was choking me. He wore a black ski cap over his face. I pulled it off and scratched his face. I wanted to be sure I had some evidence of who he was. When I took off the cap, he got right in my face and told me I'd done it. I'd sealed my fate. He threw me to the ground and kicked me in the ribs. He shot me in the back twice, and stood over me for a moment before he stabbed me in the thigh. I remember hearing the police cars coming as my eyes closed. I opened them again when I heard the man get into his car and drive away. I blacked out wondering if Agent Turner was all right."

Sam couldn't believe that after everything she'd been through, her last thoughts were of him. He rarely met people who were so giving and thought of others first. Jenna was like that and Jack was lucky to have her. Sam was lucky to have ended up in front of Elizabeth's home.

In the next moment, Sam understood the implications of what she'd told them. She'd seen him. He'd gotten right in her face. He hoped she'd give them a decent description. He waited for Vernet to ask her to describe the man.

"Miss Hamilton, let's go back to when you were under the vehicle with Agent Turner. You said he took the gun from you before you turned toward the man getting out of the car and you stabbed him in the foot. It's at this point Agent Turner shot you in the arm. Is that right?"

"Yes."

"So Agent Turner shot you when your back was to him."

"Yes."

Agent Vernet smiled, completely elated with her answer. She knew what he was trying to do. She'd let him dig himself into a hole before she tossed the truth on top of him, burying him in the grave he was digging for himself. Agent Reed and Deputy Director Davies both frowned, worried. She'd put their minds at ease in a moment. She hated to make Sam sweat. But it would only be for a few minutes.

Sam almost groaned. Vernet finally had the evidence he needed to take him down, and Elizabeth had given it to him. She hadn't been a threat at all. Her damning words sealed his fate as far as Vernet was concerned. His stomach turned sour at the thought of ever hurting Elizabeth for any reason.

## *Chapter Eighteen*

AGENT VERNET FIXED her with a sharp eye. "Just to get the record straight, Miss Hamilton, Agent Turner shot you even though you turned your back on him. You weren't threatening him with the knife, but using it to protect yourself from the assailant."

"Yes."

Agent Reed bowed his head and sighed. Deputy Director Davies watched her intently.

Bile rose to the back of Sam's throat as he listened to her answer the questions. Did she really think he shot her knowing she wasn't a threat? He'd never do that. She had a knife. He thought she'd hurt him. Didn't he? Now he wasn't so sure about what happened.

"You're telling us Agent Turner shot you on purpose?" Vernet asked, obviously loving her answering the same question again, proving Sam guilty. Or so she let him think . . . for now.

"Absolutely not." They all watched her closely. "I never said he meant to shoot me."

Sam listened intently. What was she up to?

"You said he shot you when your back was turned to him."

"He did."

"Then, he meant to shoot you."

"No." Elizabeth was actually starting to have fun with this guy. Hell-bent on finding something to hurt Sam, he didn't realize he'd missed the point of her story entirely. Deputy Director Davies and Agent Reed hadn't. She wanted to give Deputy Director Davies the proof he needed to make sure Agent Vernet was disciplined for his conduct. He was biased toward Sam, his investigation slanted. She needed to ensure the investigation was fair and accurate. She also wanted to be sure Agent Vernet wasn't allowed to do this to any other agent in the future.

"You're not being very cooperative about this, Miss Hamilton. Please answer the question."

"Don't you mean tell you that Sam shot an innocent woman when her back was to him and she posed no threat whatsoever to him? Is that the answer you want?"

"Elizabeth, calm down. Your heart monitor is going nuts," Agent Reed said, concerned.

She ignored him and took a calming breath while addressing Agent Vernet again. "Is this what you did to Sam? Did you take his statement and twist things around, so it appeared he shot me out of some kind of malice or perceived threat that wasn't there?" The guilty look in Agent Vernet's eyes made her even angrier.

"I didn't mean to upset you. I only want to make sure the facts of the case are revealed. I understand you want to protect Agent Turner, but he's stated he took the gun from you and shot you. You, yourself, said he shot you when your back was turned to him. Those are the facts of the case."

She addressed Deputy Director Davies. "Is he really this moronic? Does he really believe he can twist people's words because he has some grudge against Agent Turner?" Both were rhetorical questions. Deputy Director Davies smartly kept his mouth shut.

Elizabeth had no doubt Deputy Director Davies knew her game. Agent Vernet wasn't taking the entire scene Elizabeth set up into account. He was only hearing what he wanted to hear about Sam. He wasn't seeing the scene and how it had actually played out. Being a field agent, Deputy Director Davies would understand what happened. In Sam's altered, drugged state, he would remember the events, but maybe not as clearly as Elizabeth.

"Agent Vernet, apparently you have some desire to make Agent Turner look bad and to harm his career. I can assure you I am not protecting him in any way, but giving you my accurate account of what happened that night."

Agent Vernet, perturbed she'd dared to call him a moron, pressed his lips together until they disappeared into his mouth. His eyes went cold, and she had no doubt he would try to get her to say something that would help him destroy Sam's career.

"I have your statement. I have his statement. He took

the gun from you and shot you. He stated that he believed you were a threat because he saw the knife in your hand. But you, in fact, were not a threat with your back turned. You, obviously, were not trying to harm Agent Turner, and he shot you anyway. He'll have to answer for that."

"No, Agent Vernet, he won't."

"Excuse me, but I am conducting the investigation and because of both your statements, I have enough to take this further and file charges against Agent Turner."

"Excuse me, Agent Vernet, but you do not have grounds to file charges against Agent Turner, and he won't have to answer for his statement or mine because I can answer for him." She paused to make sure she had his attention and the other agents. "I have no doubt Agent Turner stated he took the gun from me and saw the knife in my hand before he shot me."

"Those were his words," Agent Vernet confirmed.

"Well those words are true enough . . ."

Agent Vernet cut her off. "See! You admit he's telling the truth. He shot you when you turned your back to him."

"Shut up, Vernet, and let her tell us what happened," Deputy Director Davies spoke for the first time since entering the room.

"Thank you. At least two people in this room would like to know what really happened." She pointedly looked at Deputy Director Davies and Agent Reed. "As I said, I'm sure those were Agent Turner's words, and they are true. But in Agent Turner's altered state—he was drugged you know," she said sarcastically to Agent

Vernet. "He remembers the event accurately, but out of context."

"What do you mean?" Deputy Director Davies asked.

"After Agent Turner took the gun from me, the man got out of the car. Agent Turner wasn't able to speak to me, but we made eye contact, and I knew he understood someone was coming. I rolled over with the knife in my hand and stabbed the man in the foot. At the same time, Agent Turner fired and hit my arm as I brought the knife down.

"If you picture the scene in your mind, you can play it out. Sam lay on his back behind me. I was on my left side about to stab the man, and Sam fired and hit my arm. The only way he could have hit my raised arm is if he aimed at the man's legs. He would have had to hold his arm and the gun well above his chest. If he meant to shoot me, he wouldn't have had to hold the gun so high. Look at where he shot me."

She pulled the bandage off her arm and showed them the stitched cut, which creased her from the middle of her outer arm down toward her elbow. She held up her arm in the position of holding the knife about to stab someone. "As you can see, the only way for the bullet to have grazed my arm in this manner, and leave this scar, is if Sam aimed over me toward the man. He tried to shoot the guy in the leg, but he hit me instead. If he'd wanted to shoot me, he'd have shot me in the back or shoulder. It was my fault for getting in his way. He never meant to shoot me."

Pinning Vernet with a harsh glare, she continued. "You wanted to know if I was covering for him. Absolutely not. His actions speak for themselves. He tried to protect me, even though he'd been shot and drugged and was barely conscious. He deserves a damn medal, not an inquisition into his conduct."

She yawned, extremely tired after exerting all her energy explaining herself. This had been the longest she'd managed to stay awake. Certainly the most she'd spoken in days. She hadn't expected to have to defend her statements or Sam's actions. She closed her eyes a moment to gather her strength and keep the pain in check. Her anger and the heavy dose of painkillers had left her drained.

She really wanted to see Sam. He felt guilty about shooting her, and they hadn't had a chance to discuss what happened. She had no idea he thought he'd shot her because he thought she was the threat. She wished she'd seen his face when she recounted what really happened. He must be so relieved.

Sam lay back on his bed and stared at the ceiling reeling from Elizabeth's statement. She was right. He remembered the events like snapshots, not like a movie. He saw each piece, understood their meaning, but when you knew what the missing frames of the film were, it made a different picture all together. He never meant to shoot her.

He wished he were there with her. He'd kiss her for putting the puzzle together for him and not letting Vernet alter her statements about what happened. She certainly was a judge's daughter. She stuck to the facts and recounted them without embellishment. She presented her case, and no one could dispute her evidence.

He'd tried to shoot the suspect and not her. He didn't exactly remember that, but he had no doubt the bullet wound on her arm backed up her account.

"Elizabeth, are you all right? You don't look so good. Do you want me to get the doctor?" Tyler asked, worry in his voice.

Concerned, Sam imagined this was taking everything she had, and she didn't have a lot to give in the first place. This had been too much, too soon, for her.

Elizabeth opened her eyes. "No. I'm just tired. Are we done with the investigation into Agent Turner shooting at a *suspect*, who was trying to kill us both?"

"I believe you've provided a plausible explanation for Agent Turner's actions. I'll have your statement prepared for your signature."

"Plausible explanation? Is this how you treat victims and the agents who try to protect them? You should be ashamed of yourself, not to mention fired for conducting an investigation where you are clearly biased against the subject of that investigation."

He wanted to interrupt, but she didn't let him. "Furthermore, I expect the statement you prepare will be word for word and that it will reflect Agent Turner in no way meant to harm me. If it isn't, you'll hear from all of my lawyers. I'm sure you've heard of them. They're all named Hamilton. Also, if you bring charges against Agent Turner, you can bet your ass you'll hear from my attorneys and my father. That would be Federal Judge Hamilton of the District Court. If I have to, I'll break out my address book and contact every influential person I know, of which there are many in the public and private sector, and make sure Agent Turner is treated with the respect and admiration he deserves for conducting himself in such a gallant manner and trying to save my life, even in his incapacitated state. Are we clear?"

Agent Vernet, his face red with fury, gave her a curt nod and turned off the recorder. "I've everything needed to write the report, which will reflect your statement that Agent Turner wasn't at fault for the shooting," he said, his voice tight and controlled.

Sam would probably get a commendation for his actions, and that would piss off Agent Vernet even more. The thought almost made her smile, but she held it back.

"Now, Deputy Director Davies, apparently Agent Vernet has missed the mark on what aspect of that night requires further investigation. I'm sure you, Agent Reed, and Agent Turner understand what that important matter is."

"You can identify the suspect, and he's a threat to you," Deputy Director Davies stated the obvious. Well, obvious to everyone but Vernet, she thought.

"Hallelujah! We are finally getting to the important part of this conversation. I assume an agent will be assigned to protect me until you apprehend the suspect, since I'm the only person who can identify the man who attempted to kill an FBI agent, as well as myself. I don't know what else you want this man for, but I assume he's dangerous. I'm stubborn and independent, but I'm not stupid. If this guy knows I'm still alive, he knows I can identify him. He'll try to kill me again."

"Yes, I think you're right. We'll assign a couple agents to protect you."

"Good. I'll also assume that I get the best, since I'm a federal judge's daughter and the man after me is willing to kill an FBI agent to keep his identity a secret. Which means Agent Turner will be assigned to protect me while he and Agent Reed work to apprehend the suspect. Since Agent Turner is injured, I assume he won't be assigned an undercover job until he's fully recovered. I'm sure he can handle a simple babysitting job, especially since he's already acquainted with the facts of the case and will be an asset to Agent Reed as he determines the identity of the suspect and takes the man into custody."

She smiled at Agent Reed and looked pointedly at Agent Vernet and hoped he understood she felt Agent Turner was the best the FBI had to offer and not to mess with her. Sam wouldn't be happy unless he was working again. Protecting her would give him time to decide what type of work he wanted to do in the future. He'd told her working undercover was burning him out. She had to admit, she'd also feel better having him close, until they resolved the entire ordeal.

Sam wiped his hand over his brow and into his hair, completely blown away. She was something else. After everything that happened to her, she still managed to defend him, make him out to be a hero, and now she got him back on the job as the best agent to protect her.

"Agent Vernet, since this part of the discussion is about an ongoing investigation, you can go," Deputy Director Davies's deep voice came over the line.

Being excluded from the conversation was sure to rile Vernet. Sam didn't care. Davies would ensure Vernet answered for his conduct.

"You and I will meet with your superior on Monday to discuss Agent Turner's and Miss Hamilton's statements. I will be following up with the director concerning your conduct and Agent Turner's outstanding efforts in the field regarding Miss Hamilton and this case. I expect the investigation will be closed and Agent Turner will be allowed back into the field as soon as possible. Miss Hamilton demands the best the FBI has to offer, and that's Agent Turner and Agent Reed in her opinion and mine. I'm sure once the director sees your report detailing Agent Turner's heroic actions in trying to save Miss Hamilton, he'll agree as well."

Agent Vernet fumed. Nothing he could do. He left her room without looking at Deputy Director Davies or saying goodbye.

"What an asshole!" Elizabeth announced once the door closed behind Agent Vernet.

"I believe this call is for you." Agent Reed handed the phone over.

"Why the hell aren't you here? I hope you didn't tell that maggot you shot me on purpose, because that would be really stupid, and you are not a stupid man."

Sam smiled at the phone. God, she was something. "Hello, sweetheart. How are you?"

She relaxed at his lazy soft tone. That voice did something to her. She couldn't explain it, but she liked it. "I'm fine now. I'm tired." She let out a huge yawn.

Both Deputy Director Davies and Agent Reed exchanged a look. She ignored both of them.

"Thank you for what you did for me," Sam began. "I told Agent Vernet I'd shot you because I remembered seeing you with the knife. You were right though. I took the image out of context. I remembered the events in pieces. You helped me put them together. I still don't remember exactly what happened, but I'm glad you said what you did."

"Do you think I said all of that just to save your ass? Are you an idiot? Everything I said to Agent Vernet was the unbiased truth, and I'll not have you thinking I did it to protect you, or make you feel better. You were trying to shoot the other guy, not me. I got in your way. End of story. So stop beating yourself up over what happened."

"So far you've called me stupid and an idiot. How much pain are you in right now?"

"A lot. More than a lot. Oh, God, Sam, I'm sorry."

"It's okay, sweetheart. Put Tyler back on the phone."

"Who's Tyler?"

"Agent Reed," Sam said and Tyler took the phone back.

"What's up, man?"

"She's in pain and too stubborn to tell anyone. Call the doctor into the room to give her some more drugs. How does she look?"

"Bad," Tyler confirmed. "I hit the call button for the nurse."

"Damn. Is she able to give us a description of the guy before she passes out?"

"I don't know. She's about to pass out now."

"Why are you two talking about me like I'm not here?" Elizabeth shifted her weight because she was uncomfortable. She pressed the button on the bed to lower herself. Her back hurt, so she tried to roll to her side, but that shot pain through her back and down her legs, which then sent fire screaming through her thigh. She moaned in pain. Deputy Director Davies put a pillow behind her to help her stay on her side, and he rested his hand on her shoulder.

"There now, Miss Hamilton. Is that better?"

"Yes, thank you. I need to tell you about the man," she slurred softly, having a difficult time keeping her eyes open and the pain at bay. Both Deputy Director Davies and Agent Reed came to the side of the bed where she could see them.

Fading fast, the nurse came into the room and Tyler spoke for her. "Miss Hamilton is in a lot of pain and needs some medication."

"I have it right here." The nurse held up a syringe and stuck it into the IV and pushed the contents into the line. She left the room without another word.

"I put Sam on speaker. He can hear us now. Can you give us a description of the man? Do you remember?" Tyler took out his notebook and pen.

"He was taller than me, maybe six feet or six-one. When he was choking me, I was a couple inches off the ground, and we were face to face. When I took the ski cap off his head, we were eye-to-eye. His are brown as mud. He has fair skin and his features are sharp. His lips are thin, and he had high cheekbones and a broad fore-head. Next to his left eye, he has a small mole just under the lower lid near the corner. His hair is brown, cut short with a touch of grey at the temple. He reminded me of a banker or businessman. Maybe a lawyer. You know, someone who has to look very presentable. He's in his late forties or early fifties. Thin, but not weak. Strong and lean, like a swimmer." Her voice trailed off and her eyes fluttered closed, though she fought to stay awake. The medicine the nurse had given her was finally taking effect and the pain eased away.

"Come on, sweetheart, keep going," Sam prodded, so they'd get the whole description before she was completely out.

"Sam, she's fading. We'll finish this tomorrow." Tyler didn't want to push her. She'd given them a lot of information and the doctor had warned them before they came into her room she wouldn't stay awake for very long.

"He's a coward." She'd closed her eyes, barely able to say the words. She concentrated on what she wanted to tell them. Her brow furrowed.

"Why do you say that, Elizabeth?" Tyler thought it a strange statement when the guy had shot both her and Sam.

"Because he shot us in the back. He couldn't look at us when he shot us. He also drugged Sam, which tells me he doesn't want to get his hands dirty. He kills like a woman. Men usually kill with force or weapons. Women kill using poison. They don't usually shoot people or stab them. Sorry, I'm rambling. He knocked me to the ground and kicked me, so I wasn't looking at him when he shot me then stabbed me with the knife. I don't think he would have stabbed me, except that I'd made him mad by stabbing him in the foot. You should check the hospitals and clinics to see if someone had a foot injury."

"Yeah, I'll do that," Tyler said with a smile on his face and in his voice.

She smiled up at him, her eyes drooping. "You probably already thought of that."

"It's okay. I think your drugs are kicking in."

"They are. I'm starting to float. It doesn't hurt so much anymore, or maybe I don't care that it hurts."

"What else can you tell us about the man?" Tyler hoped she could give them something distinctive. The description's good, but maybe she could remember something definitive.

"He wore expensive cologne and a gold bracelet with a logo on it. He had on dark blue jeans and a black sweater. The sweater was expensive, cashmere. I've seen him somewhere before. Did I tell you that alrea—"

"Elizabeth. Elizabeth!" Sam shouted over the phone.

"Sam, she's out. You know, I think we should make her an agent. She's good. Better than Vernet, and she doesn't have any training. I like her. I like her a lot," Tyler remarked.

Elizabeth slept, her skin as pale as the sheet covering her. Dark circles marred the skin under her eyes, but still one of the most beautiful women Tyler had ever seen. Easy to see why Sam had become infatuated and protective of her so quickly. She was smart and held her own.

She didn't allow people to boss her around, or lead her where they wanted her to go.

"Back off, Tyler," Sam grumbled. "She's a witness and a victim. What do you guys think about her description? Does it match any of our suspects?"

Sam didn't want to hear about how Tyler liked Elizabeth. He didn't want to think about him in the room with Elizabeth. He wished he were there with her. She'd had a rough time telling them all what happened. Verbally sparring with Vernet hadn't helped. If he could have, he'd have put a stop to Vernet's verbal jabs and kicked him out long before he upset Elizabeth.

"I'll go through our list of suspects and see if anything matches up. Her description matches with our profile of the unidentified subject. We assumed it was someone in their forties or fifties, well educated, someone in the business field who knows how insurance claims work, and someone who prefers to stay away from violence. Although he kills his victims, he always uses poison rather than, say, setting up a suicide using a gun or other violent means. Her personality assessment of the guy is right on. He's a coward of sorts, because he isn't able to confront his victims face-to-face. Now that he's shot you and Elizabeth, I hope he doesn't escalate to more violent crimes," Tyler stated.

"She said she's seen him somewhere. What do you think she meant? Does she know him? Where did she see him? She owns that bakery and café, maybe she's seen him there?" Deputy Director Davies asked, his concern matching Sam's. "Maybe this person knows Elizabeth as well. He could get to her more easily than a stranger could."

"We'll have to wait to ask her," Sam answered, though he wished she wasn't out cold again. "I think if she knew the guy's name, she'd have told us. She knows and is acquainted with hundreds of people, since she's invited to every benefit and society party in the state. I imagine she's met dozens upon dozens of people simply because of her name, not to mention she owns one of the most popular shops in the city."

If she knew him, they could apprehend him quickly. More than likely, she thought she'd seen him before. She hadn't sounded convinced she knew him for certain. Then again, she was pretty out of it there at the end.

"I'd like to ask her about the logo on the bracelet. Maybe we can trace it somehow. Can you believe her memory and the details she's provided. We should give her Vernet's job." Tyler had dealt with a lot of witnesses. None as good as Elizabeth. They usually got facts wrong, embellished the story in some way, or their perception of what happened was wrong. Witnesses were usually unreliable and changed their story often. He had no doubt Elizabeth recounted the story accurately and the details wouldn't change. She knew what she knew. Sedated and in a deep sleep, she probably wouldn't wake up until tomorrow.

Deputy Director Davies wrapped up the meeting. "Let's get out of here and go over the list of suspects we do have and see if we can narrow down our search. We'll have to talk to her again tomorrow. I hope she'll be up to it. Today was hard for her. I have no doubt she tried to hide her feelings and emotions about the attack. She's a strong woman, but I think she's being torn up inside about what happened. I imagine nothing traumatic like this has happened to her, or anyone in her life."

"She'll overcome this as soon as we find the man responsible, and she has some closure," Sam responded. "She is strong. The fear will subside as she deals with what happened."

"I'm not surprised she asked to have you assigned to protect her," Deputy Director Davies went on. "You should have seen the change in her when she heard your voice a little while ago. Her whole body relaxed. She trusts you. We'll need her trust if we're going to protect her from this guy."

"When are you putting me back on the case?" Sam wanted to catch this guy before he had a chance to hurt Elizabeth again. Jarred had already gotten into her room. What if the Silver Fox decided to try something? A chill ran up Sam's spine.

"Elizabeth has a hospital guard on her door. Her father doesn't want that Jarred guy to get to her again. I'm sure he thinks there's a threat from our guy. You still have to be cleared by Vernet's investigation, which should come about Monday or Tuesday. Take the next several days to heal and get your head straight. I'll put you back on the case as Elizabeth's guard and Agent Reed's backup when she gets released from the hospital," Deputy Director Davies told Sam.

"But . . ."

"But nothing. Take it or leave it. She's right, Sam, you're the best, but you've been injured and involved in a traumatic event. You need time to heal, but I think even on your worst day, you're capable of watching out for her. Shooting her messed with your head. You know now what the actual circumstances were, but I still believe you need time to work it all out. You've been on the verge of burnout for months. Because of the shooting, you feel responsible for her. I believe you're becoming personally involved with her, which could be a liability."

Sam wanted to protest, because he didn't want to admit to Davies or himself he had feelings for Elizabeth, but Davies went on. "I believe you want to protect her and that makes you perfect for the job. Let Agent Reed take the lead on finding the suspect. You concentrate on Elizabeth. You're back on the job when she leaves the hospital and not before. Set up your appointments with the mind benders," Davies ordered, not about to let him off the hook for the appointments with the psychiatrist. He obviously thought Sam needed it.

"Shit. I hate the shrinks." Hell, he'd talked more to Elizabeth in the last few days than he ever would to some doctor.

"Exactly. I don't like having the mind benders invade my head either, but it's part of the job when you've been involved in a shooting. Do the time with them, and get it over with, so you can put this all behind you."

"I'll get it done. Tyler, keep me updated on the case and whatever you uncover. When is Elizabeth supposed to get out of the hospital?"

"The Doc said she should be out by Tuesday. That's long enough for you to spend some time with your family and get your head together."

"I'll be ready to take her home," Sam said, trying not to read too much into what that really meant, or could mean.

## Chapter Nineteen

*Saturday, 2:04 A.M.*

THE HOSPITAL WAS busy even at this time of night, but he'd planned well. He took out the guard and the nurse without alerting anyone else to his presence. From the moment news reports announced Elizabeth and that damn FBI agent had survived he'd fantasized about this moment.

How did everything go so wrong? He shot both of them and still they didn't die. Well, this time he'd make sure they died, starting with the woman. He'd like to keep her, but since she met with the FBI and had possibly identified him, she'd have to go. He couldn't afford an eyewitness. Without her, the FBI had nothing to pin him to the Silver Fox murders, or the attempt on their agent's life. Too bad, though. She was beautiful. Her spirit and fight intrigued him. Used to everyone doing his bidding and worshiping his skills, he liked her defiance and strength. He found her bold and refreshing.

The dim light spotlighted the sleeping beauty beside him in the bed. This should be easy, but something made him pause. He'd never killed an acquaintance. The others were strangers, nothing to him. He steeled himself for the job ahead. With her asleep, all he had to do was inject the poison into her IV line. He pushed the needle in, but she shifted and her soft voice whispered, "Sam." Their gazes locked and he pushed the plunger. She made a grab for the needle in her arm, but he grabbed her wrist and held firm. She tried to fight him with her other hand, lashing out wildly, but the poison worked fast and she fell back limp on the pillows.

He brushed a strand of hair from her face with his fingertip. Such a waste. But necessary.

## *Chapter Twenty*

*Saturday, 10:22 A.M.*

JENNA'S PHONE RANG far off in the penthouse. Probably someone from Merrick International trying to get in touch with her. Sam had his own line in his bedroom, so he tried to ignore it. Jenna's muffled voice carried down the hall to his room. The distress in her tone signaled some kind of trouble.

Opening his eyes, he glanced at the clock. He'd slept in spurts throughout the night. He remembered waking up just after two in the morning in a cold sweat to the sound of Elizabeth's scream. He must have lain there for over an hour trying to get back to sleep. At some point he succeeded, because it was after ten now.

The dreams disturbed him. His guilt rearing its ugly head, because he hadn't protected Elizabeth. He blamed himself for her injuries, since she'd gotten them saving his hide. Maybe things would be better when she was out of the hospital and he was there to protect her. It would give him a chance to make things up to her.

A familiar chill went up his back, little devils danced between his shoulder blades. *Mind your back* played in his head. Suddenly, he wanted to know who was on the phone. Carefully getting out of bed, wearing only his pajama bottoms, he made his way out toward the living room. He'd taken his sweat-soaked T-shirt off in the middle of the night, and he didn't bother grabbing another one. Hell, Jenna had seen him half naked more than once. She could pretty much guess what the rest looked like, since Jack was his identical twin.

The penthouse was oddly quiet, since four children and four adults were living there with him at the moment. He found Jenna sitting on the couch with her hands together pressed to her mouth. She stared off in the distance.

Sitting next to her, he asked, "Where is everyone?"

"They went to the zoo. I thought you needed some peace and quiet this morning. Caleb and Summer are taking the kids back to Colorado tomorrow. Jack wants to stay until you're feeling better."

"He doesn't have to do that. I'm fine. I'm home. No major damage done. My back is better. The muscle spasms are subsiding and the meds are helping."

"He's not worried about your physical health. It's your mental state that concerns us. Deputy Director Davies said you seem better, and you've been cleared of any wrongdoing in the shooting. I knew you would be, but I'm glad you have the FBI behind you too. You must be relieved. Jack and I still feel you need some time away from your work. It's taking a toll on you, Sam."

Her comments and worry, nothing but stalling tactics. "Who called? Did something happen at work? I can tell you're trying not to tell me something."

Sam sat beside her, his chest bare, the bruises fading, and although she couldn't see his back, the look on his face told her his pain persisted. Odd, when she looked at him, she felt the love of a sister, even though he had the same face as her husband. When she looked at her husband, he sometimes took her breath away, he was so gorgeous. It goes to show love is not only a physical attraction, but a connection between two hearts. She hoped Sam would find a woman who connected to his heart. He needed someone to love him.

Stubble shadowed his jaw. He needed a shower and to eat a decent meal, and all she had for him was more bad news. She wasn't sure how much more he could take. "Everyone stayed up last night talking about how we've never seen you like this. You're like a roller coaster. You were so happy when Elizabeth woke up and talked to you, but then you go quiet for long periods of time."

He was reliving that night over and over, but they all hoped that as Elizabeth got better, so would Sam. Even on his last visit to the ranch, they recognized his depression and weariness. But now he was on some emotional pogo stick and that was a very bad sign, since Sam was such a strong individual.

"Jenna, I'm fine," Sam said, even though she didn't believe him for a minute, and he knew it.

"I don't want to tell you the news I received. It's bad, Sam. I'm not sure how you'll take it."

Those devils stomped up his spine again. "Who called, Jenna? What's happened?" He sat forward and glared her into answering him.

"Mrs. Hamilton called. Before you panic, Elizabeth is alive, but apparently, someone tried to kill her last night at the hospital." She spit it out fast, like the words were some sour fare she couldn't get rid of fast enough. Sam digested them and wished he hadn't asked to be served the news.

"Oh, my God. She's alive though." He ran a hand through his hair. His stomach pitched and rolled. Bile rose up his throat, and he swallowed hard. "What aren't you telling me?"

"Someone drugged her with the same stuff they found in your system. Because of her already fragile condition, even with the antidote, she's worse now. She's in a coma, and they've had to place her on a ventilator."

Everything inside Sam went still. Taking a breath was a monumental effort. Jenna continued with the details. "The night nurse went in to check on her because the guard at her door went missing. Someone hit the nurse from behind. When she awoke a few minutes later, she discovered Elizabeth's heart rate was dangerously low, and she was non-responsive. They suspected she was probably drugged and shut off her IV. They found the same drugs you were given in her blood-work. She's alive, Sam, but Rachel wanted you to know what happened. She's hoping that maybe you know who did this to her daughter."

"No one knows the man who did this. He's a ghost we've been trying to trap for a long time. I was so close that night, but he got away and I never saw his face. He didn't succeed killing Elizabeth the first time, so he tried to finish it last night. Davies, Tyler, and I talked about this yesterday. She gave us a description of the guy, but she fell back to sleep before we finished questioning her. She can identify him. That's why he tried to kill her again."

Sam stood and marched to his room to get dressed. He had to get to the hospital to see her, then he'd talk to Davies about how they were going to stop this bastard. For good.

"Sam, calm down. You're getting all worked up. She's alive. We'll go and see her and you'll see for yourself."

In three long strides, he stormed back to her. "Fine. She's almost been killed twice because of me. How much more do you think she can take?" His rage wanted to fly, but he took a deep breath and pulled himself back together. Jenna didn't deserve his anger.

"Sam, this isn't your fault," Jenna said softly, her big, round, sad, green eyes pleading with him to calm down and be reasonable. He couldn't do that where Elizabeth was concerned.

He glared at Jenna, turned on his heel, and went back toward his bedroom to get ready to go.

"I'll have the car brought out front. I'll go with you."

They arrived at the hospital and Sam jumped out of the car before it came to a stop in front. Jenna hurried after Sam, who had already made it to the bank of elevators and gotten into one. Jenna almost didn't catch the elevator in time, banging her shoulder against the door as she hurried inside.

"Jesus, Sam. Take it easy."

"I'm sorry, Jenna." He wrapped his arm around her and gave her a squeeze. "I have to see her. She has to be okay."

"I told you she is. Rachel said she's stable, they're waiting while the drugs clear from her system. They expect her to wake up in a day or so, like you did."

He hoped it wouldn't take Elizabeth long to wake up again.

"She was already in a fragile state after surgery. Her liver had to be repaired from the gunshot wound. Her system can't handle the drugs as well as I did."

Sam shifted from foot to foot in the elevator. "Can't this thing go any faster? It's only four floors, for god's sake." Just when he thought he'd go nuts, the doors opened onto the ICU floor and Sam took off toward the only room that had two guards posted outside. This time, the guards were FBI agents. Sam flashed his badge and stormed right past them.

Rachel hadn't expected Sam to get there so quickly. He came bursting into the room and didn't even see her. He went straight to Elizabeth, stood over her, and took her in. The sound of the ventilator echoed in the otherwise silent room. The intense look on his face told her Sam cared deeply for her daughter. His heart was breaking, like hers, seeing Elizabeth worse off than she'd been when she'd first come out of surgery.

Jenna came into the room quietly. Rachel got up to greet her, but Sam stopped her.

"What did the doctors say?"

"She's okay, Sam. They got the antidote into her system quickly." Rachel walked over to Sam and put her arm around his back. He traced his fingertips over Elizabeth's pale cheek as soft as a ladybug crawling over her skin.

"She's been through a lot. Whoever did this to her must have woken her up because she fought him. See her arm. He grabbed her and held on."

The impression of a perfect handprint with fingertips circled her forearm near her wrist. Sam rubbed the back of his neck and tried to work out some of the tension.

"What else did the doctor say?"

"Sam, she's in a coma. We have to wait for her to come back to us in her own time. The Judge is down the hall in the waiting room talking with Agent Reed about how the man got past hospital security and what they *didn't* find on the security footage," she said, frowning. "Why don't you go and speak with them? Agent Reed can tell you what happened."

"I don't want to leave her. I'm supposed to protect her and look what happened. I wasn't here when she needed me. Again."

"Sam, this is not your fault. We had a guard protecting her. Whoever did this got past everyone. You're on leave until she's supposed to go home. I can't tell you how relieved we were to find out you would be protecting her. She trusts you, and the Judge and I trust you with her. Do you understand what I'm saying to you, Sam? We trust you with the most precious person in our life."

"She wouldn't be here if it wasn't for me and the investigation I'm working."

"You'd be dead if it wasn't for her. Remember that." Rachel stood beside him, holding his arm and giving it a squeeze. "I'll leave you alone with her. The Judge expects you for dinner tomorrow night, and so do I," she commanded.

Rachel and Jenna left the room and he took the seat next to Elizabeth. Alone with her, he took her hand in his and watched her face to see if she knew he was there. "Hi, sweetheart. Can you hear me?"

He waited to see if she tapped his hand, or blinked her eyes. Something. Anything to indicate she was aware of him. She didn't move. It was too much to hope for at this point.

"Come on, honey. Give me one tap, so I know you're okay." Nothing. Not even a twitch in her pinky.

"I'm sorry. I know you asked me to protect you yesterday, and I wasn't here last night when that bastard tried to kill you again. You must be so mad at me. I'm mad at myself. We should have known hospital security wasn't enough to protect you from this maniac. I mean, how daring is that to try to kill you in a crowded hospital?

"You did so well yesterday giving us the description of the man who tried to kill us. Agent Reed is working on the suspect list. Thanks to you, he's been able to narrow the list of people down considerably. I wish I was here with you yesterday.

"You were so great with Agent Vernet. I thought I made the guy's life hell, but you really stuck it to him.

Your brother, Patrick, said you had a great sense of humor, but you really have a wicked sense of humor the way you played with Agent Vernet and his game of words. You can be a force to be reckoned with when you want. I knew you were leading him on, but I never guessed you'd completely exonerate me in the shooting.

"I don't remember the events like you do, but I know you told the truth. That's all I need to remember each time I replay that night in my mind. I never meant for you to get hurt. Now when I see myself shooting you in my mind, I remind myself I was trying to help you.

"God, I wish I was here with you last night. You must have been so scared, and you're probably scared now. Don't be, sweetheart. Two really big guys are outside your door making sure no one gets in here. This time, they're FBI agents. I haven't been cleared to work yet, but thanks to you, the investigation will be closed by Tuesday. I was hoping to take you home that day. If you wake up right now, maybe I still can. Come on, sweetheart, wake up for me, so I can take you home."

He sat holding her hand, rubbing his thumb across the back of it, and hoping he'd feel even the slightest movement in her fingers. He wasn't sure how long he'd been there staring at her when Rachel and Jenna returned along with the Judge.

"Sam, let's go home and let Elizabeth's parents spend time with their daughter," Jenna coaxed softly.

Sam didn't move or stop watching Elizabeth. He wanted to feel her move once. A strong hand clamped down on his shoulder, and he glanced up at the Judge.

"She'll be fine, son. Not to worry. I expect you at Sunday dinner tomorrow. She'll know we're all here with her. She'll come back to us. I have no doubt."

"This is all my fault, sir. I can't fathom everything she's suffered. You should have heard her yesterday. She'd make a great lawyer. Hell, she'd make a great agent. She's precise, sticks to the facts, doesn't mince words, and keeps everything to the point. She was a great witness. And as you know, that's rare. You should be proud of her."

Judge Hamilton smiled. "I am proud of her. She's great at arguing her case. I have to say, I was disappointed she didn't go to law school. She said we had enough lawyers in the family, and she wanted to do something fun, not taxing. She said she'd take cupcakes over nutcases any day of the week.

"Once, when she was sixteen, she wanted to start dating. She wasn't allowed at the time, but this one boy wanted to take her to the prom. I wasn't in favor of the idea because the boy was older than her. In order to convince me he was respectable and would treat her well, she walked into my office and presented me with letters of recommendation, like some lawyer presenting me with legal briefs. She supplied one from the boy's teacher, his mother, his best friend, and even one from another girl he had dated.

"She knows how to get what she wants, and she's fair-minded and understands that in order to make your side of the argument you have to be truthful and present facts and not emotion. That's not to say she doesn't have a heart. She's got one bigger than most. She gives more than she'll ever take.

"That's why I'm saying this for the last time. This is not your fault. You have done nothing but show concern for her well-being, and when Jarred came here to cause more trouble, you took care of him. I have no doubt that had you been with her last night you would have fought to the death to save her. I'll expect no less when it's time for her to go home and you're assigned to protect her and find the bastard who did this to her. Are we clear?"

"Yes, sir." He wasn't quite convinced, but having the Judge on his side did make a difference. "Did you let her go to the prom?" The image of Elizabeth walking into the Judge's office and presenting her case nearly made him smile.

"She presented a sound argument and the boy's references were impeccable. They had a great time, as I remember. She wore a blue gown with her hair piled on her head. She was beautiful. They were crowned prom king and queen." Judge Hamilton remembered the night fondly. "Her first dance and date with a boy. She was so excited when she got home with her rhinestone crown propped atop her head. She looked like a princess." Those were memories to cherish. And by the look of the Judge, he had a lot of wonderful memories of Elizabeth. Sam hoped there'd be a lot more to come.

A princess. Prom king and queen. Maybe they fit into Tyler's cryptic message from his 1-800-PSYCHIC and the missing girl case.

"You'll call if there's any change, or if she wakes up. I want to know right away. I'll come back and see her later."

"You know we will," the Judge assured him.

Judge Hamilton liked Sam and any man who cared for his Elizabeth like Sam did deserved his sympathy. The Judge wondered how long it would take Sam to realize he cared for Elizabeth on a deep personal level and not out of guilt or responsibility. They'd make a nice couple. He hoped to see his daughter with someone as trustworthy and honorable as Sam. Maybe something would develop between the two of them. Sam was a good man. The Judge had no doubt about it. Elizabeth was kind and sweet. She'd bring joy into Sam's dark world.

Sam kissed Elizabeth's temple and gave her hand a gentle squeeze. He hated to leave her, but her parents wanted to be alone with her, and she would want them before she'd want him. He headed for the door where Jenna waited. Rachel reached out to touch his arm as he passed. He gave her a reassuring look and walked out, leaving his heart and soul in that room with Elizabeth.

Tyler stood talking to the agents guarding Elizabeth's door. "Hey, I have a lead for you to follow on that missing girl. She's in high school, if I remember right. Check to see if she went to the prom, and whether the guy she went with was the prom king. That might tie into your King of Hearts message."

Tyler smiled. "I'm surprised you considered the message and took it seriously enough to come up with a lead. Maybe I'm not crazy for listening to Morgan after all."

Sam shrugged, so Tyler left it alone. "I'm meeting the detective in a little while to go over the case. The file contained a picture of her and a bunch of girls at a dance. Maybe she went with a date. I'll check it out.

How are you doing with all this? How's Elizabeth? Did you see her?"

"I'm fine. She's not." Sam turned to address the two men guarding Elizabeth's room. "No one but her immediate family and me goes in." He waited for their nod. Grabbing Jenna's hand, he headed toward the elevators to go home. He wanted to stay with Elizabeth, but he needed to get out of there before he collapsed on his knees by her bed and begged her, God, the universe, anyone, everyone for her to wake up.

## Chapter Twenty-One

### Saturday, Noon

HE PRESSED THE heavy weight up to the resting bar and rolled up from the weight bench. Sweat beaded on his forehead and chest. His muscles quivered from exertion, but the sense of euphoria that kept him up all night thinking about killing Elizabeth hadn't waned.

He wiped a towel over his face and body. He took pride in every sculpted muscle and believed in strength in both body and mind. He flexed his foot, the ache not so bad today.

Anxious to catch the news of Elizabeth's death, he switched off the blaring rock music he worked out to and tuned the TV to local news.

". . . survived an attempt on her life last night when the Silver Fox tried to kill Miss Hamilton in her ICU hospital room where she is recovering from serious injuries.

She's listed in critical condition and remains on life support at this hour. The entire Hamilton family is at her bedside. It's unclear how the serial killer snuck past security without anyone seeing him. A security guard and nurse were injured . . ."

Unable to control his rage, he chucked a ten-pound weight at the screen, cracking it and shutting the damn thing up.

"Shit. How the fucking hell did she fucking survive?"

If she hadn't woken up, calling out for that damn agent, she'd be dead like she's supposed to be. "Fuck."

Well, not again. Next time, he'd make her pay for fucking up his life. No way in hell was she leaving that hospital alive.

### *Chapter Twenty-Two*

*Saturday, 3:00 P.M.*

DETECTIVE SANDERS WAS going out of his mind. Two
dozen case files cluttered his desk, all demanding his attention, and the most pressing one was Dianne Wales.
The poor girl had been missing several weeks, not a single
lead indicating who might have taken her, if someone had
taken her, or where she might be. Her parents were, un-
derstandably, frantic and left him message upon message,
hour after hour. He hated telling them each and every
time he had no new leads, or even an idea about what had
happened to the seventeen-year-old girl.

By all accounts she was a good student, well liked by
her classmates. She held a part time job and had never
been late. The parents appeared to have a strong marriage, no signs of trouble at home. It didn't appear she
was a rebellious teenager, or there had been some kind of

sudden trouble. Her grades were consistently good, and she kept to a regular school and work routine.

Unhappy the FBI was coming in today, Saturday of all days, to help with the case, his frustration grew. If he couldn't find any evidence or leads, he didn't know how some hotshot FBI agent could make any headway either.

"Detective Sanders. I'm Special Agent Reed with the FBI. I'm here about the Dianne Wales case. I have some questions and possibly a lead."

"Agent Reed."

Detective Sanders shook the agent's hand and gave him a cursory once over. The guy was big. Tall and broad, his dark hair and darker eyes made him look mean, even with his neutral expression.

He thought he must appear the exact opposite of the agent. Oh, he had dark hair, more gray than brown these days, and brown eyes as well, but he was anything but tall, handsome, or strong. He'd gone the way of the doughnut many years ago. He was still sharp of mind though, and that's what mattered when you were a detective.

"I'm all ears. I don't have anything new in the case. It's as if Miss Wales simply disappeared."

"Did she have a boyfriend?"

"Her parents said she dated in the past, but no one recently."

Tyler opened his copy of the file and took out the picture of Dianne at the school dance. "Did you ask the parents if she went to this dance with a date?"

"No, not specifically. They provided several photos to post on the Internet, make up flyers, give to reporters and such. I can call them and ask if she went with a date. Why? Do you think it's important?"

"I don't know yet. According to all reports, she was a model student and person. She stuck to pretty much the same schedule, but all of a sudden one day she up and vanishes after school. No one claims to have seen her once she got off the bus. Let's start with the dance and work forward."

Tyler didn't want to tell the detective about his message from Morgan. He could tell the story only so many times before someone thought he was crazy for listening to a woman he'd only met once and spoken to for less than a minute. Even he was starting to think he was crazy. Then again, she'd proven herself right every time she gave him a lead. And since a young girl's life was on the line, he'd give Morgan the benefit of the doubt.

"Let me get them on the line."

Detective Sanders dialed and waited for the connection to go through. "Mrs. Wales, this is Detective Sanders. No, ma'am, I don't have any news. I'm here with Agent Reed from the FBI, and we have a few questions. Do you remember the photo you gave me of your daughter at the school dance? The picture was taken a couple weeks before she disappeared, you say. Did she go to the dance with a date? Chris Hillman. Did they date regularly?" He put the call on speaker for Tyler to listen.

"They spent time together before the dance, but never went on any other dates. After the dance, they stopped seeing each other. Dianne didn't say why."

"Mrs. Wales, this is Agent Reed. I'm sorry about your daughter. Do you mind if I ask you a few questions?"

"No. I'll do anything to find her," Mrs. Wales said anxiously. "What do you want to know?"

"Do you know if she and Chris were crowned king and queen of the prom?"

"No, they weren't. That went to one of her friends."

"After she stopped seeing Chris, was she upset or emotional about the breakup?"

"I don't think so. School and work kept her very busy, so her father and I didn't get a lot of time to talk to her. We didn't have any reason to be concerned. We gave her the freedom she'd earned. Everything seemed fine. I've spoken to all her friends and none of them have any idea what happened. She should have gone straight from school to her job. She never showed up. Something happened to my girl. You have to find her," Mrs. Wales begged, crying in torrents.

Tyler hated to make her cry. "We're trying. Thank you for answering my questions. We'll contact you if there is any news."

"Okay. I'm so glad you're still looking for her, that she hasn't been forgotten."

"No, ma'am. We're doing everything possible to find her," Tyler assured her.

"Goodbye."

"Goodbye, Mrs. Wales.

"Have you interviewed this Chris Hillman?" Tyler asked the detective.

"We questioned a lot of her friends, but most were

her girlfriends." He grabbed the list off the pile of papers on his desk and scanned it. "He's not here. Do you really think this kid has something to do with Dianne's disappearance?"

"I'm not sure, but I think it's worth asking some questions. Who was Dianne's best friend?"

Detective Sanders checked his notes. "Leslie Monroe."

"Great. Do you have an address?"

"Yeah."

"Let's pay her a visit and see what she knows about Dianne and Chris. Maybe we can figure out what was going on between the two of them before we interview Chris."

They arrived at the best friend's home and tried to get Leslie to open up about Dianne. Not so easy with her mother sitting next to her, making sure they didn't push too hard for answers.

"I don't want to get Dianne into trouble with her parents, or with Chris," Leslie said for the fifth time.

Tyler tried to hold on to his patience. "Dianne is missing. We need to know about her life. You're her best friend. If you know something, you need to tell us."

In the end, Leslie finally relented. "Dianne was completely in love with Chris. They'd been secretly seeing each other for a few weeks before the dance. The night of the dance they snuck away early and . . . they had sex." She lowered her head and avoided her mother's gaze. "It was the first time for both of them," she added softly, her cheeks flaming pink.

"Were they still seeing each other when she disappeared?"

"No. Once Chris got what he wanted, he broke things off with her and started seeing another girl at school, then stopped seeing her about a week later, and started seeing another girl after that. Who can keep track at this point?" she said, disgusted.

"How did Dianne take the breakup?" This could be the break they needed. Dianne might have run away to avoid Chris, or she might have harmed herself if she'd taken things badly. Either way, they needed to find Dianne.

"Dianne didn't take the breakup well, or the fact Chris was chasing after every easy girl at school. He used to be a really nice guy," she said softly. Then she added scathingly, "Now, he's a complete dog. At least, that's the general consensus. He used Dianne, and he made sure everyone knew they'd slept together. Chris is lower than pond scum."

"Do you think Dianne ran away because of what Chris did?"

"No, she wouldn't run away. I mean, she was upset, but she really loved him, even though he is a dog. I talked to her a lot. She never said anything about running away. There's no reason why she would. He isn't worth it," Leslie said, summing up her opinion of Chris.

Tyler and Detective Sanders left, thanking Leslie for the information. "Do you think she ran away because Chris decided to sow his wild oats instead of stick with her?" It was a reasonable explanation. "Her first experience with a boy, the rejection could have been too much for her to deal with at such a young age."

Tyler didn't think Dianne was the runaway type. "I

don't think it's that simple. She'd keep in contact with her parents and friends if she were just upset over a boy dumping her. It's got to be something more. I don't think we'll find this girl alive," Tyler said sadly, knowing more often than not that was the case.

"I've had that same feeling for a long time now," Detective Sanders admitted. "She's been gone too long. She wasn't a troubled teen or into drugs. We're missing something. Maybe Chris can fill us in on what that is."

They found Chris in his driveway with a blonde pressed up against a pickup truck. With his hands on her hips, he locked lips with her, not realizing Tyler and Sanders stood behind him. Tyler took a moment to assess the young Casanova. About five-ten with too long brown hair, well below his T-shirt collar. He wore baggy jeans, several sizes too big, falling down his ass, showing off plaid boxers. Barefoot, he had probably just rolled out of bed with the blonde.

The girl was pretty and fresh looking, her long hair tousled, her sundress wrinkled and well above her knees.

Tyler cleared his throat, loudly, to get their attention. The girl's head flew up, eyes wide at the sight of Tyler and Sanders. Pushing Chris away, she straightened her wrinkled dress, bit her lower lip, her eyes falling to the ground.

"What do you want?" Chris asked, unhappy about the interruption.

"Chris Hillman, right?"

"Yeah, who wants to know?"

Tyler remembered being a cocky teenager. He probably deserved a good pop in the mouth a few times for giving people attitude for no good reason. "I'm Special Agent Reed with the FBI. This is Detective Sanders. We want to ask you some questions about Dianne Wales." He looked pointedly at the girl. "Do you have a way to get home, Miss?"

"Yes, sir. Um, I'll see you later, Chris. Call me, okay," she said with a seductively sweet smile that absolutely caught Chris's eye.

"I'll catch you later." She walked away, and Chris followed the sway of her hips.

Tyler hoped the sir was because he was an FBI agent, and she wanted to be respectful. Only thirty-one, he hoped he wasn't already a sir to young ladies.

Focused on Chris, he asked, "We understand you took Dianne to the dance at school last month."

"Yeah. So."

"So, what happened that night?"

"We went to the dance, partied, and I took her home. She had a good time."

"I'm sure she did. I heard you guys left early that night. Where did you go?" Most teenage boys wanted to brag about their conquests. Tyler hoped Chris was stupid enough to spill his guts.

"We parked out by Monroe Park and did a little back-seat dancing. After, I took her home. She didn't even miss curfew."

"You guys had sex?"

"Yeah. What of it?" Chris stood, crossing his arms over his thin chest to appear tough, but looking defensive instead.

"Did she give her consent?"

"Hell yes. I don't need to force anyone. Just ask Ashley, there." He pointed to the young girl driving away from the curb in an old yellow Beetle.

"I think we'll spare her the embarrassment. Your relationship with her is quite obvious," Tyler said with a frown. He must be getting old if he thought it inappropriate for teenagers to give in to their raging hormones. He'd been young and dumb once, letting his smaller head think for his big one.

"Relationship, shit. I'm tapping that well until it runs dry. I'm not getting myself tied down. Dianne thought just because we'd done it together we were in some romantic relationship, together forever. Hell, I told her I'd pretty much gotten what I wanted. She wasn't even that good. I didn't want her clinging to me. I'm leaving this fall for college anyway."

Tyler hoped he was never this callous with the girls he knew in high school. "When was the last time you saw her?"

"All the time before she disappeared. She constantly followed me around school, asking to talk to me. The day she went missing, she came here."

Tyler was surprised by Chris' easy admission. "How did she get here? She didn't have a car. Did someone bring her?"

"She walked, I guess. The school bus lets out pretty close. It's about halfway between here and her house. I talked to her for a few minute before I took off in my truck. Last I saw her, she was standing in the driveway. The next day, her picture's all over the news."

"Why didn't you call the police, or tell her parents you'd seen her that day?"

"I didn't think anyone would care." He shrugged and shoved his hands in his pockets. "She was fine when I left. I figured she'd walk home and finish crying there."

"Why was she crying?" Tyler hoped to get the details of what really happened to Dianne, or at least a good lead he could chase.

"She wanted to get back together with me. I told her I didn't believe her lies, and I certainly didn't want to marry her. She couldn't take a hint."

"What did she lie about?"

"Said she was pregnant," Chris said reluctantly. Putting his hands out to his sides, he let them fall and slap his thighs. Maybe he had some concern for her well-being. Tyler wasn't so sure Chris was involved in her disappearance directly.

"She used it as an excuse for us to get back together. We'd only had sex once. She couldn't have gotten pregnant. It was her first time."

Chris really wanted to believe that. Being a teenager, denial was the best course of action when faced with something so life altering.

"Did you use a condom?" Tyler asked.

"No, but we only did it once. It didn't even last that long," he said, embarrassed by the admission. A car drove up, causing Chris to turn an even deeper shade of red.

"What's going on here, Chris? You do something wrong?"

"No, Dad. They're asking about Dianne. She's still missing."

Mr. Hillman approached and stood beside his son. "Well, my boy doesn't know anything. These young people today think they can do whatever they want. She probably took off with some friends."

Tyler ignored Mr. Hillman's statement and concentrated on the man's manner and stance. He was hiding something, or nervous about them being there. Maybe Chris didn't know anything about Dianne's disappearance, but Mr. Hillman did. Tyler thought his choice of words was interesting at least.

"Mr. Hillman, I'm Special Agent Turner with the FBI and this is Detective Sanders. Did you know your son saw Dianne the day she disappeared?"

"I did. She tried to cause some trouble. She's a young girl trying to hold on to her first love. Chris didn't feel the same for her. I told her it was just a crush, and she'd get over it."

"When did you tell her this?" Tyler never took his gaze from Mr. Hillman, who swiped his fingers over his mouth, startled. He hadn't meant to give up that information, and Tyler was chomping at the bit to get him to reveal even more.

"I came home after Chris left Dianne in the driveway."

So Chris wasn't the last person to see Dianne.

"I asked her what was wrong. She was upset Chris didn't return her feelings. He's attending college this fall, has a scholarship lined up. Nothing'll stop him from going to school. Not if I have anything to say about it. Isn't that right, Chris?"

"Yeah," Chris grudgingly agreed.

"What happened when you told her she'd get over it, Mr. Hillman?" Tyler thought it insensitive to say to a young woman in love for the first time with the man's son.

"She got even more upset, and I told her to leave. My son doesn't need an anchor like her around his neck, dragging him down."

"Did she leave after you told her to go?"

"I guess. I went back to my shop, since Chris wasn't home. I figured I'd get some work done and pick up dinner on the way back," Mr. Hillman rambled.

"Did you see her leave?"

"Not really. She walked down the driveway when I left. I don't know where she went after that."

Tyler looked to Detective Sanders to see if he had any other questions. This was the best lead they had so far. Looking around the front yard, Tyler noted the ugly pea soup-green house with brown trim. It needed a paint job, and not because of the hideous color. The garage door was closed. The front yard was bare, but the lawn had been cut recently. No trees, just some scraggly bushes. If Dianne was beneath the grand oak, it sure wasn't here at the Hillman house.

"Is Mrs. Hillman home? Perhaps she saw where Dianne went after you left?"

"Mrs. Hillman left years ago. We divorced. Chris was seven, so I guess it's been about ten years."

"Dad's more the love 'em and leave 'em kind. Isn't that right, Dad?" Chris's voice dripped with scorn.

Obviously, there'd been a number of women in and out of Mr. Hillman's life. From the way Chris spoke, he didn't approve. Tyler wondered if Chris realized he was doing the same thing his father had been doing for years.

Maybe only a few years older than him, Mr. Hillman was young to be the father of a teen. A teenage father, Tyler guessed.

The thing about history, it had a way of repeating itself. Dianne had told Chris she was pregnant. What if she'd also told his father?

"Mr. Hillman, what type of shop do you run?"

"I own a furniture business. We make and sell custom furniture."

"What's the name of the shop?"

"The Oak Warehouse."

Tyler gulped down hard. Everything in Morgan's message was coming together. He could feel it. "You're sure you don't know what happened to Dianne?"

A trickle of sweat slid down the side of Mr. Hillman's face before he answered. "No. Listen, I need to get a few things done around the house before Chris and I have dinner. If you have any more questions for my son, you'll have to ask them later. Chris, let's go in now."

Father and son headed for the front door. Tyler took a good look at Mr. Hillman's car. A red Mustang, maybe a '94 or '95. He took a look at the license plate; he'd use it to run a check on Mr. Hillman. The vanity plate surprised him. His whole system felt electrified when he read the letters: KNGHRTS.

"Mr. Hillman. That's quite a license plate. King of Hearts. Is that some kind of nickname from the ladies?"

"Something like that. It's a leftover nickname from my youth. It goes with the tat."

"I'm sorry. The what?" Tyler knew he meant a tattoo. He hoped he'd get a look at it to connect to the message from Morgan. God, she was creepy.

"My tattoo. See." Mr. Hillman pulled the collar of his button-down shirt aside and revealed the red heart with a gold crown surrounding it. "I got it when I was eighteen. I thought I was real hot shit back then. My wife got me the license plates when I bought the Mustang. She left me a month later when she found out I was having an affair. Said I was the King of Assholes." He shrugged and followed Chris into the house.

Tyler let him go. He didn't have any evidence that pointed to Mr. Hillman, or that he'd done anything to Dianne. All he had was the tattoo matching the message from Morgan and a hunch Mr. Hillman knew exactly what happened to Dianne after Chris left.

"Sanders, what do you think?"

"He knows more than he's saying. I don't think Dianne Wales left this property of her own free will. Did you notice how adamant he was that Dianne not drag Chris down? He appeared overly concerned Chris take that scholarship and go to college. I wonder if Dianne mentioned to Chris's father she was pregnant, and he decided to make her disappear, so Chris wouldn't give up school."

"That's my line of thinking as well. Now we need some evidence to back it up, so we can get a search warrant. I'd like to get into the house, the car, and the store.

I think he took her to his shop. Let's get a few officers to canvas the neighborhood, see if any of the neighbors remember seeing Dianne here that day, and whether or not she left with Mr. Hillman. Maybe you can hit the shop and find out if any of Mr. Hillman's staff can verify he came back that day, or if anything has been off with him since Dianne disappeared. See if you can get a judge to issue warrants on the basis Mr. Hillman was the last to see Dianne. It's thin, but maybe we'll get lucky. Make sure you put a man on him until we finish investigating. I don't want him to disappear on us too."

"You got it. I have to say, you really took nothing and made it into something. Not one person I talked to ever mentioned Chris, including her best friend, Leslie. I guess all her friends believed they weren't seeing each other anymore, so it wasn't important enough to mention. Looks like I blew this one."

"You didn't blow anything," Tyler assured the detective. "I read the file. You did a top-notch investigation. I got lucky. That's all. Let's follow up on this and see if we can't find out what really happened. Unfortunately, I don't think this case will end well."

# Chapter Twenty-Three

TYLER SCANNED UP and down the street at each of the neighboring houses, hoping someone might have seen something. Directly across the street, the drapes on an upstairs window fell back into place. The same creepy feeling he got whenever Morgan gave him a message reverberated through him.

"Sanders, let's check out the house across the street. Someone's been watching us from the upstairs window. Maybe they know something and can help us."

"It couldn't hurt. So far you've gotten me further on this case in a few hours than I've been able to get in weeks."

They stood at the front door of the two-story house. A little old lady opened the door and stood before them, all of five feet nothing, wearing gray slacks and a crisp white blouse. She reminded him of his grandmother. Tightly curled hair crowned her head, and he'd swear he smelled lavender. She held her trembling hands together in front of her.

"Are you the police?"

"I'm Special Agent Reed with the FBI, ma'am. This is Detective Sanders. Do you need to speak with us?"

"Aren't you going to arrest him for what he did to that poor little girl?"

"Which him are you referring to, ma'am? And what did he do to the girl?" Tyler's gut tightened. This was it. They had a witness.

"That terrible man who always has those floozy women over. He's not setting a very good example for the poor boy, who lost his mother. She left years ago. A nice woman, but very young. That man always yelled at her about how she ruined his life. Seems it takes two to make a baby, and it isn't the baby's fault it gets made."

"Ma'am, did you see Mr. Hillman hurt a girl?"

"Yes, he did. She had short blonde hair, very pretty, even though she was crying. Her picture was on the news. I was out clipping the roses by the picket fence. She spoke to the boy first, but he left. When the man came home and found her there, she was still crying in the driveway. He took some things out of the trunk and put them in the garage. He came back to talk with her. She must have said something he didn't like because he hit her with a hammer he took out of his trunk. She fell to the ground. He put her in the car and left with her."

Good God. "Was she dead? Could you tell?"

"I don't think so. She moved, trying to get away from him when she lay on the ground. He picked her up to get her into the car. Blood ran down her face. I thought maybe he'd do the right thing and take her to the hospital. He came back later and told me that if I said anything he'd kill me. But now that you've come to arrest him, I can tell what happened. You'll make sure he doesn't hurt me."

"Yes, ma'am, we will." Tyler took the photo of Dianne out of the file and handed it to the woman. "Is this the girl you saw across the street?"

She studied the photo for a long time. "This is the girl. This isn't the same photo they had on the TV."

Tyler exchanged a look with Detective Sanders, who walked away with his phone to his ear. This would definitely get them the search warrants they needed to search Mr. Hillman's properties and hopefully find Dianne.

Tyler turned to the detective. "Sanders, when you get the warrants, I want to search The Oak Warehouse. I think we'll find her there."

Tyler gave the older woman a reassuring smile. "Ma'am, an officer will come and stay with you and take your statement. Okay?"

"Oh, yes. I'll put on some coffee. The officer will stay until you take the man to jail, right?" Mr. Hillman had certainly made sure the death threat appeared credible.

"Yes, ma'am. We'll take good care of you." Tyler smiled reassuringly. "You go inside while we get things coordinated. I'll come back and see you when the officer arrives."

The woman closed the door and threw the bolt into place.

Unbelievable—in a matter of hours they'd managed

to find the suspect and a witness. Now all they had to do was find Dianne.

He didn't think they'd find her alive, but in any missing person case it was better to find the person dead than to not find them at all. Dianne's parents deserved closure, no matter what the outcome. Without Morgan's message, he would have never asked about Chris taking Dianne to the dance. He would have never discovered Mr. Hillman had been the last person to see her. Now, because of the part of the message regarding the grand oak, he had a feeling they would find Dianne. And it was all thanks to Morgan.

## Chapter Twenty-Four

*Sunday, 1:44 A.M.*

TYLER HAD ONE hell of a night and needed to decompress. Hell, he needed to get the image of Dianne out of his head. Sam was in a bad state, but he'd wanted an update on Dianne's case. Tyler dialed Sam's cell, knowing Sam wouldn't mind the late-night call. You couldn't tell just anybody about the types of things you saw on the job. Sam would understand without Tyler having to explain every detail. Surprisingly, Sam picked up on the first ring.

"Turner."

"It's Tyler. What are you doing up so late? Is everything all right with Elizabeth?" Tyler hoped nothing else had happened. He still couldn't get Sam's devastated face out of his mind. He didn't think he'd ever seen Sam in such despair.

"Is it late? I was sitting here staring out the window watching the city. As far as I know, Elizabeth is the same. I called and checked on her a while ago, and they said there'd been no change. Nothing. She hasn't woken up."

Still in a coma, and they had no idea *if* she'd wake up. Sam had locked himself up in his room with a bottle of whiskey as soon as he and Jenna returned to the penthouse. He'd been sitting in the leather chair by the window in his room looking out at the city. The sunset had been spectacular. He'd watched the fog roll in and envelop the city. The lights in the buildings came on and lit up the night, casting an eerie glow against the fog. He'd sat there hoping and praying and drinking, his mind always on Elizabeth.

"Sam. Are you drunk?"

"Pretty much. I'm about half a bottle of whiskey shy of oblivion. Want to come over and finish the rest with me? We could sit here wondering if she'll ever wake up again while we watch the sun come up in a few hours. I've already watched it go away, might as well see if it comes back again."

"I think you need sleep. I'll call you in the morning."

"Why are you calling me so late? Did you catch a lead on the Rose Princess? Did you find the King of Hearts, 'cause it sure isn't me. I'm more the 'see-how-many-times-you-can-get-a-woman-almost-killed' kind of guy. Or maybe I'm the guy that's really great to date because he's dangerous and mysterious with a cool job with the FBI, until he isn't around when you want and need him. Maybe Elizabeth would say I'm the guy who's never there when she's being attacked. What do you think? Which guy are you?"

"I'm the guy who'll call you in the morning and make sure you're okay. Sleep it off and remember this isn't your fault. Getting drunk won't do you, or her, any good."

"It certainly couldn't hurt. In fact, my back hasn't bothered me in hours. Come on, why are you calling?"

"I found her. She's dead."

"Shit."

"That pretty much sums it up. It's exactly how I feel. I had to tell her parents."

Sam knew how Tyler felt. No one wanted to tell a parent their child is dead. "What happened? Was it the prom king?"

"No. Believe it or not, his father. She told the boyfriend— well, ex-boyfriend—she was pregnant, so he would get back together with her. The father came home and found her crying in the driveway, his son long gone. She told the father she thought she was pregnant, and she needed to get Chris, the boyfriend, back. A teen father himself, the father decided he didn't want his son's life ruined by having a child so young. He wanted to see his son go to college and make something of himself. Anyway, he hit her in the head with a hammer. Then he took her to his workshop where he strangled her, wrapped her in plastic, and stuffed her into a wood chest and left her in the basement. When we finally got the guy to talk, he said she'd sworn she'd lied about being pregnant. She said she was only trying to get Chris to take her back. He didn't believe her.

"The coroner will determine if she was pregnant or

not. I think she told the truth when she said she lied about the pregnancy. She desperately wanted to hold on to Chris. She was a kid in love for the first time with a boy who was only looking for the next conquest. The father could have sent her home to her parents and found out later she wasn't pregnant. His own past clouded his reasoning. He killed her believing she was pregnant with his grandchild."

"I don't know what to say," Sam slurred sadly. "Maybe you should come over for a few shots. You've had a hell of a night. The young ones are the hardest. It's such a waste to lose them when they have their whole lives ahead of them. That's how I feel about Elizabeth. She should be home baking cookies, getting married, and making beautiful babies."

"That's a little sexist, don't you think?"

"Why? She owns a bakery. She should be baking up pastries and pies. She's beautiful. I don't know why she isn't married already. She loves kids. She bakes cookies every Thursday for the children's hospital. She should be baking for her own kids. She's going to be a great mother."

"Why don't you marry her if you think she's so great?"

"Funny. Actually, I told Dickweed I'm marrying her."

"You should. Who is Dickweed?"

"The stalker guy, Jarred. I forgot to ask her father if he got the restraining order restored."

"Let's hope so. He's trouble."

"Yeah. So how did your psychic do on the case? How did the father turn out to be the King of Hearts? And was the Rose Princess under the grand oak?"

"You'll love this. Morgan's unbelievable. You know Dianne was the Rose Princess, because of her name and how it relates to Princess Diana of Wales, aka 'England's Rose.' That and the pendant she wore in the picture pretty much makes her the Rose Princess. The King of Hearts reference is for a tattoo the father has of a heart with a crown."

"No shit."

"No shit. Not only that, he had vanity plates on his red Mustang that said KNGHRTS."

"No way. Your psychic chick is creeping me out."

"That's not all, don't forget the grand oak. The father owns a furniture business. It's called The Oak Warehouse. It's huge, as in grand."

"That's just weird."

"There's more. We found Dianne in a wood chest, a large oak tree carved on the lid surrounded with a wreath of roses. Very detailed, beautiful. Literally, she was beneath a grand oak. When I saw the chest with the carved roses and tree, I almost lost my mind. I couldn't believe how much Morgan had gotten right. I can't even call to thank her. If it hadn't been for her message, I would never have solved this case. Her message was the catalyst for figuring everything out and knowing where to find Dianne."

"Too bad we can't call and ask her about a few of our other cases. She'd be handy to have on speed dial."

"Nothing would please me more than to know where she is, and how to get in touch with her. I never got a chance to thank her for saving my sister's life. For some unknown reason, she won't speak to me directly. This is the sixth time she's helped me. I don't know why she chose me, or how she knows about my cases, but I'm grateful to her."

"We could certainly use her help with the Silver Fox. I want to kill the bastard for what he did to Elizabeth."

"He's hiding in plain sight. I don't know what that means exactly. It's not as obvious as the message on Dianne's case. What about the double threat to Elizabeth? Does the first attack and now the second mean there's no more threat to her, or does it mean two people are the threats? I think in this case our best bet is with Elizabeth herself. She's given us the most information. I hope she can help us more when she wakes up."

"*If* she wakes up. You didn't see her. She's worse. I wanted to die. Listening to the machine breathe for her was torture. That slow hissing sound along with the slow beep of her heart monitor were more than I could take. With each breath the machine gave to her, I was reminded I wasn't there to protect her. I promised her I would."

"You know she meant when she went home. We thought she'd be okay with security at the hospital."

Sam poured another shot and downed it while he stared out the window. He couldn't see the hospital where Elizabeth was being kept alive by a machine, but it was out there. "Yeah, well, we were wrong. I don't want to be wrong again."

"Neither do I. Hey, maybe Morgan will call with another cryptic message. Stranger things have happened."

"She's strange. I wouldn't mind hearing from her

though. At this point, I'll take anything I can get to help Elizabeth and catch this bastard. He's already killed eight people we know of for the insurance claims. Who knows how many we don't know about?"

"We'll get him. Are you going to see Elizabeth tomorrow?"

"I don't know." He couldn't tell Tyler it was too hard to see her like that, the weight of everything crushing down on his chest. "I'm supposed to have dinner with her family. Can you believe they want me anywhere near her? Well, her brother, Daniel, will probably give in to his urge to punch me after what happened."

"You better sleep it off, so you'll at least stay on your feet if he does. It's embarrassing to see an FBI agent hit the deck."

Sam couldn't help it if the corner of his mouth lifted. "Funny. He won't get a chance to take a shot at me, because I'm not going just so I can sit there watching her. She's invaded my every thought already," he admitted.

"Go. Maybe she'll wake up for you. When she heard your voice on the phone when we were there with Vernet, her whole body relaxed and her eyes softened. You two have something. Go see her. Talk to her. She needs you. It couldn't hurt. Go to sleep. I'm home now. I need to crash and forget this day ever happened."

"You solved the case. Her parents will be thankful they know what happened to her. You gave them that much at least."

"I hate cases like this one."

"We all do. Have a beer and get some sleep," Sam slurred.

"You skip the beer. Go straight to bed."

Tyler said goodbye and landed on his back on the couch. He hadn't even bothered to turn the lights on in his apartment. Propping the pillow behind his head, he put his arm over his eyes and tried to block out the day. He thought about his ghost, Morgan, and wondered where she was and what she was doing. He needed to talk to her.

The ringing of his phone startled him. He grabbed it off the coffee table and hoped it wasn't the office calling to tell him to go out on a new case.

"Reed."

"You should really try to get some sleep," came a woman's silky, low voice over the line.

Tyler shivered. A man could be talked into doing anything by that sultry voice.

"Who is this?"

"The Rose Princess wants to thank you for finding her. She left you a gift on your pillow in your room."

"Morgan? How did you know I found her?"

"She can rest in peace now that you've given her back to her family. I knew you'd help her."

"How did you know?" A million questions ran through his mind.

"I have a gift for knowing things. Don't be sad. You did a good thing, something many people wouldn't be able to do. You should be proud. Anyway, she said thank you. After the day you've had, I thought you should know. Get some sleep, Tyler."

"Wait! I want to talk to you."

"You'll only ask questions I won't answer. Some of your questions don't have answers. Others have answers you won't like. I called you tonight because I knew you were down and thinking about me. Stop thinking I'm creeping you out. You and the blonde agent are peas in a pod."

"Can you help me with the case I'm working on with him? The woman was attacked again. I've narrowed down the suspects, but I need something more than *he's hiding in plain sight*."

"That's all I have for you right now. She'll be all right. She needs that blonde agent, but he needs her more. She'll give him what he's always wanted. He'll be the man she never thought she'd have."

"He's crazy about her. It's become quite obvious to everyone but him. She responds to him. He's lucky."

"I'm sorry you're lonely tonight. Things will get better for you."

"Are you watching me?"

"Not in the way you think. I'm not stalking you. Let's just say my gift allows me to feel you. I can't actually see you, but I know things about you."

"So instead of a ghost, you're my guardian angel, watching over me. Like you always know where I am, and how to contact me. How come you don't call me direct? You always leave a message. Half the time I think you're a figment of my imagination."

He couldn't hold back his frustration. She came into his life whenever she pleased, and she wouldn't tell him anything about herself.

"Wow. You really need to get some sleep. Listen, I'll help you when I can. If you don't want my help or for me to call you anymore, then say so. I leave you messages because it keeps things simple." Morgan couldn't tell him how connected she was to him, or why. From the moment she'd touched him in that restaurant years ago, he'd become a part of her. How could she tell him, or explain it to him, when she didn't understand it herself?

"I'm sorry, Morgan. I do want your help. I was thinking about you tonight because I wanted to thank you for helping me. Not just with the Rose Princess, but also with my sister and all the other cases you've helped me solve. You're amazing at giving me clues. You don't have to leave me messages. You can call me. I'll try not to ask you too many questions."

"Like I said, the messages are for a reason. My reasons. Your sister will have a good life. She'll be happy. She made a mistake and took a turn down a path she wasn't destined to go. You can stop worrying about her."

"She's my sister. I'll never stop worrying about her. But hearing you say she'll be happy makes a difference. And what about my path? Will it ever cross yours again?"

He hoped he'd get to see her again. Soon.

"Our paths are destined to cross, Tyler, like they did in the restaurant. I'm not what you think I am. Get some rest."

She hung up before he said anything more. Yes, their paths would cross, but Morgan knew that crossing would be dangerous and tumultuous at best. At worst, it could cost her her life. He would ask her to face a past she had desperately run away from and was still running from today. She didn't know if she could take that path with him.

Tyler stared at his phone, disbelieving she'd hung up on him. She didn't give him any answers and left him feeling more alone. He rose from the couch and stood in his bedroom doorway, staring at the bed. He'd forgotten about the gift left by Dianne until he saw the snow-white rose on his pillow. Stripped of his clothes, he picked up the flower and sprawled on his back on the bed. He held the rose on his chest over his heart. The sweet, heady smell drifted up to his nose, and he inhaled deeply. Eyes closed, sleep creeping in, Morgan whispered in his head, *"You're not alone."*

with him.

### *Chapter Twenty-Five*

---

*Sunday, 3:30 P.M.*

SAM'S MIND LOCKED him into the dream again. Elizabeth, under the car with him, the knife in her hand. The shot rang out and everything went black, but he still heard her scream. The echo reverberated all around him, but this time it was different. Instead of just a scream, she screamed his name. He woke up with a start to find his niece, Lily, standing beside the bed, her eyes wide with fright.

*Should have known that flimsy lock wouldn't stop Jack.*

"Uncle Sam, are you okay? You don't look so good."

"I'm okay. Just a bad dream." He rubbed his gritty eyes, trying to scrub away the nightmare. "What are you doing in here, honey? Where is everyone?"

Sam glanced at the clock. He'd slept the day away. The

headache pounding in his head and the sour taste in his mouth told him it was the whiskey's fault.

"Aunt Jenna says it's time to get up. You're supposed to have dinner with Elizabeth."

"I'm not going anywhere."

Lily wore a frown on her angel face. "I feel bad you're so sad," she said, breaking his heart. He hated putting that look on her face.

Sam tried for a smile when he pressed her little nose like a button, letting her know in a small way he appreciated the sympathy.

"I thought you were going home today."

"We're leaving in an hour. Cameron took the jet somewhere, so we have to wait for them to get the plane ready again."

"You like flying on Jenna's plane?"

The kids loved it. Who wouldn't? It was a nice jet. Jenna tried to keep things normal for the family and the kids, but when you had money like Jenna, there were some things you couldn't give up. They made life easier and more convenient. Like having your own jet and avoiding flying commercially with four small children.

"It's a lot of fun. I get to watch the pilot fly the plane. Why are you sleeping in your clothes and shoes?"

Sam had managed to get from the chair to the bed, but apparently he'd forgotten to take off his clothes and boots. "I guess I forgot to change clothes, honey."

"It's time to get up now. Everyone wants to say goodbye. You have to go see your friend."

"I'm not going to see her."

"That's not nice, Uncle Sam. She's sick, and you should go and see her."

Assertive as any adult, but she was just a little bitty angel. "I don't want to," he grumbled.

"Why are you being mean? We came to see you when you were in the hospital. You have to go see her."

"I don't think she'll want to see me."

"Why? You're nice when you aren't grumpy, like now."

"Grumpy, huh." So everyone had sent the six-year-old to make him go see Elizabeth and stop wallowing.

"She's probably scared. I bet the doctors have given her a dozen shots by now. She'd probably feel better if you were there with her. I don't like to get shots, but it's better when Mommy is with me."

"Elizabeth is really sick. I don't think my being there will help her. Besides, her family is with her. She doesn't need me."

"Everyone needs a friend," she said, a little sage advisor in the making. "Why don't you want to go? Don't you like her anymore?" Lily put her chin on her hands on top of the bed, her big blue eyes staring at him.

"I like her. I like her a lot." He didn't want to think about that. It was futile. She'd go back to her life, and he'd go back to his. If she ever woke up.

"What do you like about her? Is it just that she's pretty? Mommy says just because someone is pretty it doesn't mean they're a good person. Tom, at school, said he liked Mary more than me because she's pretty, but I think she's mean. She's always saying mean things to people."

"I think you're the prettiest girl there ever was and

Tom is blind if he can't see that." He gave her hair a tug and smiled. The kid didn't buy it. "Elizabeth is pretty, but there's a lot more to her. She's got a great sense of humor, she's nice, she's smart, and she's got great strength. She's pretty on the outside and on the inside where it counts. Like you, honey."

"Then don't be mean to her. Go see her and tell her you think her insides are pretty."

Sam held back a laugh at her wording.

"Girls like it when you say nice things to them."

Dating lessons from a peanut. "Did Aunt Jenna tell you not to leave here until I said I'd go see Elizabeth?" Sam was very suspicious of the little angel. Relentless, he had no doubt someone had put her up to it.

Lily smiled broadly. "I don't know what you're talking about." The tone was very reminiscent of her mother's, his sister.

"I'll bet you don't. Go on now. I'll be out in a few minutes."

"And you'll go see her?"

"Yes. Okay? I give up. I'm going." Sam sighed and sat up on the edge of the bed. Grabbing his niece, he hugged her fiercely.

Lily wrinkled her nose. "You need a bath. You smell really, really bad."

"Thanks. Get out, so I can take a shower. I'll be out in a while to say goodbye to all of you." Lily headed for the door as Jack and Caleb came in. "Are you two the next wave of assault? Figured you'd soften me up by sending the kid in first?"

"That was Summer and Jenna's idea," Caleb said smiling. "We're supposed to drag your ass out of bed if Lily couldn't get you to get up on your own."

Jack took in the nearly empty bottle of whiskey sitting on the table next to Sam's chair and reading lamp. He gave his brother a once-over and determined Sam was hung over and looking like he'd had a hard night. Bloodshot eyes, wrinkled clothes. Sam rubbed at his temples, probably to ease the pounding headache. He deserved a little pain for his stupidity.

"It's not fair sending that little angel in here. I can't say no to her."

"Neither can I," Caleb admitted about his daughter. "I wanted to send the three boys in to attack you. I think in your condition, they could take you."

"You're probably right. Fine, I'm up. I'll hit the shower and go to the hospital. Call off your wives. I swear, I don't need one of my own with your two harassing me all the time. Can't you all leave me alone for a little while?"

"Looks to me like when we leave you alone you self-destruct. What's with the bottle of whiskey? It's not like you to drown away your sorrows." Sam wasn't acting like himself and it worried Jack. He nodded to Caleb to give Sam and him time alone together.

"Nothing is with the bottle. I got carried away. I've had a hard couple weeks, and now that I have some time off, I thought I'd let loose."

"Let loose," Jack said sarcastically. "You locked yourself in a room and drank yourself into oblivion—alone. Your family came to help you get through this rough time, and you've either ignored us or snapped at us. I think maybe you're right about Elizabeth; you should stay away from her. She's turning you into a drunk and an asshole. I'd rather you go back to being irritable. You'll be cleared to work on Tuesday, get back to what you do best and forget about her. Tyler can finish the case. You're better off without her."

Sam grabbed Jack by the front of his shirt, held firmly, and got in his face. "Forget about her. Hell no. I can't forget about her. She's almost died twice because of me, and you want me to go back to work and forget what happened. You think I'm better off without her. Look at me. I'm still half drunk from last night because I can't stop thinking about her. She's my every thought and . . . shit."

He was falling for her. She consumed his life. The only time he'd been happy since the shooting was when she woke up and they'd talked. Like an old friend to him already, he'd told her more about his life than he'd ever told another person. He released Jack, shoving him away, and tried to breathe, taking in deep gulps of air.

"Exactly. Now, get your sorry ass down to the hospital. Have dinner with her family and spend some time with her. Talk to her like before, let her know you're there for her. It'll do you some good too. Oh, and lay off the sauce," Jack ordered.

Sam dropped back onto the bed and put his face in his hands. Jack might think it funny, but it just hit him right between the eyes what the rest of the family already knew. He was falling for Elizabeth, and falling hard. Maybe they could build something good together. Then again, they had to get past everything happening now. Jack knew what it was like to fall in love when you were in the middle of a hurricane. He must have experienced the same when he met, fell in love with, and married Jenna. Their lives had been in such chaos, but they found each other, and eventually worked their way through the turmoil together. Maybe he and Elizabeth could do the same. God, he hoped so.

"Shit." Somehow she'd worked her way past his head and into his heart without him ever seeing her coming. He glanced at Jack's knowing smile.

"You already said that. Get cleaned up and say good-bye to the family. The kids will miss you. Summer and Caleb will be happy to be away from you for a while." Jack slapped Sam on the back. "It's not that bad. You'll live."

"Not without her. She's got to wake up and be all right. I couldn't take it if she . . ." He left the sentence unfinished because he couldn't speak his worst fear. That he'd never get the chance to see if there could really be something between them.

"You know what I find interesting? The only time she woke up and talked to anyone, it was for you. Go see her. Make her wake up. I have a feeling she'll do it for you."

Sam stood and headed for the bathroom, anxious to get to the hospital now. Maybe Jack was right and she'd wake up for him again. Then maybe she'd finally get out of the hospital, and he could take her on a proper date. Holding hands in the hospital when she was half uncon-scious didn't count.

He wanted more, a hell of a lot more.

## Chapter Twenty-Six

*Sunday, 6:00 P.M.*

SAM MANAGED TO get himself cleaned up, say goodbye to his family, and make it to the hospital in time for dinner with the Hamilton family. Gathered in Elizabeth's room when he arrived, he didn't even glance at them; his eyes went right to Elizabeth, the ventilator still doing its job keeping her alive. Her dark hair was pulled back by a white headband. No doubt her mother's way of taking care of her.

"Hello, Sam. It's so nice you could join us. We were about to eat. Come. Sit down, and we'll fill you in on Elizabeth's condition." Rachel led Sam by the arm toward the table.

"Hi, everyone." Sam took in the family sitting at the small table set up in the room. The second bed had been removed to make room for their dinner. He thought it amazing anyone could set a table with linens, silver, and crystal in ICU. But these were the Hamiltons and he imagined they could make just about anything happen.

Each place setting had a covered plate. Gerard's, one of the finest restaurants in the city, had delivered dinner. A box from Decadence, Elizabeth's store, sat on the other table.

Sam took the empty seat facing Elizabeth and tried not to stare at her. It didn't work. He couldn't help but watch her, hoping she'd wake up, move her hand, something.

The Judge cleared his throat and gave him a knowing look across the table. "Sorry, sir. How is she?"

"Better. They're weaning her off the ventilator. It's only helping her now. She's doing most the work. They'll try to take her off of it completely sometime tonight. It's the best we can hope for right now."

Sam understood the waning hope in the Judge's tone. Every second Elizabeth lay silent made it more and more difficult to believe she'd wake up and be fine.

"I hope you're hungry. Gerard's makes the best prime rib dinner with all the fixings," the Judge went on, trying to sound jovial.

"Thank you for inviting me." Sam's stomach wanted to rebel at the sight and smell of food, but he'd get through dinner and hope for time alone with Elizabeth.

Rachel removed the covers from all the plates. Prime rib dinner with all the fixings included mashed potatoes, green beans with bacon and caramelized onions, and sautéed mushrooms. Once he got a look at and smelled the food, he decided he was hungry after all. He grabbed a roll from the basket on the table, buttered it, and tried to make nice with Elizabeth's brothers. "How's it going, Patrick? Daniel?"

"Just fine, Sam. Any news on the person who did this to our sister?" Patrick asked hopefully.

"Nothing definitive. The best information we have came from Elizabeth. She gave us a very good description of the man. We've narrowed our suspects considerably. I'll be back on duty by Tuesday, and I'll help Agent Reed until we catch this guy."

"I know you guys are doing your best and giving everything you have to the case, but don't you have any idea who did this?" Daniel was still fuming about his sister, but he'd mellowed considerably since the last time they crossed paths.

"That's been the problem all along. The guy is a ghost. No one has ever seen him, except Elizabeth."

A few feet away, Elizabeth lay still. She looked like a shell, no life or glow to her, like she wasn't really in her own body.

"She mentioned she might have seen him somewhere before, but I imagine with the social obligations and other benefits she and your family attend, the number of people she meets and runs into is enormous. Not to mention the horde of people who storm her shop each day."

"Her business is very popular." Rachel beamed. "She meets all kinds of people at work and at the other social events she attends. I'd imagine trying to sort out who might have been at one of those places and attacked you both would be difficult for her to remember precisely," Rachel said discouraged.

Sam nodded and continued to eat with the family. Their conversation centered on their work and their lives, while Sam sat mechanically eating. Whenever they asked him a question, or for his opinion, he gave it, but never took his eyes off Elizabeth, waiting for any sign she was coming back from the black oblivion. Rachel served desert, a rich chocolate cake. He didn't remember eating it, or the fact he'd managed to down two cups of coffee on top of it. He couldn't remember half of what he'd talked with her family about either. He was too busy watching her.

"Sam," Daniel bellowed.

"What?" Sam jerked around. "I'm sorry. What did you say?"

"Did you accept the assignment to protect Elizabeth when she's released and can go home? I gave you a hard time, but I think you're the best man for the job. Hell, if all you have to do is watch her, you're getting a lot of practice tonight."

Daniel laughed at his expense, and Sam glared back at him, despite the truth in Daniel's observation.

"Yes. I'll be the one assigned to her if that's what she still wants when she wakes up."

"She will." The Judge said it like he had no doubt. "More importantly, her mother and I want you with her." He winked at Rachel.

It might be nice to see his daughter date a man for more than a few weeks. Sam wasn't like the other men who tried to get in Elizabeth's good graces. Sam didn't want anything from her or them. He was his own man. He hadn't asked John once who he might know in the upper ranks of the FBI, or to put in a good word for him with so and so. A straight shooter, he didn't want anything he didn't earn himself, and the Judge liked him for it all the better.

Sam hoped she would want him to protect her. The conversation around him started up again between the guys and their parents. The dream he'd had that day came back to him. He remembered waking up to find Lily by his bed with Elizabeth screaming his name ringing in his ears. He heard her sharp piercing cry now, calling out to him. A single tear trailed down the side of her face, and another, and by the time the third one ran down, he realized he wasn't seeing things. She was crying.

In the next second, all hell broke loose. She moved so quickly no one had time to stop her from grabbing at the breathing tube. She thrashed in the bed trying to get the tube out, but the tape and strap were secure. Buzzers and alarms went off like slots in a casino. Sam jumped up from his seat and made it to the bed before anyone else had a chance to get to her. He leaned over her face, whispering in her ear.

"Sweetheart. Stop. Stop. You're okay." Grabbing both her hands, she finally focused on him. Wide blue eyes filled with fear stared up at him. "They'll take it out. Stop." She gripped his hands, her nails digging into his skin, and kept her eyes locked on his. "The doctor's coming. They'll take it out. Are you okay?"

She shook her head no, but relaxed. She never took her gaze from his, or let go. At that point, he was her lifeline. He made her feel safe. He was real, and after being in the black ooze, she needed a buoy to keep her afloat, she held on to him.

"Ellie Girl. I'm so happy you've come back to us. You missed dinner. We had it right here in your room. Sam joined us, of course." Her father's happiness at seeing her awake filled his every word. She couldn't turn away from Sam. She held on with everything she had.

"Your Mom went to get the doctor. Hold on for a minute, Ellie Girl."

"Hey, Busy Bee. We're so happy you woke up. Don't worry, you'll be home in a few days. I bet you'd like that. The Muffin Man misses you. I think he hates me." She caught his weak smile out of the corner of her eye.

She wanted the tube down her throat out.

"Everything at the shop is fine, Lizzy. I've been checking in as often as I can. Amy and the rest of the staff are keeping everything the way you like it. We had one of your triple chocolate cakes tonight. It was really good."

Elizabeth was happy to hear all of them talking to her, but she couldn't shake the need to keep the connection with Sam. He kept her afloat when the black wanted to come back and pull her down. She didn't want to go there ever again. She willed herself to stay with Sam, with them all. The tube made her feel like she was choking. She tried to make a grab for it again, but Sam stayed her hands and held on to her tight.

"Stop. Don't pull at it. You'll hurt yourself. They'll

take it out. Relax." Sam was thankful to see she had so much strength. He kept a good grip on her hands to keep her from grabbing the tube. Once the adrenaline wore off, she'd be weak as a newborn baby.

Doctor Watts hurried into the room and came right to Elizabeth. "Please give us a few minutes alone. It looks like she's fighting mad to get the tube out. Let us get her settled again, and you can spend some time with her."

"Sweetheart, I'm going to let go of you. Don't pull at the tube. Let the doctor take it out. Okay?" She blinked at him once. "Okay, sweetheart. We'll be right outside the door. We'll come back in a minute." He let go of her hands and gently wiped away the tears from her cheeks. She started to panic again, and he laid a kiss on her forehead. "I'll be right back. You can't talk to me until they take the tube out. I'll be back. Okay?"

She blinked once for him and let him go. She needed to talk to him, and the sooner the tube was out, the sooner she could speak. The doctor worked quickly. Uncomfortable, to say the least, and once it was out she tried to say something, but her voice came out scratchy and her throat hurt.

"It'll take some time for your voice to come back." He held a glass of water by her head and helped put the straw in her mouth. She drank deeply. "Slow down. You don't want to make yourself sick. How are you feeling?"

"Like I'm neck deep in the sand. It's hard to move. I feel like there's a weight on me, and there's a fog in my head. My heartbeat echoes ten times louder in my ears, and I have the worst headache."

"I'll give you some meds for that."

"No more drugs. I've had enough. I want to go home," she said, knowing sitting up was beyond her strength. Getting up and walking, out of the question.

"It'll be some time before that happens." She turned her head away while he listened to her heart and lungs. She'd been through a lot and in the hospital for a long time. She wanted to get her life back on track. Forget all this ever happened. Like that was possible. "You'll be home before you know it," he assured her.

"Can they come back in now?"

"Sure. I'll check on you in a little while. If you want more medication, let us know."

Blessedly alone for a few moments, she tried to compose herself. She didn't have a lot of energy, but she needed to talk to Sam. She'd have to get through the time with her family, and hope she had a moment alone with him.

Her mother came in crying, followed by her father. He exhaled with relief and reached for her hand. "There's my Ellie Girl. You look much better. How are you feeling?"

"Tired, but fine." Her voice croaked like a frog, but at least she got the word out.

"That's good. The doctor told us you're not supposed to talk too much. You need to let your throat heal. They quickly gave you the antidote for the drugs you were given. There's no permanent damage. You needed time to recover. I told your mother you'd wake up for Sunday dinner. You wouldn't disappoint your dad, now would you? Not that you ever could." He picked up her hand

and kissed her knuckles. Her gaze went to the bruises on her arm, but she didn't say anything.

Her mother leaned over and hugged her, trying her best not to hurt her. Elizabeth wrapped her arms around her mother and held on, trying to keep from breaking down. She wanted them to believe she was okay, even though she was a mess on the inside. She'd let herself go when she was alone. Her brothers came in, but she held fast to her mother. After giving her a big kiss on the head, her mother let go. She listened to her brothers tell her about her shop and everything she'd missed over the past two weeks in their lives. Her mother cleaned up the dining table, having everything wheeled out on a cart, including the empty box from her shop. She tried to keep track of the conversation, but she struggled to focus.

"I'm tired. I think I'll go to sleep now." She couldn't hold on much longer. The emotions raged inside her and wanted to come out. Turning into a sobbing ball of fear and pain was not an option in front of them.

Sam hadn't come back like he promised. She needed to talk to him, and he'd left. Her family reluctantly said goodbye and promised to return in the morning. She didn't want them returning in the morning. She wanted to go home and sleep in her own bed, hide in her own house.

When the goodbyes and hugs were over, and she was alone in her room, she lowered the bed, rolled onto her side, and curled up. The bruises on her arm reminded her of what happened and fear washed over her again. Shaking, she put her arms over her head and sobbed. It all came up from inside and poured out in her tears.

Sam walked in quietly and found her curled up in bed crying her heart out. The wracking sobs tore his heart to shreds. He moved the IV lines and wires connected to her monitors and lay down on the bed behind her, pulling her to his chest. Wrapping his arm around her, he held her while she cried.

The second Sam entered her room, she felt him. Gently, he pulled her to him. The feel of his strong body pressed to her back, so reassuring, so warm and solid, she simply gave in and let the rest of the tears come out. He'd hold her until she regained some semblance of herself and strength. Right now, it was heaven to feel his arms around her and know she was safe, if only for a little while. She could let the tears fall and feel the fear with him. Her family would have been concerned, but Sam would understand.

He whispered to her, telling her she'd be all right, and she'd get through this. He told her to let it out, let it go, and held her close.

All the tears spent, the fear subsided. She didn't mind Sam being in bed with her, but after all the sobbing ended came the embarrassment.

"I'm sorry. I'm a mess. This is probably the last thing you needed, some hysterical woman crying all over you."

"You've been through one traumatic thing after another. I think you're entitled to a crying jag. I'm surprised you've held up so well." He liked the feel of her pressed up to him. Reluctant to let her go now that she was recovering, he stayed put.

"Traumatic is right. Some fake fiancé you turned out to be. You didn't even save me a piece of chocolate cake." She tried to overcome her embarrassment with humor.

His laugh rumbled up his chest pressed to her back. She loved the solid feel of him and his amusement made her feel lighter. He gave her a warm, soft squeeze.

"I'll get you some cake if you want it. I'll get you anything you want if you stay awake." He nuzzled his nose into her hair behind her ear and said, "I'll be the best fake fiancé you've ever had if you get better. I don't think I can take much more of you being unconscious." His lips brushed the ridge of her ear, and her whole body tingled. "I like your new sexy voice too. Talk dirty to me, baby."

He was trying hard to keep things light and make her laugh. She couldn't manage. "He tried to kill me." Shaking again, it was okay, because Sam held her tight and waited for her to go on. "He came in while I slept. I thought, maybe it was . . ." She stopped, not wanting to make him feel guilty because she thought it was him coming to see her. She'd been so excited to see him again. Only it wasn't him.

"You thought it was me," Sam finished for her. "It's okay, Elizabeth. I came to see you several times late at night. You thought I came into the room. Finish the story."

"I opened my eyes and was about to make a smartass remark about sneaking into girls rooms in the middle of the night, but it wasn't you. He'd already pushed the needle into the IV line and I tried to pull the needle out of my arm, but he grabbed my wrist. My eyes were about to close when he grabbed my hair and pulled my head up. He said . . . he said the Hamilton name wouldn't buy my way out of death. He knows who I am. I know you kept the majority of the story out of the papers, but he knows who I am. I can't help but think he knows me from somewhere else."

"So you saw him again with the lights on. You can be sure of his description now."

"I'm already sure. This time, though, he disguised his appearance. He wore a heavy, thick coat and a ball cap. His face was the same, but with the coat and hat it would be hard to say how much he weighed or the color of his hair. He's slim, but the bulky coat made him look bigger. I guess he figured that if someone in the hospital saw him, they'd get the description wrong."

"Okay, so it's the same guy. We knew it based on the drugs he gave you. They were the same thing he used on a couple of his victims and me.

"I'm sorry I wasn't here. You asked me to protect you and I didn't." He continued to hold her, his face pressed against her head.

So sincere, his voice rough with emotion and laced with guilt. "Sam, we had a guard on the door, a hospital full of security, and doctors and nurses who check on me every hour on the hour. It isn't your fault the guy got past everyone. You aren't supposed to be with me until I go home."

"I should have known he'd try to get to you. Dickweed got in, didn't he?"

"Dickweed? You mean Jarred. Well, he's a psychotic stalker who thinks we're getting married. You can't protect against that kind of obsession. I'd take you as my fake fiancé over him any day." She eased her sore body over toward him. The fog from the drugs still blanketed her mind. "None of this is your fault. I couldn't leave you lying in the street. I'd do it all again to make sure you were alive and safe."

"You like me, huh?"

"As fake fiancés go, you're not so bad. Except for the chocolate cake thing, of course."

"Of course," he mimicked her serious tone.

She wrapped her arms over his arm lying across her and leaned her head against his chin and closed her eyes. "You really know how to hold on to a girl when she's feeling scared and alone. I always feel safe when you're here with me. That's why I asked Deputy Director Davies to assign you to me. Well, that and the fact you need to work. I know you're struggling with what happened, and you blame yourself for shooting me. I thought maybe you'd make it up to me by being the one to protect me until you guys catch this maniac. That, and I loved the look on Jarred's face when you said you were marrying me. Absolutely priceless. He never gives up. Maybe now he will. One maniac down, one to go."

"So you just want to use me to get rid of Dickweed." He knew that wasn't the case. It amazed him she understood his feelings about the shooting and the importance of his work.

"No, now that I know how safe I feel lying in your

arms, I might make you sleep with me every night." The wheels started turning as she replayed that in her head and gave him a lopsided smile. "My head is foggy, and that came out wrong."

"I think it came out fine." He leaned down and kissed her long and soft. She gave herself over to him; leaning in, she melted in his arms. Nothing could have made him stop kissing her at that moment. Until she squealed in pain. He backed away immediately. "What's wrong? Did I hurt you?"

"No. I rolled onto my thigh and the pain streaked up my hip. Oh man, that's better than a cup of coffee to wake a person up."

Sam shifted to get up, but she grabbed him by the shirt.

"Don't. Don't go yet."

Her eyes pleaded. How could anyone resist her? She was so beautiful, even in her condition. He couldn't wait to see her well again. "I need to move so I don't hurt you. I'm not leaving. You couldn't pry me out of bed with a beautiful woman begging me not to go with a crowbar or a stick of dynamite. You said it before, I'm not stupid." He helped her get settled and arranged the wires and IV lines so they weren't tangled. He managed to scoot to the edge of the bed so she had enough room. "There. All better."

"No." She tried to get more comfortable and scoot closer to him. He was so warm and strong. Groggy and tired, she wanted to fall asleep before he left. Without him there, she'd stay up all night worried the man would come back to hurt her. If she could fall asleep before he left, maybe she wouldn't realize he was gone and she could sleep.

"Don't pout. What's wrong?"

"If this fake marriage is going to last, we need a bigger bed." She gave him a crooked smile while her eyes were closed. Her body began to relax and she drifted off.

"Stop it. A man can only take so much." She set his whole body to flame. That kiss had started a slow burn that flashed each time she wiggled closer. He wanted to kiss her again and run his hands over her. The only thing separating her from him was a sheet and a flimsy gown, which he'd already noticed didn't close in the back. She had the softest skin. He brushed his hand up and down her arm while she nestled against his chest. She felt so good curled up to him with her full breasts pressed against his side. Oh God, what sweet agony.

"Since I'm still foggy from the drugs, and I can use that as an excuse later, can I ask you something?"

"What?"

"Will you kiss me again when I get out of here?"

Sam groaned. He put a finger under her chin and lifted her head, so he could look at her. Her eyes, barely opened, appeared groggy and half asleep. "I'll kiss you anytime, anywhere." He kissed her softly, beginning slowly and nibbling at her lips. He traced her lower lip with the tip of his tongue. She sighed with pleasure, and he took the kiss deeper. He kept it slow and lingered over the task. She was so sweet, his mind went numb and his body raged with fire. He slid his tongue into her mouth. She opened for him and responded with long, slow thrusts of her tongue, sliding over his. They kept things slow and soft and warm. He pulled back just enough to trail kisses over her cheek to her temple.

Tucking her head in the crook of his shoulder, he said, "Go to sleep, sweetheart, before you kill me."

Kissing the top of her head, he held her while she drifted off, her hand resting on his chest over his heart. Damn if his heart didn't already rest in her hands.

He stayed with her for two hours, watching her sleep and keeping her close, everything inside him in agony being so close to her and wanting her. He found it even harder to leave her, knowing she wanted him to stay and protect her, but he couldn't let her family find him in bed with her in the morning. A nurse had already come in to check on her and gave him a wide, knowing grin. Besides, two of his fellow agents were stationed at the door. They'd never let him live it down if they caught him in bed with his witness. Clothes on or not.

## Chapter Twenty-Seven

### Thursday, 1:30 P.M.

FOUR LONG DAYS passed since she'd woken up from the coma. Monday morning she awoke to discover Sam had left her in the middle of the night. She missed him, but knew she couldn't ask him to stay with her every minute of every day just so she felt safe. She spent the day doing physical therapy, respiratory therapy, and having nurses and doctors poke and prod at her. Doctor Watts wanted to order more surgery to repair the scars on her back. He told her a plastic surgeon could make them almost invisible. She'd had enough of the hospital and the last thing she wanted was more surgery. They told her it would only take a couple of hours. Since Doctor Watts and her parents ganged up on her, she conceded.

The evening after the surgery she awoke to find herself lying awkwardly on her stomach. Sam sat in a chair next to her bed, holding her hand. He kissed her on the head and told her he'd spent much of that day in and out of meetings with his superiors, before attending his mandatory psychiatrist appointment.

So sweet, he told her he got more from talking to her than he did from talking to the mind benders. She had to laugh at the term and the disgusted look on his face. She was about to fall asleep after they'd talked for over an hour when his phone rang. He'd be back on the job the next day, so it surprised her when he told her he had to go to work. He'd kissed her on the head again and gave her butt a soft caress that made her smile and her blood heat.

Sam spoke to her guards and left her alone to worry about him and whether the elusive Silver Fox would try to kill her again while Sam was gone.

Tuesday and Wednesday were more therapy and visits from her family. Kay tried to visit, but the guards refused to let her in. Kay made a fuss in the hallway, and Elizabeth rescued her, grateful for the chance to confide her mixed up, overwhelming, strong, and deep feelings for Sam. He hadn't come to see her since Monday night. It worried her, but he was trying to find the man responsible for shooting and drugging them. She reminded herself, she wasn't his only case.

She *hoped* she wasn't only a case.

As Kay expressed her excitement about her friend's possible new love interest, Elizabeth simply hoped Sam was different from the others. She'd been proven wrong so many times. If Sam turned out to be like the others, she'd give up on men all together. Maybe it wasn't in the cards for her.

Irritable and cranky, she hadn't slept well in the noisy hospital since Sam left her Monday. The nurses checked on her every hour on the hour, and she was in a constant state of unreasonable fear. As soon as she saw her parents this morning, she announced she was leaving the hospital and going home. She refused to stay even one more day cooped up in that room.

She called Deputy Director Davies and told him he could find her at home that afternoon. She told her father to either get the hospital to release her, or she was simply walking out. Apprehensive at first, her parents saw her determination and made arrangements with the doctor for her release.

Her next call went to Patrick. Since he had been staying at her house, she asked him to bring her some clothes. He'd chosen well. Black yoga pants, a long sleeve white T-shirt, and a pair of tennis shoes. Comfort and convenience were the order of the day, since her thigh and back were still bandaged. She'd have to use crutches for several more days until the thigh muscles healed and could support her weight for longer than a few hours.

Before she dressed, she managed to take a shower and wash her hair and felt almost human. Two weeks without a proper bath, she needed one.

The shower tapped almost every ounce of her energy. She managed to get her underwear and pants on. The bandages on her back and the healing wounds prevented her from putting on the bra. She'd have to go without and find a better shirt when she got home. Her arms in the sleeves, she couldn't lift them to put it over her head. Her back to the door, it swooshed open, and she assumed her mother was coming in to help her finish getting dressed so they could leave.

"Mom, I can't get the shirt over my head. My arm hurts, and I'm too tired from the shower." She put her head down, her gaze on the floor and her bare feet. How was she going to do this at home alone? Well, she'd take her time and get it done.

With her arms in the sleeves, the shirt covered her breasts. She thanked God for small favors when a large pair of men's boots appeared next to her bare feet.

It didn't surprise her anymore to simply know without looking. Sam. "I'm stuck." She tilted her head back to see him. His mouth tilted up in a mocking half smile, punctuating the absurd situation she'd gotten herself into.

She'd had surgery on her back on Monday, but he hadn't actually seen her back until now. Black, blue, and green bruises bloomed across her skin. He wanted to remove the bandages, see for himself the damage done by the bullets. When he got close to her, he saw the long scar on her arm where he'd shot her. Nearly healed, he hoped in time the scar would fade so she wouldn't have to look at it and be reminded of what he'd done. He couldn't see her thigh, but imagined it was healing well too.

Her dark hair hung wet down her back past her shoulders. Her face was pale with black circles under her bloodshot blue eyes. She trembled from the exertion of trying to get dressed. Exhaustion had depleted all her strength. Speechless, he stared. Regardless of everything else, she was so beautiful.

"Sam, can you help me? I can't lift my arms."

"Sorry. Yeah, here let me do it. Let go of the shirt, and I'll pull it over your head." He grabbed the shirt and her arms and lifted them both over her head. He had a nice view of her lush, round breasts, but that didn't hold his attention. Well, for long. He's a guy after all.

A scar ran at least six inches along the underside of her breasts. "Oh God, honey. That must hurt like hell." He didn't pull the shirt down, but stared at the line marring her creamy skin. Red and healing, he could imagine how much it hurt and what she must have gone through in surgery.

"Sam, let go." She tried and failed not to be self-conscious about him seeing her breasts. They were just breasts, after all. He'd probably seen a lot of them. Okay, she was embarrassed she couldn't hide her response to him. Her breasts grew heavy, her nipples tightened, and her whole body became aware of his intense scrutiny.

Lust didn't hold him enthralled. No, the scar bothered him, but not her, really. "They took the stitches and staples out the day before yesterday." She pulled her shirt down and grabbed the pair of socks from the end of the bed. Unable to meet his eyes, she tried to scoot back on the bed to pull her feet up and put her socks on. With her thigh bandaged and making it difficult to move, she couldn't manage.

Sam took the socks from her and picked up one foot and then the other and helped her put them on.

He grabbed her shoes, slipped them on, and tied them. Before she slid off the bed, he planted his hands on each side of her hips and leaned down, his face close to hers.

"I'm sorry."

"I don't want to do this with you again. You didn't do this. I'm fine. See. Here I am going home."

"You're fine, huh. You can't even put your shirt on."

"Thanks for pointing that out."

Already on shaking ground because, as much as she wanted to go home, facing the street and car where she and Sam had been attacked frightened her.

"Yeah, well, we both know I'd rather take your clothes off."

"You might get your wish. I'm so tired from putting them on, I may never get them off again."

"Never fear, fake fiancé is here." He gave her a wolfish grin.

"Funny. Very funny." She laughed and gave him a playful smack on the shoulder. "You look good. I forgot to tell you I like the haircut. You've gotten some sleep too, I see."

He did look good. In addition to the black work boots, a nice snug pair of blue jeans showed off his long, muscular legs. He had a dark blue T-shirt on and a flannel shirt over that. The T-shirt was tucked in and on his belt he wore his gun and badge. He looked good. Dangerous and strong were good words to describe him, but he was also in complete control and self-assured. Things she used to be, to feel. But as of late, she felt unsure and scared of her own shadow.

"My sister gave me a haircut. Apparently I was scaring my nephews. They didn't like the fact I didn't look like Jack anymore."

"You sure do now. When he came in this morning I knew it wasn't you, but God, the resemblance is uncanny. I bet most people can't tell you apart."

"You saw my brother this morning? Why was he here?"

"He and Jenna came to thank me personally for saving your life. Jenna wants to talk to me about a business opportunity. She wanted to know what my plans for the future included for my bakery. Odd of her to ask, but she's really nice."

"I hope you told her whatever it is you have planned. She'll make it come true. She's like a fairy godmother."

"What do you mean?"

"She takes care of people and grants their every wish when she considers them family. I'd say she feels like you're family, since you saved me."

"I don't expect anything in return." Remembering what Sam had said about Jenna and all she'd done for his brother, Jack, and sister, Summer, she wondered what Jenna had gifted Sam.

"What wish did she grant you?"

"She built me a big log cabin-style house right on the lake at the family ranch. Four bedrooms, a huge Great Room, a big kitchen, and a deck in front overlooking the water. My dream house. I live there when I'm on vacation. Someday I'd like to live there full time. Right now I have work.

"How'd you know Jack wasn't me? You're right, most people can't tell us apart."

"There's no difference in your appearance, but he wasn't you. I can't explain it. I just knew."

She couldn't tell him Jack felt different. She looked at Jack and saw Sam, but he didn't make her stomach tighten or send a warm shimmer through her body. Whenever Sam came into the room, her whole being responded, and when she'd seen Jack, it was like seeing one of her brothers. She didn't have a connection to him, other than fondness because he was nice and Sam's brother.

"I'm sorry I didn't come back on Tuesday or Wednesday. Something on the case came up, and I've been working with Tyler on it in between my appointments with the mind benders. I thought I'd let you have some time with your family."

Actually, his contact, Scott, who he was meeting at the bar the night they were attacked, was found shot to death and locked inside a cargo container at the harbor. He'd been there for quite some time. Maybe even since the night he and Elizabeth had been attacked. Sam figured Scott had made him for a cop and told the Fox. Obviously, the Fox didn't like having someone set him up with a cop and had decided to do a little housecleaning. Now, without the middleman setting up the hits, the Silver Fox could close up shop or move on to greener pastures, and they'd never get him. No one knew who he was, except for Elizabeth, and that was a loose end Sam intended to make sure the Silver Fox didn't tie up.

"Thanks. I can't tell you how much I appreciate you

leaving me with four people who fuss over me and tell me I can't possibly want to go back home and to work with a maniac out to kill me. Oh, and let's not forget my stalker. Deputy Director Davies said he wanted me to stay a few more days so you guys could secure my house. No thank you. And then there's the fact I haven't slept since you left on Monday. And I feel like shit. I can't even walk without crutches, or put my damn clothes on."

She ran out of steam, her frustration spent. The whole tirade stemmed from fear and exhaustion.

She was afraid to go to sleep. The Silver Fox had tried to kill her while she slept, Jarred had snuck in while she slept, and the thought of being vulnerable like that again scared her. Who could blame her?

"You haven't slept since Monday. You want me to sleep with you when we get to your place?"

Her parents stepped into the room at that precise moment. Her mother held back a laugh, despite the smile on her face. Her father's gaze shot daggers at Sam.

"Maybe we need someone to protect her from you," the Judge suggested.

Sam smiled and stood to his full height. "Hello, Rachel, Judge. It's nice to see you again. Elizabeth says she hasn't slept well the last few days. I thought perhaps she'd like to take a nap when I get her home," he covered and tried to keep his face passive. He didn't want to make her parents think he couldn't take care of their daughter. He needed them to keep their faith and trust in him.

"It's nice to see you too, Sam. Don't mind the Judge. He's upset Elizabeth won't come and stay with us. He forgets she's a grown woman and knows her own mind. Are you ready to go, Elizabeth?"

"I was ready days ago. Mom, hand me the crutches."

"Didn't Patrick bring you a sweater or jacket? It's cold outside and, well, that shirt is rather revealing," her mother said pointedly.

Elizabeth looked down at herself and shrugged. She didn't have anything to put over the thin fabric. Without the bra, you could practically see right through it. Before she lifted her head to tell her mother she had nothing else, Sam draped his flannel shirt over her back and helped her slide her arms into the sleeves. He rolled up the arms because they were too long and buttoned a few buttons in the front to help keep in closed.

"There you go. All set."

Heat from his body and his fresh clean scent lingered in the shirt. She wanted to lie down and hold the soft fabric to her nose and go to sleep smelling him. "Thank you," she said softly and his blue eyes grew very intense. "Let's go. I want a real meal, my own bed, and to check on things at my shop. I probably have a mountain of work to do."

"No work today, sweetheart. Today we go to your place. While you sleep, I'll make sure the place is secure. I'll take you to work tomorrow for a couple hours if you're up to it."

"But Sam, I have a business to run. I've been in here for two weeks. Enough is enough. I can't put off business any longer."

"Don't worry, Ellie Girl. Daniel took care of everything at the shop. He's contacted all your suppliers and let them know you'll pay them when you return. They've all agreed to hold your accounts and make their deliveries. They know you'll make payment when you're able. The payroll company has paid the workers. Your assistant manager signed, but Daniel verified every check before he paid the employees. Everything is running smoothly, and that's because you run a good business. Things are fine. Let's take you home so you can rest."

The nurse came in with her wheelchair and Sam asked everyone to step out so he could have a word with her alone before they left.

"Elizabeth, I want to make something clear before I take you home." He waited for her nod. "We haven't captured the man who did this. He's still out there, and he wants you dead because you can ID him. I'm sorry to put it so bluntly, but I want you to understand you're in real danger."

"Sam, I know. I spoke with Tyler last night. He told me what to expect."

"You spoke to Tyler last night?"

"Yes, he came to see me. That's why I decided to leave here today. I'm no safer here than I would be there. I want to go home, Sam."

She couldn't tell him Tyler had brought a sketch artist and some photos of the suspects they had. He showed her the photographs of their suspects, and she discarded all of them without hesitation. She worked with the sketch artist to translate her description into a picture. Once they had that, she remembered the company logo on his bracelet. It took some time, but several minutes later she came up with the company name. After she knew that, it wasn't hard to remember the man's name and where she'd briefly met him.

Tyler accessed the company's website on his laptop and found a picture of him, along with a short biography. Tyler was surprised to see the sketch and picture were very similar. They planned a trap for the guy, and decided it was best not to tell Sam she was the bait. She hated lying to Sam, even by omission, but it was necessary.

"What else did you and Tyler talk about last night?"

She'd drifted off into thought, and Sam wondered if she was thinking about Tyler. He didn't like the fact she'd spent time with him alone. Tyler thought Elizabeth was beautiful, and he liked her personality. He'd been making one comment after another about her the last two days, and now he was visiting her in the hospital behind his back.

"What's the matter? He came to talk to me about the case and make it clear I should keep you with me at all times." She tried to lighten his mood. "I only have one fake fiancé, honey, and that's you. I'm a one man kind of woman." She winked. "Actually, I have two fake fiancés, but you're the only one I want."

He couldn't help himself and smiled. "Thanks. I'm a one woman kind of man, and I don't like the idea of Tyler sweet-talking you into having him guard you instead of me."

"How'd you know that's why he came?" She tried to

hide her smile and looked up at him, acting completely innocent, but he didn't buy it.

Sam thought he hid his feelings well, but she had a way of dismantling his walls. His jealousy showed, despite his best effort to keep it under wraps.

"All he's talked about is you for the last two days. I think he has a crush on you."

"Oh yeah? What about you, Sam? Do you have a crush on me?"

Uncomfortable and unable to meet her eyes, she smirked and made his discomfort worse. He didn't know how to answer. How did she maneuver him smack in the middle of a minefield?

Defensive, he glared at her and said, "Let's go. The two agents who have been guarding your room are going with us, until you and I are settled in at your house. If I tell you to do something, you do it. No questions. If I say duck, you take cover without questioning me. This guy has already shot you once, I don't want to give him an opportunity to do it again."

"Some fake fiancé. You can't even tell me you like me." He glared at her even more. "Okay. No questions. Follow whatever order you give me. It's for my own good, and you're trying to keep me alive. I got it. I'll try to be a model protected witness."

She slid off the bed and stepped forward to take a seat in the wheelchair so they could leave, but Sam grabbed her and pulled her to him. He held her tight against his chest and looked down into her surprised face. One arm banded around her, he traced his fingertips over her cheek and down along her jaw to her neck. His fingers rested against her warm skin, her pulse skittered against the pad of his thumb.

"God, you're beautiful."

Eyes locked on hers, he leaned down and kissed her. Slow and easy, when she opened her mouth to him, his control slipped, and he demanded more. Wrapping her arms around his neck, she buried her fingers in his short hair, closed her eyes, and let go. He held her by her hips, so he wouldn't hurt her back or stomach. He wanted to pull her hips to his, but they had to leave, and he didn't have time to make love to her like he wanted and his body demanded.

Frustrated, he pulled back just enough to see her face. "Does that tell you how much I like you? Fake fiancé or not, I want you. Stay away from Tyler. He can get his own girl. You're mine." He brushed his lips against hers and stepped back. It took everything he had to let her go when he wanted to keep her close.

She limped to the wheelchair and eased herself into it, her face flushed, her eyes and head dazed after their kiss. He'd rattled her, and it felt good to know she was just as affected as him.

After handing her the crutches she needed at home, Sam pushed her toward the door. "Remember what I said. Do what I tell you. No questions."

"Okay," she said, a little dumbfounded after the kiss, giving his ego another boost. "Let's go. I want to go to sleep knowing no one is sneaking up on me. Not that being there will change that," she sighed.

He stepped up beside her and put his hands on his hips and looked down at her. "I won't let anyone hurt you again." He gave her his best mischievous grin. "Besides, the only person you have to worry about sneaking up on you while you're sleeping is me."

## *Chapter Twenty-Eight*

THE QUIET, NEARLY deserted streets in this part of town
made it easy to get close to her home. Or at least what
she called home. He should buy several blocks of the di-
lapidated warehouses, level them, and build high-priced
condos. He'd make a fortune. He always did in every ven-
ture, but the prospect didn't hold any appeal. Not when
his future hinged on Elizabeth and making sure she never
testified against him. He needed her silence and one way
or another; he'd have it.

Due home from the hospital soon based on his sources,
he circled her block in the innocuous white sedan he'd
rented under a false name. He slowed at the approach to
the alley behind her home. In the distance near the trash
bins, he spotted a man stumble out her back door when a
cat rushed through his feet.

"Stupid fucking cat," the guy yelled, oblivious to everything around him.

The cat crouched, hissing and growling. One paw swatted out at the man's leg, claws catching on denim before ripping clear. The guy slammed his boot down on the cat. His screech echoed between the buildings, and the cat tore off to hide under the dumpster. The man pulled out a knife and worked in deliberate scratching motions, carving something into the door. In unrestrained fury, he worked at the task. "Take that, bitch."

"That guy is a nut." Someone else had it out for her. If he got in his way, he'd eliminate him too. The Fox drove on, shaking his head, and let go of the idea of getting close to her today. Always at his best when presented with a challenge. Elizabeth intrigued him, but a second player in their game raised the stakes.

## Chapter Twenty-Nine

SAM TURNED HER over to the aide outside her room and they rode the elevator down to the lobby. Before they left the hospital, he stopped everyone and bent down next to her.

"Can you walk out to the car with your crutches?"

"Yes." A brand new midnight-blue Suburban sat parked out front. "Nice car. Is it yours, or the FBI's?"

"It's yours."

"What? No."

"Yes, it is, Ellie Girl. Your mother and I got it for you. Yours was severely damaged and we thought you might want a new one after what happened."

Tears welled in her eyes, and she tried to blink them away. "Thank you. It's wonderful. What about my other car?"

"We had it towed away. Not to worry. We took care of everything."

"Thank you. I don't know what else to say." She had worried about going home and seeing the car all smashed up and remembering what happened. At least she wouldn't have to deal with it.

Sam took both her hands and helped her out of the wheelchair and placed the crutches under her arms to support her. Her fingers tingled after he'd touched her and her heart fluttered with awareness, but she tucked it away for later. Sam's guard mode rubbed off on her. She scanned the faces in the hospital entrance, her nerves kicked in and the fear came back. Sam noticed the subtle shift in her mood and stepped in front of her, looking at every person around them. He angled his head to glance at her behind him and she gave him a half-hearted smile. Because she wanted to, she ran a hand over his shoulder to reassure him—and herself—that everything was fine.

"Let's go."

"I'll walk out first, you stay right behind me," he ordered. "Both agents will remain right beside you. Go straight to the car and get in the back seat. John will sit beside you, and Mark will follow us in the other car."

"Okay."

She convinced her parents she was in good hands. They said their goodbyes and left first. Sam made her wait until they cleared the cars waiting out front, then they made their way outside. He timed the exit perfectly. Only one other couple waited out front with their newborn as Grandma placed multiple flower vases in the back of their SUV. The new father placed the infant car seat in back and helped his wife into the car. Not even the family escaped Sam's intense scrutiny. He watched everything at once. His diligence in protecting her went a long way to tamping down her building fear.

Everything went according to plan, and they got into the car together. Sam had to help her into the high seat while John stood guard beside them. On the drive home, her anxiety heightened. When they turned onto her street, sick with worry, her stomach churned. Sam pulled up in front of her house and turned off the car. The other agent, Mark, went inside first and made sure everything was as it should be and no one else was inside. He poked his head out her front door and gave Sam an all-clear wave.

"I'll get out first. Get out after John. Go straight into the house. Ready?"

Fingers clamped together, her palms wet and held tightly in her lap, she stared out the window seeing Sam lying in the street, the car bearing down on them. She hated thinking about it, seeing the replay in her mind. Her throat closed when she imagined the man's grip around her throat. Fear made her heart thunder in her chest.

"Elizabeth."

She gasped, her vision cleared, and Sam turned toward her in the front seat. "What? Yeah. Get out of the car behind John and go straight in. I got it. John, please take the crutches out first. That way I won't fall on my face."

"No problem. Stay behind me. Sam will walk behind you."

"I got it. Let's just go."

Her heart continued to pound, and she could barely take a breath. She seriously considered she might have an anxiety attack over getting out of the car and going into her own house. She stared out the window once more, down the street to where the dark SUV had been parked. No such car today, everything appeared as it should.

Sam got out before she followed John out the door and headed inside. She stepped into her living area and immediately backed up again and ran right into Sam. He put his hands on her arms to steady her.

"Ouch!"

He instantly let go of her injured arm. "Oh, God, sweetheart, I'm sorry. What's wrong? Why are you backing up?"

"Something's wrong?"

"What's wrong?" He scanned the room looking for any threat or sign something was out of place. "Mark checked the place. No one is here. You're safe."

"I'm telling you, something is wrong. I can feel it." She tried to back up more, but Sam was a wall behind her. His breath blew through her hair. Because the other two agents stared at them, he didn't put his hands on her, but stayed close. The heat of his body comforted her, but didn't erase the strange feeling stealing her good sense and making her panic.

"Is something out of place? Patrick has been staying here. He left this morning because you're coming home. I know the flowers are half dead, but he wanted you to see how much everyone cares about you."

"It's not that."

Her kitchen was at the far back of the huge open space, a Decadence cake box sat on the counter. Everything appeared the same, but something was still . . . off. She couldn't put her finger on it. Her heart raced and the hairs on the back of her neck stood on end. All three men watched her. She was acting ridiculous, but the creepy feeling coursed through her. Maybe after all that had happened, she was looking for something to be wrong.

"I don't know. It's something. I don't know. Never mind. You said no one is here, so I'm sure it's fine. It's fine," she repeated, wondering if her nerves could take this.

"Elizabeth, I know you're scared and uneasy about being here after what happened. You'll settle down once you've gotten accustomed to being home again. Mark and John will watch the outside of the building. You won't see them, but they'll be out there just the same. I'll stay here with you. Wherever you go, I go. Tyler will be in and out too. We're all here to protect you."

"I know. I'm being stupid. John, Mark, I'm sorry. You guys can do whatever you need to do. You're welcome to come in and raid the fridge and coffee pot whenever you want."

"They won't make their presence known, Elizabeth. They aren't hanging out with us. We want to protect you, but also make it seem like this guy can come after you, so we can catch him. You do understand that, right?"

"Yes, I'm tired. I'm not thinking clearly. Please, feel free to go to Decadence and have all the free coffee and food you'd like. I'll call the shop and tell them. I'm sure you know it's not far from here." She hobbled toward the kitchen. Maybe she'd whip something up and she'd feel better. She always felt better when cooking.

"Okay. Thanks, Elizabeth," John said. "And remember, if you see us in the shop when you're there or outside, pretend you don't know us. We're keeping watch over you." He and Mark left after that to take up their posts outside.

"They'll search the area around the building and make sure no one is watching the place. They'll also check out the neighboring abandoned warehouses to make sure they're empty," Sam explained to satisfy her doubts and fears.

She made it into her kitchen and leaned the crutches up against the counter. Maybe she'd make Sam and herself some lunch. Then she'd take a nap. Sam spoke with the agents and closed and locked the front door. He pulled the curtains shut, which made the room darker, but the second story windows kept the place fairly well lit.

Sliding the bakery box closer, she opened the lid and gasped. Someone had carved the word BITCH into the chocolate icing. She stood frozen, eyes locked on the ominous cake. Finally regaining some of her composure, she looked up toward Sam, who had turned on the big screen TV in the living area. He was about to sit on the couch and watch a ball game when she called out to him, "Sam, did you get this cake?"

Her voice shook with fear, making him turn to her. She never took her eyes off the cake, like it might somehow attack her if she looked away.

"I asked Patrick to pick it up this morning from your shop. You were giving me a hard time about us eating the cake on Sunday, so I thought you might like a welcome home cake. Why?" he asked concerned.

"I really prefer it when you call me sweetheart to this," she indicated the cake.

Sam came over and slammed his hands down on the counter. "Shit! Someone's been here."

And then it dawned on her. "Sam, have you seen the Muffin Man?"

He raised an eyebrow and asked, "Who is the Muffin Man?"

Any other time, she'd have teased and asked, "Do you know the Muffin Man?" But this wasn't the time and she couldn't joke when she felt like she was standing in someone's crosshairs.

"My cat is missing. He always comes out to see me when I get home."

"Maybe Patrick let him out this morning when he left?"

"He doesn't go out, except . . . maybe he's on the roof. I have a sitting area up there and he likes to come up with me. Maybe Patrick had his coffee on the roof this morning and the Muffin Man got locked out. Patrick can sometimes forget about him because he doesn't like him."

"Patrick doesn't like your cat?"

"The cat doesn't like Patrick, or anyone for that matter. He only likes me."

"Who doesn't like you, sweetheart?" He gave her a smile and hoped she'd forget about the cake for a minute.

"I'll go upstairs and see if he's up there. Maybe he's curled up on your bed or something."

"He hasn't seen me in weeks. He'd come down. He always comes when I get home. Something is terribly wrong. I know it." Her hands shook, and her stomach felt like a river swirled around inside.

Sam's warm hands cupped her face. "We'll find him. I'll go upstairs and check. You check the rooms down here. Maybe he's hiding because of all the strangers."

The kiss he planted on her forehead allowed her to exhale and breathe again. With a soft push from him, she started toward the spare room.

"Take your crutches, sweetheart."

"I can walk a little. My leg gets sore quickly, but the therapist said to keep using it to get the strength back. I'm fine."

Sam went upstairs and checked the first door leading into the master bathroom. He never went in, but closed the door and headed down the open landing. He paused in front of her bedroom. With his hand on his gun, he opened the door and went into the room. Elizabeth waited for him to come out. He did a minute later, and made his way up the set of stairs at the end of the landing and through the hatch, more like a large skylight, which opened up onto the roof. He disappeared, and she checked the downstairs spare room where Patrick had slept.

The room was empty. She checked under the bed and went through the adjoining bathroom. She exited into her living area and went to her office.

Opening the door slowly, she searched inside and under her desk. He wasn't there. Patrick knew better than to let the cat out, but maybe he had run out without Patrick seeing him. She unlocked and opened the back door and stepped out into the back alley where Patrick liked to park his car.

"Muffin Man," she called to the cat and listened for his meow. "Here kitty kitty."

Nothing. No soft meow. Not even a hiss of displeasure, telling her he was mad she'd been gone too long. Dejected, she turned to go back inside and stopped midstep, frozen by the horrific bold letters carved into the paint on the door: I'LL GET YOU NEXT TIME.

A soft mewling drew her attention to the wood palette beside her garbage cans. Her little Muffin Man's nose poked out of the crevice he'd wedged himself into between the wood and brick building. Her knees buckled and she sank to the ground. She reached out for him and he sprang forward, but landed hard on his chin when his front paw gave out. She grabbed him and pulled him to her chest, his front leg bent at an odd angle. She gave him a squeeze to keep him steady and he growled in pain. She buried her face in his neck and cried. This would never end, until they found the man responsible and put him away for the rest of his life.

Sam checked the upstairs and roof and found nothing. His devil friends stomped up his spine. Elizabeth was worried and looking to him to make things safe. Here, in her own home, she should feel safe, especially with three FBI agents watching her and the house. But someone had gotten past them and written a threatening message in the cake and her cat went missing. Not a good start to his assignment to protect her.

On his way down the stairs, the hairs on the back of his neck rose when he scanned the empty living space. The creepy feeling danced up his spine again.

"Elizabeth." He called out to her, but didn't hear anything. The back door stood open a crack, and he raced to it, hoping no one had come in and taken her. He flew through the door and stopped short when he found her on the ground crying, a ball of fur in her arms. At first, he thought she'd hurt herself, and then she looked up and behind him. He turned around and faced the ominous message.

"Shit."

He grabbed an empty cardboard box from beside the recycling bin and kneeled down beside her. She gently laid her cat inside and gave him a soft pet on the head. Weak from pain and his injuries, the Muffin Man backed into the corner of the box and stared, his ears laid back in warning.

"I think he's got a broken leg and rib."

Her trembling voice tore at his heart. He wanted to rage at whoever had done this to her and the cat. Not only had this guy tried to kill her, but now he terrorized her with threats and cruelty to her beloved pet.

"We'll get him to the pet hospital, sweetheart."

"He's going to pay for this," she threatened, her eyes wide with fear, hurt, and a determination he admired.

Sam stood and pulled her up by her hands. He picked

up the box and ignored the hissing cat. Her feet dragged from exhaustion. No matter what else was happening, he needed to take care of her.

He thought he'd lost her again and his heart nearly thundered right out of his chest. Holding her close with his arm around her waist to support her weight, he pulled the door open and took her inside.

She settled on a stool at the kitchen counter and he sat the box in front of her. She peered over the edge and spoke in a gentle reassuring tone to the cat, brushing her fingertips along his head between his ears.

At a loss for what to say, Sam kissed her on the temple twice before pulling out his cell phone and dialing John. "Get in here, we have a problem. Someone's been in the house. They left a message in the cake and back door and hurt Elizabeth's cat." He hung up and stared down at Elizabeth's bent head. Her shoulders slumped and her crooning voice grew weary. Unable to stand it any longer, he scooped her into his arms and carried her out of the kitchen.

"My cat," she protested, her sad eyes pleading with him.

"I'll take care of him after I take care of you."

With her arms wrapped around his shoulders and her face buried in his neck, wet tears dampening his skin, he carried her upstairs to her bed and laid her on the soft cover. He pulled the blanket draped across the end of the bed over her and kissed her soft lips. He brushed the hair away from the side of her face and kept his hand against her head. With a sweep of his thumb, he wiped the tears from her too-pale cheek. The dark circles under her eyes worried him.

"You just got out of the hospital. You need to sleep, sweetheart." She opened her mouth to protest, but he kissed the words away. "Please, I will protect you, even if it's from yourself."

Too tired to fight him, she settled into the pillow and mattress with an exhausted sigh.

Her eyes drooped closed and he watched her for a moment before he went downstairs to deal with the cake and cat. When he got his hands on the person responsible for this, they would wish they'd never hurt his Elizabeth.

## Chapter Thirty

ELIZABETH WOKE TO the dim light of sunset darkening her room. Sam sat in the rocking chair in the corner watching her, his blue eyes intense. She sat up on the bed and faced him, hoping it had all been just a bad dream. She'd met him at some party, instead of lying in the street.

"The cops are gone," he began in an unfamiliar flat tone. "They took the Muffin Man to the animal hospital. The vet called and said in addition to his broken leg, he's got three broken ribs, but they think he'll pull through. I'm sorry about your cat, sweetheart. The cops printed the cake box and the back door, but if it's the same guy who came to the hospital, there won't be any. I don't know what to say. We checked the place top to bottom before we brought you home. The alley is easily accessible. After John left us off here, he checked the alley to be sure no one was there. There's no place to hide, so he didn't come all the way down to the door. He didn't see the words on the door or the cat. I'm so sorry, sweet-heart."

Not a dream at all, she thought, but a living night-mare that got worse and worse. She held her hand out to Sam because she needed him close. When he was near, nothing else mattered. She waited for him to come to her. He rose slowly and sat on the edge of the bed. Taking her hand, he leaned down and kissed her palm. She didn't say a word. Fisting his shirt in one hand, she pulled him down on top of her as she lay back on the bed. She wrapped an arm around his neck, leaned up, and planted her mouth over his. When he tried to pull back, so he didn't crush her, she pulled him closer. She wanted to feel his weight and taste his lips and forget the rest of the world. Safe. Warm. Strong. All those things and so much more for her. She wanted him like she'd never wanted anyone.

Life was too short not to grab hold of something as good and precious as what she felt when she and Sam were together.

Intoxicated by her scent, the feel of her soft skin, the taste of her, everything. If he didn't stop soon, he wouldn't be able to stop at all. She held on to him with all her might as he crushed her into the bed. She didn't seem to care and pulled him as close to her as possible. He didn't object to being there. He ran his hand over her head and down her cheek to her neck and shoulder. Pressing her down into the bed, he lifted his head and stared down into her eyes.

"I don't want to hurt you, sweetheart. Your back is still bandaged, and so is your thigh." She rocked her hips against his hard cock, and he groaned. With his forehead against hers, eyes locked, he said, "Honey, you're not making it easy for me to be a gentleman and let you recover."

She rocked her hips against him again and again to let him know she didn't want to stop. She leaned up and kissed his neck, grabbed his hair and pulled his mouth back to hers. Her hands skimmed down his hard back to his waist. She pulled the T-shirt out of his waistband and up and over his head and let it sail off the bed to land on the floor. She ran her hands over the smooth muscles in his back. So much strength in him. He kissed his way down her neck to the V in her shirt and the top of her breast.

"I want every inch of your skin against every inch of mine, Sam. I don't want you thinking about the scars. I want you wanting me."

"I do want you, sweetheart." He came up and leaned on his elbows, holding himself over her. "I don't care about the scars. You're the most beautiful woman I've ever seen."

His hot, wet mouth pressed against the swell of her breast, his tongue swept across her skin, leaving a blazing trail of heat. His big hand cupped her breast and his thumb swept over her nipple, bringing it erect. She shivered from the ripple of passion radiating through her and moaned when he continued to rub his thumb over the sensitive pebble in slow circles.

"Oh God, Sam. Show me how much you want me, because I want you more than I want to breathe right now."

She leaned up and kissed him again, her hands trailing down his hard chest, over his flat, taut stomach to his belt. She undid it and his jeans. When her hands went to his hips to push the jeans down, she accidentally grabbed his gun.

Consumed with her, Sam had forgotten all about his gun—at least the one on his hip—until she went absolutely still in his arms. He leaned back and pulled the gun from his belt and put it on the table beside the bed.

He waited a moment to see if she'd changed her mind.
*Should have known better. Thank God.*

In an attempt to drive him even crazier, her nimble hands glided over him again and again. He went back to her, gently pulling her pants down her legs and trailing kisses down her uninjured thigh. Grabbing her hands, he pulled her up and took his flannel and her white T-shirt off. He bent to her and took her taut nipple into his mouth, sucking and licking while he wrapped an arm around her back and lowered her gently to the bed. He cupped her breast, brought it up to his hungry mouth, and feasted. Always careful where he touched her and put his weight, he gave in and caressed every inch of her with one reverent stroke after another.

He moved to her other breast, savored the taste of her. Smoothing his hand down her stomach, he found the very treasure he sought. He hadn't removed her panties, so he stroked her through the thin barrier while she rocked her hips against his hand. Her body responded, hot and wet for him, he moaned with pleasure and dined at her breasts. Kissing his way up to her throat and jaw, he made his way up to her mouth. Stroking his tongue over hers, he slipped his hand into her panties to rub and slide one finger, then two, into her slick core. Hot and tight, he wanted to be deep inside her—now.

When his finger entered her, she thrust forward and welcomed him. Muscles trembling, that familiar ache increased.

"Oh God, Sam. I want you. Don't stop." She felt so free and cherished. So gentle and demanding at the same time, he coaxed her to respond to every reverent touch. Her whole body flamed, and with each stroke of his fingers that fire burned hotter.

He rubbed his thumb over the sensitive little nub and sent her skyrocketing over the edge. She bucked and moved against him, wave after wave of heat rocked her.

As the trembling subsided, he leaned back away from her. "I don't have any protection with me. Do you have something?" He wanted her, but he was always careful and the last thing she or he needed was a baby on the way.

"I'm on the pill." She had a momentary second thought about its effectiveness, since she'd been in the hospital and missed several days. Then he moved over her, and she could only want. "I haven't had sex since my last year of college, and even then, only with one guy. You're safe with me."

"I'm blown away. You've only been with one guy," he said, completely surprised. "Are you sure you want to do this? Maybe you're just upset, or . . ."

"Sam, I don't care if you've been with one woman or a hundred. I know you're smart and careful, and you don't use people." She slipped her hand into his jeans and took him into her palm, gently squeezing. Her hand stroked up and down his hard shaft. Heat and strength radiated from him, and she loved how he felt in her hand and the sound he made deep in his throat as her palm and fingers worked over the smooth skin.

She kissed his neck and nibbled her way to his ear. "I know what I want. It's you, Sam. I've never wanted anyone more. I want you inside of me and wrapped around me. Please, Sam, don't make me beg."

Something snapped inside of him, and in the next second her panties disappeared along with his jeans. Still holding him as he came back to her, she guided his hard length to her before she gripped his hips and pulled him hard and deep inside her. She felt wonderful and powerful. She'd never been so daring or adventurous.

Sam took her mouth in the same instant he slid into her with one powerful thrust, her nails biting into his hips. He didn't know what he'd expected, but as he pushed into her, she came up to him and took him deep and moaned into his mouth. He was lost to everything but the feel of her.

Cradled between her thighs, she pulled her knees up, allowing him to plunge deeper. It was like diving into molten lava, she set him on fire. She rocked her hips, keeping pace with him. Her hands rubbed over his back, down to his hips where her nails dug in. She arched up to him. He made love to her with everything he had, hoping to erase every thought from her mind except her need for him.

He tried to keep the pace slow, but her hands were everywhere, driving him mad. Each time he thrust forward, he didn't think he could get closer to her. She pushed toward him and proved him wrong. Her long legs wrapped around his waist and pulled him in deeper.

Quickening the pace with his face buried in her neck, he kissed her and thrust harder, slower, longer, faster. She tightened around him, he thrust hard and fast until she cried out his name and went rigid around him with wave upon wave of spasms. He rocked against her, but never pulled out, and she crested a second time. Her heavy sigh echoing in his ears, he finally let himself go and spilled himself deep inside her with a satisfied groan.

Their coming together had been the most perfect joining. Connected to her in a way he'd never experienced with any other woman scared him to death.

He'd emptied himself into her, yet he felt so full.

Exhausted, he'd set her whole body on fire and turned her to liquid gold. She loved the feel of him inside of her. His breath whooshed out in ragged pants at her neck. She stroked his back lazily, up and down, loving the feel of all those rigid muscles. Leaning on his arms, he tried not to crush her. Cradled between her legs, she slowly slid them down his thighs and calves, using her feet to rub his legs the whole way down.

"I can't stop touching you, Sam. You feel so good against me."

"Sam's dead. A beautiful woman killed him. She seduced and ravaged him. It was the sweetest death."

Giggling in his ear, she hugged him fiercely and said

shyly, "I didn't know it could be like that. I've never, you know. And now, I did three times."

She'd never had an orgasm, and she'd only been with one guy. He couldn't be this lucky to have such a beautiful woman, who was so giving, want him so much. Still smoothing her hands over him, his groin stirred even now, after they'd had the most amazing sex ever.

"You're killing me all over again. You've never had an orgasm?"

"I've had three now. Thank you. That was wonderful. I didn't realize I could be so free and want so much. You're amazing."

She really knew how to make a guy feel a hundred feet tall. The sincerity and warmth in her voice made it all the more sweet. Possessiveness, male pride, her honesty, all of it made him want to give her more pleasure. This was making love, not merely enjoying a bout of sex. Kissing his way from her neck to her cheek, he found her mouth, and began the journey to ecstasy all over again.

His flesh swelled inside her. She sent him to the brink when she whispered in his ear, "That's the most amazing, unbelievably erotic feeling," and pressed her hips to his.

"Sam, I need to get off my back. It's starting to hurt."

He couldn't pull out of her, even if bombs were going off around them. He wanted her too much. Holding her hips with one hand, he lifted her, shifted over on the bed, and rolled with her, careful to go over her good thigh and leave the bandaged one over his hip. Landing on his back, he helped her get situated on top of him.

He held her hips and she found her rhythm and

slowly drove him crazy. Head back, eyes closed, her body moving steadily with his, not a bit of self-conscious shyness or reservation in her movements. He ran his hands over both her breasts, sat up and took one hard nipple into his mouth. She wrapped her arms around his head and held him to her breasts while she rocked back and forth on top of him.

A fire burned inside both of them. Her body tightened around his and she rocked harder against him. Lying back on the bed, he caressed her with his hands and moved his hips to the rhythm of hers. He gripped her hips and used the pad of his thumb to gently rub the wet nub where they were joined. Her head fell back, and she crashed over the edge of sanity, her mouth partially open, a heavy sigh escaped her.

Beautiful and so carefree, her body locked tight around his. Unable to hold on any longer, when she rocked forward again, he thrust up deep inside her and let himself fall over the edge. She crashed down on top of his chest and lay there holding on to his shoulders. Her breath came out soft and warm against his throat. He wrapped his arms around her and held her, thinking he'd never let her go.

The shadows lengthened in the room until they filled every corner. Her hands in his hair massaged his head, hypnotic and so relaxing he thought he might fall asleep with her on top of him, and him inside of her.

Gently sliding out of her, he used his fingers to stroke the soft flesh he'd just left. She moaned with pleasure and he stroked her hot, wet center again and again.

He continued to touch and tease and coax her to make those wonderful sounds. He slipped two fingers inside, pulled out to stroke the soft flesh before he pressed his fingers back inside of her again. She continued to moan and whimper and call his name until he pulled out, stroked the soft nub with a circle and sweep of his finger. He pushed back into her, and she tightened around him, and dug her nails into his shoulders as the tightening spasms crescendo and subsided.

Her lips moved against his chest when she smiled. "You sure know how to play me like an instrument. I feel like spaghetti. I don't think I can get off you. Ever."

"You're fine where you are."

When she didn't move, he gently rolled to his side and let her slide off him. He nuzzled her ear and laughed. She'd been exhausted from the shower that morning and hadn't been able to get herself dressed. After making love and having multiple orgasms, he was surprised she wasn't comatose. Limp beside him, a tremble rippled through her. It worried him he might have hurt her, or set back her recovery.

"Honey, I'm so sorry. I shouldn't have been so rough with you."

"You couldn't have been more gentle or wonderful. I'm fine. You are a beautiful man, Sam. I can't decide if I like looking at you or touching you more."

"Stick with the touching." He couldn't help the cocky grin from turning up one side of his mouth. She made him feel so good.

She lay on her stomach with her arm on his chest, her

eyes closed. Cherished, cared for, she felt loved. She never wanted to lose this feeling. "I wish you didn't have such a dangerous job. Of course, then I wouldn't have met you." She didn't know what she'd said, but his whole body went rigid and the fingers that had been softly rubbing the back of her hand stilled. "What's the matter? What did I say?"

"You don't like my job?" Here we go. They'd shared an amazing night, and now she'd tell him how she couldn't live with the work he did.

"I think your job is fine. It's just that since I've seen firsthand what kind of danger you put yourself in, I wish you didn't have to. I'd hate to see anything bad happen to you again. I know you love your job, and you're good at it, great even, but your job is dangerous. I'm worried about what could happen to you."

"So what you're saying is you wouldn't want to be stuck at home wondering where I am for days at a time, or what kind of danger I might be in." That's what she meant to say. She wouldn't be happy with a man who spent days away on a case. She didn't want to have to worry about him every time he went to work.

Frustration and something else filled his voice. Something he didn't want her to hear, but there all the same.

"Well, as your fake fiancé, what kind of woman would I be if I didn't worry about you?"

She gave him a pinch to let him know she was joking with him. He didn't bite though. She sighed. Time to explain and convince him she didn't mind his job, which meant admitting the deep feelings she already had for him.

"I care about you, and I'd hope you'd expect nothing less." He tried to get up, but she was faster. She moved her body on top of his and pinned him with a look, and he went limp beneath her, waiting. "I, on the other hand, won't be waiting around for you to get your butt home. I have a business to run, charity work I do, social functions to attend, and a dozen other things that occupy my time. I don't know what the other women in your life were like, but I have my own life. That isn't about to change if we decide to have a relationship. I'm perfectly capable of being alone without beating you up because you went to work."

"You say that now, but sometimes I'm undercover for days, even weeks. I'll miss taking you out to dinner, or to some fancy party you have to attend. You'll resent the fact I'm not here. Then you'll resent my job, and what I do. We'll argue about how important my work is to me, and you'll say it's too dangerous, and you can't live with wondering if I'm dead or alive."

"Well, I'm glad we're getting this fight out of the way now. It will save us from having it in six months." She waited for him to look at her. When he wouldn't, she took his face in her hands and made him. "If that's what you think will happen, you're wrong."

His eyes remained cold and steady. He didn't believe her, so she tried again to convince him.

"How about the fact after we've been dating six months, you'll be begging me not to make you attend another dinner party dressed in a tux? Or maybe you'll decide that after you've been gone for three or four days, and we've made love all night and you wake up alone because I've gone to work at three in the morning I'm not giving you enough of *my* time, or putting *you* first, when we only have a little bit of time together. Maybe when all the bandages come off, you'll decide you can't stand the site of all these scars. Maybe . . ."

He stopped her words with the press of his mouth to hers. All worked up and disgruntled, trying to prove him wrong. Hell, maybe he was wrong. Maybe she could handle it. Right about one thing, the other women he'd dated didn't have as full a life on their own as she did. He really wanted to make it work with her, like he'd never wanted to with anyone else. And maybe that made all the difference.

"You could have a thousand scars and I'd still think you're the most beautiful woman I've ever seen. I'll wear a tux for you whenever you want *if* I get to take you out of whatever sexy dress you're wearing. And why the hell would you go to work at three in the morning?"

"I run a bakery. I have to bake early in the morning for the breakfast crowd. I have people who do the early morning shift, but occasionally I have to cover for them. The point is, you might be gone for several days, and when you get back, you'll find I'm busy. That could be a problem for you, since our schedules will be unpredictable. I want you to understand I get it, and I have my own life. I'm sure you don't expect me to sit around waiting for you to come home."

She kissed him again and laid her head down on his chest. Exhausted after a long and stressful day, she let out a huge yawn to prove it. "I started this conversation because I wanted you to know I care about you, and I don't take our sleeping together lightly. If you don't want to be my fake fiancé and only want a casual bed partner, you have the wrong girl. I think we could have something amazing. But I don't want you thinking every time you go on an assignment. I'll be angry with you when you get back. Your job is a part of who you are. It's part of what I love about you, your commitment and your devotion to your family and your work." She yawned again and closed her eyes.

*Did she say she loved him?*

He didn't hear her right. Tired and not thinking straight after a long and difficult day, she only meant she cared for him and admired his committed to his family and job. *Right?*

Concentrate on the fact she wants a relationship, not a casual affair. She wanted to be with him, committed with him.

"I want you all to myself. I'm a possessive man when it comes to you. If you think you can handle my work and the long hours and days I'm gone, I'd like to see if there's something special between us."

She mumbled her agreement, sound asleep on his chest seconds later. Her head lay over his heart, and he wrapped his arms around her, pulling the covers over them. He kissed the top of her head and settled into the bed, the moment, the happiness building inside of him, and slept.

## Chapter Thirty-One

---

*Two weeks later . . .*
*Thursday, 6:07 P.M.*

"SAM, YOU BETTER come down. Tyler will be here any minute. You need to get ready to go." He'd been up on the roof talking on his cell phone for almost an hour. Elizabeth had dinner ready and Tyler would be at the house by six thirty.

Tyler tried, unsuccessfully, to find the man she'd identified more than two weeks ago. While Tyler discovered a lot of public information on the company owned by the Silver Fox, he'd had a difficult time wading through the overload of shell companies and dummy corporations to find any personal records that led them to the man. The Fox had gone into hiding, and they couldn't locate him.

Sam had the sketch of the person they suspected, but only Tyler and the other two agents assigned to watch her and Sam from a distance knew who the man is and had an actual photo of him. She didn't know why Tyler felt it necessary to keep the photo from Sam, but he thought it better to have Sam watching out for any kind of threat, rather than focused on a single person. They assumed, since the middleman had been murdered, only the killer remained to be apprehended. If they didn't catch him, he'd get away with all those murders and trying to kill her and Sam. Elizabeth was the only person standing between the Fox's freedom and life in prison.

"Sweetheart, you don't have to yell." Sam came down the steps from the roof.

She stood in the doorway of her bedroom, and God, she got more beautiful every day. She didn't have to use the crutches anymore. Her long legs and hips were outlined nicely by her tight blue jeans. The low-cut red shirt she wore shaped her breasts nicely and gave him a glimpse of their swell above the fabric. Her hair was tied up into some kind of knot on the back of her head. Wisps of dark chocolate hair escaped around her face. She had diamonds in her ears. He wanted to run his tongue over the ridge of her earlobe and nibble his way down to her breasts.

As he walked toward her, she put her hand up to stop him. "I know that look, Sam. Didn't you get enough last night?"

"As if that will ever happen." They'd gotten into a regular routine over the last two weeks. He took her to work every morning and stayed with her. He tried his best to keep her out of the café and the crowd in the dining area.

He wouldn't allow her to work all day, so she'd bring home whatever paperwork she needed to do and bake at home while he watched TV or worked over the phone and computer with Tyler. Every night they slept together in her bed and made love, usually more than once. She couldn't get enough of him and the feeling was mutual.

"You're like a drug. Every time I see you, I want more and more. Come here, sweetheart. Stop backing up."

"Tyler will be here in a few minutes. We don't have time for this." Her laughter belied her words. She enjoyed this just as much as he did, so he continued to stalk her across the room.

"I love a challenge." He gave her a wicked smile and made a grab for her before she escaped his reach and pulled her to him.

Capturing her mouth, he distracted her and backed her up to the bed. When her legs hit the edge, he gently laid her back onto the mattress and trailed kisses down her neck and over the swell of her breasts. She put up a token resistance, until he took her straining nipple into his mouth, suckling hard. Her shirt long gone, he continued kissing down her stomach to where he undid her jeans. Hungry for her, he worked them and her panties over her hips and down her silky legs. Thankfully she wasn't wearing shoes, so they slid right off. He rose above her and kissed her mouth again. His wandering fingers trailed up her thigh to her wet, hot center. Moving his fingers over and into her until she writhed on the bed, he trailed kisses down her middle and replaced his finger with his tongue. He possessed her with his mouth and held her hips in his hands, kneeling beside the bed. Moaning and calling his name, she pleaded with him not to stop when her hips pushed toward him, and a wave of spasms wracked her body.

Still recovering, he undid his jeans and pushed into her with one hard thrust and took her mouth in a deep kiss. He took her fast and hard, and she pulled his hair and screamed his name when they came together. He dropped on top of her completely spent. The doorbell rang.

"You better get that, sweetheart. Tyler's here." He hovered over her with a cocky, self-satisfied smile sure to rile her.

"You did that on purpose." She smacked him on the shoulder, and laughed straight from her gut. "I must look like a mess."

"You're gorgeous." He kissed her softly. All playing aside, sometimes she took his breath away. Especially when her cheeks flushed and her eyes went dreamy after they made love.

He stood, pulled up his jeans, leaving them unzipped. He stared down at her lying on the bed. She was about to get up, but he laid a hand on her stomach and used a finger to trace the long scar running across her middle. He would never forget how she'd gotten that scar and the others. Every time he looked at them, he remembered she wasn't safe, yet. He leaned over and kissed the scar, his mouth soft against her skin.

Without a word about her injuries, he helped her up. "Hurry up. I've got to get cleaned up before I go."

He always did that, ran a finger over one of her scars and looked forlorn. She hoped one day he'd look at her and not see them anymore. She wiggled into her clothes and Sam tore his off. His fine ass and the rest of his gloriously naked body disappeared into the adjoining bathroom.

The doorbell rang again. She sailed down the stairs without a thought to her injured leg. "I'm coming, Tyler."

She opened the door without looking through the peep hole and came face-to-face with Jarred. She wanted to take a step back and slam the door. Probably should, but she didn't want to give Jarred the satisfaction of knowing he scared her.

A rush of adrenaline ignited in her veins and made her heart thunder.

The shower went on upstairs. Sam wouldn't hear her if she screamed at the top of her lungs. She hoped the other agents were out there watching her. She didn't know where they were, only that they kept surveillance on the house.

"What are you doing here?" She blocked the door so he couldn't step into the house.

"I came to see how you're doing. I know you've been home for a few weeks, and you're back to work."

"I've seen you around too. You're supposed to stay away." She tried to keep her voice firm. She hoped only she heard the slight tremble.

"We both know you never renewed the restraining order. You're too busy shacking up with your FBI agent. Seems to me, if you planned to marry him, you'd have a ring on your finger." He stroked his fingers over her left hand on the door, sending a quiver of fear through her system. When he took a step closer, she froze. "You belong to me. Don't ever forget it. I know you aren't engaged, but playing more games. You'll regret playing them with me. We could have been good together. Maybe you'll come to your senses before it's too late."

He leaned down close, his breath washing over her face. She didn't back away, couldn't. When had she become this docile, allowing fear to immobilize her where she'd normally stand her ground and fight? A whisper away from her mouth, he grabbed the back of her head and pulled her mouth to his, kissing her hard, punishing her in a small way. She struggled against him, bit his lip, and finally managed to push him away. Jarred pressed his fingertips to his swelling lip and raised his other hand, palm out, to smack her.

"You better leave before Sam's friend gets here."

She nodded toward John coming up behind Jarred, his purposeful stride eating up the distance.

She wiped the back of her hand across her mouth, hoping he didn't see it shaking.

"I'll see you soon." He scurried down the street and disappeared around the corner. Relief swept through her when he ducked out of sight.

John looked her up and down, undoubtedly seeing the fear in her eyes. He'd seen everything, including the kiss. "Are you all right? Where's Sam?"

"It's okay. He's an ex who hasn't given up thinking we can get back together. It's fine, really. He left." She tried to sound confident, but inside fear shook her to the core, even though she did her best not to show it.

Tyler pulled up in front of the house and got out of the car. "What's going on, John? Why aren't you at your post?" He shared a knowing look with John, but kept his attention on Elizabeth. Their exchange wasn't lost on her. She knew better than to open her door without making sure who was on the other side. It could have been worse. At least she hadn't opened the door to a killer.

"A man was here with Elizabeth, and I didn't see Sam. I thought something might be wrong. She says she's fine."

Both men stared at her. "I am. Nothing to worry about. Tyler, I'm so glad you're here. Dinner is ready," she said to distract him and change the subject, trying her best to sound cheerful.

John shrugged and headed back the way he'd come, letting Tyler take over protecting her. From herself, since she was stupid enough to allow Jarred to get that close to her again. She should have slammed the door in his face.

Tyler wasn't entirely convinced. He'd let John take care of the rest while he and Elizabeth ate. By far the best cook, the thought of dinner was enough to set his concern aside. "What's on the menu tonight?" he asked and made sure to lock the door behind them.

"Pot roast, mashed potatoes, and roasted vegetables. Sam should be down shortly."

"What's with your hair? It's falling out all over. What were you and Sam doing upstairs?" He gave her a cocky grin.

Happy for them, Tyler knew exactly what they'd been

doing together. They'd found each other and made something wonderful out of something terrible.

"Will you excuse me a minute? I have to go up and see Sam."

Upset, but trying to hide it, he had no trouble seeing past her ruse. "Elizabeth, I was kidding around. I didn't mean to hurt your feelings or embarrass you."

"You didn't. I'll be right back."

Elizabeth met Sam halfway up the stairs and tried to pass him, but as a trained FBI agent, he knew when someone evaded by not looking at him.

"What's the matter?"

"Nothing. I'm fine," she said to his boots.

"I'm up here." He waited for her to look him in the eye.

"I hurt my leg coming down the stairs too fast. It's nothing. Don't worry."

Worried anyway, he placed his hand on her hip and rubbed down her leg. "The doctor told you to take it easy. That leg is going to take weeks to heal all the way. You have to be more careful. I don't want you falling down the stairs."

She'd lied, but he let her have her space, for now. Taking her into his arms, he held her close, hoping she'd trust him and tell him the truth.

She wrapped her arms around his neck and held him tight. He was about to let her go, but she held on. "Not yet. Just hold me for another minute."

He held on to her, both arms banded tight around her. "Sweetheart, what's wrong? You can trust me. Tell me what's the matter."

She pulled back from him, held on to his neck, and looked him in the eye. "I trust you with my life." She put her forehead to his. "You know that, right?"

"So tell me what's wrong?"

She stood back from him and thought about everything that had happened in the last month. God, had it only been a few short weeks. How could that be? How could she have fallen in love with this man in just a month? She did love him too. And that's why the circumstances surrounding them were so hard to handle. She wanted some normalcy. She wanted to go out on a date with him, see a movie, and make out the whole time without worrying someone might take a shot at them. She wanted to go to a restaurant and eat a lovely meal by candlelight. She wanted to have Kay and her other friends over to the house, so they could meet Sam and see how happy she was with him. She wanted . . . She wanted so much. She wanted her life back.

"I'm tired of all of this. Hiding in my own home. I can't step out the door without you and two agents on my heels. A customer can't even walk into my store without my having to look up to make sure it isn't someone coming to hurt me. I'm afraid all the time. I want this to be over. But I'm afraid when it is, I won't have you."

He cupped her face in his hands and gazed deep into her eyes. "You do have me. I'm not going anywhere. We'll get this guy, and you and I will be together." He held her tighter to reassure her. "Maybe we can go away together, just you and me. Anywhere you want to go."

She opened her mouth to say something, but closed it

at the ring of his cell phone. He cursed under his breath. Upset, she wanted to talk to him, and he didn't want to leave her hanging. Unfortunately, his job took precedence. Reluctantly, he let her go and answered, because he had no choice.

"Turner." He listened to John on the line and his gut knotted and his anger flashed. Elizabeth walked away, up to her room. He didn't like what John had to say. "I'm on my way. Give me fifteen minutes to leave, and we'll meet up."

After he hung up, he took one last look at the bedroom door where Elizabeth disappeared. Frowning, he went down to the kitchen where Tyler waited.

"Did you talk to John about what happened before you came down?" Tyler asked.

"It won't happen again," Sam said with a feral smile.

"Is she mad at me?"

"Why? What did you say to her?" Furious at even the thought Tyler upset her, Sam caught himself before he got in his friend's face.

Tyler put up a hand to ward Sam off. "I made a joking comment about her tousled hair and asked what you two were doing upstairs. I didn't mean to upset her. Is she mad I know about the two of you?"

"She probably thinks everyone knows about us. This whole thing is wearing on her. She hasn't completely healed from her injuries. She said she's scared all the time someone is out to hurt her. She's afraid when all this is over, we will be too." Sam rubbed the back of his neck, wishing for some way to reassure her everything would work out. But he couldn't make any promises, because nothing was certain so long as the Silver Fox was out there gunning for them.

"You aren't planning to break things off with her, are you? Because let me tell you, I'd snatch her away from you in a second."

"You even think about touching her, I'll bash your teeth in, cut off your balls, and stuff them down your throat."

"Graphic. Have you told her you're in love with her?"

Sam sputtered some incoherent denial, which Tyler ignored and went on. "Never occurred to you, did it?"

He hadn't told her any such thing. She knew he cared about her. Didn't she? Maybe that was why she wasn't sure about whether they'd still be together when he wasn't assigned to protect her anymore. Maybe she thought this was a short-term deal that expired along with his assignment.

Damn, he needed to talk to her about his feelings. How the hell was he supposed to do that? Did he love her? Probably. Something deep inside him called her *mine*.

He thought about how he felt when she was in the hospital and about what life would be like without her. He thought about what he wanted in his future and the truth hit him square in the heart.

Damn, he loved her all right. Facing a future without her was unthinkable.

"I can tell by the look on your face the wheels turning in your head have finally grinded to a halt on the right answer. I can't believe you just figured it out, and you still haven't told her. She's an amazing woman. And, God, she can cook. If we bottled the smell in this kitchen, we'd make a fortune. You'd be a fool to let her go."

Sam didn't hear Elizabeth come up behind him.

"Let who go?" she asked, stepping into the kitchen.

"You okay?" When she nodded, he backtracked the conversation. "Tyler here is jealous I've got you and the only woman in his life is a psychic ghost."

"Are you being haunted, Tyler?" Elizabeth asked, joking.

Tyler sighed, "Yeah, I am. I talked to her again, a couple weeks ago. She actually called me."

"You get this far-off look on your face when you talk about her," Elizabeth teased. "Whoever she is, she's got you interested. Why do you call her a psychic ghost?"

"It's a long story. She knows things. When she does, she contacts me and gives me messages. Each message has resulted in my solving a case."

"I'd love to hear what she thinks about my case. I don't care if she's a psychic or a ghost if she can help me get my life back."

"I never thought to tell you before now. She said you have a double threat, and the guy we're after is hiding in plain sight. Sam and I agree: the Silver Fox and Jarred are those threats."

Her silence disturbed them. She made a plate for Tyler and herself. Sam wasn't staying for dinner. He'd told her he had a case to work on, and that's why Tyler came to watch out for her. Part truth, he couldn't tell her the rest. Not yet.

She handed him two large thermoses and a small bakery box. "What's this?" Sam asked, surprised she'd made something for him.

"One thermos is coffee, one is stew I made with the pot roast, since you won't be here to eat with us. In the box is a piece of apple blueberry pie. There's a fork and spoon inside the bakery box."

"Elizabeth, I would have stopped for something to eat later. You didn't have to do this."

"I didn't have to, I wanted to. You should eat a good meal. You didn't say where you're going tonight, so I made the meal portable. You can keep it in the car and eat it whenever you want. The thermos will keep the stew and coffee hot. If you're up late, the coffee will come in handy," she shrugged. "Kiss the cook."

Sam kissed her on the lips and Tyler kissed her from behind on the top of her head, making Sam scowl over Elizabeth at him.

Tyler gave him a cocky smile and headed to the table with his plate. "What? She said, 'Kiss the cook.' You think I'd ignore an order like that from a beautiful woman? She might not cook for me again." He winked at Elizabeth.

"Keep your hands to yourself tonight."

"Just tonight. Can I have her tomorrow?"

Too good to pass up a chance to rile Sam, Tyler skated on thin ice, but Sam held back the fist he wanted to plant in Tyler's smug face. He'd just realized how serious his feelings were for her, and now he had to leave her with another guy for the night.

"Do you want to eat that food or wear it?" Maybe

leaving her alone with Tyler wasn't such a good idea. He hated that nagging voice inside, telling him he was being unreasonable.

"Don't you have to go to work?" Elizabeth asked, an attempt to diffuse the situation. He hated even more being this transparent.

Sam stopped glaring at Tyler long enough to look at Elizabeth. She hadn't even asked what he had planned for tonight. No questions. No hounding him for information. Nothing.

"Don't you want to know where I'm going?"

"You're going to work. Aren't you?"

"Yes, but you didn't ask me where I'm going, or when I'll be back."

She held back a laugh, knowing he was serious. Over the past two weeks they'd talked a lot about his job and how hard it was to have a relationship with his work constantly getting in the way.

"Sam, we talked about this. You work undercover, so I assumed you can't tell me those things."

With her arms wrapped around his waist, she went on. "You said tomorrow morning sometime, so I assume you don't know exactly what time, but you'll do your best to be here when you say you will. I've made sure you have a good meal and enough coffee to get through the night. Those are the things I can control. I'll worry about you while you're gone. That I can't control. You'll come back as soon as you can, and I'll be waiting for you. You can count on that." She leaned up and gave him a long soft kiss.

"Lucky bastard," Tyler called to Sam.

Absolutely. Not many women understood what it was like for him working undercover. He wanted to spend time with whatever girlfriend he had at the time, but the job came first in a lot of cases, and most women couldn't accept that. Elizabeth understood very well. She did come first, Sam had to take care of some business, and he'd come back to her.

Sam cupped her face in his hands, running his thumbs over her jaw. "I am the luckiest man alive. You and I need to talk when I get back." He leaned down and kissed her again. Reluctantly releasing her, he went to the counter where his other gun and shoulder harness lay. He strapped it on and glanced at Elizabeth to gage her reaction. She watched him interested, but not overly worried. He slipped his jacket on and went to her and kissed her goodbye.

As he went to leave, he turned back to Tyler. "Keep her safe."

"I just might keep her."

Sam glared, his hands fisted at his sides. Nearly at the end of his rope, Tyler pushed, raising his hand like he was swearing, promising, "I'll keep her safe and sound. She'll be as perfect as she is now when you get back. I promise to sleep on the couch, and I'll only make two or three passes at her while you're gone." Before Sam turned away, he crossed his heart with his index finger. "Want to pinky-swear on it?"

"I'm about two seconds away from shooting you, and I'm heavily armed. You should remember that." He winked at Elizabeth and headed out the door.

"Don't forget to pick up your tux at the penthouse before you come back here tomorrow," Elizabeth reminded him.

"I will." He walked out the door completely focused on the job ahead. He would take care of one of those threats against Elizabeth tonight. He wasn't coming back until he did. And coming home to her was a very good reason to eliminate that threat quickly.

"He'll be fine. Don't worry," Tyler said, as if his command would make her feel better about Sam going off on another dangerous assignment.

"I'm not," she said, mustering up her confidence. "He said he'll be back tomorrow. I know he will. How come you didn't go with him on this assignment? You guys are partners, right?"

"We are sometimes. He didn't trust anyone else to watch you."

"It didn't sound like he trusts you, the way you two went back and forth tonight."

"He knows I'm messing with him. I'd never go after another guy's girl, and you're his. No doubt about it. It's written all over the both of you. You really understand him and his work, don't you? You actually get it."

"I think I do. Don't get me wrong. Until he walks back through that door with all his fingers and toes, I won't stop worrying about him. I understand what he does is important and it comes at a price to him, emotionally and personally. I can either ask him to be something he isn't and lose him, or I can be supportive and patient and trust him to do everything he can to make it home."

"You're one in a million, you know that? I meant it when I said he's a lucky man. Most people in law enforcement end up not finding someone to share their life with, or even when they do get married, they usually end up divorced. I have a good feeling about the two of you."

"We'll see if you feel the same way after tomorrow night."

"Everything will work out. We've got his house under surveillance. He's on the list of attendees to the Governor's Ball. We've had the Hamilton name in the papers along with many of the other prominent families attending. He'll be there, because he knows you'll be there. He won't pass up the opportunity to get close to you at the ball."

"I don't like leaving Sam out of the loop. You need to tell him our plan for tomorrow night."

"Deputy Director Davies agrees with you. We'll fill him in right before we leave. He won't have a chance to object, but at least he'll know who we're after tomorrow night. You'll be protected no matter what. Agents will be posted all over the place."

"All right. Let's get on with it. What do you want me to do?"

"I'll give you a wire to wear, so we can hear you. If you get into trouble, you won't even have to yell, we'll hear you. If he comes after you, you might have the opportunity to get him to incriminate himself in the insurance murders. We have him on the attempted murder of you and Sam, but we'd like to nail him on the others as well.

If you can't get him to talk, we'll simply arrest him for the attempted murder charges."

She hoped it worked out like Tyler explained. She wanted to end this nightmare and be with Sam and have her life back. That's all she wanted. She hoped it wasn't too much to ask.

## *Chapter Thirty-Two*

---

*Saturday, 1:38 A.M.*

SAM SAT IN the car a block away from Jarred's house, waiting for the prick to come out. Tonight he had a different partner. John sat beside him, watching the quiet street and Jarred's garage. The stakes were just as high tonight as they were when he went to meet Scott in that bar and wound up in front of Elizabeth's home.

"That smells good," John said, pulling him out of his thoughts.

"Elizabeth made it." He poured a portion of the stew into the thermos lid and handed it over to John with the fork from the bakery box.

"She sure can cook."

She cooked up amazing things in the kitchen, in their bed, and somehow she'd cooked up some sort of spell to cast over him.

He loved her. Ever since Tyler goaded him into admitting it, he couldn't stop thinking about it. The expected panic didn't rise up to choke him. Instead, he felt content. Settled. Like everything was right. He loved her. It was that simple and made everything right in his life.

"The lights upstairs went out."

Well, everything would be right as soon as he eliminated the double threat against Elizabeth and they could live their lives without fear. Tonight he'd put a stop to Jarred's escalating stalking and intimidation. All he had to do was catch him in the act.

"There. The side door, leading to the garage."

His purposeful strides carried him across the short distance to the garage door. Momentarily caught in the streetlight's glow, Sam saw something besides the innocuous duffle bag that made his gut burn.

"Is that a gun case he's carrying?" John asked, staring through the binoculars.

"Yes. The day after I caught him in Elizabeth's hospital room, he went to a local pawn shop and bought a handgun. He signed all the papers and waited the required ten-day waiting period." He turned to John and met his steady gaze. "That asshole psycho is armed. Watch your back. There's no telling what he's got planned."

"Whatever it is, we'll stop him," John assured him.

No assurance necessary. "Damn right. Today was the last day he ever gets close to Elizabeth."

He wanted to kill her for opening the door to Jarred earlier. Didn't she know the risks? Hadn't he told her a hundred times over the last couple weeks to always be vigilant? Never, ever, go anywhere without him. Don't open the door. Anyone, including the Silver Fox, could have been standing on the other side. And there he was, taking a shower, relaxed and happy after making love to her, none the wiser to the scene downstairs. Lucky for him, John stepped in to protect her. Still, it could have been a hell of a lot worse if she'd opened the door and Jarred had shot her on sight. That nightmare chilled his blood every time he thought about it.

The garage door slid up. No light from the automatic door opener came on. Jarred backed his car down the narrow driveway and onto the quiet street. Sam gave him a good lead before he followed. He expected the left turn and the right, but every turn closer to Elizabeth's home made his anger hum and his heart flutter with fear.

Sam grabbed his cell, hit the speed dial for Tyler and put the phone on speaker. His gaze on Jarred's taillights in the distance, he kept his focus on the target even as he warned Tyler.

"He's on the move, headed straight for you. Is she okay?"

"Safe and sound, asleep in her room. We might actually get this done without disturbing her."

"Let's hope. The last thing she needs is another terrifying night to add to her collection of bad memories."

"How long?"

"Less than five minutes. Be ready."

"I already am."

"Whatever happens, your only job is to protect her."

"I won't let anything happen to her. I'm looking forward to the wedding—and whatever cake she makes for it."

Tyler disconnected and Sam shook his head. "If he gets his mind off his stomach, we might actually pull this off without her knowing."

"She makes a damn fine cake—and pie and stew and her double chocolate chip brownie cookies are beyond amazing," John chimed in.

Sam let out the pent-up stress with a short laugh. "Yeah, I got it. Everyone is in love with her cooking."

"But you're in love with her."

"This may be an FBI operation, but for me it's personal."

"Then let's take this guy down once and for all."

Sam gave John a nod and felt better knowing he understood his feelings about Elizabeth and how important it was to keep her safe.

Sam pulled over two blocks from Elizabeth's home. He and John jumped out and ran down the street, keeping close to the dark buildings. Their black clothes and jackets kept them hidden in the shadows. They stopped at the last building, hugged the wall, and stared across the street.

Jarred cut the headlights and backed into the alley behind Elizabeth's place. He stepped out of his vehicle and surveyed the empty street. Perhaps sensing their presence, he stood for over a minute, listening, waiting, and scanning every building. Sam held his breath. Satisfied he was alone, Jarred popped the trunk and pulled out a few items. Too far away to see if he had the gun, Sam's gut tightened, knowing he had it, but unsure if he'd actually have the guts to use it.

"If he pulls that gun, shoot to kill. Don't take any chances with this guy."

John nodded, checked his weapon, and held it by his side. Sam did the same and they moved in, stealthy as a hawk swooping down to catch a rat.

JARRED SCANNED THE deserted street one last time, shaking off the paranoid feeling of being watched. No one was out there. He'd planned everything down to the last detail. This might be the hardest part, but he'd get past Elizabeth's "*fiancé*" and she'd be his. He'd tried to do things the civil way. She'd driven him to this.

He grabbed his supplies from the trunk and left it open for when he brought her out. Gun at the ready, he gripped it tight, liking the weight of it in his hand. The powerful feeling rushed through him with a wave of adrenaline, propelling him to Elizabeth's back door. He used the key he'd stolen from the pegboard in her kitchen. He'd been inside her home a number of times without her knowing. He liked being here, amongst her expensive, but still comfortable things. Most of his visits he'd kept to her office. He'd learned a lot about her personal finances and investments. If she'd agreed to marry him, he wouldn't be in this position.

The nightlight by the coffeepot cast a dim glow to the dark expanse in the kitchen. Unable to see the stairway at the front of the living space in the blackness, he pulled a penlight from his pocket, clicked it on, and pointed it to the stairs, spotlighting a man holding a gun pointed directly at his chest. Momentarily frozen, his heart pounded, and he raised his gun.

While Tyler's presence distracted Dickweed, Sam tackled him from behind, grabbed his wrist, and slammed his hand against the hardwood. The gun skittered across the floor, stopping under the kitchen table.

Jarred fought him, but he held tight and shoved his knee into Jarred's back to keep him down.

Sam pushed the barrel of his gun into the back of his head and whispered ominously, "Say one word, or call out in any way, and I'll kill you."

He wouldn't, but Jarred didn't know that. Though they'd made some noise, Elizabeth hadn't come out of her room. He hoped she slept in peace, blissfully unaware of the danger too near to her.

Jarred struggled and grunted under Sam's weight, but went still at his words. Tyler turned on a single lamp on the end table next to the couch. Jarred's eyes went wide when he saw both he and Tyler with their bulletproof vests and guns drawn, FBI stamped across their chests, badges on their belts.

Pissed off, but still in control, Sam holstered his gun, yanked Dickweed's arms behind his back, and cuffed him. "You're under arrest, asshole."

Jarred opened his mouth to say something, but Sam clamped his hand over it and, still whispering, said, "I told you to shut the fuck up."

Sam ignored the glare and the urge to seriously beat

the shit out of Dickweed. He settled for knowing the guy faced years in prison for Elizabeth's attempted kidnapping.

John's soft voice came from the backdoor. "Cops are here. No lights or sirens, like we requested. I'll take him."

"Read him his rights and search him. No telling what other surprises he's got on him."

Tyler handed over the gun to John and helped Sam haul Jarred up from the floor by his arms. About to put up a fight and start protesting, Sam got in his face and glared. Dickweed thought better of it and snapped his mouth shut with a click of his teeth. Satisfied, Sam backed off and let John take him out the back door where four police officers waited.

Sam's gaze went up to the landing and Elizabeth's closed bedroom door before he turned back to look at Tyler.

"Well, that was easier than I thought it would be. Go up and see her. I'll coordinate things out back until you come down."

Grateful for Tyler's understanding that he couldn't just walk out and not see her and prove to his unreasonable mind that she was safe and sound.

He entered her room and stood beside the bed looking down at her. She slept, but restlessly, her arm outstretched to the empty space he'd slept in for the last few weeks. It did something strange to him to know that even in sleep she wanted him near and missed him in his absence. As much as he wanted to crawl into bed and make love to her, satisfying his urge to touch her and feel the intense connection they shared, he still had work to do to ensure Jarred paid for what he'd done and for even thinking he could harm Elizabeth and get away with it.

Unable to leave without one touch, he leaned down and softly kissed her temple. She sighed and settled deeper into sleep. His heart eased and with one last look, he turned and went to finish things with Dickweed.

From the moment Sam stepped out of Elizabeth's house and joined the officers at Jarred's car at the end of the alley, Jarred hadn't stopped griping, loudly, that he'd been set up. Sam ignored his every scathing word until Tyler and John came over and handed him what they'd found in Jarred's car. He read the ransom demand and scanned the storage unit receipt, which included the code for the security gate, the locker number, and combination for the lock.

Sam didn't say a word to Tyler or John. Several long strides took him directly in front of Dickweed. The two officers keeping an eye on him by the patrol car backed off at his menacing approach. Sam tried to contain his rage, but it filled every word out of his mouth.

"You son of a bitch. Not only were you going to kidnap her, but you planned to stick her in a storage locker and just leave her there until her family paid the ransom."

Jarred's face paled and a bead of sweat trickled down the side of his face. His breathing went shallow and his pale complexion turned green. Sam's stomach turned, knowing Jarred's plans had been much more ominous and Jarred had only just realized how crazy and fucked up he'd become.

"What is in this locker?"

"I wouldn't have done it," he swore. "This is a mistake. I wasn't really going to hurt her."

"No? What was your plan? Shoot me while we slept and take her?"

Sam swore when Jarred turned an even more sickly shade of green.

"I needed the money. The economy tanked and all my investments went bust. Everyone she knows is rich and powerful. If she'd only introduced me to some of them and given me a recommendation, I'd be back on my feet. With friends like hers, the sky is the limit."

"Those people are her friends because she doesn't use them the way you've tried to use her. She's kind and generous and if you got to know her even just a little bit, you'd have never been able to do this to her."

A sinister smile climbed Jarred's face. "You really did fall for her."

Irritated, Sam snapped, "You messed with the wrong woman. I'm going to make sure you pay for that mistake." Sam turned to the cops waiting nearby. "Take him in. Throw the book at him, breaking and entering and attempted kidnapping to start."

"I didn't do anything to her. She's fine."

The protests went on and on, but Sam walked away, knowing one threat to Elizabeth's life had been eliminated.

Tyler met him by one of the cop cars. Sam read the dire expression and hated to ask, knowing Tyler had more bad news. "What's wrong? Did Elizabeth wake up?"

"No. I checked on her, she's sleeping."

"Okay. We'll be out of here in a few minutes, once the cops finish their investigation of the scene and tow Jarred's car. So what's put that look on your face?"

"John and another officer went over to check out the storage unit. It's not good, man." Tyler handed over his phone. Sam scanned through one ominous photo after another of a crude pine box.

"I'll kill him."

Tyler jumped in front of him and gabbed his shoulders to hold him back, despite Sam's best effort to push past him and seriously fuck up Jarred.

"Stop. You got him. He's in custody. He can't hurt her now."

Sam took a ragged breath and tried to calm the raging need to do bodily harm to Dickweed for even thinking about killing Elizabeth and putting her in that coffin and locking her away forever.

"Tell John to meet me at the police station with the photos and any other evidence they collect."

"Sam, let the cops handle the details. You got him. It's over."

"It's not over until the charges are filed and that ass-hole spends the rest of his days behind bars."

Sam walked to his car and pulled out his phone. He hated to ask Elizabeth's father for a favor, but in this case he had no trouble enlisting the Judge to help him ensure Jarred got the maximum sentence.

## *Chapter Thirty-Three*

ELIZABETH AND TYLER had gone over the plan and the layout of the hotel ballroom a dozen times last night. He showed her how to wear the wire, so the FBI heard anyone with her. Once they finished, she turned in early. Stressed about the ball on Friday and worried about Sam, she let the quiet settle around her and tried not to think. She hadn't slept without Sam in the two weeks she'd been home from the hospital. No surprise she had trouble falling asleep, tossing and turning most of the night and wishing for Sam and his warm, strong body wrapped around hers. At one point during the night, she'd thought he'd come home and kissed her, but she must have been dreaming, because when she woke in the morning the bed beside her was still empty.

Sam didn't come home in the morning like she expected. By the time she and Tyler arrived home from the bakery after lunch, she still hadn't heard from him.

Afraid to ask Tyler to find out where he was, she wanted Sam to know she trusted him. Just when she thought she couldn't handle her overwhelming worry, Sam not being home, and everything planned for that night, the phone rang.

*Please be Sam.* "Hello."

"Hey, sweetheart. Is Tyler behaving himself? He better be, or I'll kick his ass."

"He's a perfect gentleman. He only kissed me twice since you left."

"What?"

"He kisses me on the head each time I feed him. It's kind of cute." Sam wouldn't want to hear that, but she didn't want to lie. Besides, she found Tyler's affection sweet. She thought of him as a brother. "Are you on your way here?"

"No. I've been up all night. I'm closer to the penthouse than your place and I need to crash for a couple hours. Jack, Jenna, and I will pick you up in the limo. Will that work for you?"

"I don't know. I'll have to ask Tyler. He's supposed to go ahead of us to make sure everything is okay at the hotel."

"He'll have time. Jenna wants to talk to you before we leave your place tonight."

"Why does she want to talk to me?"

"I don't know. She's being very secretive about the whole thing. Knowing her, she's about to make one of your dreams come true."

Elizabeth didn't know what that could be, or why

Jenna would do anything for her. They'd only spoken the day she'd left the hospital. She'd find out later. "I'll be ready when you arrive. Sam?"

"Yeah, sweetheart?"

"Did everything go all right last night?"

"Better than all right. I'll tell you all about it later."

"So you're okay?"

"Yes, sweetheart. I'm fine. Were you worried?"

"Just a little." More than a little, actually, but she wasn't about to tell him. She was used to seeing him with the gun strapped to his belt. Seeing him put on another gun told her he was expecting trouble, and that hadn't sat well with her. She'd also missed having him in her bed last night.

"I hate to admit it, but it feels good knowing you're worried about me and want to know if I'm okay. I missed you. I'll see you tonight."

"Okay. I love you. Bye." She hung up and immediately realized what she'd said. She looked across the dining room table at Tyler, who'd been sitting there listening the whole time. "Did I say 'I love you' to him and hang up?"

"Yes you did, darlin'." Tyler gave her a huge smile. "You look so pretty when you're in shock," he teased.

"Oh, God. What have I done?"

"You told him the truth when your defenses were down. He's probably as stunned as you are."

"Stunned. Great. Maybe he didn't hear me. Maybe he'll think I didn't mean it. You know, it was part of the goodbye."

"Maybe nothing. He heard you loud and clear, and I

bet he's happy as hell. He'll probably gloat about it for a month."

"Sure he is. What man wouldn't want to hear the woman he's been seeing for, what, less than a month really, is in love with him. He's probably running as fast as he can. He probably won't even show up tonight. You'll be my date."

Tyler chuckled and gave her a huge grin. "I'd love to be your date, but I'm afraid you're stuck with Sam. If my guess is right, you'll be struck with him the rest of your life."

She laid her head on her arms on the table and groaned in frustration and embarrassment. "I really screwed this one up. Couldn't I keep my big mouth shut? Couldn't I wait to tell him in, oh, say a year? He must think I'm crazy."

His smile broadened when she looked up and glared at him. "I have to say, I'm enjoying sitting on the sidelines of this game of love. You're a great match. Maybe I'll get lucky one day."

Frustrated, she stood and went into the kitchen. She needed to work off some of her energy and think about everything. She'd come up with an explanation for what she'd said if he asked. Maybe he wouldn't ask. Maybe he'd let it go. That's it. They'd pretend it never happened.

She aimlessly took canisters out of the cabinets.

"What are you doing?" Tyler asked.

"What would you like? A pie, a cake, maybe some cookies? Oh, I'll make them all and you can decide once they're done."

Too much was happening all at once; she needed to sort it out. They had the ball tonight, a murderer wanted her dead, Jarred was stalking her and deluding himself into thinking they'd get married, Sam's sister-in-law wanted to speak to her, and—oh yeah—she told Sam she loved him. Good God, what a day.

## Chapter Thirty-Four

*Friday, 6:30 P.M.*

SAM LED JACK and Jenna into the living room. He scanned the baked goods filling every baker's rack and available counter space. He spotted Tyler on the landing, walking out of Elizabeth's room. "What the hell are you doing up there?" Sam asked, about to blow a blood vessel.

"I didn't expect everyone to show up early. You weren't supposed to be here for another half hour."

Tyler planted both hands on the railing, leaned over, and gave him a cocky grin. "What kind of gentleman would I be if I didn't help a beautiful woman zip up her dress? I have to say the bullet wounds are healing nicely. I assured her no one could see them, even though that dress is a knockout."

Sam was halfway up the stairs before he finished the

last part of the sentence. Tyler threw up his hands to ward off Sam coming at him like a freight train.

"Get a grip, Sam. Think about what she said to you today. Do you really think anything happened in that room other than my zipping up her dress?"

Sam had thought of nothing else but what she'd said to him on the phone. She loved him, and he'd hoped all day it was true. Apparently, Tyler believed it.

He stopped short in front of Tyler, sighed, and ran a hand through his hair. He didn't have anything to say. She loved him. She wouldn't do anything with Tyler. She was his.

"And reason returns." Tyler clamped a hand on his shoulder. "Good. Now come downstairs. I need to tell you about tonight's operation."

"Operation? I'm supposed to protect her while she goes to the ball. The place will be crawling with security. She'll be fine." Tyler's intense face said he was about to put the weight of the world on Sam's shoulders. After last night, Sam wasn't sure he could take much more. All he wanted was for her to be safe.

"She won't go unless I fill you in. You won't like this, Sam, but it's necessary, and the only way to arrest this guy."

"What are you talking about? We don't even know who he is."

"We do. We have since Elizabeth identified him before she left the hospital."

Shocked, Sam mumbled, "She knew who attacked us. She knows the identity of the Silver Fox." They'd arrest him, and this would all be over. Finally.

"Davies and I both made her swear not to tell you or the other agents watching her. We weren't sure how many other people might be involved, besides Scott at the insurance company and our suspect, so we wanted you to watch for any threat."

"She knew the whole time she was in the hospital?"

"No. She worked with a sketch artist the day before she came home." Tyler steered Sam toward the stairs, and they headed down to where Jack and Jenna waited in the sitting area.

"Once I had the sketch, I compared it to some of the photos we had of suspects. He wasn't part of our suspect pool, but Elizabeth had an idea of where she'd seen him. She studied that sketch for a long time, and then it got interesting. She remembered the logo on the bracelet he wore. The guy's company logo to be exact. I set up an impromptu photo lineup, and she picked the guy out, no problem. He's been in hiding ever since the night he tried to poison her in the hospital. We've had his homes, his place of business, and his known haunts staked out, but he hasn't shown himself.

"He's on the guest list tonight. We've spread the word in every newspaper and advertisement about the ball that the entire Hamilton family will attend. He knows she'll be there. He won't pass up an opportunity to grab her in public."

"You're using her as bait." His stomach turned to stone. "Was this your idea? Davies?"

"No, Sam. It was hers."

"Hers? Are you kidding me? She wants to offer herself up as bait?"

"She wants this to be over."

Sam understood why she wanted it over. Having someone follow you around everywhere you went and watching your back constantly was no way to live. Even if Sam was the one with her all the time, it wasn't any way for them to have a relationship.

"Sam, I for one know what it's like to be afraid someone is out there waiting for a chance to hurt you," Jenna said, reminding him of how he'd helped save her from her ex-husband. "She's got to be scared, not to mention feeling very much alone. I had people around me, but I was always so scared something would happen to them because of me.

"It's why I isolated myself. Elizabeth wants to end this so her family and friends will be safe. She wants to make sure you're safe," Jenna said, putting her hand on his chest.

Tyler pointed to the other room. "Look at that kitchen. She did all of that in about four hours because she's scared to death she'll lose you and she'll never have her life back. She baked about two dozen different pies, a dozen cakes, and I don't know how many dozen cookies. I've never eaten so many sweets in my life. She's up there scared to death this won't work, and she'll spend the rest of her life afraid of this guy. She's even more scared you'll hate her for lying to you about all of this."

"That's ridiculous. I'm pissed you kept me in the dark, but I'm not mad at her for keeping the secret you asked her to keep. I know how these things go down. I didn't become an agent yesterday, you know. It just proves how trustworthy she is. I hate the idea of dangling her in front of this psychopath."

"You don't have a choice," Elizabeth said from behind the group.

She came down the stairs while they were talking. She wasn't sure how Sam might feel once he found out what they had planned, but hearing him say he wasn't angry she'd kept it from him made her feel better.

She'd spent most of her time upstairs, hoping he wouldn't comment about her blurting out she loved him. He had feelings for her, but she didn't know how deep they ran. She didn't want to mess things up before they really had a chance to bloom.

Since they hadn't seen her come down the stairs, she had time to get a good look at everyone. Sam and Jack were identical in their tuxes. No one would tell them apart. She could, and she bet Jenna could, but others would see identical images of the same man.

Stunning in purple, Jenna's dress was a sleeveless V-neck, snug around the waist before it draped and flowed down to the floor. Gorgeous. Her hair was pinned up in an elegant French twist. She wore green amethyst jewelry, the same pale shade as her eyes. The heart-shaped pendant on her chest sparkled like dew on a blade of grass.

Sam turned around to talk to her, but stopped dead, struck speechless at the sight of her. More beautiful than he'd ever seen her, she wore a white gown with tiny gold roses stitched into the fabric, connected by a line of gold thread, glistening in the light. Strapless, her breasts swelled over the top with each breath she took. The dress hugged her body to her knees before softly flaring out at the bottom and swaying as she moved.

He always thought the expression trite, but she literally took his breath away. Chocolate curls fell here and there from the knot on top of her head, framing her angelic face. Light makeup enhanced her soft skin and beautiful blue eyes. Still wearing the same diamond earrings he'd seen her in before, she'd added a diamond tennis bracelet and a diamond cocktail ring. He'd never seen her look so expensive. He never really thought about who she was, besides his witness and a bakery and café owner. But she belonged to the Hamilton family, and that meant money. Not for the first time, he thought she was completely out of his league.

"Aren't you going to say anything?" Elizabeth fidgeted self-consciously.

"You're beautiful." Sam couldn't think of anything else to say but the obvious.

"I've been telling her that every ten minutes since you left, man. You can do better than that," Tyler chided.

Tyler loved giving him a hard time. This time Sam didn't rise to the bait. He was struck speechless by the sight of Elizabeth. Something about her glowed. She radiated wealth in that gown and those jewels, almost royal.

"Until this moment, I didn't really understand who you are. I didn't realize what your being a Hamilton means."

She wanted to throw something at him. What the hell did he mean by that? If he thought because she had money they were somehow different, he had another think coming.

Jenna and Jack exchanged a look, and Tyler stared at the floor.

"Being a Hamilton means the same thing as being a Turner."

"Let's face it, sweetheart, it isn't exactly the same."

She ignored that statement and made one of her own. "Do you mean being a Turner doesn't mean you're smart, trustworthy, strong, honorable, dependable, and reliable? Because that's what being a Hamilton means to my family and me. The rest is just a bunch of green paper and stuff. I'm the same person you knew yesterday. Look at Jack and Jenna. Do you think it really matters to Jack that Jenna has all that money? No," she answered for them. "I run a bakery. I go to fancy parties because of my name, but most of the events I attend are to support a charity. I give food to the local shelters and food banks."

"Looks like they'll eat well, too." He nodded toward the kitchen where every available space had a pie, cake, or cookie on it.

Heat rose in her cheeks when she saw what she'd done. She glared at Tyler. "Why didn't you stop me?"

"Stop you? You were a woman on a mission, and I stood back and got out of the way before you baked me into one of those pies." He looked back at the kitchen and her again. "What did you want me to do? Tell you to put the spatula down and come out of the kitchen with your hands up?" Tyler smiled, along with everyone else but Elizabeth.

"Excuse me." Embarrassed, she picked up the phone and called Kay. "Hey, it's me. Can you do me a favor tonight?"

"What do you need? I thought you and Sam were attending the ball. I'm surprised to hear from you."

"We are. I seem to have baked a few extra things today. Could you come by and take them over to the shelter? I'll leave the keys to my car on the counter."

"Sure. Is everything okay?"

"Everything is fine. Why do you ask?"

"No reason. I have a question for Sam, is he there?" Kay asked casually.

"Yeah, hold on. Oh, I don't have time to pack things up. You know where everything is though." She gave the phone to Sam. "Kay wants to ask you something."

Sam didn't know what Kay wanted, but she was Elizabeth's best friend and probably wanted him to reassure her the FBI was doing everything possible to keep her safe. "Hi Kay, it's Sam. What's up?"

"Without letting Elizabeth know what we're talking about, how much did she bake? Enough for a family, a pie eating contest, or a corporation?"

"Definitely the last one. Why?" His suspicions rose.

"Because when she bakes at home it means she's upset. The volume of what she bakes tells you how upset she is. What happened? What did you do to her?"

"Nothing. I don't know. I wasn't here."

He didn't know how to answer. He had no idea Elizabeth went nuts baking when she was upset. Based on the state of her kitchen, she was really distressed, and he hadn't done a damn thing to make her feel better since he arrived. She had so much to be worried about that he couldn't pick out the one thing that might be upsetting her most.

"Are you going to find out what's wrong with her, or do I have to talk to her and find out?"

"I'll take care of it. Don't worry. We'll talk to you later." Sam would take care of it too. He'd start right now.

Elizabeth sat at the kitchen bar, speaking with his brother and Jenna and feeding them cookies. He needed to talk to her alone for a minute and grabbed her hand, pulling her with him toward the massive stone fireplace and as far away from Jack, Jenna, and Tyler as he could get her without dragging her out of the house all together.

"Sam, I was talking with your family."

"They can wait."

He pulled her into his arms and kissed her. He only meant to give her a quick kiss before he talked to her, but as soon as his lips touched hers, he took it deeper and lingered over her mouth and the sweet taste of her. Her scent, something sweet and flowery, wrapped around him. Damn, she even smelled expensive. She opened to him, and he dove in without thinking about anything but having more of her. Regaining some semblance of sanity, he slowed the kiss and gave her a few light brushes of his lips over hers.

He leaned back. Her eyes fluttered open and held a dreamy wonder. He continued to hold her waist and looked into her eyes. "Did I tell you how much I missed you last night?"

"No. Instead you implied that somehow between yesterday and today I turned into someone you don't know because you saw me in a dress," she grumbled.

"You look like a million bucks in that dress, and it occurred to me you're probably worth that much too."

"More actually. Much more. But that has nothing to do with who I am and the woman you know," she snapped.

This wasn't going well. "I realize you're the same woman, and the fact you have money shouldn't bother me. It does because I'm an FBI agent with a decent salary, but nothing near what you must make, or what the people you know earn."

"I think the same thing I thought every other day I've known you. When I look at you, I don't see a paycheck, or what you have or don't have. I see you, the kind, caring, strong, dependable person I met in the hospital. I see the man who calls me sweetheart and makes my knees weak when he kisses me. I see the man I love. There, I said it." Throwing her hands up and letting them fall, she went on. "If all of this is because I said I love you on the phone and you can't deal with it, I'm sorry. I do love you. I don't care if you're an FBI agent with a decent salary, or an Internet mogul with millions."

About to turn away, Sam stopped her by pulling her into his arms and kissing her again.

He didn't know what to say. She blew his mind. Could he deal with the fact she loves him? Hell yes. It's what he wanted more than anything. "Elizabeth, I . . ."

"I'm sorry to interrupt," Jenna cut in. "There's something I want to speak to you about, Elizabeth, and we don't have much time before we leave."

"Jenna, can't this wait? I'm trying to talk to her about

something important." Sam kept a firm grip on Elizabeth's waist.

"You both will have to wait," Tyler interrupted this time. "I need to go over a few things with Elizabeth and Sam before we go. I need to make sure both of you understand the protocol for tonight."

Sam's blood pressure rose dangerously high. Elizabeth stepped away, slipping from his grasp, their conversation left hanging.

Sam wanted to throw them all out and take Elizabeth upstairs, get her out of that million-dollar dress, and make love to her the rest of the night. Could he tell her he loved her? He'd never said the words to a woman. He'd never felt this way about anyone else.

"Tyler, you've gone over everything with Elizabeth already. We can recap in the car on the way. I want another minute with her," Sam said with frustration, but Elizabeth was already walking away to grab her wrap from a chair.

"We don't have time. We have to leave. I'm going ahead so I can change and be in position when you arrive. It has to be now."

"Shit." Sam went to help Elizabeth out to the car. She seemed more than willing to leave their conversation unfinished. He hated to think it was because she thought he didn't have anything to say back to her after she'd confessed she loved him.

So far, he was zero for three: he'd come home and not seen she was upset, he'd insulted her for being wealthy, and he hadn't responded to her declaration of love. When he got her home and alone, he'd fix everything with three words.

## *Chapter Thirty-Five*

THE FOX STOOD before the mirror and straightened his blood red bow tie. He slid his arms into his black jacket. His white shirt glowed beneath the dark, rich fabric. A piece of lint on his sleeve marred his perfect image. He flicked it into the trash and his frown turned to a satisfied smirk. With a last brush of his hair, he set the antique silver backed brush in its exact spot on the bureau. Unable to help himself, he adjusted the mahogany framed mirror just a smidge to the left.

Perfect.

Just like his life would be again after tonight.

Plans in place, his secret rented house in the hills was the perfect place to spend time alone with her. He thought of the chair he'd nailed to the floor, the leather straps banded around the chair back, and the pain he'd inflict. Oh, the screams he'd elicit from her beautiful lips.

She'd pay for all she'd done, surviving twice after

he'd tried to kill her. She'd ruined his perfect setup with the insurance man. He'd only just begun to realize his full potential. He needed more time to perfect his craft. When he had her alone tonight, he'd explore a whole new aspect of his darker half.

Outside, the elegant limousine waited. He slipped into the back seat and sank into the luxurious soft leather. A dark smile tugged at his lips. He liked this part of his life: wealth, privilege, power. Tonight he'd use his power in a whole new way. He'd use his cunning, imagination, his need to inflict pain and suffering, and he'd silence Elizabeth forever—and he'd do it with pleasure.

## Chapter Thirty-Six

*Friday, 9:13 P.M.*

SAM BROODED DURING the car ride and Jenna made Elizabeth's dream come true. Jenna offered her restaurant space in the Merrick International building in downtown San Francisco. Prime real estate for any business, and Jenna had offered up a huge space in her building. The current lease expired in another month, and Elizabeth could take over the space and open a new bakery and restaurant. The location was better than perfect and three times the size of her current shop. She and Jenna would iron out the details with Cameron Shaw, the president of Merrick International, and in about three months she'd be open in a bigger location. It's what she always wanted.

They arrived at the Governor's Ball. A beautiful spectacle of champagne-carrying, tuxedo- and gown-clad who's who of politics and high society. The more she introduced Sam, the more uncomfortable he became at the sheer number of people she knew.

Crowded, people crushed in on her at times. She tried to keep track of where she was and the people around her, but she simply couldn't, and it added to her anxiety. Each time a cork popped, she flinched, thinking someone was taking a shot at her. Sam had to tell her every five minutes to relax.

She and Sam danced together, enjoyed a wonderful meal, and spent time with Sam's family as well as her entire Hamilton family. Sam was a wonderful dancer, and she loved being in his arms. It had been the only time all night she'd felt safe. Her thigh wasn't completely healed, so as the night wore on she leaned heavily against him. Her high heels probably weren't the best choice.

"What's the matter? You're like a falling tree." He loved having her pressed to his side, but it worried him. Every man in the place stared at her. All of them saw she only had eyes for him, and that was a powerful feeling for Sam.

"My leg. These shoes are making my thigh hurt. Sorry, I hope I'm not bothering you."

She liked feeling him hold on to her, so he did it often. Scared to find the man who had tried to kill them, she was also afraid of not finding him. Feeling his arm around her gave her strength, and Sam would do anything to let her know she had him.

"You can lean on me all you want. I wanted to make sure you're all right. Have you spotted our guy yet?"

"No. The guest list includes over three hundred people,

so it's been hard to get a look at everyone. He's got to be here. This has to end."

"Don't worry, sweetheart. Even if he doesn't show tonight, we'll get him. I promise you."

He wasn't sure he could keep the promise. The guy might go into hiding and never surface again. If he left the country, they'd never track him down. Nothing this guy did would surprise Sam. The man was unknown right up until he decided to take down an FBI agent and failed.

"I need to visit the ladies' room." She kissed him on the cheek and pulled free of his arm.

Before he let her leave his side, he whispered into her ear, "Remember the drill. I'll be a few steps behind you all the way. If anything happens, signal me and the other agents." She stepped away, and the familiar little devils danced up his spine. Minding his back, he kept her in his sight and followed at a distance. The hardest thing he'd ever done was let her go, so a killer could make his move.

Elizabeth wound her way through the crowd. Just about every other person stopped to say a few words to her. She knew most of them by name, if not by sight. The crowds at the charity events she attended consisted of many of the same people attending the ball tonight.

About ten feet from the exit, leading out into the hallway, someone grabbed her arm from behind and propelled her through the double doors. Startled, she looked up, thinking it was Sam, and found herself face to face with a killer.

She held up the glass of champagne in her hand above

her head to avoid someone walking by. At least that's what she wanted the man beside her to think. She was actually signaling Sam and every other agent in the room. She handed off the glass to a passing waiter.

He may have been dressed in a tux with expensive Italian leather shoes and a Rolex watch, but a killer hid beneath the facade. The FBI suspected him in eight cases, and now the attempted murder of her and Sam. All those deaths on his hands, and here he was, a respected businessman and philanthropist. He gave to a number of charities. But he was also known for investing in shady business deals that usually turned out to make an astronomical profit. Many CEOs and business managers sought his business advice. Everyone respected him, and women flocked to him. He appeared in the society pages in many major cities across the country.

She didn't pay attention to such things. She'd paid for that by not being able to identify him immediately. She didn't attend parties and benefits to network and make business deals. While others craved their picture in the papers and magazines, she liked her quiet life. Tomorrow the newspapers would print a very different headline about him:

RESPECTED BUSINESSMAN ROBERT CHAINY
ARRESTED FOR MURDER

"Why do you do it?" she asked. He had everything. He led a rich and full life. Why would he become a contract killer? For sport? For fun? For the thrill? Or was he a cold-blooded murderer?

"Do what?" He pretended not to understand.

Undeterred, Elizabeth pushed on. "You know what. You kill people for money. Why would you do that? You don't need the money?"

His grip tightened around her arm where Sam had shot her. Pain shot down her elbow and up into her shoulder.

"You're right. I don't need the money. Making money is easy. I can do it in my sleep, and I do. It's all become so tedious."

"Tedious. You kill people because you think your life is boring. You're crazy. If you want a thrill, go skydiving."

He leaned in close to her ear so no one overheard them. "You have no idea what kind of thrill it gives me when I take a life. The first couple of times, I found it exciting. Now, it's an art. The police can't figure out if the death is an accident or murder. They can't trace them to me. I'm one step ahead of them all the time."

He made few mistakes in his life. Those he did make he fixed, learned from them, and continued to succeed, excelling in everything he did. But this thing consumed him, clouding his reasoning.

"You almost screwed everything up for me. That stupid insurance agent tried to set me up with a cop. He got what he deserved, and I would have finished off the cop if you hadn't stuck your nose in my business. I'll take care of you tonight. No loose ends, you see. Once you're out of the picture, I can go back to my boring financial enterprises, and no one will be the wiser. Even if you've identified me to the police, all they have is suspicion. They can't tie me to anything. They might think they know what I did, but they don't know. If they can't prove it, then they have nothing. Nothing," he rambled, growing more agitated. "Without you to testify, well, let's just say my lawyers will have a field day if they try to charge me with nothing more than circumstantial evidence."

"Then why go after Sam in the first place?"

"The ultimate challenge. A trained agent. I had him until you interfered," he said through clenched teeth.

Sam had been for sport. A challenge Robert couldn't pass up. No sympathy, empathy, no regret. No soul. Completely out of his mind. If she didn't stop him, his sociopathic tendencies would drive him to keep killing. He'd never stop. He'd pick a new place and a new way to do it and elude the police again.

He continued propelling her down the hallway to where it ended in an emergency exit. She couldn't allow him to take her out the door. If she did, he might succeed in killing her before the agents reached them and arrested him. She stopped dead in her tracks. His only choices, drag her or stop. Surprisingly, he stopped and faced her. His back to the wall, the hallway and the emergency exit on either side of them, she stalled, knowing Sam would rescue her.

"You really think you can get away with killing all those people? It's not going to happen." Out of the corner of her eye she spotted Sam heading their way. She turned so Robert was between her and Sam. "The FBI is on to you.

They can hear everything we've said." The light dawned in his eyes. "That's right, I'm wired. You've admitted to the contract killings and to killing the man from the insurance company. You've admitted to the attempted murder of an FBI agent and trying to kill me. Oh, and let's not forget the threat you've made to my life tonight. This is over." She took a slow step away, and then another.

"I'll kill you." He lunged at her and grabbed her wrist. "If for nothing else, I'll kill you for setting me up and making me say all those things."

Something in his eyes wasn't quite right, a reflection of the madness driving him to kill. It chilled her to the bone.

She'd gone too far. Releasing the rage, he spun her around to face Sam, grabbed her around the throat, his arm cutting off her air. His breathing quickened and his heart pounded against her back at her shoulder.

He fumbled behind her, his grip around her neck tightening. He pulled a gun out of his tuxedo jacket pocket and held it to her temple, the muzzle cold, hard against her skin. Frightened, she locked eyes with Sam and the fear eased.

Sam had never been so scared in his life as he was at that moment, seeing the man they called the Silver Fox with a gun to Elizabeth's head. "FBI, drop your weapon. You don't have anywhere to go. If you shoot her, I'll kill you. Slow."

"You'll drop your weapon if you want her to live."

"I can't do that." Sam wished that's all it would take to get Elizabeth back.

Sam watched Robert Chainy closely for any movement he made toward shooting Elizabeth and looking for a way to take him down.

"You will, or I'll kill her right here. You've been with her day and night. She's a beautiful woman. I'll bet she's a wildfire in bed," Robert taunted. "Is she? Maybe I'll keep her for a while, see for myself."

Robert brushed his lips against the side of Elizabeth's head, and the agent's eyes flashed fire and promised death. Robert lived for this kind of adrenaline rush. The situation was deteriorating to the point of no return, and it was going to be Elizabeth's demise or his. He'd prefer to go out in a blaze of glory, but he had money and a dozen lawyers to keep him out of jail long enough for him to leave the country and disappear. All he needed to do was get out of the hotel. The thought never crossed his mind that he shouldn't have come in the first place, or gone after the agent at the bar. He'd craved this kind of excitement his whole life, but never found anything quite like it until he'd planned and executed his first murder.

"Touch her again, and I'll drop you where you stand." Sam tried to figure out a way to get Elizabeth safely away from this guy without someone getting hurt. He didn't want that someone to be her. He'd do anything to save her. Anything.

"Sam, I want to go home now."

Elizabeth's panic and fear shot straight through his heart, shattering it into a million tiny pieces. "I know, sweetheart. Don't move. Keep still."

He didn't have a clear shot. If he tried to shoot Robert,

he might hit Elizabeth. All his training, all his experience came down to this one moment. Get the hostage away from the suspect. He needed to take her out of the equation. How? He couldn't shoot Robert in the head because he held a gun on her. Robert's head was too close to Elizabeth's anyway. He needed a clear shot to the guy's heart, but Elizabeth was a perfect shield in front of him.

Elizabeth didn't know what to do. The grip around her throat cut off her air and Robert pressed the gun so hard to her temple a headache bloomed and throbbed. It wasn't supposed to go this way. He'd admitted everything. Now it was supposed to be over.

Elizabeth tried to take her weight off her feet and let Robert hold her up. Maybe he'd get too tired of holding her, and he'd have to drop her. Instead, his grip grew tighter around her throat. She had no choice but to stand on her feet to prevent him from choking her to death.

She loved cop shows and crime scene investigations. Enjoyable, and very helpful when a madman wanted you dead. Her life had turned into a TV drama with all the necessary components: a serial killer, the FBI hunting him, and a woman in peril. She hoped, in this case, for a happy ending.

Sam needed to kill him. She knew it, and Sam knew it. She also knew Sam was an excellent shot.

Her shoulder was over Robert's chest. Sam could shoot her and the bullet would go right through. Sam had only one choice in order to save her.

*Shoot the hostage.* She kept her eyes locked on him, but Sam's narrowed gaze remained on the Silver Fox, waiting for any opportunity to take him down. Robert took a stronger hold on her. She smelled his fear, it hummed through his body pressed against hers. Or maybe she was the one shaking. She clawed at the arm around her throat, but she was no match for his strength. She'd never free herself.

"You're going to be fine. Stay still," Sam pleaded, never looking directly at her.

If she moved to her left, he'd have a clear shot. Her throat and lungs hurt from trying to suck in gasps of air. She continued her futile struggle to get away, clutching and scratching at the hand at her throat.

He didn't want to do it. He didn't have a choice. Several other agents took up their positions to the sides and behind Sam. Men wearing jackets that read FBI filled the hallway. Probably a dozen more agents waited outside the emergency doors, ready to burst through them. If they did, she'd be dead for sure. Her best chance was Sam. She trusted him. He'd make a clean shot and she'd be okay. She would make it through this. She trusted him completely with her life.

"Shoot him. You can't let him get away," she rasped out. "He'll run, and you'll never find him again. He needs to be punished for what he did to all those people, to you, and to me," she gasped and struggled to get the words out.

She wanted Sam to think like an agent, not like the man sleeping with her.

"Stay still, Elizabeth. You'll be fine." *Please, Elizabeth. Stay still.*

Sweat trickled down Robert's face. "Don't make promises you can't keep. I'm taking her with me. You'll never see her pretty face again. If anyone tries to stop me, I'll kill her. Now drop your weapons!" he shouted.

Robert backed up toward the doors, dragging Elizabeth. Too heavy to hold on to her for much longer, he needed to get away before the agents overtook him. If he could get her out the door to his car, he could make his getaway.

This wasn't supposed to happen. He was rich. People did what he said, no questions asked. They wanted to be part of his circle. They listened to him, admired him, envied him.

She'd make a nice consolation prize for all the trouble he'd gone through because of her. If she hadn't taken his mask off that night, so long ago now, he could have continued this enterprise with the cops none the wiser. This was her fault.

She'd ruined everything for him, and now she was about to get him killed. When they were safely away, he'd teach her a lesson she'd never forget.

"Agent Turner, shoot!" Elizabeth yelled the moment before Sam fired. The bullet tore through her flesh, blood immediately stained her snow-white gown red. The Silver Fox's gun went off, a blast of fire and smoke as the bullet exploded from the chamber at her head. Robert dragged her down and she fell hard to the floor. Sam, frozen in that moment, stood with his weapon held out in front of him. His heart stopped. His mind grinded to a halt. Something else entirely took over. It had to be a dream. Some kind of nightmare conjured while he slept, Elizabeth safe beside him, her skin against his, not lying on the floor dead.

Agents burst through the door and came from behind Sam, surrounding the Silver Fox and Elizabeth. He hardly registered any of it. He stood there with his weapon at his side, the weight of it like an anchor dragging him down to the depths of hell. He'd shot her. Blood poured across her chest and down her head, covering her beautiful face.

*She's dead. I shot her. She's dead.*

He didn't have any other options. It's what the other agents would have done. He thought maybe he'd be lucky enough to just wound her, but all that ominous blood confirmed he'd killed her.

Someone spoke behind him, a muffled sound layered behind the echo of emptiness consuming him. His whole world tunneled in on him, his focus on Elizabeth. An agent put something over her and tried to stop the bleeding. She lay on her side facing him, both arms flung over her head. Barely able to make out her face, the blood oozed down from her temple, covering her eye and cheek.

"Sam! She'll be okay. Give me your gun." Tyler had seen and heard everything. Sam didn't have a choice. He had to take the shot or risk losing Elizabeth. The wound to her side wasn't bad, but Sam was in shock and clearly not thinking straight.

Sam's eyes remained clouded over. He wasn't really seeing Tyler standing in front of him. His flat voice chilled Tyler to the bone.

"I shot her. I shot her again."

He held his gun up to his head, scratching it as if

trying to figure things out. "She actually yelled at me to shoot her. I love her, and I shot her. How can this be? How does someone shoot the woman they love?"

Tyler didn't like seeing Sam with the gun held up to his head. Jack came toward them, and Tyler hoped maybe Sam's brother could help.

"You didn't have a choice. He was going to kill her. The only way to stop him was to shoot him in the heart. You did. It was a clean shot. She'll be okay."

Tyler hoped he was right. Elizabeth moved just in time to save herself from serious injury. The shot sliced open a huge gash in her side, right along her right breast and into Robert Chainy's heart. He'd dropped like a stone, but not before he'd squeezed the trigger and fired his gun. Elizabeth's head had been right next to the barrel and the bullet opened a large wound at her temple. The concussion from the shot could do serious damage to her brain, and Tyler hoped she would be okay for her sake, as well as Sam's.

"Give me your gun," Jack pleaded, waiting until Sam really saw him. "Give it to me." He held out his hand, but Sam made no move to hand it over.

"I shot her. She's dead." He backed up until he hit the wall nearby and slid down with his knees up and put his hands, gun and all, to his face. He sat there holding on to the gun he'd used to shoot the woman he loved. He smelled the gunpowder and felt the hot metal against his forehead.

He never told her he loved her. How much he wanted to have a life with her, make babies with her, and have a real home together, like his brother and sister had in Colorado with their families.

"Sam, please don't do this. Give me the gun. She's not dead. She's unconscious. Let's take her to the hospital. You have to go with her."

Jack hunched down in front of Sam. His mirror image, Jack would understand how he felt. "She's dead." His despair laced in his voice, a single, lonely tear sliding down his face.

"No. She's not. Look at me." Sam's eyes cleared, allowing him to actually focus on Jack. "She's alive," Jack said, but Sam knew he lied. "We have to take her to the hospital. Give me the gun," Jack pleaded.

Sam dismissed the gun in his hand and his brother's request, focusing on Elizabeth. She didn't look like the beautiful woman he remembered seeing not ten minutes ago. Her blood stained the gorgeous white gown.

Paramedics rushed down the hall. He didn't want them to take her away from him.

"Sam. Give me the gun. Now!" Jack's voice penetrated the hollowness in Sam's ears.

Jack's eyes were fierce, his mouth drawn into a sharp line. He turned the gun over without a word, rushing to Elizabeth's side. He pushed several people out of his way, grabbing Elizabeth and holding her to him. Rocking her back and forth, he looked down at her bloody face.

"I'm sorry, sweetheart. I'm so sorry. I never meant to hurt you. I never meant to kill you."

He kept a tight hold on her and couldn't hear anything around him. The world had closed up to him and

Elizabeth. As far as he could see, hear, and feel it was only the two of them. No one would take her away. He used his left hand to brush away the blood from her cheek, smearing it more than anything. He ran his hand over her hair.

"Sweetheart, I'm so sorry. I never meant to kill you. I love you so much."

"I love you too. Let me go," she said weakly.

He held her close, his strong arms around her and hearing him say he loved her filled her heart and soul with such warmth, it burned bright just for him. He rocked her and with each beat back and forth her head pounded. A scorching pain seared through her side, and for a moment she thought she'd been stabbed again. His arm pressed on whatever burned and throbbed like a hot poker. She wanted him to let her go so the pain would stop. On the other hand, she wanted him to hold her for the rest of her life and tell her he loved her. They were the sweetest words she'd ever heard. Barely able to keep herself above the black ooze, she fought to open her eyes and see the man she loved.

"I'll never let you go." Sam rocked and held her tight. He was losing it. He'd killed her, and now her ghost pleaded for him to let her go. He couldn't do it. They'd take her away, and he'd never see her again.

"Sam. Let her go, man. You're hurting her. They have to take her to the hospital." Jack crouched behind Elizabeth and put a hand on Sam's shoulder. "Sam, she's awake. Talk to her. Let her go before you hurt her."

Sam focused on his brother. "Hurt her?" How could he hurt her if she was dead?

"Sam, look at her. She's alive. We have to get her to the hospital."

"No more hospitals." Her words came out barely above a whisper. Her eyes fluttered open, looking into Sam's. "I want to go home. I love you so much. Take me home, Sam."

"You're alive." He couldn't believe it. Everything rushed back to him, and the world around him that had once enclosed just him and Elizabeth now exploded into reality. His brother, Tyler, the paramedics who wanted to get to Elizabeth, and about twenty other agents all came into focus. Robert Chainy dead, blood running down his chest and pooling on the floor. His eyes were open, but the life inside them had extinguished.

"Sam, let her go. Give her over to the paramedics. She'll be okay."

This time Sam heard and understood. He placed a kiss on Elizabeth's forehead, and as gently as if lying down a sleeping baby, he set her on the floor. Unconscious again, but at least she'd gotten through to him. Tyler thought the way he touched her, and the way he stood not even a foot away from her with that tender look in his eyes, spoke volumes about how much he loved her. He couldn't imagine the many emotions going on inside Sam after shooting Elizabeth for a second time.

Tyler would have to speak with Jack and make sure they kept an eye on Sam a little longer. Elizabeth's head wound was serious. A large gash across her temple swelled to an egg shape, opening the gash even more and spilling more of her blood over her face. The wound under her arm and across her ribcage had a padded bandage over it and the paramedic applied pressure to stop the bleeding.

The paramedics lifted her onto the gurney. Sam stepped forward once they strapped her in and kissed her forehead again. He held her hand and followed alongside to the waiting ambulance.

Tyler grabbed Jack and Jenna and they followed behind the ambulance. The entire Hamilton family waited outside, desperate to get a look at Elizabeth before they took her away. Tyler had no doubt they'd give him and Sam a tongue lashing when they got to the hospital. He hoped he wouldn't have to be the one to tell them this had all been Elizabeth's idea.

## Chapter Thirty-Seven

*Saturday, 8:07 A.M.*

SHE BARELY SLEPT through the night, even with the painkillers. She woke up several times from nightmares and the sound of gunshots in her head. Each time she opened her eyes, Sam was with her, holding her hand, telling her she was safe and he loved her.

Caught in the same dream again, she tried to tell herself it wasn't real. Robert Chainy had a gun to her head, Sam stood in front of them, his gun trained on Robert. The awful pop of gunfire exploded, and the searing pain burned her head and side. She woke up with a start. Her eyes flew open only to see Jack sitting in the chair beside her bed instead of Sam.

"Where's Sam?"

Jack smiled. "Most people can't tell us apart, but here you are half out of your head with pain, and you knew immediately I wasn't Sam." Shaking his head, he sat forward. "We sent him home. Jenna came and got him about an hour ago. She'll bring him back once he's cleaned up, and she's made sure he's eaten a decent meal. I promised I'd stay in his place. I thought if you woke up, you'd see him and go back to sleep."

"You aren't him." She couldn't hide her disappointment, sure Jack understood she needed Sam. "I'm glad you're here though. Is he okay?"

"He's getting there. We haven't left him alone. He stayed by your side the whole night. Tyler stayed with him until I came a few hours ago to take a shift. He won't be satisfied until he hears you say you're okay and you don't blame him for shooting you. Had it been anybody else he had to shoot, it would have been easier for him to accept.

"He loves you, and hurting you on purpose is a weight he can't bear. Everyone knows he didn't have a choice. Chainy would have killed you. Sam took the shot to save you."

"He needs to stop blaming himself when it isn't his fault," Elizabeth agreed.

"I think it would do him a world of good to hear you say it."

"Oh, he'll hear from me."

She put a hand to her head, still pounding away like the cadence of a marching band. She had stitches across her temple and a goose egg to boot. The bullet wound along her ribs next to her breast had been stitched closed. She looked terrible. Her hair was in tangles and half the pins were missing or falling out. Her gown was completely ruined, she was sure. Her eye was all puffy and probably black and blue. The entire right side of her face hurt.

Jack leaned forward and held her gaze. "Don't be too hard on him. He thought you were dead. He thought he killed you last night. Tyler and I had to talk him into giving up his gun. It took some doing, but he finally gave it to me. He picked you up from the floor and rocked you while he told you how sorry he was for killing you. We couldn't convince him you were alive until you spoke to him."

That sank into the depths of her soul and filled her with overwhelming sadness. Poor Sam. She hadn't been hurt as badly as she could have been, because she'd trusted Sam to take the shot and do as little damage to her while still killing Chainy. She was proud of him. She'd been right to trust him. He'd saved her life.

He'd taken shooting her the first time so hard, and now he'd actually thought he'd killed her.

"I had no idea he thought he killed me. I'll take care of him. I'll make sure he knows I'm okay, and I don't blame him. I'll have to thank him too. One murderer down, and a stalker to go," she said with a sigh. Already getting tired, the pain radiated through her head and side. Maybe she'd take another nap, and then, with or without permission from her doctor, she was going home.

"You should look at this." Jack handed over the newspaper he'd been reading. "My wife knows a lot of people. She had a reporter talk with Deputy Director Davies last night about Sam's operations the last two days. He's a hero, thanks to you. Again, that is."

She took the paper and read through one eye the front page headline:

## ELIZABETH HAMILTON SAVED BY FBI—TWICE

She covered her open mouth with her fingers, her eyes wide with surprise.

"Read the story. It's quite remarkable. You know about last night, but I bet you don't know where he went the night Tyler stayed with you."

She read the story through once and glanced up at Jack, who'd been watching her intently. Then she read the story again, unable to believe the unbelievable.

In addition to what happened with Chainy the night before, the night Sam had left her with Tyler, he'd gone after Jarred and arrested him for stalking and attempted kidnapping. Apparently Sam and Tyler, in conjunction with local police, had discovered Jarred was in dire financial trouble. Set to kidnap Elizabeth the night Sam arrested him, he intended to ransom her to her family for millions.

They found him at her house armed with a gun, rope, duct tape, a hunting knife, rubber gloves, and a ransom note he'd pasted together using letters from magazines and newspapers. The most ominous discovery: a receipt for a storage locker at a local storage yard paid in full for five years. When they searched the storage locker, they found a crudely fashioned pine box coffin lined in plastic and a hammer and nails to seal the lid. She wondered fleetingly if he'd meant to seal her in that box alive or dead.

Ill, she remembered Jarred coming to the door and giving her that menacing kiss. He might have taken her then, but John and Tyler showed up. A chill ran up the length of her spine and the hairs on the back of her neck stood on end. She'd come so close to death three times. Each time she'd survived.

In the midst of all that had happened, she'd fallen in love with Sam, and he loved her. One thought rang in her head, she was one lucky woman.

"When will he be back? I need to see him," she said on a yawn.

She closed her heavy eyelids for what she thought was a few seconds. When she opened them again, Sam stood in Jack's place. She closed her eyes and opened them again. Sure enough, Sam stood before her, his face marred with frown lines and dark circles under his eyes.

"Some fake fiancé you are. It's not nice to play tricks on someone with a concussion. I may be seeing double, but I know the difference between you and Jack. You can't leave a copy of yourself and hope to pass it off as the real thing." She smiled and held out her arms, waiting for him to come to her and hold her. He didn't move. She dropped her arms, disappointed.

Carefully, she sat up in bed and waited for the room to stop spinning. Her focus restored, she took a good look at him. Clean-shaven, his hair still damp from his shower, he wore blue jeans, a dark gray T-shirt, and his black leather jacket. She couldn't figure out what was wrong with the way he looked. Of course he was as handsome as ever, but something in his appearance wasn't quite right. It hit her all at once. She'd never seen him without his badge and gun strapped to his belt. The solemn look in his eyes disturbed her even more.

"Aren't you going to say anything?" He'd never used that harsh tone with her.

"I did say something. I really would have rather woken up and seen you sitting by my bed. I know you were here with me all night. Every time I woke up, I felt better just knowing you were beside me. You look tired."

"I look tired. That's all you have to say. I look tired."

"Sam, calm down. That isn't all I have to say." She wanted to tell him how much she loved him. He wasn't ready to listen. She'd start with last night and work her way toward the rest of their lives. "Where are your gun and badge?" His eyes flashed with some emotion she couldn't identify. Anger, frustration, maybe resignation.

"Deputy Director Davies has them. I gave them to him last night. Well, Jack gave him my gun. I turned over the badge myself."

"Did you quit your job?" *Please, Sam. Don't quit your job. You love it.*

"Let's talk about something else. Are you in pain? You look like you're in pain. I can get the doctor if you need something."

About to lose it, she snapped, "Did you quit your job?" She hadn't meant to raise her voice, but she couldn't allow him to give up his life's work. Pressing the heel of her hand to her head, she glared at him until he answered.

"Yes, damnit. I can't do it anymore." Sam turned his back on her, crossing his arms over his chest, shutting her out.

Deputy Director Davies and Tyler walked into the room. Their expressions turned grim when they felt the heavy tension in the room too. She intended to clear things up for everyone, especially Sam. Right this minute.

"Deputy Director Davies, I'm glad you're here. I believe you'd like to take my statement about what happened last night."

Sam kept his back to all of them, staring out the window. His shoulders and spine completely rigid. Even though her head throbbed, she had to make this right so she and Sam could move on with their lives.

She set her jaw and determination filled her eyes. Davies remembered the last time he'd come to take her statement about the first shooting. She'd given quite a performance that day, and he expected nothing less today. She'd put Sam in his place. He knew it. She looked pointedly at his coat pocket. The woman didn't miss anything.

"Why don't you start with when you met with Chainy in the ballroom, and he walked you out to the hallway? We have the recording of his confession that he was responsible for the insurance murders, as well as the attempted murder of you and Agent Turner. I'd like to hear about what happened when Sam caught up with you two in front of the emergency exit."

Davies knew she wanted to start here. It would be difficult for her to recount, but she'd put things into perspective for Sam. He was too close to her. His emotions made it impossible for him to think rationally. Elizabeth had a knack for sorting things out and putting them into a logical order. She'd done it before, and he had no doubt she'd do it again. He was counting on it, in fact, because he didn't want to lose one of his best agents.

She eyed Sam's back and turned to both Deputy Director Davies and Agent Reed. She nodded to Davies and began.

"Let's keep this simple. Chainy had his arm around my throat, choking me. I could barely breathe." She touched her fingers to her sore throat. Taking a shaky breath, she went on determined to get it out and get Sam back. "He dragged me against him. With his head right next to mine, he held a gun pointed at my temple. He said he'd kill me, and we all know he meant to, whether in that hallway or once he got me through those doors and away from the hotel. Agent Turner"—she used his last name to let him know she took this seriously—"ordered Chainy to drop his weapon and let me go. Chainy wasn't about to comply and wanted Agent Turner and the other agents to drop their weapons. Agent Turner followed protocol by identifying himself as an FBI agent, ordered Chainy to drop his weapon again, and with no other alternative but to kill Chainy, he shot him."

Deputy Director Davies led her where she wanted to go. They both understood the only way this would work on Sam was to keep things on a professional level. There would be no misunderstanding her all-business tone, despite the sweat breaking out on her face.

"You do understand, Miss Hamilton, Agent Turner shot you."

Sam's shoulders slumped and his head went down a few notches. This must be so hard for him, but she'd make it right.

"He did not shoot me, Deputy Director Davies. He shot Chainy. My side happened to be in the way."

Out of the corner of her eye, Sam turned around. She didn't look at him, but kept her gaze on Deputy Director Davies and Tyler, who stood in front of her hospital bed, looking professional. They conducted the interview like they'd never met her.

"Agent Turner is, absolutely, one of the best agents the FBI has, and he would never shoot an innocent person. His aim was true. I did my best to get out of the way, but Chainy had quite a grip on my neck. I knew Agent Turner would have to shoot Chainy, and I even yelled for him to shoot him. At no time did I feel Agent Turner wouldn't make the shot, or that my life was in any danger from Agent Turner, even if that meant he had to shoot through me to get Chainy."

Out of the corner of her eye, she saw Sam's mouth drop and a surprised look took over his handsome but tired face.

"I expect the FBI will honor Agent Turner for the outstanding work he's done the last two days, as well as Agent Reed. They've performed their duties in an outstanding manner and should be rewarded for their bravery and investigative work."

"So you feel Agent Turner and Agent Reed protected you and solved both cases to the best of their ability." Deputy Director Davies waited to hear her answer, his only response a slight tilting of his mouth at the corners.

Sam's eyes went wide, shell-shocked by what she'd already said. She continued, never looking at him. "I assure you the entire Hamilton family, including myself, are grateful for the outstanding job Agent Turner and Agent Reed have performed. Agent Turner not only saved my life last night, but stopped my potential kidnapping by Jarred." She paused to let that sink in with Sam before she continued. "I understand Agent Turner was not thinking clearly last night after the shooting. No doubt a traumatic incident, even for the most seasoned of agents. I understand he asked you to *hold* his badge for him." Deputy Director Davies's mouth turned up ever so slightly. "I think you'll want to return that to him, in addition to his weapon. Agent Reed"—she waited for him to nod to her—"I expect you'll need to take Agent Turner to the shooting range. His aim seems to be about an inch off." She indicated her arm and side with a nod and a smirk. "Perhaps some practice will get him back on track."

She smiled at Tyler. Sam's aim was dead on, and they all knew it. She couldn't help getting a little dig in at Sam and letting him see the humor in what happened.

Tyler winked. "I'll be happy to escort him to the range for a proper tutorial, Miss Hamilton," Tyler teased.

Deputy Director Davies laid Sam's gun and badge at the foot of her bed, but she wasn't quite finished yet. "Deputy Director Davies, I hope I've answered all your questions satisfactorily." He nodded yes to her. "Please tell that internal investigator, what was his name, Vernet, I look forward to discussing Agent Turner with him again." She gave Deputy Director Davies a wicked grin. She did look forward to sparing with that weasel. No one would ever hurt Sam, not if she could help it.

Deputy Director Davies shook his head. "Agent Vernet has been," he held for a diplomatic pause, "reassigned."

"Excellent. I'm sure whomever you send to conduct the internal investigation will be fair and open-minded. Now, if you don't mind, I'd like to kiss your agent, and I'm sure you don't want to be present, since getting involved with a witness is frowned upon by the Bureau." She smiled at Deputy Director Davies and nodded her farewell.

Tyler, always up to something, sure enough started toward her, bent to kiss her, but Sam pushed him away.

"Don't even think about it, Tyler. It appears I'm armed again, and I can only handle so many shootings in a matter of days."

Blown away by Elizabeth, Sam hadn't lost his mind enough to allow Tyler to kiss his future wife. She didn't know it, but a diamond ring was burning a hole in his pocket. He'd come into her room ready to beg her forgiveness, and beg even more to make her his wife. He loved her. And job or no job, he wanted to make a life with her.

"I wanted to give her a kiss goodbye—on the cheek. Man, you are so uptight. Relax. Elizabeth is fine." He leaned down to her. "I will miss your home cooking though. I've never eaten so well in my life."

"You're welcome at Decadence any time. I'll have you to the house for dinner often. Once the new restaurant is open, you'll have a seat whenever you like. You'll be my guest at both restaurants. I mean it. I better see you there. Often." She brushed her hand down his arm in a friendly gesture. Grabbing his shirt, she pulled him down and kissed him on the cheek as he'd wanted to do to her.

Tyler followed Deputy Director Davies out the door. Sam ran a hand over the back of his neck, overwhelmed. "Elizabeth, I . . ."

"Not so fast, buster. I don't want to hear you say you're sorry for what happened. You don't owe me an apology. I made the decision to go last night and catch that evil bastard."

She got up on her knees on the bed. Her head and side probably hurt like hell. In pain, she winced, but didn't let it deter her from facing him and looking him right in the eye.

"Elizabeth, get back into bed. Listen . . ."

"Not one more word until you get over here and kiss me and hold me." Her voice cracked.

Desperation laced her voice. She'd managed to get through talking with Davies with boldness and confidence, as if she'd been conducting a business meeting, but she'd used up all her stores of courage and needed him. He took the few steps to her and gathered her in his arms. She clung to him fiercely. He leaned down and kissed her like she'd asked. Gentle with her, he brushed a soft kiss against her lips, then pressed harder and drank her in. He pulled back but kept his arms around her, feeling the bandage around her breasts and ribs. The suffocating guilt overwhelmed him.

"Sweetheart..."

"If that sentence has the word sorry in it, I don't want to hear it. As far as I'm concerned, this whole episode is over, and I'm closing the book on it." Her voice turned serious. "I owe you my life, Sam. Thank you for what you did. Not only for last night, but for Jarred too. I can finally breathe easy knowing no one is out there trying to hurt or kill me."

She held his face between her hands and leaned in and kissed him. "I love you," she said against his lips, then took it deeper.

Sam couldn't get enough of her. He wanted to lay her down in bed and make love to her. He remembered the ring in his pocket and brought the kiss to an end with a nibble at her soft lips before he leaned away. She wouldn't leave this room without making him a promise.

"I love you." He kissed her gently again. "I have one problem. I'm tired of you calling me your fake fiancé."

"No problem. You took care of my stalker fiancé. There's no reason to carry on with the whole fake fiancé bit. I promise, I won't make jokes about that anymore." She crossed her heart with her index finger and leaned in to kiss him again.

He leaned back and dodged her lips. He needed to get this out. "That's all well and good, but you see, I do like the fiancé part."

"What? What are you talking about?" she asked, confused.

Anxious and feeling mischievous, he pushed her back onto her heels. The surprised look on her face helped ease his nerves. He kneeled beside the bed and took the ring out of his pocket. Holding it up to her with one hand, he held her other hand in his and said, "I love you, Elizabeth Hamilton. I want to make a life with you. I want to have a family and grow old with you. I can't live without you. Will you marry me?"

She never took her eyes from his, even though he held a gorgeous diamond ring up to her. She couldn't care less, and that said everything about her priorities.

A brilliant smile bloomed on her lips when she said, "Yes. Oh, yes, Sam, I'll marry you."

He let out a deep breath, slipped the ring on her finger, and stood and gathered her into his arms. Last night his future looked bleak and dark, and now he saw a bright and happy future with this woman, with his Elizabeth. He kissed her forehead and both her eyelids even as tears spilled down her cheeks. He wiped them away with the pads of his thumbs, careful of the swelling around her right eye. Kissing her cheeks, he finally found her mouth.

"Ellie Girl, your ass is hanging out the back of your gown." The Judge covered a laugh with a cough.

Elizabeth didn't care whether she was buck-naked standing on the Embarcadero in front of Pier 39 at that moment. She and Sam were getting married.

"John. That's our daughter you're talking about," Rachel laughed out. "Elizabeth, darling, please cover yourself. Hello, Sam. How are you today?"

Sam held her face and kept his forehead to hers.

Elizabeth settled back into bed. After covering her and making her comfortable, he brought her hand up to his lips and kissed her palm. "I'm perfect, now."

"Dad, Mom, Sam and I are getting married." Her parents' eyes lit up, and they both came to the bed and held her close.

"Congratulations, Elizabeth. I knew you two were perfect for each other," Rachel said, beaming.

"Are you sure, Ellie Girl? I can have him locked up for something if you'd rather," the Judge teased in a serious voice. "I'm sure I can frame him for something."

"I'm sure, Dad. Sam is my future. We're getting married, I'm going to open a new restaurant in his sister's building, and soon we'll have babies." She smiled at Sam as he smiled back at her.

"Well, those are some big plans. We'll get started on the wedding as soon as you're well." Rachel's eyes went misty thinking of her little girl walking down the aisle.

"Dad, will you do a couple of things for me?"

"Sure, Ellie Girl, anything."

"Go use that wonderful Hamilton clout and get me out of here. I'm going home with my fiancé." She ran a hand over Sam's hair and down his cheek. She wasn't about to spend another minute without him, and she certainly didn't want to spend another day lying around a hospital room.

"Elizabeth, you're seriously injured, and you have a concussion. You can't leave the hospital," Sam said, worried about her.

"He's right. If they won't let you go home in a few days,

I'll spring you," her father said lovingly. "What else do you want me to do? You want something else very much, and I can tell by the light in your eyes it's a doozy."

"You know me so well. I want you to marry Sam and I next Saturday at his family's ranch in Colorado."

"Elizabeth, we can wait until you're feeling better," Sam said, shocked she wanted to marry him immediately. "You have time to plan the wedding you want."

"That is the wedding I want. I want to be married on the ranch you love with your family and my family. I don't want to wait to be your wife."

Her mother smiled down at her. "Elizabeth, a wedding on the family ranch is a splendid idea, but you haven't considered a few details. Darling, you can't be serious about doing it next Saturday. We have to get you a dress and order flowers and food, not to mention getting permission from Sam's family to use the ranch and setting things up."

"I'm sure between you, me, Jenna, and Summer we'll get everything done. Sam, your family won't mind, will they?"

"Hell no. They'll be thrilled. I'd marry you anywhere, but the ranch is perfect. I have a house at the lake. We can stay there before and after the ceremony. Jack and Summer both have spare rooms for your brothers, and there's the cabin for your parents. There's plenty of room for everyone."

"Sam, I love your enthusiasm," Rachel chimed in, "but Elizabeth, you've forgotten something important. Your face. You don't want all of your wedding photos to show your bruised and swollen face. I don't think a week is enough time for it to heal."

Elizabeth wanted to marry Sam right away, but she didn't want to look back on their special day and have any of the past few days' ordeal mar any part of their wedding.

"All right, make it three weeks, but not a day longer. I'm going to be Mrs. Sam Turner by the end of the month."

## *Epilogue*

SAM AND TYLER arrived at his home in Colorado. Expected to join Elizabeth there in another week, he and Tyler had closed their case early, thanks to the help of Tyler's psychic ghost, Morgan. The racket from his family rolled all the way out to the porch. When he stepped into the house, the sweetest family scene greeted him. Toys littered the floor, the smell of good food cooking, including his wife's baking, wafted on the air, and the noise that only a family can make.

His sister, Summer, rocked her baby by the huge stone fireplace. His newest niece, Rose, lay on Summer's chest sleeping with her little mouth open. Lily and Jacob, Summer's other two children, sat at the long farm table in the kitchen with their father, Caleb, decorating cupcakes with Jenna's boys, Sam and Matt. Jenna was supervising the children from the head of the table with Jack sitting beside her, helping little Sam put candies on his cupcake

in the shape of a happy face. Jenna was decorating a cupcake, a comical sight because at eight months pregnant
she barely reached the table while she sat in the chair.
Beautiful in her pregnancy, she glowed.

The real beauty, though, stood in the kitchen with a
baby held in one arm nursing under a blanket and a pie
in the other hand she'd just taken out of the oven. The
Muffin Man rubbed at her legs and purred loudly, hoping
for a treat.

Elizabeth looked up when the screen door at the front
of the house banged shut. She'd been staying at their home
in Colorado on her maternity leave, and she was enjoying
a day of baking and playing with all the children. All six
of them. She put the pie down to cool and smiled at her
husband and Tyler, who came in behind him.

"You're home. You weren't due back for at least a
week." Happy to see him, her heart quickened.

Everyone in the house shouted one kind of greeting or
another at Sam and Tyler as they made their way into the
house. Sam headed straight for her.

"Morgan helped us tie things up faster."

"Tyler, what are you doing here?" Elizabeth loved
seeing him. He came to the new restaurant at the Merrick
International building in San Francisco often.

"You said you'd feed me a home-cooked meal any
time I wanted. I was hungry, so I came along with Sam."

"You eat at the restaurant all the time." Elizabeth had
made sure Tyler always had a seat, no matter how busy
things were, and never got a bill. He was family.

"Sam said he was taking his family leave, and I had

a few days' vacation coming to me, so I thought I'd tag along and see my best girl." He stepped away from Sam before he got jabbed in the ribs by an elbow. Elizabeth smiled. Some things didn't change. Those two were always joking with each other.

"I think Tyler's in love with Morgan. He came here to hide out from her, if that's even possible. She's got him all tied up in knots." Sam winked at Elizabeth. She waited for Tyler's denial, though it had become very obvious something was brewing between Morgan and Tyler.

Jack almost dropped his cupcake. He coughed to cover the smile on his face. Tyler had come to the ranch to hide from Morgan. Jack wondered what Tyler would say if he knew Morgan was their neighbor.

Jack wanted to tell them he'd seen Morgan, had actually run into her that very day. He'd promised her he wouldn't tell them and hated lying, but it was important. Her prediction correct, Sam and Tyler had arrived unexpectedly.

"She won't tell me where she is, or how she knows how to get in touch with me," Tyler grumbled. "It's like she's invaded my head and knows my every thought. It's getting downright creepy. Sometimes all I have to do is think about her and she calls me."

Sam chuckled, "It's *getting* creepy? It's been creepy since the beginning."

Tyler shrugged and headed for the table to shake hands with Jack. "Might as well decorate a cupcake and play with the kids. I'm not thinking about Morgan anymore," he said, mostly to himself.

"Sure you're not," Sam teased. "Give it up already. We all know she's all you think about."

Sam laughed when Tyler opened his mouth to say something nasty back to him, but Jenna stuffed a cupcake in his mouth. All the kids laughed along with the adults. Tyler good-naturedly ate the cupcake and swallowed the comeback.

Sam finally made it into the kitchen and greeted his wife, "Hello, sweetheart. How are my girls today?"

Elizabeth kissed him for a long moment. He hadn't been gone that long, but she'd missed him every moment he was away, like he'd missed her.

"We're good. Grace is not living up to her name, however. She's a little piggy and has been nursing non-stop. I think it's her way of protesting your absence."

Sam lifted the blanket to peak at his daughter. Sure enough, she sucked away at her mama. Her little fist rested on Elizabeth's breast next to her mouth. Her eyes were closed, completely content against her mother's skin.

"Who could blame her?" Sam bent his head and kissed the swell of his wife's breast above his daughter's face. He kissed Grace on her forehead. When he met his wife's eyes again, he gave her a look, telling her she would be all his tonight when they were alone. She blushed and he leaned in and kissed her lips, holding her and their daughter in his arms.

They'd been married more than a year when little Grace came into their lives. True to her word, he and Elizabeth were married exactly three weeks after her release from the hospital. They spent those three weeks making love and planning their wedding. He'd been so happy the day he and Elizabeth had gotten married in the midst of Jenna's flourishing garden, surrounded by their family with her father presiding over the ceremony. The day Grace was born, he was sure he couldn't get any happier. Today came close, seeing everyone spread out in his house. It wasn't the first time Sam had taken stock of his life and counted himself blessed.

"I love you, sweetheart," he said, his voice gruff with emotion.

Sam's eyes grew serious and she leaned her forehead to his. "I love you too." Leaning back, she tried to lighten Sam's mood. "So do you really think Tyler has a thing for Morgan, even though he hasn't seen her in more than four years?"

"I think there's something there. She calls him direct now. No more messages at the Bureau. Of course, Davies has her name flagged in the system, so if she does call the main number she'll be put through to him. Davies doesn't want to admit she's the real deal, but I don't think he can ignore all the help she's given us, either."

"Maybe Tyler will be lucky like us."

He took in the room filled with their family. Sam held his wife and daughter close. "If he finds the kind of love we share, he will be lucky."

## Chapter One

SHELLY SWIPED THE lip gloss wand across her lips, rolled them in and out to smooth out the color, and grinned at herself in the mirror, satisfied with the results. She pushed up her boobs, exposing just enough flesh to draw a man's attention and keep it, but still not look too obvious.

"Perfect. He'll love it."

Ah, Cameron Shaw. Rich and powerful, sexy as hell, and kind in a way that made it easy to get what she wanted. Exactly the kind of husband she always dreamed about marrying.

Shelly grew up in a nice middle class family. Ordinary. She desperately wanted to be anything but ordinary. She'd grown up a plump youngster and a fat teenager. At fifteen, she resorted to bingeing and purging and starved herself thin. Skinny and beautiful, boys took notice. You can get a guy to do just about anything when you offer them hot sex. By the time she graduated high school, she'd transformed herself into the most popular girl in school.

Destined to live a glamorous life in a big house with servants and fancy cars and clothes, meeting Cameron in the restaurant had been a coup.

Executives and wealthy businessmen frequented the upscale restaurant. She'd gone fishing and landed her perfect catch. Now she needed to hold on to him and reel in a marriage proposal.

# Chapter Two

NIGHT FELL OUTSIDE Cameron's thirty-sixth floor office window. Tired, he'd spent all day in meetings. As president of Merrick International, long hours were the norm and sleepless nights were a frequent occurrence.

The sky darkened and beckoned the stars to come to life. If he were out on the water and away from the glow of the city lights, he'd see them better, twinkling in all their brilliant glory.

He couldn't remember the last time he took out the sailboat. He'd promised Emma he'd take her fishing. Every time he planned to go, something came up at work. More and more often, he put her off in favor of some deal or problem that couldn't wait. He needed to realign his priorities. His daughter deserved better.

He stared at the picture of his golden girl. Emma was five now and the image of her mother. Long, wavy, golden hair and deep blue eyes, she always looked at him with such love. He remembered Caroline looking at him the same way.

They'd been so happy when they discovered Caroline was pregnant. In the beginning, things had been so sweet. They'd lay awake at night talking about whether it would be a boy or a girl, what they'd name their child, and what they thought he or she would grow up to be.

He never thought he'd watch his daughter grow up without Caroline beside him.

The pregnancy took a turn in the sixth month when Caroline began having contractions. They gave her medication to stop them and put her on bed rest for the rest of the pregnancy.

One night he'd come home to find her pale and hurting. He rushed her to the hospital. Her blood pressure spiked and the contractions started again. No amount of medication could stop them. Two hours later, when the contractions were really bad, the doctor came in to tell him Caroline's body was failing. Her liver and kidneys were shutting down.

Caroline was a wreck. He still heard her pleading for him to save the baby. She delivered their daughter six weeks early, and Caroline suffered a massive stroke and died without ever holding their daughter.

Cameron picked up the photograph and traced his daughter's face, the past haunting his thoughts. He spent three weeks in the neonatal intensive care unit grieving for his wife and begging his daughter to live. Week four had been a turning point. He felt she'd spent three weeks grieving the loss of her mother and decided to live for her father. She began eating on her own and gained weight quickly. Ten days later, Cameron finally took his daughter home. From then on it had been the two of them.

Almost a year ago, he decided enough was enough. Emma needed a mother. He'd dated several women since Caroline's death. More so, he took a few women to bed and felt no emotional connection to any of them. They provided a physical release. Nothing more than empty encounters between two consenting adults. Perhaps that's what made him feel emptier each time. He didn't want to examine it too closely. It hurt too much, this loneliness.

He didn't know if he was capable of giving anything more than his body to any woman anymore. It hurt too much to have his heart ripped out of his chest when Caroline died. He figured there was literally nothing left of it.

The women knew it, understood it, and took what they could get from him. No shortage of women who wanted to be seen with him, sleep with him, enjoy the money he had, and casually slip away when the time came. The problem with that was none of them would make a good mother to Emma.

He hadn't lost his head over a woman since Caroline until a month ago. He'd had a hard day and ended up right here, sitting in his office looking out at the night and thinking about Caroline and how much he missed her. He'd drowned himself in her memory and what it felt like to be her husband and to love her and be loved.

He'd gone downstairs to Decadence to have dinner alone at his reserved table. When he'd entered the restaurant, he'd seen a woman at the bar who reminded him so much of Caroline that he almost believed it was her. He struck up a conversation, and they'd ended up going at it on the sofa in his office. It had been the one and only time he'd lost his head that way.

When it was over and he'd realized what he'd done, he apologized to the woman and offered to drive her home. She'd made things easy and asked him to dinner.

So began his relationship with the blonde beauty, Shelly Ramsey. They'd been seeing each other regularly for a month. He took her to several charity benefits and social functions he attended for business purposes. So far, they enjoyed each other's company.

He scheduled dinner with Shelly and Emma downstairs at Decadence and awaited his daughter's arrival. He stared at the picture of Emma again and wondered if it was too soon to introduce her to a woman he was seeing.

He thought about Shelly. Nice, well spoken, and beautiful, if not too made up at times. Caroline often made jokes about herself to make others feel comfortable around her. Shelly didn't have a sense of humor about herself. She took things too personally.

The more Cameron thought about Shelly, the more he realized his interest in her ran more to her resemblance of Caroline. The longer he spent with her, the more he realized her looks weren't enough to keep him interested.

Always nice to him, but not necessarily to others. That was a problem for Cameron. At every business function they attended, Caroline went out of her way to befriend everyone. She was a warm fire on a cold night. Everyone wanted to gather around and feel her warmth. He missed that about her. He'd bask in the praise and compliments about what a wonderful woman he'd snagged. They'd tell him how lucky he was and how they thought she was great. He hadn't needed anyone to tell him he was lucky. He knew it.

So far, Shelly hadn't shown that side of herself. If she even had it in her. He sometimes suspected some sort of hidden agenda.

Cameron sighed and put the picture of his daughter back on the corner of his desk and considered himself a royal jackass. Yeah, the sex was good, but he spent the whole time pretending Shelly was his wife. After the first time, he hadn't lost his head quite so completely. In fact, now he could take it or leave it. He chalked Shelly up to supreme stupidity and a deep longing for his dead wife.

He wished he'd realized Shelly was just a substitute for Caroline before he'd agreed to introduce her to his daughter. Emma would arrive any second, and he couldn't cancel now.

He continued to stare out the window at the ocean in the far distance. A row of lights appeared very small on the water. A ship, lights lining the mast. He imagined a sailboat and wished he were aboard right now.

MARTI STARED OUT across the water and sighed. She loved the ocean, the sound, the smell, the solitude, and most of all, the sheer size of it. You could lose yourself out here on the wide-open sea. She had for the past year, and now it was time to find herself back on land.

The saltwater spray swept up from the bow and misted her face. Her last day on the ship. Tomorrow she arrived in nearby San Francisco.

She'd seen the world from the ocean and from port to port. She'd explored every wonderful place she'd ever dreamed of visiting: England, Ireland, France, Greece, Italy, Egypt, Fiji, Brazil, Chile, Australia, Japan, China. Everywhere her heart desired, she'd gone and explored.

Some people dreamed of a trip around the world and never did because they couldn't afford to, or just didn't take the time. Three hundred and sixty-five days at sea. On day three hundred and sixty-six, she'd dock in San Francisco, sign the estate papers at the lawyer's office, and make a life on dry land—alone. Her heart ached over the loss of her grandmother, and soon the sea.

She'd rather not go back to the city, but the year was up and she'd fulfilled her grandmother's last wishes. How could she refuse such a wonderful request? But she couldn't spend the rest of her life sailing from port to port. She wanted to, but needed to get back to her life. Actually, she had to start her life. She was ready to stay in one place for a while and make some friends.

"Marti, we've dropped sail and anchored for the night. The fog's rolling in and we should get settled. What time do you want to get underway and drop anchor in the bay in the morning?"

"Let's not make it early," she said over her shoulder to her trusted captain. "How about eleven? I can watch the sun come up and spend a quiet morning with you and the crew. It'll be our last breakfast together for a while."

"You look sad. It's been quite an adventure, wouldn't you say?"

Captain Finn understood her reluctance to leave the ship and begin an unfamiliar life.

"A grand adventure. I'm going to miss it as much as you salty dogs."

"I think we can call you a salty dog after a year of sailing. You handle this ship as well as anyone. You make a great mate."

"I learned from the best." She smiled to let him know how much she appreciated him for treating her like a part of the crew and not keeping some sort of boundary between them because she was technically the boss. "How long until dinner?"

"A few minutes. We're set up on the back deck."

"Perfect. We'll watch the fog roll in and play our last poker game."

"Will the men keep their money for shore leave?"

"They may just leave with a bonus tonight." She winked and he laughed.

An experienced card sharp, she'd make sure all the men left with her money.

Captain Finn caught her looking longingly at the water. "She'll still be here come tomorrow night when you're tucked into some hotel room. Stay aboard."

"I have things to do. I need to find a place to live on dry land. If I stay on the ship, I'll only want to sail away again."

"I understand and know just how you feel." He belonged to the sea and she was cut from the same cloth.

"The ocean, she calls to you, but you have to find your way now that Sofia is gone. She gave you a gift, Marti. She would be proud to see you embraced it with your whole heart. I've never seen anyone take to the open water like you, or enjoy the adventure of exploring a new land with such enthusiasm. She understood your spirit."

"Yes. She did. She left me in good hands too. You and the crew have been wonderful to me. I couldn't have gotten through the first few weeks without your kindness."

"Kindness was easy to give to someone like you. You earned my respect, and that of the crew, when you insisted on becoming a sailor. Your Uncle Anthony doesn't deserve either kindness or respect from you. Remember that tomorrow and all the days after that. He'll come after you. He wants what Sofia gave to you."

"Did he call?"

"This morning. We told him you went diving and couldn't be reached." He gave her one of his lopsided smiles.

"You tell him that every time he calls."

"It's been true a time or two." Captain Finn's mouth tilted up in an unapologetic grin.

"Thank you, Captain Finn, for everything."

"I loved your grandmother. I've taken her all over the world and watched her create some of her masterpieces. And now I've had the pleasure to take you around the world and watch you do the same in your own way."

Marti thought fondly of her grandmother, the world-famous painter. Her paintings hung in galleries and museums all over the world. She'd taught Marti how to paint from the time she was old enough to hold a brush. A smile touched her mouth at the sweet memories. How she'd loved painting with her grandmother.

Marti was an accomplished artist in her own right, but the public wouldn't know it. She'd never shown one of her paintings to anyone. To her grandmother's frustration, Marti painted for herself. Truth be told, she was scared to death to let anyone see her paintings and compare them to her grandmother's masterpieces.

Marti kept her talents on an anonymous level, writing and illustrating her own series of children's books. She wrote the series under a pen name. No one except her publisher knew the author was the granddaughter of one of the greatest painters in the world. Marti hoped she'd get to keep the secret. A hope she knew wouldn't come true. No secret stayed hidden forever.

"I only wish she could have made this journey with you," the captain said.

"I've wished the same since we left. She watched over us. I know she did." Marti gazed up at the darkening sky, the stars beginning to wink and twinkle to life.

Captain Finn walked back across the deck behind her.

Tomorrow would be a new beginning and facing it alone scared her. Instead of looking out at the ocean and the fog about to envelope them, she turned to the land and the city by the bay. San Francisco was lit up in the distance. She stared at those lights and wondered what all those people were doing right then. Working in their offices, going out for a night on the town, spending an evening with someone they loved, their family and friends.

Maybe they were lonely like her and wishing to have something more in their lives.

Tomorrow she'd become a part of that world. Tonight, she belonged to the sea.

She stared out across the water to one of the tall buildings reaching up to the stars. For the first time, she felt as if something, or someone, was drawing her back.

CAMERON WAITED FOR his daughter to arrive, dreading the evening ahead. He watched the ship on the water, drawn to it like a beacon.

Jennifer lives in the San Francisco Bay Area with her husband, three children, her dog, Bella, and cat, Shadow.

When she isn't writing a book, she's reading one. Her obsession for both is often revealed in the state of her home and how late dinner is to the table. When she finally leaves those fictional worlds, you'll find her in the garden, playing in the dirt and daydreaming about people who live only in her head, until she puts them on paper.

For more information about Jennifer and her upcoming releases, visit www.jennifer-ryan.com.

Visit www.AuthorTracker.com for exclusive information on your favorite HarperCollins authors.

Give in to your impulses . . .
Read on for a sneak peek at a brand-new
e-book original tale of romance from Avon Books.
Available now wherever e-books are sold.


## ALL OR NOTHING

A TRUST NO ONE NOVEL

*By Dixie Lee Brown*

An Excerpt from


# ALL OR NOTHING
## A Trust No One Novel

*by Dixie Lee Brown*


Debut author Dixie Lee Brown launches
her *Trust No One* series with this tale of
a hunted woman and the one man who
can save her life . . . if she'll let him.

"Trust me. This is the safest way."

Everything required trust with Joe. So, did she trust him? If she ever got back on the ground, she might be able to answer that question. Cara looked over the edge of the platform. *There's no way!*

"Take your time. Go when you're ready . . . unless you want me to give you a little push."

"You wouldn't dare!" She wrapped her arms around the pole.

"You really don't trust me, do you?" He laughed.

"I was starting to, before you said the word 'push.' "

"There's hope then? If I choose my words more carefully?"

"Maybe . . . if I ever get down from here."

"Let's sit for a minute. Things will look different from that perspective." He sat, dangling his long legs over the side. Cara positioned herself beside him, her hands nervously flexing on the rope that joined her to the zip line.

"Jumping doesn't seem any more reasonable from here." Too bad, since sitting close enough to rub shoulders with him made her nearly as uncomfortable as the stupid zip line.

"We'll just hang out and talk for a while then. That okay?" He gripped the edge of the platform and leaned forward, turning to look at her.

"The last time we talked, it ended badly."

"Now we know which subjects to stay away from."

"Yeah, anything to do with either of our private lives."

"I think it was your ex-husband and my desire to protect you from him that got us crossways with each other."

Cara glanced sideways at him. He was looking at her. Their eyes met. The strangest emotions coursed through her. Somehow, it didn't sound so bad when he said it like that. Who didn't want a knight in shining armor? She was afraid for Joe, but he sounded so confident that he could protect her, and himself, she almost believed it. Recognizing the danger in that, she tore her eyes away from his.

"We're making progress. You didn't rip into me that time." A grin came through in his voice.

"It doesn't do any good to try talking sense into you." She wanted to sound serious, but her heart was no longer in it. She forced her mind back to the task at hand, considering the likelihood that she'd ever be able to *zip* off this ledge. What was the worst that could happen? The cable could break, and she'd plummet thirty feet to the ground. End all of her problems. More likely, it would be a gradual descent, with the jump from the platform the only really exciting part. She could do this.

"We've got unfinished business, you know. We might as well take care of it while we're sitting here."

"What's that?"

"I almost had you talked into dinner that night we met."

"You weren't even close."

"I think you were as intrigued with the idea as I was." He grinned. "I also think we stood a good chance of ending the evening with a kiss."

"That's a stretch. You're making the same mistake you made that night. Going from confident to arrogant in about two seconds flat. There was no chance in hell you were going to get a kiss." Cara smiled at his wounded look.

"Will my chances ever improve?" His eyes met hers again.

She'd forgotten what a good-looking guy he was. The same mesmerizing pull she'd experienced the night she met him overcame her better judgment now. For a moment she wondered what it would feel like, his lips on hers, his arms holding her close, while they lost themselves in each other.

Cara drew herself up short. Was she completely crazy? She was barely free from one dangerous man. Why would she get involved with another? There was an attraction between them she couldn't deny, but nothing could ever come of it.

"Maybe." The word slipped out, almost on its own.